THE TWISTED STAR

by

Don LoCicero

FIRST EDITION

Copyright 1992, by Don LoCicero
Library of Congress Catalog Card Number: 92-70490
ISBN: 1-880664-00-3

E.M. Press, Inc.
14891B Washington Street
Haymarket, Virginia 22069

FORWARD

The Twisted Star is a compelling story in which the reader is caught up in the drama of Germany and especially its Jewish citizens from W.W.I through the Nazi era as if he or she didn't already know the outcome. The skillfully told plot weaves together the step by step process of Nazi accession to power and the gradual elimination of opponents and all Jews from the life of the nation, with a Jewish family's varied efforts to cope with a situation over which they had no control. Readers experience the trauma of these German-Jews entrapped by love of their homeland and friends, stubborn defiance of Hitler, the indifference of the rest of the world, and above all by hope. The humaneness of the victims stands in stark contrast to the inhumanity of the "master race."

Without heavy-handed rhetoric, the book makes a strong case for the need to fight against evil at its earliest manifestation.

> Alice L. Eckardt, Professor Emerita of Religion Studies, Lehigh University, and co-author of *Long Nights Journey Into Day: A Retrospective on the Holocaust*

To my brother, Vince

"A pestilence isn't a thing made to man's measure; therefore we tell ourselves that pestilence is a mere bogy of the mind, a bad dream that will pass away. But it doesn't pass away and, from one bad dream to another, it is men who pass away...because they haven't taken their precautions." (Albert Camus: *THE PLAGUE*)

"So you hope to defeat evil? Fine. Begin by helping your fellow man. Triumph over death? Excellent. Begin by saving your brother..." (Elie Wiesel: *THE OATH*)

PRELUDE

I know that I will never be able to truly sleep again, that my nose will always be filled with the putrid stench of burning flesh, my ears forever assaulted by the screams of terrified women and children, my lungs coated with the ashes of death. I know that my lips and tongue will forever balk at the attempt to form the words of *kaddish*, that the words will die before they are formed. But what I do not know, what I probably never will know, is why *they* stand out so much more vividly and painfully than all the rest. Than all the thousands. Than all the thousands of thousands. Why when I lie awake at night trembling do *their* images hover above me as if painted on the air, *their* eyes knifing into mine like an unvoiced accusation? *They* were, after all, the blood kin of the executioners. Why do I weep for *them* now, so many years later? So many tears later? So many corpses later? Was I not *their* victim? Or have I, in my torment, overlooked some vital point, some damning piece of information that might provide the clue? And, no matter how much I beg and plead with the Lord of the Universe to give me the answers, He remains silent and invisible, as silent and invisible as He was in that twisted, horrible nightmare they called Treblinka. Treblinka... How could so odious and unspeakable a place have had such an enchanting name? Treblinka... How could it have been possible?

My name is Heinrich Hartstein: a fine German name, don't you agree? Oh yes, my parents were proud to be Germans; my father in particular revered his adopted country and its wonderful heritage. After all, this was the land of poets and thinkers. The land of Goethe, whose *Faust* is the ultimate symbol for the indomitability of the human spirit; the land of Lessing's *Nathan der Weise*, which became a rallying cry for tolerance in a world consumed by bigotry. It is no wonder that my father willingly, even eagerly, spilled his blood for Kaiser and Reich in The Great War, appreciative that he had been granted the honor of sacrificing a leg for the just cause, and well satisfied at the more than generous exchange that left him the Iron Cross First Class in its place.

I recall well those years when my father would gather my sisters and me around him and remind us in a trembling voice how blessed we were to live in a land where one need not fear. How unlike the Russia of his birth it was, where the word Jew was synonymous with *pogrom*, and where pain and death were daily companions. *Yitgadal veyitkadach schyme raba* (May his name be blessed and exalted). While he wasn't a religious man in the traditional sense, my father carried a small store of such pious phrases he learned as a youth, although he truly believed that by becoming a German he had done more to guarantee that God would be on his side than he could have through any number of prayers. After all, he had written proof of this on his thick army belt, displayed for a long time alongside his Iron Cross in the glass showcase in his study: *Gott mit uns* (God is with us). And it was undeniable that the name Hartstein had a more legitimate ring than his original family name of Szmulski.

My mother, formerly Esther Feinberg, was the perfect balance for my father. A second generation German, she lacked the outward zeal of the convert. But she was as loyal a subject of the Reich as was her husband. Her family had made a prominent name in the bustling south German metropolis of Munich; throughout Germany and Europe the name Feinberg had become synonymous with quality heating equipment for home and industry.

The youngest of three daughters, my mother was the most spirited; even as a child she made it clear that she was not one to be easily dominated. In spite of her headstrong nature, or perhaps because of it, she was the family favorite, spoiled by parents and sisters alike. Nevertheless, it was still a great surprise and shock to the Feinbergs when the eighteen-year-old Esther announced at one evening meal that she had fallen in love with a soldier. The idea of their daughter marrying someone in the military was so alien to both her mother and father that they reacted emotionally. Jacob Feinberg waved his arms around as if to ward off a swarm of attacking bees, while his wife, Sarah, wrung her hands and rocked back and forth in her chair prayerfully, her face drained of color. They were somewhat placated to learn that Lieutenant Hartstein was, after all, a Jew, and that he was in the army primarily because he desired to become a German citizen. Still, they were disturbed that he was a foreigner who had seemingly renounced his true heritage.

But love prevailed. Young Erich Hartstein was an intelligent, gregarious fellow who undoubtedly loved Esther without reservation. In addition, he compromised with my grandfather by agreeing to a traditional Jewish wedding, was properly humble toward the Rebbe before, during, and after the ceremony, and did not automatically reject Jacob Feinberg's suggestion that when he finished playing soldier he might consider accepting a place in the family firm. It was 1904, not the Middle Ages, and Munich's 600,000-plus population was more interested in culture and commerce than in war. It was generally agreed upon throughout Europe that in these two areas Munich was second only to Paris.

After my father completed his military service he accepted a position in my grandfather's firm, ready to start a family of his own. And on a beautiful spring morning in May, 1906, I was born — a healthy baby boy who would perpetuate the new family name and honor.

The following years were happy ones for the Hartsteins. My father proved equal to all challenges offered at Feinberg's Ovenworks. His diligence and capabilities were amply rewarded. My grandfather, by then convinced that his Esther had not made a terrible mistake in her choice of a husband, began to groom my father as his successor. As a result of their growing prosperity, the Hartsteins were able to celebrate New Year's Day, 1913 by signing a lease for a beautiful, spacious apartment on Jägerstrasse in the exclusive Hofgarten area.

Events were moving very swiftly and inexorably, however, and by the summer of 1914 Europe had drifted into hysteria. The sides had begun to form for what threatened to be a fierce military struggle. Munich reflected the prevailing mood of Germany. Big business, labor, intellectuals, students, the military — all were united as never before, each group repeating the demand for justice that appeared in the press on a daily basis. Even the anti-military Jacob Feinberg found himself caught up in the nationalistic fervor as he stood in front of the Feldherrenhalle on August 1 and heard the announcement that the Kaiser's plea for peace had been rejected. Germany was now officially at war with Russia.

At one point my grandfather even found himself waving his hat and shouting with the others, *"Heil dem Kaiser! Heil dem Heer!"* ("Hail the Kaiser! Hail the army!"), although when war was declared on France two days later he had already begun to have doubts. While my grandfather never doubted that his country was justified in defending itself against the forces allied against it, and though he realized that from a business standpoint he stood to gain from the coming struggle (the government would be needing many stoves and other articles produced by his firm), he maintained the basic belief that war, even for the best cause, was inherently evil. He feared for his family, particularly Esther. Her husband's regiment, The 16th Bavarian Reserve Infantry, was being hastily readied for battle. He had to admit to himself, moreover, that Feinberg's Ovenworks would be hard put to replace his son-in-law, and that he would miss the young man, God grant that he return safely to them. And in all likelihood, Erich would not be home by early winter for the birth of his second child.

My father's experience as a front line soldier was brief. Although critically short of equipment (they had few machine guns, some outdated telephone equipment and very few steel helmets to replace the recruits' oilcloth caps), Erich Hartstein and his company set out from Munich's main railroad station in high spirits. As the train began to move, the air was filled with powerful male voices. The young men sang as if on their way to a festival and not off to kill or die in a foreign land.

I can still hear my father's description of the beautiful castles and picture book towns he and his comrades saw during their journey along the Rhine. They detrained at a point near the Belgian border and entered the hostile country without incident. After a grueling, forced march during which they saw very little to indicate that they were in a war, the Bavarian unit arrived at the outskirts of the Flemish city of Ypres and prepared for a major assault on the British and Belgian garrisons there.

Only years later, his patriotism all but gone, did my father reveal the true, unspectacular story of his part in the Battle of Ypres.

On October 28, 1914, Lieutenant Erich Hartstein was part of the main German attack force. Their objective was to secure the city, setting into motion a vast flanking movement that would envelop Belgium and Holland. This would be followed by a lightning assault on France and victory for the Central Powers. The men were anxious to meet the enemy, anxious to punish the Belgians and, even more so, the traitorous British whose entry into the war had awakened the cry, "*Gott strafe England*" ("May God punish England") throughout Germany. My father longed to prove himself worthy of his country, and as he led his men through the thick fog on that early morning, his only fear was that he wouldn't be equal to the task. He didn't hear the incoming shell that killed two of his comrades instantly and reduced his leg to bloody shreds. And so, after approximately two minutes of action, Lieutenant Erich Hartstein was on his way back home a hero, back to a loving wife and an executive position in Feinberg's Ovenworks.

A month after my father's release from the hospital in Munich, my mother gave birth to beautiful twin girls. In his heavily accented German, my father proudly boasted to his wife's beaming parents, "I lost a leg, but God has seen fit to replace it with my two girls. Not such a bad bargain, don't you agree?"

Fitted with an artificial limb, my father was forced to follow the war vicariously. At first he smiled with confidence as reports of victory came back from the front daily. But soon he became aware that things were not going as well for Germany as her leaders claimed. The French and British stubbornly held the line before Paris and the Marne River, which had altered the nature of the war. He knew, based on the relative strengths of the belligerents, that trench warfare would eventually doom his country. Nevertheless, the great successes of the German army in the East, commanded by the military genius General Paul von Hindenburg, were sufficient cause to dispel any feelings of impending disaster. By 1915, moreover, German submarines were decimating enemy shipping. My grandfather's repeated concern that America might be forced into the war if unrestricted submarine warfare persisted was shrugged off good-naturedly. After all, what could a businessman know about the realities of war?

***

I don't remember many specific incidents from that early period of my life, and I am not even certain how much of my recollection is derived from the family stories I heard recounted so often that they became the fabric of my experience. Did I actually hear those heated discussions between my grandfather and father, or did I construct them in my mind from the vague impressions of a child? And why, regardless of the answer to this question, do I feel this need to pass them on to another time and place? I think I know why. I think I know...

It happened from time to time in Treblinka, often deep in the night, that for no apparent reason someone would begin to scream, not in a human voice, but in one that seemed to contain the pain of the entire universe. Within minutes, the single cry would be joined by another, then another, until finally every throat was vibrating. It was as if this combined scream were the only possibility of waking the Creator. At such times even the most sadistic guards were uncertain and often did not make the attempt to beat us into silence. Perhaps they sensed that they were listening to the cries of an army of corpses, that their fists and cudgels could not coerce those who were already dead. No, I don't wonder at the fact that we shrieked out our torment to the bleak night; I only wonder that any of us were ever able to be silent again. But I cannot. I must continue the scream. From the deep night. From Treblinka, here, on these pages.

***

One particular discussion between my father and grandfather remains vivid in my mind. We were at my grandparents' for our usual Sunday visit. My father and grandfather were sitting in the comfortable living room of the large apartment on Schwanthalerstrasse. I was positioned on my father's lap, the stump of his amputated leg hooked over the edge of the sofa.

My grandfather held the newspaper out toward my father and began to speak animatedly. "And I suppose you feel that it's perfectly all right that this Ludendorff has been made quartermaster general. Why, the man is an avowed anti-Semite. I tell you, Erich, he's a devil!"

My father smiled gently, much as one might at a child who has made some obviously naive remark. "Come now, Jacob, don't get yourself all worked up. Germany is at war, and in a war military men are much more useful than moralists. Even you have to admit that we're lucky to have a man with his capabilities on our side. Whatever you might think, he is first and foremost a patriot. Words are cheap. People say a lot of things they don't mean."

My grandfather's face reddened perceptibly as he responded. "People say exactly what they mean when it comes to Jews. You of all people should know that. Didn't you leave Russia because there were people like Ludendorff in every village there? What makes you think it's any different here? Haven't you read what is written about him, or don't you care because you've convinced yourself that you ceased to be a Jew just by changing your name?"

My father lifted me from his lap and set me down on the carpet. Then he leaned forward, his face now also red, and replied in a semi-shout, "Please, spare me the sermon! I understand your fears, but I tell you there is absolutely no comparison between Germany and Russia. And as for what I am — I am a German first, and then a Jew. Whether you like it or not, Jacob, you are too, in spite of that Zionist nonsense you've gotten yourself mixed up in. This is our country, not some imaginary land somewhere in the desert. Believe me, there is no difference between Jew and German when the bullets start flying." He began to rub his thigh vigorously. I had seen him do that often, usually in the early evening after a trying day at work.

Before my grandfather had a chance to respond, my mother walked into the room. She wagged her finger in an arc that encompassed both men. "At it again, you two? Shame, shame! Instead of arguing, why don't you both come in and have some of Mama's rice pudding. Come on now, kiss and make up like good little boys."

My mother helped my father reattach his artificial leg. And by the time they reached the kitchen, both men were smiling broadly, my mother between them with an arm around each of their waists. Such was the power of her loving nature at that time so long ago.

As 1916 drew to a close and in the first months of 1917, the mood on Jägerstrasse reflected that of Munich as a whole. The famous Bavarian cheerfulness, the prized *Gemütlichkeit*, had gradually been replaced by a feeling of bewilderment and resignation. In the taverns where previously there had been laughter and music, now there were raucous political discussions. Strong opinions were exchanged, but little clarity shed on the true picture of the war's progress. The Battle of Verdun had raged throughout the year, yet despite the reports of spectacular victories over the French, the German armies could not break through to Paris. Everyone agreed that the French appeared beaten and that the Russians were being slaughtered in unbelievable numbers. But the war continued. What at first had seemed like a lark had evolved into a grueling, indescribably bloody exercise in futility. And as weeks and months passed, more and more families bore the familiar expression of grief on their drawn faces as husbands, fathers, brothers, and sons were torn apart by shells and bayonets, or had their lungs and eyes burned out by mustard gas in the see saw battles over some meaningless slits in the earth. They were unaware that their government had secretly sent out peace feelers, and that these had either been rejected or discouraged by the absurd conditions demanded by the opponents. No good German could have accepted the condition demanding the dismemberment of the Austro-Hungarian and Turkish empires. And why should Germany pay excessive compensation, as if she alone were to blame for the war? Almost nightly, my father gave vent to his growing frustration and anger, not quite sure whom to blame for the stalemate at the front.

"Can you believe it, Esi?" he would say, rubbing his thigh and wincing. "We had them by the neck and then let go. We could have crushed them into the earth if we had followed through. What the hell is wrong with our generals? Have they lost their courage and sense of purpose? And take a look at these new recruits. They're disgraceful. Not like the men I served with in the Battle of Ypres. To add to all of that, we have a growing band of defeatists among us here in the Reich. I've read their filthy little pamphlets, the swine! Can you imagine, they want us to capitulate like craven cowards!"

My mother listened to these tirades patiently, hopeful that they would remain general in nature. Invariably, however, my father turned his anger closer to home.

"And then there are people like your father and his fanatic Zionist friends who are more loyal to some imaginary place swarming with Arabs than they are to their own country. Don't they see what they owe Germany? They've been successful and prosperous here, don't they realize that? Where would people like your father have wound up if they were in Russia or Poland? It's no wonder that so many people say bad things about the Jews!"

At such points my mother usually interrupted, admonishing him gently not to let the children hear negative things about their grandfather. After grumbling for a few minutes about women's lack of understanding of important matters, my father would pick up his newspaper and disappear into his study to reread accounts of the latest military developments.

Soon my father began to invent reasons not to accompany us on our Sunday visits to Schwanthalerstrasse. When he did go with us, there were usually loud disagreements between him and my grandfather. One such incident stands out in my mind: I was in the spacious kitchen with my twin sisters, Jutta and Ursela, watching my mother and grandmother bake bread. This was always a special treat for me as I was permitted to help. I loved to punch the large mound of risen dough and watch it deflate like a pierced balloon. My father and grandfather had gone into the latter's study and closed the door behind them. The shouting began almost immediately; even the thick oak door couldn't muffle their angry voices.

"No, it is you who has to face the facts! There will be no winners in this damned war, Erich!" shouted my grandfather in response to some remark that we had not been able to hear. "We are all the losers, can't you see that? The Kaiser and his generals have betrayed the people. The idea that we were forced into it is a bare-faced lie, and no intelligent person could believe it. As if there ever was glory in killing and maiming. Wake up, Erich, and stop playing the Prussian fool!"

My father was angrier than I had ever heard him before. "That hasn't stopped you from reaping the benefits, though, has it, Jacob?" he replied. "I don't see you straining the dishwater to get a few pieces of lard, or eating bread made from sawdust. That's just for others to do. And how many government contracts have you rejected recently, or is anything justified so long as it profits your group of traitors? I suppose, too, that when the Arabs swoop down on you in The Promised Land you won't blow them to pieces. Hypocrite!"

"What do you know of these things?" my grandfather asked, his voice meeting the level and intensity of my father's. "You, who renounced your family, your name and your heritage for less than a dish of lentils. Where is your sense of identity? How can you speak of traitors and loyalty? Can't you see that you will always be nothing more than a stinking Jew here? Face the truth if you dare."

"Truth? Whose truth do you mean? Zionist truth? Or maybe you mean Messiah Sebi's truth? He was a good Zionist and Jew, wasn't he? So good that he converted to Islam. But even that didn't dissuade the zealots. Or is it Herzl's truth you mean? If I'm not mistaken, though, he was too moderate for the fanatics. You see, I've read up on your cult, so don't think you can pull the wool over my eyes."

"Your eyes are already blind, Herr Hartstein," retorted my grandfather, his voice shaking. "Perhaps you should read what your nationalist friends are writing, your fellow convert to the Reich, Mr. Houston Chamberlain, for example. He claims that this miserable war is a war against the Jews. According to him, we are out to enslave the world. And many of the decent citizens of Munich agree. Do you really think they believe that you were able to change your skin like a snake? On the contrary, one day, if they have their way, they will show you who you really are — Yem Szmulski, a miserable Jew from a little Russian village who didn't realize that he was running from the jaws of a tiger into the arms of the devil!"

Although at the time I understood very little of this violent exchange, it often came back to me with shattering clarity in later years. My father remembered it too, although a long time passed before he ever made reference to it.

My father avoided Schwanthalerstrasse for a long time after that day. He continued to work at Feinberg's Ovenworks, but it was clear that he was no longer the heir apparent of the firm. This role was given to my grandfather's new favorite, Solomon Vogelsang, the accountant who had married my mother's sister Rachel. Uncle Solomon, a distant cousin of the Feinberg's, had been exempted from military service because of a birth defect, a deformed leg which had left him with a permanent limp. What he lacked in the physical sphere, however, was more than compensated for by his keen sense of humor. Try as he did, my father rarely was able to engage Uncle Solomon in any serious argument; the latter could exploit the light side of every situation.

"Now, Erich," he would say, when my father attempted to get him into a discussion of the war or asked his opinion about their father-in-law's dedication to Zionism, "neither a victory in this war nor a homeland for the Jews in Palestine will get you your leg back or straighten mine out, so why don't we just hobble over to the liquor cabinet, have a glass of schnaps and talk about women."

***

The spring of 1917 was extremely successful for the Central Powers. Russia was on the verge of total collapse, the Italians were proving themselves no military match for Germany and her allies, and the unrestrained U-boats were taking a devastating toll on Allied shipping. In school we sang patriotic songs and listened to our teachers repeat over and over again that victory was within the grasp of our valiant armies. Many of the young boys were sad that the war would end before they had a chance to show their bravery in battle. I had very mixed feelings. On the one hand I wanted to join my schoolmates as they played war games during recess and spoke of heroic exploits, but no matter how I tried I always felt like an outsider. Perhaps my grandfather's influence was at work. Perhaps he had helped me to recognize the reality of my situation: the others considered me different because I was a Jew. I recall no overt hostility, not at first. Looking back, I realize that I was tolerated because my teachers and schoolmates knew of my father's war experience. Hirsch Grünfeld, the other Jewish boy in my class, did not fare so well. The children teased him, called him names, and continually threatened to beat him up. Luckily for Hirsch, the teacher usually interceded, though he did not punish the guilty ones. This troubled me. Finally, I told my mother about it, hoping that she could explain why the others were always picking on Hirsch, and why they seemed not to like me very much either. Her reply was unconvincing. She said simply that children were sometimes unintentionally cruel, but if I remained cheerful and courteous they would accept me as a friend. The sadness in her eyes, however, told me more than her words.

I wondered especially why my father was so unhappy at that time. If what my teachers said about an imminent German victory were true, he should have been elated. Formerly, he had always found time to sit and play with me and my sisters, or chat with me about my school day. That had stopped. He would come home from work, immediately vanish into his study, often not emerging for our evening meal. My mother explained to us that he needed time to relax. The truth was, however, that he was secretly drinking himself senseless, either to deaden the constant physical pain from his war wound, or to blot out his growing doubts and fears. It was April. The United States of America had entered the war.

The winter of 1917-1918, the one historians refer to as the Turnip Winter, was difficult. The mood of resignation had become one of gloom and utter weariness. My father's drinking had increased to the point that he was no longer able or willing to get himself out to work in the morning. My mother reminded him of his obligations to his family and warned him of the ill effects his drinking would have on his health. When this approach failed she chided him for his weakness and failure to meet his responsibilities. When not too drunk to speak, he answered her with loud profanity, expressing regret that he had survived the war only to be nagged to death by a crazy woman. We children cowered in our room as our parents shouted at each other. The arguments usually ended with my mother weeping as my father stumbled out of the apartment and headed unsteadily for the corner tavern where he remained until he had drunk himself into a stupor and had to be assisted home by anyone who was available at the time.

"Have you gone completely out of your mind, Erich?" My grandfather's voice awakened me from a sound sleep. It was a cold winter night, the first time he had visited our home since that terrible argument with my father. I sat up in my bed and listened. "You are destroying yourself and your family. Can't you see that? Or don't you give a damn?" I heard my mother's faint sobbing in the background. "I tell you," he continued, "if you don't snap out of it right away there will be a tragedy here."

My father answered, his voice thick, his words slurred by drink. "Just who the hell do you think you are, you bastard? What right do you have to come here and judge me? When I think that I spilled my blood for people like you." His voice trailed off, like a radio whose volume is turned down. I had crept to the door and opened it a crack. My father was sitting at the dining room table, his head between his hands. There was a half-empty bottle in front of him. My grandfather stood about three feet to the side, one arm draped about my mother's shoulders. His hand trembled.

"Yes, you spilled your blood, like the damned fool you were. I know all about it. You believed the asinine slogans they fed to you, the promises of glory. And I almost believed them too. But where are the slogans now? The only slogan I hear now is, *'Lieber ein Ende mit Schrecken, als ein Schrecken ohne Ende.'* Where is the glory? Is it so glorious to be a cripple and a drunk? This is what you have to thank your great Kaiser and our country for. This is what they did for you."

My father's voice rose even higher. "*Our* country? Don't you dare say that, you turncoat! You and your friends would like to see Germany go under. Communists, Zionists — call yourselves what you want, to me you are a bunch of traitors!"

For a good minute the two of them were silent. My mother sobbed quietly, her head lowered.

I had to strain to hear my grandfather's next words, spoken in a low, sad voice. "No, Erich, we aren't the traitors. We didn't betray Germany. On the contrary, Germany and the other countries have betrayed us, all of us: Jews, Germans, French, English...all of us. Human beings are being massacred and no one understands why. But you know this all too well, don't you, Erich? And you can't drown your knowledge in liquor. It doesn't work, does it? All it does is submerge your humanity and drown your soul. Please, for all our sakes, don't let this terrible thing continue. If you can't stop it because you are a good Jew, then do it because you are a good German. Or better still, do it because you are a good human being."

My grandfather walked the few steps to my father and placed his hand on his arm. My father looked up, his eyes glazed from drink and emotion, then let his head sink with a thud to the table. His shoulders heaved violently. It was the first time I had ever seen my father cry.

Life on Jägerstrasse underwent a metamorphosis after that night. Although he did not immediately return to work at Feinberg's, my father no longer spent his days lost in a drunken stupor. Peace returned to our home, if not to the world outside. My mother blossomed. Somehow she managed to provide us with nourishing meals, in spite of the growing food shortages. She also saw to it that my father's uniform was always freshly pressed for the frequent meetings he now attended in various parts of Munich. We began to have visitors, important looking men who would sometimes sit and loudly discuss the world situation with my father until the early hours of morning. They would leaf through the books and maps they brought with them and write down ideas for future speeches. My father had entered the world of politics.

***

"We'll finish this business off very soon now, Esi. The British have had their ears pinned back for certain. This time not even those cocky Americans will be able to pull their chestnuts out of the fire. We've reached the Marne and soon we will storm the gates of Paris." My father smiled broadly, his face reflecting the pleasant spring weather. The German army had made a massive assault against the French and British lines, advancing to the Marne River — only the second time in the war they had gotten so far. What my father did not know, however, was that the advance had cost over one million casualties and left the German army depleted. In contrast, the strength of the opposing armies was increasing to the tune of 300,000 fresh American troops per month. I was very confused. On the one hand, my father and my teachers were speaking about victory, while at the same time my grandfather was taking quite a different position. My mother did not understand any of it; just as she didn't understand years later when they ordered her and my father to prepare for resettlement in Bohemia, and certainly not when she and my father were taken from there to a place in Poland called Auschwitz.

Oh God, how could she have understood such a thing? How could anyone? And how can anyone ever forgive *You* for it? How can anyone ever believe that *You* exist? How can anyone ever believe? Or is it possible, perhaps, that *You* didn't understand either? Is it possible that, as a result of Treblinka and Auschwitz, *You* no longer believe in *Yourself*?

***

My father had no reason to rejoice as spring became summer and the tide of battle shifted for the final time. The Central Powers suffered one defeat after another and were on the verge of total collapse. In late September, Generals Ludendorff and Hindenburg informed the Kaiser that Germany had lost the war and advised the government to seek an immediate armistice. The war was over. Germany had been defeated.

The streets of Munich became a battleground. Different groups vied for control of Germany's remains, like stray dogs fighting for scraps of food in a garbage pail. All semblance of order disappeared. It was as if someone had suddenly pulled a master switch, extinguishing the light of reason. My school was closed many days that fall due to the disturbances in the streets, and when the teachers did show up they were sullen and distracted. They spoke repeatedly and with angry passion of the treacherous Communists and Jews, and they vowed to avenge the "stab in the back" these groups had dealt the army and country. The hostility of my classmates became more and more overt. It reached a high point one morning in October.

Our teacher, Herr Kulp, had not yet arrived at school. The children were boisterous and rowdy; they shouted and threw paper, erasers, and other objects around the room. Suddenly a loud cry rang out. I looked across my desk to the other side of the room and saw Hirsch Grünfeld standing in the aisle, crying out in pain. He held his hand to his face; blood was oozing out between his fingers.

"Serves you right, you dirty kike!" Otto Eberthal, the class bully, shook his fist in front of the Hirsch's injured nose.

Hirsch continued to cry, simultaneously attempting to stem the flow of blood and escape the threatening fist.

Herr Kulp suddenly entered the room. "What's going on here?" His angry shout sent all of the children scampering to their seats. Only Hirsch Grünfeld remained standing. He continued to hold his injured nose and whimper. Blood had dripped down the front of his shirt and onto the floor. Herr Kulp looked over at him with disgust. "Are you up to some mischief again, Grünfeld?" He took a few steps forward and stood next to Hirsch. "You seem determined to be a troublemaker, don't you?" Hirsch's eyes pleaded for, but received no mercy. "As if we didn't have enough of *your* kind in Germany. Now wipe your dirty nose and sit down!"

Several of the children giggled. Otto Eberthal took Herr Kulp's pronouncement as a signal and began to mock his victim by pretending to whimper along with him. This provoked some more scattered giggles.

"Enough of that, children," reprimanded the teacher. Then, still glaring at the hapless Hirsch, he added, "If you don't stop that sniveling, I'll give you something real to bawl about." Herr Kulp raised the heavy metal ruler he held in his hand and waved it menacingly. Then he turned to me and said in a hissing voice, "You had better teach your friend to behave, Hartstein!" There was hatred in his voice. My face flushed, my stomach sank. I looked first at Herr Kulp and then at Hirsch. The latter's eyes met mine beseechingly. I turned away, confused and embarrassed. Most of all, however, I was angry, not so much at Herr Kulp as at Hirsch Grünfeld. It was his fault, I thought, that the others didn't like me. His fault. But why was the teacher comparing me to him? We were not even friends.

Later that day, during recess, Otto Eberthal and a group of his friends began to shove me around and call me names. As far as they were concerned, they taunted, I was no better than any other *Yid*, and if I didn't watch my step they would flatten my big Jew nose for me. I was humiliated and terrified, but I stood my ground. The bell rang before they could make good on their threats.

I pretended to be ill the next day. I felt empty and ashamed. My worried mother repeatedly tiptoed into my room to ask me what was wrong. Finally, I could hold it in no longer and tearfully described what had happened at school on the previous day. At first my mother was bewildered by my disjointed explanation. When she finally understood what I was saying, her bewilderment turned to anger. There was an uncharacteristic fury in her eyes as she embraced me and promised that I would never have to go through such a thing again.

At dinner that evening, she told my father everything. I had chosen to remain in my room. Besides lacking any appetite, I was afraid that my father might blame me for what had happened, just as Herr Kulp had blamed Hirsch Grünfeld. My heart pounded as the door opened. My father stood outlined in the doorway for several seconds, as if uncertain whether to enter. Finally, he limped over to my bed. I pulled the covers up toward my face and hunched up my shoulders, awaiting the violent outburst. To my amazement, however, he merely reached down, placed his hand on my head and let it remain there for several seconds, rubbing gently in a circular pattern. Then he withdrew it, turned, and without having said a word, left the room.

I returned to school two days later. Although my mother assured me that my father had taken care of the matter, I was still quite upset when I walked into the classroom. I had no doubts that my problems were far from over when Eberthal and the others approached me only moments after I had sat down at my desk. Resuming their verbal abuse where they had left off three days before, they soon began to make threatening gestures. I picked up a pencil I was prepared to use as a weapon to defend myself, but before this became necessary Herr Kulp's voice boomed from the doorway, "Get into your seats, you worthless riffraff. And don't let me see you bothering Herr Hartstein again, unless you don't want to sit down for the next week." Eberthal and the others looked questioningly at Herr Kulp for a few seconds before retreating to their places. He meant business. While my father had apparently succeeded in halting my persecution, it seemed as if his influence had not been powerful enough to remove the loathing from Herr Kulp's voice when he spoke my name. Automatically, I looked over at Hirsch Grünfeld and was startled to see him staring at me as one would at an enemy. I had never felt more alone in my life.

***

"It's an outrage, Esi. I tell you this is the limit. Can you believe it? That ridiculous caricature Eisner has staged a revolution here in Munich and King Ludwig has run away with his tail between his legs. The dirty coward. And the soldiers stood by like puppets and let the Communist rabble take control of the city. To top it all off, now there is talk that the Kaiser is going to abdicate. Everything is crumbling. Germany has gone insane."

It was November 7, 1918. My father's lips quivered as he reported the latest news to my mother. Kurt Eisner and a group of Utopian revolutionaries had declared Munich a republic after a successful, bloodless coup, and now they were riding through the streets, their red banners waving in triumph. Most of the war-weary inhabitants of Munich went numbly about their business without noticing. Even a revolution could not stir them out of their lethargy.

"What does it mean, Erich? What will happen next?" my mother asked, as she read the latest report in the daily newspaper.

"What does it mean?" he shouted, rolling his eyes wildly. "It means that again a Jew has done his best to bring down the roof on all of us, Esi. Goddamn that dirty bastard!"

My mother winced at the violence of his reaction and asked, "But why should anyone blame us just because of one individual? Surely this Eisner didn't act alone; surely his followers are not only Jews. It just doesn't make any sense at all."

My father shrugged impatiently, obviously unwilling to carry the conversation any further with someone who could not possibly comprehend. He was already putting on his army greatcoat.

"I have an important meeting to attend," he said gruffly. "I don't know what time I will be back." He limped out of the apartment mumbling more profanities under his breath.

Three days later my father's greatest fears were realized. The Kaiser abdicated and fled to Holland, taking with him five hundred years of imperial rule. The German monarchy was dead. One German city after another tumbled into anarchy. Although the killing in the trenches was finally over, the year 1919 did not bring peace; brutality and murder were the twins that ruled the home front. In Munich, which had been spared major violence until then, Kurt Eisner was assassinated by a young anarchist while on his way to the National Assembly to deliver his resignation after the resounding election defeat of his Independent Socialist Party. There was violence in Berlin as well. The radical Communist leaders of the Sparticus League, Karl Liebknecht and Rosa Luxemburg, along with many of their followers, were murdered by a newly formed and increasingly powerful group that called itself the Free Corps. The Free Corps — prototypes of future mass murderers. The first time I heard of their existence was during the New Year's gathering that year at my Aunt Rachel and Uncle Solomon's apartment.

In spite of the chaotic conditions, or perhaps because of them, most people attempted to maintain a semblance of order in their lives. That New Year's Day it was my Uncle Solomon and Aunt Rachel who were to host the annual family affair. To my mother's surprise, my father agreed to accompany us without any prodding.

The meal was pleasant, if not elaborate, the table conversation light and humorous. Uncle Solomon was in superb form, recounting the latest political jokes with the skill of a professional comedian. My grandfather found the jokes aimed at the Kaiser more humorous than those that poked fun at the Zionists, while my father's laughter was reserved primarily for the latter. He guffawed loudly when Uncle Solomon told of the German-Jewish settler in Palestine, who, after ten years had not been able to learn Hebrew.

> *'Aren't you embarrassed about that?' inquired a new arrival.*
> *'Terribly embarrassed,' answered the settler.*
> *'Then why don't you learn Hebrew?' asked the other.*
> *'Because it is easier to be embarrassed than to learn Hebrew,'*
> *came the response.*

It was my grandfather's turn to snicker when Uncle Solomon declared that the Dutch would no longer have to depend on nature for the hot air to move their windmills now that the Kaiser was in Holland. And everyone enjoyed the gentle, off-color fun he poked at my blushing Aunt Yaffa and her new boyfriend, Konrad Lutz, who had been a master carpenter in Stuttgart before the war.

After dinner, the men retired to my uncle's den. I felt proud when my grandfather asked me to accompany them.

"He is almost a man," he exclaimed, smiling and winking. "We can't have him bustling around the kitchen with the women, can we?"

My father frowned, but did not protest.

At first, the pleasant mood from the dining room continued. Uncle Solomon produced some glasses and a bottle, and proceeded to pour out drinks for the adults. I was given a glass filled with seltzer water.

"To a happy and healthy New Year, gentlemen. *Lehaim!*" he exclaimed, whereupon they all touched glasses. Several more toasts followed. Gradually, the conversation took a more serious turn.

Aunt Yaffa's boyfriend, unaware of the family tensions lurking just beneath the surface, and feeling quite relaxed as a result of the liquor, remarked innocently, "I am relieved that the war ended when it did. My unit was being readied for the front. I don't mind telling you that I would rather be here than in some muddy trench."

My uncle's eyes went up to the ceiling in dismay. Before he could change the subject, though, my father responded. "And I suppose," he began, his voice tinged with irony, "that you are relieved that Germany was defeated. I suppose you are happy that your country will be picked over by the vultures like a rotting corpse in the desert."

The younger man was confused by the unexpectedly hostile response. Uncle Solomon attempted to restore the former mood with a lighthearted remark, but my grandfather interrupted. "I think, gentlemen, that Erich is right. This is a solemn moment in our history. With all due respect to your efforts to keep the peace, Sol, it seems that we should use this opportunity to clear the air in an intelligent, constructive fashion. We are still all in the same boat, and there is the real possibility that we'll all sink together."

My father motioned me with his head to leave the room. As I reluctantly turned to obey, my grandfather turned to him. "Please let him stay, Erich. If he's to get on in this world he'll have to learn to deal with it as it is. Perhaps it isn't too late for us to teach him that people can disagree and remain civilized. We haven't done too good a job at that up till now. In fact, both our generations have rather poor models. I think we have to put aside our personal feelings for the time being. We owe him that much."

My father hesitated for what seemed a very long time. Then, to my surprise, his expression softened. He looked at my grandfather and nodded. "Yes, you are right, Jacob. It is time to show that there can be sanity in the world." Then, to my even greater amazement, he turned to me and said, "Sit down, Heinchen, and listen carefully. Your grandfather is a wise man, and your father is trying very hard to become one. As for you, Solomon," now he turned to my smiling uncle, "you have lived up to your name. Probably, though, you were just plain *meshuggah* to invite the two of us here together. And our poor carpenter never knew that he was in the middle of a civil war." Everyone chuckled while Konrad Lutz shifted uneasily from one foot to the other, not certain what was happening.

"I don't expect to convert you, Erich," my grandfather smiled as he spoke, his eyes fixed on my father's. "All I ask is that you hear me out. Then I'll do the same for you. Perhaps we can find some common ground to sow together. We've had our fill of war. Now it is time for peace."

"Agreed," responded my father, bowing formally.

My grandfather walked over to him and extended his hand. As they shook hands, Uncle Solomon quipped, "Now that you have shaken hands, you can come out fighting. I would hate to see an old family feud fade away without one good final round."

"Yes, it is true," began my grandfather, "that when you emigrated here Germany looked like paradise in comparison to what you had known. I think I understand."

My father interrupted immediately. His voice was steady, but the slight tic at the corner of his mouth betrayed emotion. "Unless you have been there, Jacob, you can't understand a damn thing about it. You can't begin to feel the terror of a seven-year-old seeing his father beaten to a pulp, and his sister raped by a gang of drunken Cossacks. Can you really imagine how it is to live every day in fear that it could be your last? That your existence might be blotted out on the sudden whim of a bunch of thugs who decide to beat up or kill a few Jews for recreation? No, Jacob, you do not understand."

My grandfather shook his head sadly and stroked his greying beard. "Perhaps you're right, Erich, but I don't think you have to experience something directly to understand it. Besides, brutality comes in many forms. There is a brutality which is less visible, but all the more insidious —

a brutality of the spirit. It doesn't strike out of the blue like a drunken Cossack's sword or boot, but it is there, eating away at your defenses like acid on metal, until one day you crumble at the slightest touch. While Russia was and is a barbaric place, particularly for us Jews, Germany also has its dark side, its brutal underbelly."

My father had grown more animated by these words. "Everything you say shows that you consider yourself to be a Jew living in Germany," he said with disgust. "I prefer to view myself as a German who happens to be Jewish through the accident of ancestry. If we begin with such a differing premise, how can we ever reach any common ground? Can't you see that by separating the Jew from society you condemn him to remain on the outside?"

My grandfather waited for my father to complete his thought. Then he replied, "What matters isn't how we view ourselves, but how others view us. That is our real problem. Those who believe that the future for Jews lies in assimilation are destined to be cruelly disappointed. It hasn't worked before, and it is not working now. History teaches us that at best we are tolerated. At worst...well, you know what happens."

My grandfather paused to let his words take effect. Uncle Solomon sat alongside Konrad Lutz on the large leather sofa, both concentrating intently on the discussion.

My father had also sat down. He rubbed his thigh as he responded, "How can you say that? If I'm not mistaken, Jacob, you are the owner of a successful firm and a respected member of your community. What more should one expect? At the risk of offending you, I must say that you are more German than you would like to admit. You read Goethe and Schiller, you enjoy Beethoven. Your thinking has been formed by these influences as much as it has by this Johnny-come-lately Zionism. Movements come and go. One's country remains."

"You continue to miss the point," my grandfather said, measuring his words carefully. "It isn't what I think or even what I am that determines my fate. No matter how thoroughly I read Goethe and Schiller or how rapturously I listen to Beethoven's music, to the overwhelming majority of citizens in this deteriorating Reich I am still Jacob Feinberg the Jew. Just as you are Erich Hartstein the Jew, no matter what you have done or what you believe. Zionism did not appear mysteriously one day to seek me out. It is a force that has always been within me, waiting for me to discover and harness it."

"Excuse me, Jacob, but I have a question," Uncle Solomon said, his voice uncharacteristically serious. My grandfather nodded for him to speak. "As you know, Jacob," he began, "I try to avoid such discussions, but I find it very difficult to play the role of bystander for more than five minutes at a time. My question is this: If there is no future here for Jews, what the hell are we doing here? Unless I'm mistaken, very few of us, whether we are assimilationists, Zionists, or whatever other-ists, have left for The Promised Land. It has been said by some, in fact, that the few German-Jews that are in Palestine are called *Bei-uns niks*, because they never miss a chance to brag about how much better it was in their former, exalted fatherland."

My father's eyebrows went up at this unexpected support. My grandfather smiled. There was a twinkle in his eye as he responded, "So, Solomon, you have been doing your research. And all this time I thought that you only found my speeches useful for catching up on your beauty rest — just as Herr Lutz is doing right this minute." All eyes turned to the carpenter from Stuttgart who had put his head back against the leather sofa and fallen soundly asleep. "But let me attempt to answer your question as best I can," he continued, looking from Uncle Solomon to my father, and then to me. "It will not be easy, since I'm a simple businessman, not a college professor." He smiled again. "And what is involved here is an extremely complicated combination of psychology, history, pragmatism and idealism — in short, a witch's brew that can boil over at any moment."

At this point, my grandfather's eyes met mine. His glance indicated that his next words were directed at me. I had a mystic feeling that he was sharing a precious possession with me. His gentle, sad smile told me that he, in turn, knew that I had understood. He stroked his beard and continued, "I'd like to relate an incident from my own life, since I feel that it bears directly on your question, Sol. Sooner or later virtually every Jew faces a similar situation, although we don't all respond in the same way. You see, when I was younger, I believed much as Erich does." He shifted his gaze momentarily to my father. "Yes, I was also convinced that I was a model German. What you said before was correct. My ideas were shaped by Goethe and the other great minds from this land of poets and thinkers. I truly believed that I belonged here as much as any Hans, Fritz or Wilhelm. After all, I was born here."

I looked over at my father and uncle; they were both listening carefully. Konrad Lutz had awakened, but seemed to be having some difficulty focusing his eyes.

"When I was a young man," my grandfather continued, "our family had a live-in maid whom we considered more a relative than a servant. But she, apparently, did not share our feelings. She was a good Bavarian Catholic. Out of the blue one day she confided in me that she regularly went to confession to beg forgiveness for working for a family that belonged to the race that had killed God. I was bewildered, although it took years for me to suffer the full effect of her revelation. It was a gradual, subconscious process, an erosion of self-esteem that ultimately caused me to doubt my very identity. The crisis became acute when I realized that I was living my life as if our maid had been correct. I avoided anything that would identify me as a Jew. In fact, I often went out of my way to camouflage my Jewishness. I refused to speak Yiddish with acquaintances of my parents, pretending that I did not understand, and felt ashamed whenever the subject of my heritage emerged. I led a double life, not only with the world outside, but even with myself, just as you do, Erich."

"That isn't true." My father tried to get to his feet, but his artificial leg refused to cooperate. He sank back into the easy chair. "There is no comparison between your story and my present situation. None at all. For one thing, I never had a Catholic maid, or any other kind for that matter. I came to this country seeking refuge, with little more than the clothes on my back. And with my blood and sweat, I became a German. You, on the other hand, were born a German and choose to be regarded as a Jew. That is the problem. How can we expect to be accepted as Germans if we keep shoving our Jewishness down everyone's throat? You can't have your cake and eat it too. Which do you want, Jacob, to have it or eat it?"

I sat spellbound, wondering how my grandfather would counter this. On the one hand, I agreed with my father, but I was also aware from experience that my grandfather's observations were equally true.

It was Uncle Solomon who answered. "It seems that we have a bit of a paradox here. Unfortunately, I can't cut your arguments in two and offer half to each of you as my biblical namesake did with a disputed child, but I would like to summarize what we have up to this point in the discussion." Uncle Solomon stood up and began to pace back and forth in front of the leather sofa like an attorney. "First," he began, in his familiar, playful tone, "we have the fact that we Jews are still held guilty for murdering the Christian God, a God who was himself Jewish. It seems that Christian anti-Semites have even more of a paradox on their hands than we do. But that is their problem. Next, we are told not to call attention to the fact that we are Jews, because if we do we shall be recognized as such and prevented from being that which we want to be. No wonder we are called The Chosen People. No one in his right mind would volunteer for such craziness. It seems to me that we are confronted by the old dilemma of trying to determine which came first, the chicken or the egg. Can we really blame anyone for seeking refuge in sleep?" Uncle Solomon pointed over at Konrad Lutz, who had dropped off into dreamland once more.

"What the hell is your point, Sol?" To my surprise, my father's tone was more amused than angry. "Are you trying to say that we are all idiots?"

"Not at all, not at all," answered Uncle Solomon, a feigned expression of surprise on his face. "My point is that Jacob hasn't answered my original question, even though his maid story was quite interesting. Not spicy enough for my taste, but interesting. I would still like to know why we are here if the situation is so hopeless? Why aren't we on a boat heading to The Promised Land? You see, Erich, for the time being I am your ally, and for a good reason. While our esteemed father-in-law has only to contend with being a Jew, we have the double distinction of being Jewish cripples." He patted his deformed leg gently. "But don't count on my continued loyalty," he added. "We genetic cripples, unlike you heroic ones, are a very unreliable lot."

"Why are we here? Why are we here?" My grandfather repeated the question to himself, as if expecting the answer to jump out of his mouth on its own. Then, apparently satisfied it would not, he went on. "When I say that the Jew doesn't belong, I don't mean to suggest that he isn't human. On the contrary, our history proves that we have been all too human in our inability or unwillingness to shape our own destiny. We have followed a foreign piper many times in our history, and as often as not his music has led us to the river. Our passivity demonstrates that man is a creature of habit, simultaneously gifted and cursed with an uncanny ability to rationalize any and every situation. Thus, some of us stay here because we feel comfortable, because we have fooled ourselves into equating comfort with security, and security with happiness. Others of us remain because we no longer have the will to make the decision to leave, a decision that may someday be made for us. Yet others of us stay because we are unaware of an alternative, or simply do not care to acknowledge our awareness. And finally, some of us stay because we believe that our presence and efforts here will eventually make it unnecessary for any of us to ever be forced to leave. We stay to ascertain that we will eventually have a choice between staying and leaving. We stay..."

"Whoa! Hold on for one moment, Jacob." My father rocked forward, his hand upraised. "I'm afraid you lost me somewhere along the way. Are you actually trying to say that the Zionists will eventually ensure a place for Jews in Germany? That is outright sophistry. You are no mere businessman. You are either a visionary or..." My father tapped the side of his head to make his point.

"Strange as it may sound," answered my grandfather softly, "I mean exactly that. Can't you understand? By establishing a Jewish homeland in Palestine we will translate an ancient vision into a present reality. We will make it possible for Jews to live in dignity anywhere they choose, because they and the rest of the world will know that they have a homeland, an anchor that can withstand any storm. Jews who remain dispersed throughout the world will exist in a reciprocal spiritual relationship with their root culture in Palestine, providing the manpower and the material means for its upbuilding. They, in turn, will receive their energy and strength from Palestine. It will mean, perhaps, the sacrifice of comfort, but the end result will be true security, the security that comes from knowing that one belongs."

A momentary silence followed.

Finally, Uncle Solomon spoke. "Bravo," he said, clapping his hands together and nodding. "That was a speech worthy of any Bavarian politician or rabbi. Since both are a mystery to me, though, let me reserve judgment for the time being. Try as I may not to fall into a stereotype, the accountant in me is still searching for the elusive bottom line. On the other hand, the cynic in me fears, dear Jacob, that you have simply proved what you said a minute or two ago, namely, that man is the master of rationalization."

My father was about to respond to my grandfather's exegesis when a thunderous clamor from the other side of the house diverted everyone's attention.

"What happened? What is it?" Konrad Lutz walked shakily into the living room, rubbing his eyes. We had all gathered at the two large windows overlooking the street. It was a parade, complete with drums, brass instruments, and singing.

"Look," shouted my sister Jutta, pointing her little finger and jumping up and down gleefully. "They have stockings up over their knees!" I watched the rows of colorfully dressed marchers go by, four abreast, singing in deep voices to the accompanying music. Some of them carried large banners and wore hats with feathers sticking out of the sides. Others were dressed in military uniforms, complete with battle helmets. Some of their helmets were decorated with a strange symbol — a twisted cross.

"So those are the lunatics they call the Freikorps," muttered Uncle Solomon, shaking his head from side to side scornfully. "I have heard that they are going to rescue us from the Communist peril. I suppose they intend to sing them to death."

"Don't underestimate them," interjected my grandfather. "Hate can be a very powerful weapon when it is organized and put on parade. If one is to believe the reports coming from Berlin and elsewhere, there are many more where these came from. God help us if they ever get too powerful. You see, they equate Communists with Jews. In fact, they equate all of the evils of the world with us, so let's not cheer them on."

My sisters pouted and whined as they were led away from the window. I concealed the fact that I was just as disappointed as they not to see the rest of the parade. My father made a few short remarks to the effect that my grandfather was overreacting, and that these so-called Freikorps were nothing but a bunch of hooligans who couldn't even march in formation. Before a new discussion could be started, though, we had forgotten all about them. My Aunt Rachel had announced that dessert was ready and ushered us all into the dining room.

***

We were to learn later, too much later, that what we had seen that day on Schwanthalerstrasse was the prologue to an inferno that would make Dante's pale beside it. Not even my grandfather, with all of his educated fear, not even he could have begun to imagine what unspeakable horrors were being incubated by that hatred about which he warned. *Yitgadal veyitkadach schyme raba*. Poor, dear Grandpa, what torments did you have to endure before you were laid to rest? Were your heart and spirit already broken before you were snatched up from that Munich street on that cold November day, or did you continue to have faith even then? Did you still believe in the ultimate triumph of good as your senses were assaulted by the sights and sounds of death in Buchenwald? Did your tired heart finally give out in despair, or did you at least have some final moments of peace, knowing that Grandma had not had to experience such horrors? Into which pit were your meager remains cast, not to fuse with the earth of The Promised Land, but with the filth of an alien, forever hateful place? Or does a part of you still float above the clouds, belched out of the crematorium chimney into an indifferent sky, a sky I can no longer look at without thinking of your broken dream and wondering why. Why is it not your face, but *theirs* that visit me in the night? Why is it not your voice, but *their* voices that scream me awake and awake and awake, never to sleep again?

***

Within weeks, my grandfather's fears proved justified. According to the newspaper reports, several Freikorps units had marched into Berlin and ousted the Communist revolutionaries who were on the verge of taking complete control of the capital. Unsatisfied with mere victory, moreover, they then sought out and brutally murdered the leaders of the insurrection.

"I think it's terrible. Violence is never an answer." My mother's voice shook with emotion as she read the newspaper article my father had placed in front of her on the dinner table.

"What did they expect, the fools?" he replied angrily. "Even an idiot knows that if you play with fire you can expect to get burned. Again, though, because of a few bad apples, most people will conclude that all Jews are to blame. Damn that Luxemburg bitch! If you ask me, she got just what she deserved — a free trip to The Promised Land. What kind of a woman spends her time with such nonsense?"

My mother's reaction startled everyone. She jumped up out of her chair and glared at my father. "I won't have this, Erich. I am sick and tired of hearing about killing, sick and tired of all this talk about fatherlands and promised lands. All I know is that I am a mother with children to feed, clothe, and teach to be decent people. God knows how difficult the first two tasks are in these crazy times, but when it comes to the third, you continually do your best to make it impossible. You think that because I am a woman I am incapable of having any ideas of my own. You think that because I keep silent I have nothing worth saying, no independent thoughts. Well, you are wrong, Erich, so very wrong." Her voice trailed off momentarily. Tears had welled up in her eyes.

My father sat there as if transfixed. He reached under the table to massage his thigh, as he always did when he was upset. Her outburst had caught him completely off guard. He was about to respond, but she interrupted.

"You are not the only one who has been wounded by the war. There are invisible injuries that are just as real, just as painful. I'm sure you understand how painful it is to see someone you love deformed, not so much physically, but spiritually. That is what the war has done to you, Erich. It has twisted and broken your humanity. You have let it take a great deal more than a leg from you."

My father winced involuntarily at her reference to deformity. "I don't understand," he said. His voice betrayed a degree of uncertainty I had never heard in it before. As if he noted this, too, he looked at me for a brief moment and then turned away in embarrassment.

"I mean," responded my mother softly, "that you and all of your comrades have brought the battlefield home with you and carry it within yourselves like some malignant disease. Your bitterness poisons the air more effectively than the canisters of mustard gas ever did. Is this the legacy you wish to leave your children? If it is, then I can only grieve over the fact that they were ever born." She shook her head from side to side and began to weep quietly.

At first my father didn't react. He seemed to be preoccupied with some faraway thought. Finally, he cleared his throat and said, almost in a whisper, "You should have said something to me sooner. I didn't know." He made no attempt to comfort my mother, but his sad eyes showed that he had understood.

Once again my father sank into a deep depression. He became taciturn, scarcely speaking for hours or even days at a time; his interest in politics faded away almost as suddenly as it had begun. Often he would sit in his easy chair and stare into space, an open, unread book propped on his lap. He seemed to have withdrawn into some private refuge.

***

An incident from that particular time stands out in my memory so vividly that it might have taken place yesterday. I had been sent home from school early one morning with influenza-like symptoms. The worldwide epidemic of the previous year, which had claimed twenty million lives, had left such a residue of fear that a few sneezes or coughs were sufficient to arouse a near panic.

My mother put me to bed at once, disregarding my protestations. I was lying there with the thermometer under my arm when my father came in.

"How are you, Heinchen?" he asked shyly. I assured him that I was fine, and that I didn't understand why such a fuss was being made over a simple runny nose.

He smiled gently and limped over to my bed, seating himself with some difficulty on the edge, his artificial leg outstretched. He hesitated for several seconds, then began to speak again. "I know I haven't been a perfect father to you and your sisters," he said, his eyes focused on some invisible point on the floor. "But sometimes adults forget that they were once children. They forget what it was like, or what it should have been like, and they allow themselves to get caught up in their own self-importance." He began to rub his thigh at the point where his artificial leg was joined to the stump. I sat up in bed, my interest greatly aroused. He continued to stare at the floor as he spoke. "Soon, you will make *bar-mitzvah* and be a man yourself. I only hope that as the years pass you will be strong enough and wise enough not to forget the child that you were." He sat there silently for several minutes, lost in thought. Then he stood up and left without another word.

I know now what you were trying to tell me, Papa, though you could not say it out loud. I understand your silence, and I regret that I was unable to give the proper response, the response I held within me and will hold within me until the end of time, although I shall never be able to tell it to you. The words were always there, even in the darkest death hours, they were there — the simple, "I love you too, Papa. I love you too."

***

The next few years were happy ones for me, in spite of the constant turmoil surrounding us. The statesmen of Europe had done their work at Versailles, setting the stage for a future conflagration, one that was to make the Great War seem like a skirmish. But as a result of Jacob Feinberg's foresightedness, the Hartstein family suffered less than most. Not only was my grandfather able to avoid the ruin that was the fate of so many other German industrialists and businessmen, but as a result of his investments in foreign capital, he was actually able to profit significantly from the rampant inflation. The German mark, which had stood at four to the American dollar at the beginning of the war, rose steadily and astronomically. The government presses worked twenty-four hours a day printing new currency to pay the 132 billion gold marks in reparations demanded by the victors. By 1923, the exchange rate stood at an unbelievable sixty-two billion to the dollar. Home and business mortgages were no longer worth the paper they were written on; life savings were wiped out overnight. There were food riots throughout the Reich. Customers battled with shopkeepers and each other for a scrap of meat. Under threat of invasion, Germany and her allies had been forced to accept sole moral responsibility for the war, and now had to reimburse her opponents for all losses and damages inflicted on them as a result of it.

My father seemed to drift further and further away as conditions worsened. Whereas formerly he would have rejected any attempt by anyone to assist him financially, he now seemed content to allow my grandfather to provide for his family. He suffered a gradual disintegration of faith, a growing awareness that everything he had formerly held sacred was being exposed as profane. His final attempt to resurrect the dying flame of his belief ended in near tragedy.

It was a bitter cold day in late February, 1920. I had just returned from school and was attempting to sneak into the bathroom to clean myself up a bit before my mother could see me. Following some unerring maternal instinct, she confronted me at the door.

"Heinrich," she cried out in dismay when she saw my disheveled clothes and bruised face. "Have you been fighting?"

I sighed, dreading the inevitable lecture to follow. At the same moment, my father emerged from his study.

"What happened, Heinchen?" he asked, his sad eyes holding mine unsteadily.

As I began to tell my story, however, I saw some of his former animation gradually resurface.

"It was that shithead, Eberthal again," I blurted out, forgetting myself momentarily. My mother gave me a reproving look. My father smiled, though his eyes remained sad. "He tried some of his usual tricks," I continued, trying my best to sound heroic. "But this time he didn't get away with them. I don't think he'll be bothering me for a while."

"And you actually sent him off wailing?" My father smiled broadly now.

I had come to the high point, describing with only slight exaggeration how I had interceded when Otto Eberthal and his friends began their daily persecution of Hirsch Grünfeld. "I told them to leave him alone and stop calling him such nasty things. Then they turned on me, but I was ready for them. I put my head down and charged like a bull. Otto didn't know what hit him. When his friends started punching me I swung my knapsack around in a circle and hit a couple of them in the face once or twice. Believe it or not, Hirsch joined in the free-for-all, and didn't even cry when they bloodied his lip. The best part, though, is that Karl Linsdorff, the judge's son, jumped in on our side. He's the best fighter in the class. Otto and his friends backed down pretty fast then, and after it was all over Karl told me and Hirsch that if they ever bothered us again we could count on him for help. I think he wants to be my friend." By this time words were pouring out of my mouth like air from a punctured balloon. In spite of herself, my mother was smiling.

When I finished, my father put his hands on my shoulders and drew me toward him. "Good work, son," he said softly. "I am very proud of you. That's the only way to deal with swine." To my great surprise, my mother nodded in agreement.

Invigorated by my example, perhaps, my father decided to attend a political rally scheduled in the Hofbräuhaus a few days later. For some time now, bright red leaflets and posters, adorned with the increasingly familiar swastikas, had appeared in Munich announcing an important speech by a member of a new party calling itself the National Socialist German Worker's Party. The evening of the rally, my mother listened nervously as my father described the featured speaker.

"His name is Hitler. He's an ex-trench soldier," he explained. "I've heard that he fought at the First Battle of Ypres; he earned not one, but two Iron Crosses First Class. We have a little bit in common, Herr Hitler and I. Perhaps we have even met. If so, I'll know him by sight. At any rate, I would like to hear what he has to say." In spite of his limp, my father managed a military swagger as he smoothed out his freshly pressed uniform with the palms of his hands and attached the Iron Cross to his jacket at a spot just above his heart.

I was still awake when he returned that evening. I heard the door bang noisily, followed by a thud. Suddenly, my mother screamed out in a voice so shrill that it sent shivers down my spine. I ran out of my room to find out what had happened and saw her crouched down on her hands and knees next to my father who lay slumped over on the floor by the door. His face and the entire front of his greatcoat were stained crimson; fresh blood oozed from a large, ugly gash that extended from the middle of his forehead down over his eye to the middle of his cheek. There were several other, smaller wounds on the other cheek and on his chin.

"Quickly, Heinrich," my mother shouted over her shoulder, trying desperately to gain control of herself. "Heat a large pot of water. Quickly!"

I raced into the kitchen and did as I had been told, my hand shaking as I filled the pot with water and set it on the stove. Tears streamed out of my eyes as I returned to the foyer.

I was somewhat relieved to see that my mother was calmer. She had opened my father's coat, placed a cushion behind his head, and was dabbing his wounds with an already blood-soaked towel. While she did this she mumbled words of comfort to him, much as one might do with an injured child. He seemed oblivious to her attentions; he sat there without moving and repeated again and again, "The filthy swine. The filthy, rotten swine."

Somehow my mother managed to cleanse the wound and stem the flow of blood, and together we half-dragged, half-carried my dazed father to the bedroom. I learned what had happened later. Dr. Griep, our family doctor, was about to leave after having taken more than forty stitches to close the lacerations in my father's head and face.

"My needle and thread are very busy these days, Frau Hartstein," he said, shaking his head. "This is the fifth or sixth person I have stitched up this week. I have lost count." Dr. Griep shook his head again and buckled his black bag. "These days going to hear a political speech can be as dangerous as it was fighting in the trenches." He turned to my father and smiled. "I suggest, Erich, that you limit your activities to something less dangerous, like mountain climbing."

"Do you want to tell me what happened?" asked my mother. I stood just outside the doorway and peered in nervously as my mother placed the breakfast tray on my father's lap. He was in a sitting position in the bed, his swollen face criss-crossed by bandages. When he answered, his voice sounded raspy and distant.

"It was unbelievable, Esi, unbelievable. That man is a spellbinding devil. I have never witnessed anything like it in my life." He sighed loudly and continued with considerable difficulty. "There must have been almost two thousand people there in the main Festhall of the Hofbräuhaus," he began. "Everyone was drinking beer, talking politics and waiting for this Hitler fellow to speak. I have been to many political rallies and I can tell you this one was different. Along with the National Socialists there were Communists, Socialists, and others from many different parties. A group of war veterans, in uniform like myself, invited me to sit with them." He took a sip of steaming coffee and winced with pain before continuing. "The first speaker was so damned boring that hardly anyone was listening after the first few minutes. And then Hitler was introduced. I was disappointed when I saw him. He wasn't in uniform as I had expected. He was wearing an old blue suit, and looked more like a shopkeeper than a soldier or politician." He paused and flexed his jaw for a few seconds. It was obviously painful for him to speak. He seemed, however, to be under some kind of compulsion to verbalize his experience, as if by so doing he might better understand it himself. "But when he spoke, Esi, I tell you he had the crowd in the palm of his hand. Many of the things he said were things I had thought myself, but could never put into words. He spoke of the treachery that had cost Germany the war, and about the terrible problems imposed on us by the disgraceful peace. Those who had obviously come just to start trouble, mostly Communists, were taken care of quickly by his tough henchmen. They had clubs and whips and knew how to use them." He reached down to rub his thigh, then shook his head. "Then he began to present his party's program. It was the usual stuff, nothing really exceptional. I had heard most of it a hundred times before: equality for Germany, revocation of the Versailles Treaty, law and order, the kind of thing no one could really disagree with. I found myself nodding my head enthusiastically."

He took another sip of coffee and winced again. For a few seconds he gazed at the ceiling, as if struggling to assemble his thoughts. Finally, he spoke again. His voice had a weary echo to it.

"When he began to talk about the Jews my heart sank. I had read in the newspapers that he was an outspoken anti-Semite, but I suppose I was hoping that it wasn't true." There was another pause before he continued. "He intimated that they...we...were responsible for all the problems facing

Germany. He said that Jews should be treated as aliens, that we should not be allowed to hold public office, and if necessary we should be deported for the good of true Germans. And most of the people in that hall cheered, Esi. They raised their glasses and cheered." His voice trailed off at that point.

My mother had moved over to his side and removed the breakfast tray. Now she held his hand in hers and stroked his arm gently. I moved into the room to hear better. My father's voice was growing fainter.

"Among those who cheered the loudest were the uniformed veterans at my table, my so-called comrades. Of course they had no way of knowing that I was Jewish, but that really has nothing to do with it. When Hitler made his statement about Jews being aliens they lifted their beer mugs and shouted approval. Their faces were twisted with hatred. I felt as if someone had suddenly pulled a carpet out from under me." My father's face grew pale; his upper lip twitched as he continued. "The next thing I knew I was shouting uncontrollably at them, at Hitler, perhaps mostly at myself. I called them the dirty swine they were. They answered with their truncheons and whips. Someone threw a beer mug into my face. I think it was one of the veterans." He closed his eyes and sighed deeply, utterly exhausted. I barely heard his next words, which were whispered into the pillow. "Your father was right, Esi. He was right from the beginning."

***

At last I had a real friend. Karl Linsdorff was my opposite in just about every way. Although he had just turned fifteen, he was already almost six feet tall, more than a head taller than I. His steel-blue eyes and light blonde hair contrasted sharply with mine, which were dark brown and black respectively. In spite of these differences we became inseparable. Together we experienced the indescribable wonder and pain of puberty that summer of 1921.

The beautiful Munich countryside stretched out before us as we pedaled our bicycles tirelessly along the narrow road leading to the little town of Dachau. In our knapsacks were the fresh rolls, wurst, and canteens of cool water my mother had given us for our journey. We were on our way to visit Karl's aunt who lived in the modest cottage she and his uncle had worked so hard to build, but did not live to enjoy. The war had dictated a different scenario: Karl's uncle had been killed in the battle at Verdun by French machine gun bullets.

"My parents keep asking Aunt Siegelind to move in with us in Munich, but she refuses," explained Karl. "She says that she feels as if Uncle Rudolf is still with her in their house. My mother thinks she is being foolish."

We stopped beside a large barley field to take a drink of water and bite off a chunk of wurst before finishing the last lap of our journey. As we were rebuckling our knapsacks and getting ready to set out again, a high-pitched female voice called out a greeting from somewhere to the side of us. We both turned around in surprise at the unexpected sound. A pretty, red-cheeked girl dressed in a traditional Bavarian dirndl emerged from a little path I had not noticed. Although it was difficult to determine, I guessed her age at about seventeen or eighteen. She brushed aside a strand of reddish-blonde hair that had worked its way out of her peasant cap. "And what, may I ask, brings two city boys all the way out here to the country?" she added, her manner playful as she scanned our city clothes with her lively eyes. I felt the blood rush to my cheeks.

"We're on our way to visit my aunt in Dachau." Karl, whose face was also red, attempted unsuccessfully to keep his voice at a low pitch; he was at the age where it fluctuated between the deeper tones of an adult and the squeaking timbre of a child.

"And how about you, little Blacktop?" She turned to me, her large breasts straining at the tight, frilled bodice of her dirndl. "Do you also have an aunt in Dachau?"

I blushed more deeply and mumbled an embarrassed, "No," my eyes sweeping down to her wide hips as if drawn by some magnetic force. We stood there like two oafs, shifting nervously from one foot to the other.

She seemed to be enjoying our discomfort. She smiled coquettishly and asked, "And where are your girlfriends? Don't tell me two handsome boys like you don't have a whole army of them chasing after you." As she laughed, several tiny freckles seemed to dance gaily on the end of her nose. In spite of the fact that she was teasing us, I was not offended. She had an outgoing manner that put us at ease. Very quickly we were jabbering away with her as if she were an old friend, answering her questions about life in Munich with typical teenaged embellishment. The conversation ranged from Munich's Marienplatz to horses, and when she suggested we go with her to see the colt that had just been born on her family's farm, we immediately agreed. She hopped gingerly up onto Karl's crossbar and we set off on the path from which she had come.

"There's our barn," she called out happily, when we had ridden about a kilometer. Karl was puffing heavily from the combined strain of the extra burden and the bumpiness of the road. Just ahead was a typical wooden Bavarian farmhouse, and a few hundred feet to its left a large barn. "My parents are at the market; they won't be back until later this afternoon," she volunteered. As she dismounted, her short skirt momentarily fluttered up over her firm thighs. "Come on, the colt is in here." We left our bicycles at the side of the path and followed her into the barn.

At first my sense of smell was assaulted by the unfamiliar aroma of farm animals. A sleepy looking black and white cow occupied one stall to the front. As we passed her she gave a half-hearted moo and flipped her tail at some annoying flies.

"That's Hessie," laughed our new friend. "And by the way, my name is Heike. What about you two?"

We, too, laughed as we gave her our names. Hessie had taken our entrance as the signal to release a cascade of urine onto the hay beneath her, mooing again in accompaniment. "The colt is over there, at the end." Heike skipped gingerly over to a stall on the other side of the barn. "This is Schmutzi," she announced, as we arrived. There in the stall was a large brown mare; underneath her powerful body, enjoying his midday meal, was a spindly-legged colt of the same color. "We aren't quite sure what to name the colt yet. Can you think of a good name for him? For a few minutes we stood and watched in fascination as the colt continued to slurp away, trying to think of a proper name for the little fellow. We were unaware that Heike was no longer with us until we heard her voice from somewhere up above.

"When you are finished down there why don't you come up here to the hayloft? I have something interesting to show you both. There is a ladder just to your left."

Curious to know what could be so interesting in a hayloft, we raced over to the ladder, jostling each other playfully. Karl managed to elbow me out of the way and scampered up the ladder with me right behind him. When he got to the top, however, he stopped short and remained with just his head protruding above the loft floor.

"What's going on?" I yelled, slapping at his feet to get him moving again. Finally, he covered the final distance and pulled himself into the loft. When I got there seconds later, I saw what had stopped him dead in his tracks: at the far end, stretched out on a blanket that she had placed over a pile of hay, was Heike, minus her dirndl and whatever else she had been wearing.

We didn't realize at the time that our popularity was due to the fact that the war had depleted the supply of older males in the area. When we said our good-byes sometime later, both of us were convinced that we were the greatest lady-killers in the world, and we were determined to visit Karl's aunt on a regular basis. The world was a wondrous place for me that summer; each day was filled with discovery. I was young, in love (I believed fervently that I loved Heike), and had my whole future before me. I did not know, nor would it have meant anything to me if I had known, that in that very same month Adolf Hitler would become the undisputed Führer of the steadily expanding, but still relatively insignificant Nazi Party.

Munich, like the rest of Germany, continued to suffer from an ongoing nervous breakdown, and yet I felt that my life had never been so full of promise. War reparations, inflation, changes in government, political assassinations — as far as I was concerned these were the affairs of adults. At any rate, we were repeatedly assured that everything would work itself out favorably. Our teachers, formerly so adamant in their support for the

Kaiser, were now championing the New Republic. Our constitution, they assured us, was the most progressive in the world, based as it was on the dignity of the human person. Class privileges had been eliminated; in their place were social equality, personal freedom, and justice. The *Grundrechte* guaranteed the rights of national minorities, as well as freedom of speech, the press, and freedom to worship as one wished. The Weimar Constitution even went so far as to safeguard the rights of young people in the Republic. To me, in the summer of 1921, that latter safeguard meant the right to make a weekly trip to the familiar farmhouse on the outskirts of Dachau. To both Karl's and my disappointment, though, this right was revoked all too soon, but not by the government. Heike's passion, reflecting the weather, cooled with the approach of autumn. Finally, she let us know in as pleasant a way as possible that our visits would no longer be possible. She had, she informed us proudly, become engaged to a poultry farmer from the nearby town of Fürstenfeldbruck. He was the eldest son of a family friend. And so, as abruptly as it had come into being, our summer *ménage à trois* was disbanded.

***

How short the happy times are; how soon we are forced to admit that our hopes and dreams, yes, our lives are like smoke in the wind — like the smoke from the fire pits of Treblinka, where night and day the insatiable flames consumed the dead and dying flesh. And although I have defied the odds by surviving those flames, they continue to burn through me as thoroughly as if I had been cast into them. Thus, there is no joyful memory, no major or minor event which I can conjure up that is not eaten up by the fires of Treblinka and turned to smoke. My mind cannot, for example, rejoice in the memory of Heike's beautiful nakedness, for no sooner do I recall this vision than it is metamorphosed, transported like smoke in the wind to that other place and time, replaced by other naked women, equally beautiful, some more beautiful, but all of them trembling in terror rather than from passion. And always, and always, I see *her*, running along with the others beneath descending whips, heroically attempting to keep her two screaming children at her sides, thinking perhaps, insofar as thought was possible during those final, insane moments, that she might still be able to protect them from the unimaginable horror beyond the gas chamber door.

***

"There is nothing new about it, nothing at all. It's a reliable old formula that works wonders wherever it is applied, and it is the model of simplicity: If you have problems, beat up a Jew. If that doesn't work, kill one. It might not solve your problems, but it makes you feel so much better."

My father half-frowned, half-smiled at Uncle Solomon's remark, massaging his thigh gently with the tips of his fingers. We were in the front office of the Feinberg Ovenworks on Baaderstrasse waiting for my grandfather to arrive.

My father had resumed his old position with the firm, and now during school vacations I sometimes helped. I enjoyed running errands for him, my uncle, and my grandfather, and was quickly and eagerly learning the various aspects of the business.

"It gets more and more difficult to understand any of this nonsense," muttered my father, shaking his head in disgust. "They wanted to get rid of the Kaiser, and now that he's gone they want to get rid of the Republic. What the hell do they really want?"

"There's still some of the old nationalist in you, isn't there, Erich?" taunted Uncle Solomon in his usual playful tone. "I thought the Nazis, or whatever they call themselves, had knocked some sense into your head. Take my advice and leave politics to those who have no sense of smell; they're the only ones who can survive the stench it makes. Besides, you have to have a head made of concrete to survive in German politics today."

My father's hand went up to his face involuntarily. The scars, although gradually losing their angry red coloration, were still visible.

"Let's just say that it would take a lot more than a few bats on my thick head to change me completely. You really don't think that everybody in Germany is like those assholes in swastika armbands, do you?" replied my father.

At that moment, my grandfather strode into the office. Uncle Solomon, unable to resist, blurted out, "Speaking of assholes, here is our esteemed leader. Hello Jacob!"

My grandfather, undaunted by the irreverent welcome, wagged his index finger at his son-in-law and countered, "When my daughter asked my permission to marry you, I thought she was crazy. Now that I've gotten to know you, though, I can say with confidence that I know she was." After a few more minutes of similar banter, he became more serious. "Take a look at this, Erich. He handed my father the newspaper he had been holding. "It's the new official rag of the Hitler group; they call it *Der Stürmer*. I think you are familiar with their philosophy."

My father took a brief look at the paper and tossed it over into the large wastepaper basket by the desk.

"You shouldn't waste your money on trash like that, Jacob. It's just so much shit. No intelligent person would pay any attention to it."

"One never knows," responded my grandfather, stroking his beard thoughtfully. "You said yourself that Hitler is like a magnet. It's best to know what the enemy is up to." He stepped over to the basket, fished the newspaper out and placed it on his large oak desk.

"But what I wanted to talk to you both about this morning is business. I want you to listen too, Heinrich. You can learn some things here that you won't be taught in school or, for that matter, in the countryside near Dachau." My grandfather smiled at me and winked. My mouth opened in surprise; I could feel myself blushing. How did he know about that, I wondered. Or was he only guessing? Thankfully, he continued before the others became aware of my confusion.

"The way I see it, the mark is going to drop like a lead weight, at least over the near future, and if we are not careful we may find ourselves in a very bad situation. Until now we have managed to keep our heads above water because of our foreign business, but I'm afraid that there will be a very difficult period ahead. Some of our German contracts, including those with the government, will either be unwilling or unable to pay in anything other than marks. That is a fact. And it leaves us with two options: either we can renege on our agreements and face litigation, or we can meet the orders and accept payment in worthless paper. Either way, it can be unpleasant. We have to keep in mind, though, that this negative economic situation cannot last forever; there will be better days somewhere down the road. Erich, since you are involved in advertising and sales, I'd like to have your input."

My father hesitated a moment or two before responding. "I would say that the temporary losses are worth the potential gain in the future. If the economy doesn't straighten out, the country is kaput, and so is Feinberg's future here. On the other hand, our Swiss and American accounts will more than balance out the ledger even if we lose close to everything here. Fulfilling our commitments is an investment in future good will."

"Bravo! Well spoken," chimed in Uncle Solomon, tapping the side of his head with his index finger. "We wait for Germany to rise again like the mythological Phoenix, but in the meanwhile we thank the gods for Switzerland and America. You have come a long way from that little Russian village, brother Erich."

"Am I to understand, Solomon," interjected my grandfather, "that you disagree with this suggestion? Are you suggesting that there is no hope for Germany?" My grandfather's voice had a slight trace of sarcasm.

"Quite the contrary, quite the contrary," countered my uncle. "I only fear that our Phoenix might rise too high, and that the goodwill we buy will not be sufficient."

"Sufficient for what, Sol?" My father looked questioningly at his brother-in-law.

"Oh, I don't know," answered the latter. "Perhaps Jacob has gotten through to me more effectively than he realizes. I wouldn't be surprised if, before too long, I decide to pack my bags for the trip to Palestine." He smiled ironically at my grandfather, who nodded as he looked down thoughtfully at the newspaper on his desk.

***

"You'll love it, Heinrich, you really will. The lake itself is magnificent, and there is a tropical island there called Mainau with banana and orange trees and other exotic plants. We can take a ferry out to see it." Karl's excitement was infectious. For weeks he had been asking me to get my parent's permission to accompany him and his family to the summer cottage they had rented in Lindau, on the northeast shore of Lake Constance.

"All right," I answered. "I'll ask my parents today. But I will have to take off from work." We were walking home from school along the busy Brienner Strasse. The year 1922 had passed the halfway point; in a few weeks we would have our summer vacation break.

"The hell with it," Karl said and slapped me on the shoulder. "Feinberg's Ovenworks will survive without you for two weeks. Besides, how often does one get to go to the tropics without leaving Germany?"

"And you are sure that your parents won't mind?" Although I had asked Karl this question several times before, I now offered it as my last bit of resistance.

"Mind? They will be ecstatic. My father is quite impressed with you, you know. You are the scholar he wishes I would be. It must be pretty difficult for Judge Linsdorff to realize that his eldest son is much more interested in athletics than academics. Maybe he feels that you are a good influence. Let's face it, thanks to your tutoring my grades have been almost respectable this past year. But you have to admit, too, that your left hook has improved since I became your boxing coach." He laughed again and put his hands up in the classic boxing stance, flicking out a few quick jabs that grazed the side of my head. We sparred playfully for several seconds and then parted, Karl running the final few hundred meters to his home on Wittelsbacher Platz, while I trudged on to Jägerstrasse, some two blocks away.

"I don't know, Heinrich. Two weeks is a long time. After all, it isn't as if they are family." My mother looked over at my father and indicated with her eyes that she was leaving the final decision to him. He was in an exceptionally good mood that evening. My mother had prepared his favorite meal, a kind of borscht complete with sour cream, a rarity in those Spartan days. My sisters, who did not share his appetite for borscht, complained to one another and fiddled with their spoons.

"I think it would be good for him, Esi. Everything I have heard and read about Judge Linsdorff leads me to believe that he is a good man. Even your father has only positive things to say about him. Yes, I think it is very healthy for Heinchen to see that there are still a few good people in Germany." While the fists and clubs of the National Socialists had destroyed his beliefs, they had not yet totally destroyed his desire for faith.

Karl had not exaggerated; Lake Constance was magnificent. We arrived in Lindau in the early afternoon after a comfortable train ride and were quickly settled into the cottage, which turned out to be a large tudor structure, much more a castle than a cottage.

"A good friend of the family owns it," explained Karl, when I expressed my surprise. "He's a very important political figure in Berlin now, but he grew up here. My father and he were classmates at the University of Tübingen, and later they practiced law together in Munich. He's a nobleman. His name is Baron von Reichlin, but I always call him Uncle Gustav."

I was impressed at how nonchalantly Karl said this; as if it were perfectly normal to know a Baron and call him Uncle. We had been told in school that titles of nobility were no longer meaningful in the new Republic, but it seemed to me as if the addition of von before someone's name still carried some weight.

Karl and I explored the area for the remainder of the day, and went to bed early in anticipation of the trip we would be taking in the morning.

"I thought you had made the whole thing up just to get me to come," I said, fascinated by what I saw. The steamer had just let us off on the island of Mainau. Karl's mother and father were several steps behind us with his two younger brothers. I looked from side to side, scarcely able to believe my eyes. There were orange and banana trees, as well as palms, just as Karl had said. And everywhere, there were beautiful flowers. As we walked along we came to a quaint church surrounded by the lush vegetation.

"These trees and flowers can grow here because of the Gulf Stream, at least that's what they say. This is the Schlosskirche." Like a practiced tour guide, Karl extended his arm toward the baroque structure. "Come, I'll show you the rose garden and the tulip fields. Maybe we can take a rowboat out and explore. And later, when we get back to the house, I have a little surprise for you!" We set off toward the rose garden at a trot.

We arrived back in Lindau in the early evening. That day and the ones that followed remain for me among the most enjoyable of my life. They were days I was to recall often during times of despair, times when I was unsure whether to continue my dreadful existence, and needed to remember that there had been another life before the nightmare world of Treblinka. I needed to be assured that my feelings had once been human and alive. Often, while I worked feverishly on the ramp of the train station to sort the clothing and other possessions of those who had arrived on new transports, or ran full speed to the burning pits, bent under the weight of a newly murdered victim, I would go back in my thoughts to Lake Constance, and remember how beautiful flowers were, and how wonderful it was to smile and to laugh and to love...

"You said you had a surprise for me." I tried to sound nonchalant. Karl and I were sitting on the front step watching a beautiful sunset. The sun seemed to submerge itself in the rim of the lake, as if cooling itself after completing its work of the day.

"Patience, little Blacktop, patience," said Karl. "As Herr Kulp used to say: 'The longer the wait, the greater the victory.' I wonder where the old pervert is today." We both laughed at the thought of our former teacher who had been dismissed from his position a year or so earlier as a result of certain "improprieties" with a number of his male students. As we were talking, a sleek automobile pulled up in front of the house.

"Here they are now." Karl stood up and stepped briskly over to the car, leaving me to wonder who the new visitors were. A middle-aged couple stepped out of the front and now, one after the other, they greeted Karl and embraced him warmly. Just as I was coming to the conclusion that this had nothing to do with the promised surprise, the rear door opened and two young girls emerged, giggling happily as they said their hellos.

"Uncle Rolf, Aunt Marthe, this is my friend Heinrich," Karl said. I stood up awkwardly as they approached. The two older people shook my hand vigorously and uttered the usual salutations before making their way into the house. In the meantime, the two girls were waiting their turn to be introduced. In a mock formal tone that produced another volley of giggles, Karl announced, "Klara, I would like you to meet my comrade, Heinrich Hartstein The First. Heinrich, this is Klara Gottweil, the great love of my life." Klara giggled again and shook my hand, playfully poking Karl in the ribs with her free elbow. Her long blonde hair seemed to bounce as she moved, creating the illusion that it consisted of one piece rather than thousands of strands.

"And this is my surprise," continued Karl, once more in his pseudo formal voice. "Heinrich Hartstein, I would like to introduce you to your future wife, my cousin, Birgit." He swept both arms out in front of himself, one toward each of us, and bowed like a stage actor. For a second or two I was nonplused. Recovering control, I took her extended hand, bowed and kissed it the way I had seen it done in films.

"Well done, Herr Baron von Hartstein," shouted my friend, smiling broadly. "Now let us make our entrance." Like true nobility, we entered the house with our ladies' hands gracefully resting on our forearms.

I was happy just being with Birgit, relaxed in a way I had never been with any other girl. She was not as physically pretty as Heike, nor as well endowed by nature (she was fifteen at the time), but the combination of her joyful temperament and gentle spirit generated a beauty that radiated to everything around her. Her brown hair and eyes indicated a southern heritage, which was confirmed by a conversation we had about a week after we met. The four of us had been hiking along the shore of the lake when we came to a clearing.

"Beyond that point is Austria." Birgit indicated a spot in the near distance. "My grandfather was an Austrian. Actually, his family originally came from somewhere in northern Italy. He lived in a small village near Innsbruck before he met my grandmother. Isn't it strange how people divide themselves with imaginary geographic lines? I never could understand that."

"My father says that it's all a question of business," offered Karl. "He claims that when you have a lot of countries, you always have the possibility of war, and that war is the most profitable business there is."

"And my father says that the Jews start all the wars," chimed in Klara, not wanting to be left out. Karl made a face at her and shook his head.

"Should we conclude then that our Heinrich is a warmonger? Take a look at him — why, he's as peaceful as a kitten." Karl tried to hide his annoyance behind a grin, but his voice betrayed him.

"Are you really Jewish, Heinrich?" Klara was more surprised than embarrassed. I nodded without answering. It was the first time since I arrived in Lindau that I had even thought about being Jewish. I glanced over at Birgit and noted an expression of mild curiosity on her face.

"As Jewish as Moses was," I answered, in as flippant a way as I could. In reality, I was extremely upset, not so much by Klara's insensitivity as by my own reaction to her question. A part of me had wanted to deny my heritage, to say no, no, no, I am not Jewish, but German, just as you are. I recalled my grandfather's description of a similar experience in his life and how it had changed his thinking. Before I could follow this train of thought, however, Birgit took hold of my arm and pulled me gently toward her.

"Come on, Moses," she said in a soft, chiding voice. "Let's continue our little hike." And then she put her head up close to mine and brushed her lips against mine so gently that I wasn't even sure that she had kissed me.

"Careful, cousin," teased Karl, wagging his finger at her. "You wouldn't want to ruin your spotless reputation." The temporary tension was relieved. However, as we set off back to the lake, I noticed that every so often Klara would look at me in a strange way, as if trying to decide something in her mind.

Two days later I had the opportunity to speak with Birgit alone. Klara had had to accompany her parents on a visit to some relatives in Konstanz on the other side of the lake. Judge Linsdorff was already back at his post in Munich (for the remainder of the summer he would spend only the weekends in Lindau), and Karl's mother was in the kitchen busily baking some of her special pastries. We were seated on the back veranda, looking down onto the yard at Karl who was trying to teach his yelping brothers some basic soccer maneuvers.

"I will be terribly depressed when you leave next week," she said, her clear eyes smiling sadly. "It will be dull around here without you."

I smiled back, beginning to feel melancholy. Although I missed my family, the thought of going back to Munich filled me with a sense of loss. I wondered if I would ever see her again.

"I don't think Klara will be so sad," I muttered, unaware at first why I had said such a thing. Then I realized that I was really trying to get Birgit to tell me what she thought of me.

"Oh, you mustn't pay too much attention to what Klara says," she answered, laughing. "She doesn't mean any harm. She's my best friend, but she always did talk too much. Sometimes she says things without thinking about them first. The truth is, she really likes you, Heinrich. She told me so. Her father is the one to blame for that business the other day. He's a fanatic, the leader of some group who believes in purity of blood and other nonsense like that. Naturally, no one pays much attention to him. I'm sure my parents don't agree with his ideas. How could they in view of the fact that my mother's ancestors were Italian? Anyway, for what it's worth, I certainly like you...very much." She placed her hand in mine and we sat there for many minutes without saying another word.

The silence was finally broken by Karl's shout from below, "Come on, you two, stop acting like an old married couple. Get down here and play ball with us." Still hand-in-hand, we made our way down to the yard.

I left for Munich with Karl's father that Sunday. Karl, who would be staying in Lindau for another two weeks, promised to "keep an eye on my bride" for me. Birgit and I had said our farewells the evening before, and although our parting scene lacked the grandeur of classic opera, our adolescent kisses and repeated promises to write to each other did have the flavor of high drama. Judge Linsdorff, sensitive to my depressed mood, tried to cheer me up somewhat during the drive back. He pointed out in his best courtroom manner that his niece would probably find some way to convince her parents to visit their Munich relatives in the very near future, and that when they did I would be an honored guest at his home.

***

The political situation continued to remain beyond my interest or comprehension as 1922 inexorably became history. Looking back, one can only wonder that anyone was able to function under the conditions that existed. Hatred, bitterness, despair — these were the gods ruling Germany, as her people became increasingly fragmented in the search for a way out of the postwar morass. Hatred, bitterness, despair — these were the lessons that seeped through the thin veneer of optimism our teachers pretended to exude. Hatred, bitterness, despair — the new trinity for a generation growing up under the shadow of shame and defeat. Everyone was diminished; men were no longer designated by their names or their deeds, but rather by the labels their changing affiliations stamped on them. Centrists, Communists, Socialists, Monarchists, Nationalists...who can remember all of them or what they really signified? And of course, at the bottom rung of this convoluted ladder was the insidious force that almost all of the others viewed as the cause for the growing catastrophe: the Jews, always the Jews.

***

As Karl's father had predicted, it was not long before I saw Birgit again. True to our word, she and I wrote to each other faithfully, pouring out our thoughts and feelings to each other as we could to no one else. And then, about a month after my return from Lindau, a happy letter arrived announcing that she would be coming to Munich. Her father, she explained, was going to attend a medical convention there and had agreed, no doubt with some encouragement, to include a visit to his brother and family. It struck me for the first time that I had not even known what her father's work was. When I questioned him about it, Karl explained to me that his uncle was not just a doctor, but a very prominent surgeon.

"Yes, my Uncle Rolf is another shining light in the Linsdorff galaxy," he said, with just a trace of irony. "He used to be chief of surgery in a large hospital in Nuremberg before moving to Lindau. Now he heads a research laboratory there, and according to the family grapevine, he is involved in some very avant-garde medical research. I suppose having an uncle who is a surgeon and a father who is a judge makes it only logical for me to want to become a boxer or soccer player." He laughed and made a few elaborate movements with his feet at an imaginary soccer ball. "By the way," he added, almost as an afterthought. "You are invited to dinner next Friday. Unless, of course, you have a previous engagement."

My mother's reaction to the news of Birgit's impending visit surprised me. Caught up in my own happiness, I didn't realize that she was disturbed by my glowing description of the two weeks I had spent at Lake Constance. She had listened silently and said something to the effect that I was only sixteen and should be concentrating more on my schoolwork, that it was nice that I had friends, but much too early to start thinking seriously about girls.

"I don't think you should go there Friday," she declared, when I told her about my invitation to the Linsdorff's. She was setting the table for dinner. We were home alone; my father had not yet returned from work and the twins were at their piano lessons with Frau Wenzel, an elderly spinster who had an apartment on the third floor. "You can tell them that you have to help out at your grandfather's factory."

"That's ridiculous, Mama," I responded incredulously. "Didn't you hear me? Birgit will be there." I was unaware that this was the very reason why she didn't want me to go.

"I just think it would be better for you to forget all this nonsense," she blurted out with uncharacteristic severity. "This Birgit may be a very nice person, but she is just not your kind." Large red blotches had broken out on her neck. Her eyes were simultaneously angry and pleading.

I was crushed. So that was it, I thought. That again. Rage welled up inside me. I felt as if a thick, black curtain were being drawn around me.

"Kind — what do you mean by kind? What kind am I, Mama?" my voice shook with emotion; tears of anger and frustration formed in my eyes and started to trickle down the sides of my face. "Haven't you always told me that I was as good as anyone else? And how can you talk about Birgit when you don't even know her? It's not fair!" I was shouting.

"You are a Jew, that is what you are. And when it comes to Jews there is no such thing as fairness." Her voice had become deceptively calm. The red blotches were larger and had fused in spots, leaving an angry, map-like pattern on her neck.

My self-control gone, I pounded my fist down onto the table, rattling the dishes and silverware.

"A Jew! A Jew! A Jew!" I repeated, pounding the table again. "I hate being a Jew! I'm sick of it, and I hate it!" My mother was startled by my violent response. A glass had tipped over and rolled over the edge of the table, shattering into hundreds of pieces on the floor below. I stared down at the fragments of scattered glass, shaking first one foot and then the other to remove a few splinters from my shoe tops. I felt suddenly empty, as fragmented as the glass beneath me. I looked over at my mother, making no attempt to hide my tears, and said pathetically, "But I love her, Mama. I love her."

She came over to me and put her arms around me as she had done when I was a child. "I know, I know, Heinchen," she whispered, looking up sadly, as if her heart were breaking. "And I am sure she loves you too, just as I do." Then she added, almost inaudibly, "I just don't want to see you get hurt."

***

I hear your words again, dear Mama. I hear them as I lie awake during these endless nights, straining my eyes to pierce the evil curtain that began to descend as the hated, twisted cross spread its poisonous tentacles across Europe, choking all traces of goodness in its path. I hear your words again, dear Mama, as I am assaulted nightly by hordes of nameless ghosts — ghosts still smeared with blood and excrement as they were when I pried their lifeless bodies from the pyramids of death they formed in a vain attempt to gain one final breath of air before the carbon dioxide constricted their lungs and blotted out their beings. I hear your words again as my back shudders under the memory of the whips that drove me on to do the devil's work, like a blind, unthinking beast. And invariably your words become *their* screams — the screams of three yellow-faced phantoms eerily emerging from the pile of excrement and blood-covered death to condemn me to an existence that has no substance, an existence devoid of life.

***

I knew immediately that something was wrong. Birgit appeared pale and nervous as she greeted me with a short handshake and a few set phrases. Her parents were cold, even hostile. Her mother sat at her side like a hired bodyguard, determined, it seemed, not to allow me to get within a meter of Birgit. Her father did not even acknowledge me. He immediately disappeared with his brother into the latter's study. Karl tried to break the somber mood with some humorous quips, but he was not successful.

The dinner conversation was forced and sparse. Surprisingly, Karl's father and uncle did not exchange more than a few words during the entire meal; any conversation that did take place was trivial, as if they had purposely agreed to limit themselves to banalities. I was relieved when it was time to leave. Karl accompanied me to the front door, and as I stepped out into the street he patted my shoulder and said, "Well, it looks like you are a free man again." From the serious look on his face, I knew that he was not joking.

Birgit and I wrote a few letters to each other after that disastrous evening, but all efforts to recapture our former familiarity failed. Everything had changed. Gradually our correspondence ceased.

In typical sixteen-year-old fashion, I dragged my battered emotions around for the next month or two, suffering unspeakably. My family suffered with me. My mother was tortured by ambivalence. On the one hand she was clearly relieved that my relationship with Birgit had come to an end without further complications, while on the other hand she shared my pain. To my surprise, my father also became unexpectedly solicitous toward me during that difficult time, though he could not seem to find the words to express his sympathy. Even my sisters showered me with little attentions.

Gradually, the pain subsided as the memory of Lake Constance became dimmer. I immersed myself in my schoolwork more than ever, my thoughts already directed toward the Abitur. Encouraged by Judge Linsdorff and supported by my parents, I had decided to attend the University of Munich to study law.

***

The year 1923 began ominously for the struggling Weimar Republic. Claiming that Germany had defaulted on the terms of the Versailles Treaty, the French sent in troops to occupy the Industrial Ruhr area. And when the furious German mine and factory workers of the Ruhr went on a government-sanctioned general strike to protest this action, the French increased their occupation force. There were reports of violent confrontation and bloodshed.

"The French are bastards, plain and simple. And dumb ones at that. Don't they realize that this criminal action will bankrupt Germany? I say that it is an outright act of revenge." My father sat back in his chair and rubbed the stump of his leg. "Everyone knows it is just a pretense," he continued, now fidgeting with his grey moustache. "They have wanted to take over the Ruhr all along. Now they use the fact that Germany is late in delivering a few telegraph poles and some coal to send in their army. This is going to lead to unbelievable chaos — the idiots are cutting off their own noses to spite their faces." My father had regained his former vigor, if not his faith. Since his experience in the Hofbräuhaus he had become bitter; his rancor included not only the enemies of Germany (which he recognized as virtually every other country), but Germany itself. Unlike my grandfather, moreover, he had no Utopian dream to blunt the edges of his disillusion.

Uncle Solomon sat across from him smiling enigmatically. "So you think you have problems," he responded, shaking his head from side to side. "How would you like to be in my place? These days are enough to challenge the ability of a mathematical genius. The value of the mark is dropping like a stone, and I am supposed to balance the books? Why, if it keeps up like this we will have to give our workers wheelbarrows to take home their pay at the end of the week. And how will a person be able to buy a wheelbarrow if he doesn't already have one to carry the money it will take to pay for it? Perhaps our future lawyer can solve this paradox." Uncle Solomon turned to me with an expression of mock expectation. In spite of the teasing tone, I knew that my uncle felt very close to me and respected my opinions. My mother often told me that he and my Aunt Rachel had more or less adopted me when it became evident that their marriage, then in its twelfth year, would remain childless.

I looked from my uncle to my father. The latter continued to play with the ends of his moustache.

"Judge Linsdorff says that the government will have to step in to subsidize all the people on fixed incomes if this inflation isn't stopped," I ventured, trying to organize my thoughts. "That would include anyone on government pensions, civil service workers, teachers, army officers, retired people...the list seems endless. He says that they won't be able to survive on their own, and that if steps aren't taken quickly there is going to be a bloody revolution."

My father frowned as I spoke. His reply betrayed irritation. "The judge is a good man, but when it comes to politics he is no better able to predict than anyone else. It seems to me from what you say about him, Heinchen, that he is a bit of a socialist. Be that as it may, though, does he ever tell you who is going to lead this bloody revolution?"

"As a matter of fact," I answered, sensing a note of jealousy in my father's voice, and tactfully trying to sound as if I didn't totally agree with my friend's father, "he says that Hitler and the NSDAP are the ones to watch out for."

"Hitler again," my father muttered thoughtfully, running his thumb along the scar on his face. "His name seems to be coming up more and more in Munich these days. You can hardly go out without seeing some of his Storm Troopers stirring up trouble. But as far as a revolution is concerned, corporals don't know the first thing about leading an army. Why, he is nothing but a glorified messenger boy. A clown."

"If Hitler is a clown," interrupted my uncle, "it is probably because this country is turning into a circus. The Communists want to set up a separatist government in the center of the country, while here in Bavaria we see a tug of war between the Monarchists and the so-called Nationalists. The Monarchists want to put Crown Prince Ruprecht on the throne, and the fanatic Nationalists like Hitler want to set up a dictatorship. Of course, all agree that the new order must be freed from the shackles of democracy, socialism, and last, but certainly not least, Jewish capitalism. I'm afraid, Erich, that the judge might not be so far off the mark. After all, Herr Hitler is being helped along by the 'dumb bastard French,' as you so aptly dubbed them. With such enemies, he doesn't really need any friends." Then he turned to me again and asked, "Tell me, Heinrich, what do your fellow students think about it all? It seems to me that the younger generation has as great a stake in this as we do, if not a greater one. And to tell the truth, I don't think that we old fogies have been nearly as good at solving problems as we have been at creating them."

I looked at my uncle blankly. Then, without intending to be funny, I answered, "I suppose when you really get down to it, we are just as fouled up as you are."

Uncle Solomon laughed. My father seconded his reaction with a chuckle or two of his own, leaving me uncertain whether they considered my observation profound or pointless.

***

"It is absolutely preposterous. Out of the question." My grandfather paced back and forth, flinging his arms out animatedly. The family was gathered in the large living room on Schwanthalerstrasse. There was an air of crisis in the room. My grandfather stood now at one side and addressed the others. "She is thirty-eight years old; she should have more sense than to even consider such a thing. It would be a catastrophe. I will never consent to it, never." He stamped his foot in frustration.

My grandmother sat calmly on the large sofa across from him, flanked by Aunt Yaffa and my sisters. My aunt's jaw was set in a determined expression. My parents and I were seated on a second, matching sofa, and next to us on an adjacent loveseat were my Aunt Rachel and Uncle Solomon.

We had just been given the news that had caused my grandfather such turmoil: Aunt Yaffa had received a proposal of marriage. They now awaited arrival of the prospective groom, who hoped to win their approval and blessing. Apparently, my grandfather was not inclined to grant either.

"She has had many opportunities, but whom does she pick?" he complained, looking around the room for support. "A widower with two children. As if there were no suitable men around." He paused to let his words sink in. Then he continued, "Not only that, but an American no less. And she intends to follow him across the ocean." For a moment it almost appeared as if my grandfather would slump to the floor under the weight of this idea. I looked over to Aunt Yaffa to see her reaction. If anything, her jaw was clenched even more firmly. My sisters sat like two matching bookends, showing no outward reaction to the tirade.

"Calm down, Jacob." My grandmother smiled softly, extending both hands toward him. "Why don't we try to discuss this calmly? We must be reasonable."

My grandfather wheeled to face his wife. His voice rose as he replied, "Reasonable? What is reason? Is there any reasoning with a...a..." He paused, groping for the proper word. Then he blurted out, "Woman?" His expression was a comic combination of anger and perplexity. For several seconds there was silence. I looked around the room. Uncle Solomon caught my eye and smiled, obviously enjoying the spectacle. Aunt Rachel fidgeted with her necklace, her eyes averted.

It was my mother who finally broke the silence. "If I am not mistaken, Papa," she began, making an effort to choose her words carefully, "when you faced a similar situation some years ago you had the same reaction. Things didn't turn out all that terribly, did they?" She placed her hand affectionately on my father's, waiting for a response. My father sat impassively, refusing to acknowledge that what was happening had anything to do with him.

"That was a completely different situation and you know it," my grandfather shot back. "Even though Erich has difficulty acknowledging it sometimes, he is still a Jew. Americans are a different race altogether, whether or not they claim to be Jewish as our Mr. Harris does. And there was never any plan to take you away from your family and plant you in some uncivilized land. I would never have given my blessing for something like that, anymore than I will give it to your sister now." He fixed Aunt Yaffa with a stare; she returned his gaze without flinching.

"Since we seem to be adopting the spirit of the Weimar Democracy here, may I, as the only son-in-law who seems to have received your unqualified blessing, make a comment?" Uncle Solomon leaned forward, a wry smile creasing his lips. My grandfather put his hand to his forehead and looked up at the ceiling, as if seeking some aid from that direction. Taking the ambiguous gesture as permission to speak, my uncle went on, "You seem to forget, Jacob, that it was you who introduced Yaffa and Victor to each other."

"What the hell is that supposed to mean?" spit out my grandfather, his face reddening. "Does it mean that she should chase every business associate I introduce her to to New York?"

Uncle Solomon waited for the outburst to subside before responding. His tone was openly playful. "Forget about the personal aspect for a minute and think of it in another way. From the business perspective, a union between Yaffa and Mr. Harris would be most advantageous to Feinberg's Ovenworks. You, Jacob, would not be losing a daughter, but gaining a more secure market foothold in the new world. As for Mr. Harris himself, he seems to be a splendid fellow."

"So, Sol," interrupted my grandfather, placing his hands on his hips and frowning. "You have been working behind the scenes as usual. How is it that you are so informed about all of this? It seems as if you always know a little more about everything than you should."

Uncle Solomon put his hand to his chest and feigned a hurt expression.

"You have wounded me, Jacob. Do you think that I would sneak around behind your back? How could you suggest such a terrible thing?"

My grandfather waved his hand impatiently. "For God's sake, Sol, stop the nonsense. Say what you have to say and be done with it. I'm really not in the mood for a comedy show right now."

"Stop it, Papa. Stop it right now." Everyone's head swiveled around toward Aunt Yaffa, who had jumped up to her feet and now stood with her hands balled to fists. My grandmother reached out and tried to pull Aunt Yaffa gently back down to a sitting position, but the latter jerked free and continued to speak. "You said yourself a few minutes ago that I was thirty-eight years old, Papa, but you treat me as if I were seventeen. What makes you think that you still have the right to tell me what to do?" She paused, then turned toward my uncle. "And I hardly need Solomon to lead my life for me." Yaffa's voice trembled.

My grandfather looked up at the ceiling once more, but divine aid was still denied him. Uncle Solomon's smile had faded; he shifted in his seat uncomfortably as Aunt Rachel cast a reprimanding glance at him. A loud knock at the door prevented my aunt from going on.

Victor Harris did not fit the larger-than-life American stereotype that I had expected. He was of medium height, with dark hair and deep-set, lively eyes. His dress, like his person, was unstriking; his wrinkled suit gave away the fact that he had recently been living from a suitcase. What did impress me, however, was his easy, relaxed manner, which contrasted markedly with the rather stiff European counterparts I had met. As my aunt nervously introduced him, he responded in a strangely accented, but grammatically correct German, seasoned with a Yiddish phrase here and there. The remainder of the day went smoothly. Our visitor's natural ability to put himself and others at ease enabled him to blend into the family very quickly, and before many hours had passed, even my grandfather seemed to have discarded any traces of his former hostility.

Uncle Solomon summed it up when, in a conspiratorial voice, he remarked to my grandfather, "Keep a positive attitude, Jacob. At least this one stays awake when you speak to him. Just think what it would be like if Yaffa had decided to marry the sleepy carpenter from Stuttgart."

***

By the autumn of 1923 the economic chaos in Germany had reached a peak. The government presses could no longer print money quickly enough to keep pace with the runaway mark and to circumvent this, old notes were simply stamped with new numbers. Thus, as if by magic, an official would stamp a ten thousand mark note and transform it into one worth ten million, or ten billion.

"It looks like Mephistopheles is at work again," remarked Uncle Solomon one evening. He and Aunt Rachel had stopped in to say hello. I was at the table in the dining room doing my schoolwork. He limped over to me and picked up my copy of Goethe's *Faust*. "Only this time," he added, "there is no Kaiser or buried treasure involved. Tell me though, Heinrich, what is an aspiring lawyer doing with a book like that? Shouldn't you be spending your time with the Justinian Code?"

I smiled and greeted him and my aunt with a hug, impressed as usual by his flexible, inquisitive mind. "Don't forget, Uncle Sol," I countered, imitating his bantering tone, "Goethe was a lawyer, too, and yet he wrote one of the most important poetic works of all time. So the least I can do is read it, no? At any rate, it isn't a matter of choice. As you know, every German worth his salt can quote chapter and verse from *Faust*."

"Yes, that is all too true," he said, a benign smile playing at the corners of his mouth. "It is something like the *Bible*, I suppose. Everyone quotes from it, but few ever read it. And be careful when you say that Goethe was a lawyer. Remember, he was also a poet, a playwright, a novelist, a painter, a statesman, a scientist, and most important of all, an insatiable lover, even at the age of eighty. He admitted himself that he particularly liked the southern ladies when he was younger. I take it you are trying to challenge his accomplishments in that particular area. You and your friend Karl seem to have compiled an impressive record already."

I put my index finger to my lips to shush him. My mother had just come into the room and was greeting her sister.

Uncle Solomon was obliquely referring to Carla Schupp, Karl's latest surprise for me. He had introduced her to me as a consolation prize for the loss of his cousin Birgit. Carla was a talented artist, and as I found out, able to do a more than adequate job of consoling me physically. I had confided in my uncle about her.

Carla belonged to the large artist colony in Munich, and although several years my senior, her childlike temperament made her seem more like a chronological peer. Karl and she had met under innocent enough circumstances; she had been commissioned by his father to do his official government portrait. Predictably, however, before very long Karl had "allowed himself to be seduced by the older woman."

"It makes me appreciate my father's liberal attitudes. If he were not so modern, he would never have hired a female painter," quipped Karl, after having introduced us to each other. Carla kissed him playfully on the neck as a reward, and smiled her warm, mischievous smile at me. Little did I know that before the day was out, she and I were to make love repeatedly in her quaint Brümelstrasse studio.

"She's married, you know," Karl informed me several days later, laughing at my astonishment. "But her husband is even more Bohemian than she is — a sculptor. Right now he is in Florence, studying the classic masterpieces that line the marketplaces there. And I'm sure he is also studying a bit of Italian anatomy in his spare time." He laughed again, making a suggestive gesture with his hands. "As for cara Carla," he continued, "she seems to prefer the classic Aryan type, although from what she tells me, she also finds a certain Semite quite charming...and *very* energetic."

I continued to see Carla periodically. On one of these trysts, she made a surprising revelation to me. "My mother is half-Jewish, so I guess that makes us distant cousins," she remarked casually, standing in front of me with her small, firm breasts already bared while she calmly pulled up her skirt. "Her other half, probably the lower one, is Italian," she added with a crisp laugh, noting my surprise. "I guess I share her fascination for blonde, blue-eyed warriors. Karl looks more like my father than I do. It could be that there is something incestuous about my attraction for him. As for you, you might very well be another sublimation for my incestuous tendencies; you could be a substitute in bed for my Jewish mother." She loved to shock me with outlandish statements like that, and when I reacted in the way she expected, she would throw back her head and emit a throaty laugh.

On another occasion she asked me to take off my clothes and began to look me over from head to foot with the eye of a professional painter. Then, leading me by the hand to the little cot in the corner as if I were a schoolboy, she pulled me down onto her and said, "I want to paint the two of you one day, Karl and you. I'll call my finished work 'Black and White Nudes.'"

***

"It doesn't look good at all for the short term." Uncle Solomon was obviously tired. He adjusted his eyeglasses and continued in a flat voice, "Unless we can find new suppliers, we are going to have to consider an indefinite suspension of all our operations. As for the long term, it isn't even certain that there will be one. Things have gotten to the point that if you miss your tram, the next one along costs you three times as much." He removed his glasses and rubbed his eyes.

It was late October, 1923; we were sitting in my grandfather's office. Business had been extremely slow at Feinberg's. Many of our financially pressed suppliers could no longer deliver critical production materials to us. Others had simply gone bankrupt. For the first time in the history of his firm, my grandfather had to suspend acceptance of new orders and was finding it increasingly difficult to meet existing contractual obligations.

"If it weren't for Victor," interjected my father, rubbing his thigh rhythmically with the palm of his hand, "we would have lost our American accounts already. But even he won't be able to hold the line for us indefinitely." He handed my grandfather a folder. The latter opened it and began to thumb through the papers inside it.

"I am beginning to think that Yaffa was the smartest one of all of us," my grandfather remarked, flipping the folder onto his desk. "America doesn't seem like such a bad idea at all these days."

"On the bright side, though," interrupted Uncle Solomon, regaining some of his customary spirit, "we have done very well with our real estate investments. Our foreign capital has made us land-rich, that is, if there is a land left when the dust settles. Feinberg's Ovenworks even owns a medieval castle on the Rhine. If worse comes to worst, we can always retreat to our castle and live out our lives like the kings of old."

My grandfather frowned. "You can be sure," he answered, "that many of our countrymen here would take great pleasure in storming our castle. The fanatic press is calling for the blood of all 'Jewish exploiters.' It matters little that most of the big industrialists who are capitalizing on this runaway inflation are what they call 'racially pure,' whatever the hell that means, not to mention the non-Jewish foreigners who are making a killing on our misfortune. Most of the Jews in Germany are suffering as much as the rest of the population."

"Who knows," concluded Uncle Solomon, smiling at my grandfather. "Your evaluation of Yaffa might very well turn out to be the understatement of your life. Someday we all might have to join her in the barbaric new world."

***

In retrospect, it is obvious that Uncle Solomon was already, at that early date, planning for what he considered to be the worst possible scenario for the future. I know, though, that even in his most pessimistic projections he could not have foreseen even a hint of the reality that was to become Treblinka. Only a madman would have had the capacity for such a vision, only one stripped of all reason and humanity.

Treblinka. It lurks behind every word I write, every thought I have. If only I could forget. It is not difficult to comprehend why God also tried to escape that place and time, refusing to acknowledge that His well-intentioned creation had borne such bitter, poisonous fruit. Did He not, perhaps, cover His eyes to avoid seeing the agonized contortions of the dying victims whose final moments of life were not spent singing joyful praise to His name and work, but suffering in the grip of a twisted evil sufficiently powerful to fill Him with disgust and despair? Did He not, perhaps, stop His ears so as to prevent Himself from hearing His children's final sounds, not prayers of thanksgiving, but shrieks of disbelief and agony? Was He able to bear the pervasive odor of suffering and death that poured uncontrollably from the victims' broken bodies and spirits, fouling their lives and the lives of all who would follow them? To which haven did He flee? Certainly not to Sobibor, or Majdanek, or Auschwitz, or Belzec, or Culmhof, or Mauthausen, or Stutthof, or Bergen-Belsen, or Buchenwald, or Plaszow, or Ravensbrück, or Flossenburg, or GrossRosen, or Dachau, or, or, or... No, He could not escape either; He could not and cannot escape anymore than we can. We who will carry the camps within us for all time. Beyond time. And when we ultimately confront Him with the question that burns through us with the intensity of the flame pits and the crematoria — the question why, why, and why again — will He be able or willing to give us an answer? Or will He simply indicate that He, too, was a victim? Will He lament that He, too, will be tortured for eternity by the memory of *their* contorted faces, *their* screams of pain and terror, and the stench of *their* death and dying, as I am today, and will be every day, and every day...

***

It was a cold November afternoon. Wet snowflakes fell sporadically as Karl and I elbowed our way back to Brienner Strasse through the milling crowds lining the sidewalks of the Odeonsplatz. People leaned out of the windows overlooking the square, many waving small red, white, and black flags, the old colors of the monarchy with twisted Nazi crosses added in their centers. We paused at a spot across from the Feldherrnhalle. A green-uniformed member of the Landespolizei, one of a large group, waved us back impatiently with his bayoneted rifle.

Karl turned to me and remarked, "Look up ahead; here they come." I craned my neck to look in the direction he indicated and saw a column of marchers, four abreast, making its way up the Residenzstrasse, but the crowd surged forward, obscuring my view before I could distinguish any particular individuals. I was about to suggest to Karl that we move closer when a series of sharp sounds rang out, like exploding firecrackers. Instantly, the square was turned into bedlam. People began to run in all directions, screaming and lashing out wildly at anyone in their way, breaking through windows and doors to reach the safety of the surrounding buildings. There was another volley of gunfire accompanied by even louder screams. Within seconds the square had emptied, except for the Green Police and a number of prone or writhing figures strewn about on the cobblestones. I looked over toward the spot where Karl had been standing, but he was no longer there. Suddenly I felt a sharp, burning pain in my hand, just below the wrist, and in the next moment felt myself falling to the ground as if someone had pulled a carpet out from under me. As I struggled to push myself up, the pain in my hand became more severe. Dazed, I looked down to see what was causing my distress and discovered, to my surprise, that my hand was covered with blood.

"You were very lucky, Heinrich. A little lower and you might never have been able to become a concert pianist." Dr. Griep smiled as he expertly bandaged my wounded hand. Karl stood to one side, his face reflecting both fascination and concern. But for his quick action, I might still have been lying in the Odeonsplatz. He had reappeared at my side a few moments after I was wounded, pulled me to my feet and led me away from the scene at a trot. Although in a state of shock, with his assistance I was able to run the several blocks to the doctor's office on Finkenstrasse.

"It is just a superficial wound; it looks a lot more serious than it really is," continued the doctor, completing his work and patting me on the shoulder. "You were probably hit by a ricocheting bullet. But tell me, what were you boys doing out in the middle of all that lunacy? Don't you know that revolutions are dangerous?" He smiled kindly and waited for a response.

"We decided to take part in history." Karl tried to sound jocular, but his voice betrayed emotion. "I did get to see General Ludendorff for a second or two before all the commotion started. He looked a lot smaller and fatter than I thought he would."

Dr. Griep shook his head. "Heroes never look as impressive as we think they should," he said, wiping his forehead with his sleeve. "When we in the medical profession see them, they look very much like any other sick patients. I have yet to see or hear of one who did not bleed when his skin was broken." He walked across the room and began to wash his hands in the small sink in the corner. "By the way, did either of you get to see the rabble-rouser who organized this whole sorry mess?" When neither of us answered, he turned and added, "From what you have told me, I don't think any of us will be seeing Herr Hitler or anyone like him in Germany for a very long time to come. I'll never understand why he didn't stay in the Beer Hall instead of trying to take over the government. I prefer a good stein of beer over a revolution any day of the week. At any rate, if he isn't already dead, he may as well be. I hope they lock him up and throw away the key. I'm getting tired of repairing all the damage he causes."

Later in my grandfather's study, I finished giving my account of the fiasco in the Odeonsplatz.

"Well, I am glad those gangsters finally got what was coming to them. And good riddance to them." My grandfather looked at my bandaged hand and frowned. Several days had passed since the "Beer Hall Putsch," as the Nazi's premature effort to take power was labeled. Hitler was already tucked away in Landsberg prison, nursing the shoulder he had injured while fleeing from the police and awaiting trial. Almost without exception, the Munich newspapers expressed the judgment that the National Socialist Party was a thing of the past. It was now time, they urged, to unite in support of the constitutional government.

"They certainly showed themselves to be the miserable cowards they are." My father ran his finger along the jagged white scar on his face and limped across the room to the leather sofa. He let himself down with a grunt and stretched his artificial leg straight out. "If they had had any real courage they would have made a fight of it," he continued, his voice rising. "They could have used the buildings, windows, and roofs to their advantage, and then formed skirmish lines with their reserves to harass the police troops. You don't have to be a military genius to figure that out. But instead they chose to turn tail and run like frightened children. And their great leader, who vowed publicly that he would be master of Germany or dead within twenty-four hours, is now neither. He is nothing more than another petty criminal in jail."

"I don't know very much about military tactics or fanatical vows," countered my grandfather, "but I do know that it isn't that easy to get rid of a pestilence. It seems to me that this Nazi movement is more of a symptom than a disease. Unless all the germs are killed, there is a chance that it will flare up again at any time...and who can predict how severe the next outbreak will be? Unfortunately Hitler already has a few followers who consider him a kind of folk hero because of his idiotic little farce. The fact that that pompous ass Ludendorff was part of it makes it even more difficult to call it the treason that it was. I'm afraid that before this is over they will find some way to turn it into a noble, patriotic act."

Once more my grandfather's apprehension proved to be justified. It became evident very quickly that the so-called Putschist trial was nothing more than a propagandistic farce. For more than a month Germany and the world were entertained by Hitler's antics. Karl's father, who always encouraged me to discuss any legal questions with him, was uncharacteristically curt one day when I asked him if he thought that Hitler and the others would be convicted of treason. His reaction startled me.

"Convicted! That is the biggest laugh of all. We will be lucky if that swine who likes to be called the Führer isn't made the new Kaiser before this disgraceful spectacle is finished. The German legal profession has become the laughing stock of the entire world because of it. Hitler is being permitted to use the courtroom as a podium for his distorted ideas. It is an international scandal." After a short pause he continued, his voice more controlled. "There is more to it than meets the eye. Pressure is being exerted from all sides. The Minister of Justice is pulling the strings that make those three puppet judges dance, you can be sure of that. They have allowed Hitler to turn the tables on them, to the point where it now seems as if the state is on trial. To allow him to spit out his nonsense for hours at a time — it is simply inconceivable. He is making fools of us all. Can't anyone see that this trial is promoting Adolf Hitler from an insignificant local troublemaker to a serious political figure with national stature? Any thinking German should be trembling for his country right now."

The mild verdict handed down (ironically enough on April 1), was met with either indifference or patriotic joy by the majority of solid middle-class burghers in Munich. Few had believed that the great war hero Ludendorff would be convicted, and their faith was justified when the court judged him innocent and set him free. As for the five year sentence passed on Adolf Hitler, the minimum possible for the crime involved, it was common knowledge that the full term would not be served.

"He will be free within a year," predicted my Uncle Solomon, as we walked through the Hofgarten on a mild April day. "And the fact that his party and its scandal sheet have been outlawed will only make them that more attractive to a great many people. In a way, they have made a martyr of Herr Hitler. You have to give him credit — he is probably the first man in history to become a martyr by merely dislocating a shoulder."

***

The traditional family gathering on New Year's Day, 1925, took place on Jägerstrasse, and was happier than any I had known up to that point. Everyone seemed convinced that 1925 was destined to herald a new, happier era for us all. With the introduction of the new Rentenmark, the devastating economic chaos had finally been checked in the closing months of the outgoing year. One of these new notes equaled a trillion of the former, inflated variety.

"Well, Erich, we're no longer trillionaires," joked Uncle Solomon, sipping a glass of wine. "So let's all drink to this latest paradox. Our loss is our gain." He took another long sip and turned to me. "You see, Heinrich, Mephisto's plan has come full circle. Our politicians think they are geniuses for coming up with this solution, but we Goethe scholars know that it was proposed by the devil almost a hundred years ago."

"You have to admit, Uncle Sol," I answered, "that this is an even simpler plan than the one Goethe envisaged. Our new mark is not backed by buried treasure, but by the land itself. When you stop to think about it, it really is ingenious."

"Ingenious my missing foot," grumbled my father, not wanting to be left out of the conversation, although it was obvious that he was unfamiliar with our references to Mephisto and Goethe. "The next thing you know they will be issuing money with the sky as collateral. I don't understand any of it."

"There is no need to understand money, Erich," my grandfather said from across the table, "so long as you know how to earn it and spend it. You don't have to understand air in order to breathe, do you?"

"And you don't have to understand women to make love," added Uncle Solomon, smiling at his wife, who had just come into the room with my mother and grandmother. She blushed and gave him a reproving glance.

"And you don't have to understand men to know that they are really all naughty little boys," quipped my mother as she set a platter with steaming vegetables down on the table in front of my uncle.

For most of the remainder of the meal the conversation continued in this cheerful vein. I had never seen everyone so lighthearted before; even my grandmother joined in the lively conversation, telling stories from the days of her courtship with my grandfather. As for me and my sisters, for the first time in our lives it seemed as if the time of struggle was finally coming to an end. The economy was in better condition than it had been since before the war, and, as my grandmother repeated several times, we were all healthy, thank the Lord. She read aloud a recent letter she had received from my Aunt Yaffa, who reported that she was adjusting very well to life in the United States. She proudly informed us that she could already understand and make herself understood in English, and was enjoying her role as stepmother very much, although she missed us all. She would, she added happily, try to accompany Victor on his next business trip to Europe, which, God willing, would be soon.

It was Uncle Solomon who eventually brought the conversation around to politics.

"I see, Erich," he said, turning to my father during a lull in the conversation, "your Iron Cross comrade was released from prison several days ago. They say he has turned over a new leaf. As one of the conditions of his parole he had to promise not to lead any more revolts against the Republic. You would think that he would have enough brains to avoid another such fiasco without being told."

"The only way to get such a man to keep his word is to keep a gun pointed at his head," responded my father through clenched teeth.

"No," corrected my grandfather. "You don't control the likes of a Hitler simply by pointing a gun at him. You have to pull the trigger, and keep pulling it until you are sure he isn't going to get up again. I have read enough of his trash to know that he will never change."

I had never heard my grandfather speak like that. His voice was hard, his eyes determined. It seemed as if he would have liked to have the gun he spoke about in his hand. A moment later, however, his features softened and he added, "A better way to see that he keeps his word is to make sure that we do not allow conditions to deteriorate again. The Nazis are like scavengers; their carrion is discontent and failure. A satisfied, successful society cannot be led by such human dregs because it cannot identify with them. Scapegoats are only needed during bad times. They won't be able to capitalize on their hatred for us Jews when things are going well. The most effective weapon against their lies and hatred is a simple one — happiness."

"Hear, hear, as our British cousins say," offered Uncle Solomon, clapping his hands in mock applause. "But as much as I would like to feel secure with your line of reasoning, Jacob," he added, "I can't help thinking that happiness is far from simple, and at best an extremely temporary condition."

For the next few years it seemed as if Uncle Solomon's view of happiness was overly pessimistic. Gloom had been replaced by hope, sparsity by abundance, hostility by conciliation; everywhere one looked there was evidence of the miraculous metamorphosis. Even my grandfather, the skeptical Zionist, seemed transformed by the New Germany, as it was dubbed both at home and abroad. Evidence of this could be seen in the spring of 1925 when he and my grandmother moved into their luxurious new apartment on the fashionable Prinzregentenstrasse. When his American son-in-law next visited him, Jacob Feinberg was living in a style befitting an increasingly successful leader of German industry.

"You must come to visit us the next time, Jacob." My Uncle Victor took a pack of American cigarettes out of his shirt pocket and tapped one out to offer to my grandfather. "It is about time you saw the country that has done so much to contribute to your prosperity." He smiled broadly and lit the cigarette for my grandfather. "And you, too, Erich," he added, extending the cigarettes to my father, who declined with a shake of the head. "Our mutual brother-in-law, Solomon the Wise, suggested that the two of you might come together and try to get some work on Broadway as a dance team."

"Now hold on for just a minute." My grandfather chuckled as he spoke. "Are you trying to break up the Feinberg cartel by drawing away its top executives?" Then, in a more serious tone he said, "I want you to know how much I appreciate your support during the critical times, Victor. Without your backing we would have had a difficult time holding our heads above water." My uncle tried to wave him off, but he continued. "Thanks in good part to our American sales, we have been able to completely retool and expand our plant without having to borrow heavily as many others in similar circumstances did. I think it is time now to set up an independent American branch of Feinberg's, and I want you to be in charge of it." He paused to let his words sink in. "We are going to sell off most of our real estate holdings here to finance the project. I've asked Solomon to go over all the figures with you."

Several days later, Feinberg's Ovenworks undertook the first steps in becoming a multinational corporation.

***

The new prosperity extended beyond economics. Peace and cooperation became the bywords throughout Europe. In 1926, Germany rejoined the civilized world by becoming a permanent member of the new League of Nations. My personal life paralleled the times; I received my Abitur with honors, and began my studies at the University of Munich. To the great relief of his family, Karl also passed his qualifying examinations and enrolled in the University of Constance. To celebrate our graduation, my grandfather gave a party in our honor.

It was a traditional German party, with toasts, speeches, and endless conversation. My parents proudly accepted congratulations from dozens of guests, many of them strangers to me, but as my grandfather assured me, important people whose acquaintance could benefit my future career. Uncle Solomon was more witty and eloquent than ever, laughing and joking with the Linsdorffs as if they were childhood friends. And yet, from all of it I remember best a few introductory words exchanged between two men who shared a vision, words which turned out to be prophetic.

"It is a pleasure to meet you at last." My grandfather extended his hand as I introduced him to Judge Linsdorff; they both bowed slightly as they shook hands. "My grandson is a great admirer of yours, Judge Linsdorff, as am I. It is comforting to know that there are still some men in Germany who strive to strike a balance between law and justice."

The judge bowed again, obviously pleased by the compliment. He looked from my grandfather to me and replied, "And it is comforting to me to know that I am not alone in this struggle, Herr Feinberg. You see, Heinrich has told me a thing or two about you, too. And although our avenues of approach are quite different, I am convinced that our ultimate destination is not. I hope that one day we will be able to meet on a common road."

***

Karl had already said his farewells to his family. The two of us stood alone on the platform waiting for his train to arrive. We were silent, having spent more than half the night talking of our plans for the future and sentimentally vowing to each other that we would keep in touch. Karl explained the reasons why he had given up his plans to become a professional athlete in favor of a career in medicine. He wanted, he said, to pit himself against pain and suffering, much as a boxer confronts a powerful opponent. When he had first told me of his change of heart, more than a year before, I thought he was joking. At that earlier time, he had cited our experience on the Odeonsplatz as the motivating factor. If he had had medical training, he said, he wouldn't have had to waste so much energy carrying me to Dr. Griep's office.

Soon after that, however, Karl's desire to become a doctor was neither a joke nor a whim. In his final year of Gymnasium he had applied himself to his studies with uncharacteristic diligence. His Uncle Rolf, he explained, would guide him for a year or so with his introductory studies and then, should he show promise, use his influence to have him admitted to a first-rate medical school.

Karl leaned out of the window as the train began to move slowly away from the Munich station. "So long, Blacktop," he shouted, his blonde hair blown flat back against his head by the wind. I waved back for a few seconds, choking back my tears as I watched him grow smaller and smaller in the distance.

***

The next two years passed with the swiftness of a happy dream. It was difficult to believe that this was the same land that so recently had teetered on the edge of an abyss. A new world had opened up before me, a world in which I could control my own destiny. In addition to my legal studies, I had immersed myself in literature, devouring the works of all the great writers of Germany and the continent. The air of Munich seemed to exude the freedom and vitality I felt within myself.

***

"I still plan to paint you and Karl someday, hopefully before I am too old to hold a brush, or you two are too old to take off your clothes." Carla smiled her familiar, mischievous smile. It was January, 1928. We were seated in a student restaurant in the university area. Colorful frescos of Bavarian outdoor scenes adorned the walls on all sides, framed by dark, polished wood. "Have you heard from our prodigal son lately?" she added, lifting the large beer mug to her lips and taking a long swallow. Although we continued to see each other from time to time, the nature of our relationship had changed. Carla's husband was back from his pilgrimage to Italy, and, as she put it, they had agreed to try out the conventional bourgeois life-style, at least for the time being.

"As a matter of fact," I answered, "I haven't gotten a letter from him for about three months. I did see Judge Linsdorff last week, though, and he told me that Karl would be coming to Munich in the early spring. He has been extremely busy. Not only are his courses difficult, but his uncle has him working obscene hours as a kind of apprentice in his research laboratory. The last time we saw each other, about six months ago, we really didn't have much of a chance to talk. He looked tired and nervous, and didn't seem anxious to discuss his work."

"To tell you the truth, Heinrich," she answered, her voice dropping almost to a whisper, "I'm a little nervous myself these days. I try to tell myself that it's because I am an artist, and that artists are only happy when they are in the midst of suffering, but I am not so sure it is so simple. Something just doesn't feel right."

I heard similar sentiments from my Uncle Solomon that same winter. Unlike Carla, however, he expressed his concern as a rational probability rather than a premonition.

"Don't let all of this superficial tranquility fool you, Heinchen," he told me, removing his glasses to polish them with his handkerchief. "Underneath it all there is a sleeping monster."

"And I thought you were a realist, Uncle Sol," I responded, smiling. "I didn't know you believed in supernatural monsters."

He did not change his expression. "Oh, but this monster is not supernatural," he explained. "It is a man-made one, but very powerful nonetheless. Because we do not see It does not mean that it is not there. On the other hand, we have been hypnotized into believing that what we see is reality, while it is really the illusion." He finished polishing his glasses and placed them back on his nose.

"I don't understand," I said.

A slight smile played at the corner of his mouth. "I am just a simple accountant," he said, "so I tend to reduce a situation to its mathematical components. One does not have to know very much about mathematics, though, to know that it is a losing situation when you put yourself into such deep debt that there is no possibility of paying back what you owe. And that is exactly what Germany has done, to the tune of over twenty billion marks." When he had assured himself that I was properly impressed by the large figure he quoted, he went on. "Luckily, your grandfather was a wise enough man to listen to at least one of his gimpy sons-in-law and not make the mistake of keeping all of his eggs in the German basket. Your father, in spite of everything, still believes that the tooth fairy wears a Prussian uniform. He is still unconvinced that our American venture was the best solution. I think he secretly longs for a return of the good old days of the monarchy. Unless I am mistaken, though, the future is not going to be found anywhere on this rotting old continent, but across the sea."

"I don't know, Uncle Sol," I answered, trying to show off my grasp of current events. "Isn't it a fact that production is way up, unemployment is down to its lowest point in decades, salaries are higher than they have ever been, and taxes are going down? Perhaps my father has a point."

"I admit that it looks good if you don't look too closely," he responded. "But there is still something unsettling about it all. Don't you see a pattern emerging?" He paused to let me think.

I shook my head, puzzled. "Up and down, up and down," he said. "It's a question of gravity, plain and simple." He laughed when he saw that his enigmatic comment had confused me even more. "As a lawyer you will have to train yourself to think in analogies, Heinrich." He patted my arm affectionately. "What goes up must come down, that is gravity. Newton didn't realize, though, that gravity is a law that involves more than just physical objects. It applies to human institutions as well, particularly economics. We in this country should be more aware of that than anyone else." He smiled again.

"Everything will be fine," he continued, "as long as everything is fine." He paused again, letting me savor his truism. "But what happens when the bill collector comes to the door and demands payment? Will he smile and say it is all right when you tell him that you cannot pay? Will he open his wallet and offer you some more money to hold you over until you can? I think you know the answer to that one." Before I could respond, he added, "To use a more popular analogy, Germany is like a dike with a weak spot. If that spot develops into a crack it will not be long before the water pushes its way through and collapses the entire structure...and woe to anyone who is in the way of the released flood." He sat back and waited for me to reply.

"You know, Uncle Sol," I said, "you should have been a professor. That was one of the best lectures I have heard all year." Then I smiled, and trying to imitate his voice, added, "But I have an artist friend who said very much the same thing you did, only she did it in one sentence. The way she put it, 'something doesn't feel right.'"

Uncle Solomon laughed heartily and, not to be outdone, retorted, "Perhaps she has been feeling the wrong thing."

***

Karl was calmer and more self-assured when I saw him in the spring. At first our reunion was a bit awkward, but in a very short time we were exchanging anecdotes. Only one or two specific memories of those few weeks have stayed with me clearly, such as a short comment he made in passing one afternoon which struck me as rather odd. I did not think it significant at the time, and let it pass without comment. At one point, while we sat in a café on the Marienplatz, Karl smiled conspiratorially and remarked, "Your ex-wife asked me to give you her best wishes." Then he winked and added, "And I had the distinct impression that she would give you a lot more if it weren't for my uncle's genetic fantasies."

Karl stayed in Munich for three weeks, but due to our demanding schedules we only saw each other sporadically. He had informed me in passing that at the end of the semester he would be leaving Constance in order to continue his medical studies in the north German city of Hannover. I congratulated him, glad to see that he had found his direction in life, but nevertheless I could not help feeling hurt by the fact that he had not confided in me about his plans sooner. And even though I realized that our drift in different directions was to be expected in the normal course of things, I felt a sense of loss. This feeling was heightened on the day that he left to return to Constance. I accompanied him to the main station as I had done more than a year before, but this time we parted with a semi-formal handshake and a few hackneyed phrases. I did not wait on the platform for the train to pull out of the station.

***

For the remainder of 1928, the upward spiral continued, not only in Germany, but throughout all of the industrialized nations. The world had become sane at last; there would be no more war among civilized countries. Perhaps gravity was not an infallible law after all. Perhaps it had already been overcome by the goodwill and dedicated work of enlightened men. As if to give further credibility to this conquest, in October the German dirigible Graf Zeppelin transported a nation's pride along with twenty passengers across the ocean to America. And who could say with certainty that what went up could not keep going up indefinitely? The sky is endless, we thought; there were no limits to the heights one could reach, just as there are no limits to human hopes and dreams. Human hopes and dreams. Where did the dreams end and reality begin? We did not realize how applicable to us the words of the great German-Jewish poet Heinrich Heine were to become: "*Ich hatte einst ein schönes Vaterland: Es war ein Traum.*" ("Once I had a beautiful fatherland: It was a dream.")

***

Uncle Solomon peered out of the front window of my grandparents' apartment. "I understand you now have a famous neighbor, Jacob," he observed, an amused glint in his eye. "And a rich one, at that," he added, turning around to face my frowning grandfather. "But since when does a petty politician have enough money to afford a fancy new automobile and a chauffeur?"

"Didn't you know, Sol? He's a successful author as well as a respectable statesman," answered my grandfather sarcastically. "He spent his time in the Landsberg hotel with his cronies, converting his idiotic ramblings into a book, and people are actually buying it. I hate to admit it, but I am guilty of complicity in his literary success — I bought a copy when it first came out in '25. *Mein Kampf*, that's what he named his masterpiece — nothing but the same old nonsense one finds every day in his Nazi newspapers, written in typically poor German. I never could get through more than about fifty pages."

"I doubt that he has made enough money in royalties to afford such luxuries," responded my uncle, again gazing at the street. "More than likely, our Austrian Messiah has been pocketing some of his party's funds like all the rest of the politicians. The joke is on him in any event. I wonder how he would feel if he knew that one of his neighbors was a Jew, and a Zionist at that."

"If he feels half as upset as I do about having the leader of the Nazi Party living right across the street from me, that will be my consolation. The more I think about it, the more I begin to believe that fate is an even bigger comedian than you are, Sol."

"There he is now." Uncle Solomon motioned with his head for us to come over to look. My grandfather shrugged him off and disappeared into the kitchen to say something or other to my grandmother. The rest of us crowded around the window, a scene reminiscent of an earlier time and place. A shiny, new, black Mercedes Benz was parked at the curb. A man in a light trench coat stood at the side of the car with his back to us, apparently waiting for the young woman who was just coming out of the building. When she reached him, he turned to open the car door for her. For a few seconds he appeared to be staring up at our window. I recognized him at once from the pictures I had seen of him on posters and in the newspapers. There was no mistaking him. On the advent of the Jewish year 5690, from a window of an apartment on Prinzregentenstrasse in Munich, Germany, my family saw proof that the devil did exist. Little did we know that he would soon become the unchallenged leader of Germany, and that we would become part of his kingdom of death.

***

It would be easy to believe now that Adolf Hitler's presence on that particular occasion was an evil omen, a warning of the approaching catastrophe. And yet, I cannot accept it as such; to do so would be to give credence to the idea that there was a prescribed order to the events that began to unfold in the following weeks. To do so would be to accept the idea of a cosmic plan, ruled not by the forces of good, but by the very opposite. To do so would be to accept the idea that God can, even temporarily, be vanquished from His creation. No, I cannot accept this. I must not accept this. I must reject the notion of a plan that includes bashing out babies' brains, or immolating little children. I must reject an order of existence that compels human beings to kneel, not in prayer, but before a ditch that is quickly transformed into a blood-soaked mass grave when they are gunned down like animals. I must reject a God who is able to permit, or unable to prevent, such things, for only in that rejection can I ever hope to accept and believe in Him again.

***

The first crack in the dike did not occur in Germany, as Uncle Solomon had predicted it might, but on the other side of the ocean. On Tuesday, October 30, 1929, the newspaper headlines and radio broadcasts announced that the American stock market had crashed on the preceding day, and, as we were to learn, with it the hopes of the world for continued prosperity or peace. By the spring, water had already begun to force its way through the widening crack.

"The difference now is that no one is going to bail us out. Quite the contrary, now they are going to throw us overboard because they are in the same sinking boat that we are." Uncle Solomon slammed the large, leather bound ledger shut and handed it to my grandfather, who swiveled around in his chair and breathed a loud sigh.

"Calm down, Solomon," he said, smiling. "It isn't exactly as if we have never seen bad times before. We'll weather this storm just as we have all the others. Victor has sent good news from America. He's almost certain that he will be successful in getting a furnace contract with the New York Board of Education. And that added to the orders from the Transit Authority should give us some breathing room. The man is either a magician or a genius."

"You misunderstood me, Jacob. I wasn't referring to Feinberg's, but to Germany as a whole. The country is in debt to the tune of almost thirty billion marks, most of it in the form of short-term loans. This was all well and good while our creditors were prospering, but now that the bottom has fallen out for them too, they are not going to listen to anyone who cries poverty as a reason for not paying them back. The poor have very little sympathy for their fellow poor. And what we see is just the tip of the iceberg. Unemployment is already soaring. By this time next year we are going to be in worse shape than we were in '23."

"Aren't you exaggerating a bit, Sol?" My grandfather stroked his beard and thumbed through the ledger before him.

"I don't think so," responded Uncle Solomon. "At least in '23 we could look for help abroad. This time we are going to have to solve our problems on our own, and I'm afraid to think what that can mean. You can see for yourself what is going on here in Munich and in many other cities. It isn't safe to be out on the street anymore. Your Nazi neighbor's brown-shirted thugs and their Communist counterparts are waging a minor civil war out there."

My father, who had hobbled into the room during this exchange, entered the conversation. "What can you expect from a government of mealy-mouthed liars and hypocrites? If they weren't such a pack of cowards they would have run Hitler and his degenerate gang out of the country long ago. They could have shipped him back to Austria after his trial instead of putting him into a hotel. Why he lived better in Landsberg than most people do in Munich."

My grandfather had risen from his chair while my father spoke and now paced back and forth at the side of his desk. Finally he stopped, leaned his hands on the desk and turned to me. "And what do things look like on the academic front, Heinrich? Do your professors and fellow students have as bleak a view of the situation as your family does?" he asked, in a tired, dejected voice. "I didn't invite you here just to let you hear the old folks ramble on." I looked from my grandfather to the others. When I saw that they were seriously awaiting a reply I grew ill at ease. It became clear to me that my apprenticeship was over, and that I was no longer an observer at these meetings.

"For the most part," I began slowly, trying to order my thoughts a bit, "there is still an ivory tower attitude in the university, although there are indications that this is changing. Unfortunately, though, the changes that I do see are not for the better." My observation had surprised even me. It was as if I were expressing ideas that lay buried beneath my consciousness, ideas that I had not wanted to confront. I added, "While we haven't come to the point here in Munich that some of the universities in Prussia have, there is a marked swing to the right in certain circles."

"You mean they haven't come around to demanding an 'Aryan Paragraph' yet, barring Jews from the universities?" interrupted my grandfather, narrowing his eyes angrily. "How decent of them."

"That among other things," I replied, somewhat uncertainly. "I don't think it will ever come to such an extreme in Munich. For the most part the professors and students seem to be indifferent to economics and politics, but lately there have been some disturbing incidents." I paused for a second. They were all listening intently. Growing even uneasier, I went on. "Maybe I am overreacting. I guess that tendency exists for everyone in this family." I looked at each one of them in turn before continuing and forced myself to smile. "The other day I was walking along Ludwigstrasse with a classmate I had always considered to be both decent and intelligent. Suddenly we saw a group of Storm Troopers on the corner in front of us.

They were all decked out in their brown shirts and swastikas. One of them was haranguing a crowd of students with the usual Nazi nonsense — Jews and Communists were responsible for rising unemployment, Munich should follow the lead of Thuringia and elect Nazis to office — that kind of trash." I paused again, growing more disturbed as I thought back on the incident. "I wanted to pass right by without acknowledging their presence, but when the others stopped, I did too. It was comical. The SA speechmaker could hardly put a proper sentence together, let alone make sense when he did. At one point I laughed out loud, expecting my classmate to join in. He remained silent. In fact, he actually seemed annoyed at my reaction and told me to keep quiet so he could 'hear the fellow's position.' I left him standing there, wide-eyed and with a rapt expression on his face."

There was a pause before anyone spoke. Finally, Uncle Solomon leaned toward me and asked, "What else have you come across? I believe you indicated more than one disturbing incident." I knew from his tone of voice that he was genuinely concerned.

"I can't really pinpoint anything else," I answered, although that was not entirely true. "I suppose it's more of an attitude than anything concrete. There have been several times during lectures when I got the distinct impression that the professor was hinting at things that the Brown Shirt on Ludwigstrasse came out and said openly. But as I said before, I could be overreacting."

"No, Heinrich," my grandfather said sadly. "You aren't overreacting. A Jew can never overreact when it comes to these people." He opened his desk drawer and pulled a large volume from it. "If you have the stomach for it, I suggest you read this hateful book. I finally brought myself to finish it, much to the detriment of my digestive system."

I walked over to the desk and took the volume of *Mein Kampf* that he extended to me.

"And when you finish with it, Heinrich," added Uncle Solomon, "give it to me. I can use it for toilet paper."

There was another "incident" that I did not mention that day in my grandfather's office: I had seen Birgit again. I did not recognize her at first. The Birgit I remembered was a cheerful, vivacious girl; the person whom I saw at the Linsdorff's on that spring day in 1930 was a woman with troubled eyes and a melancholy smile. I had gone there to return some law books that the judge had loaned me for one of my courses.

"Hello, Heinrich," she said, extending her hand as I entered. Her voice was familiar, yet I could not place it. I must have had a peculiar look on my face, because she giggled; I recognized that sound at once. Except for a lack of youthful joy, it was the same giggle I had come to know so well that summer on Lake Constance.

"My uncle told me that you might stop by this afternoon, so I decided to wait," she explained, when she saw how surprised I was. "My mother and I had to do some shopping in Munich. But don't worry," she added. "She isn't here right now. She and my aunt are still out there somewhere looking for bargains. They will probably be gone for hours. Just to avoid complications though, why don't we go for a little stroll?"

It was a chilly, clear spring day. As we walked, she asked about my studies and my goals, indicating by her questions that she already knew many of the answers. I concluded that Karl had kept her informed, but was puzzled and, I must admit, pleased by her interest. My puzzlement turned to confusion when she matter-of-factly informed me that she had become engaged, and that she had spent the morning in the city selecting her trousseau. Although I did not understand why, I suddenly felt depressed. I hadn't really thought that much about her the past few years, and had hardly lived monastically during that time. Nevertheless, I felt a terrible, sinking sensation in the pit of my stomach.

She must have noticed my changed expression, because she added, almost apologetically, "His name is Dieter. He is really a very nice fellow; I think you would like him." Her nervousness was evident by the red blotches that had broken out on the side of her neck and throat.

We continued to walk for a few minutes without speaking. Finally, I broke the silence by asking her if she wanted to sit for a while. We had reached the Hofgarten; directly ahead at the side of the path were some benches. She nodded without answering and we made our way to one of them.

"I have wanted to explain to you for a long time," she said, almost in a whisper. "I really am sorry that it has taken this long." She turned her face toward mine; her eyes seemed to be pleading.

"There isn't anything to explain," I lied. "We were just children." I felt bewildered by it all. Why had she wanted to see me? Why did she feel this need to talk about something that couldn't possibly have anything to do with us now? We really didn't know each other; perhaps we never had. And yet I knew that my need to hear what she had to say was just as great, possibly even greater, than her compulsion to say it.

"I tried my best not to hurt you, Heinrich," she continued, her head drooping slightly forward.

I looked at her soft, brown hair and had all I could do to stop myself from running my hand through it as I had once done. And then it suddenly dawned on me. It was absurd, ridiculous, I thought, but true nevertheless: I still loved her. Moreover, I knew at that instant that I had never stopped loving her, and that I probably never would. But I also had a sinking premonition, as I sat there struggling to compose my thoughts and feelings, that this was the last time I would ever see her.

"I never blamed you," I replied, this time truthfully. "I know it was not your doing."

She lifted her head and turned her face to me. "It was my father." Her voice was so soft I could hardly hear it. "I never knew he felt the way he did...the way he does," she continued, shaking her head from side to side. "I never knew."

I don't remember the exact words from this point on; I don't think I heard most of them. It had happened about a week after I returned home from Lindau. Her father, she explained haltingly, had told her that she should not see me again, at first giving her age as the reason. No amount of reasoning or pleading could change his mind. Finally, furious that she persisted in her "stubborn idiocy," he had admitted the true reason for his hostility. In no uncertain terms, he let her know that he did not want her to become too friendly with a Jew.

"What could I do?" she asked, directing her question more at herself than at me. "When I tried to talk to my mother about it she told me that it was my duty to listen to my father. But I continued to write to you, and managed to get most of your letters before they could be intercepted. And then we came to Munich..."

Our unhappy reunion came back into my mind. Mechanically, I asked, "Why did they let you see me at your uncle's house if they felt that way?"

"They had no idea you would be there," she replied. "My Uncle Paul knew my father's attitude by then, so he didn't tell him. I suppose he thought he could show him the light, but it didn't work out that way at all. They had a terrible argument after you went home that night; they scarcely speak to each other now." Then, looking at me with her sad eyes, she said softly, "I am sorry, Heinrich. I am very sorry."

Before I could reply, she leaned over to me, kissed me lightly on the lips, got up from the bench and ran down the path toward the street. I sat there for what seemed hours, running my fingertips gently over my lips and staring vacantly at the angry, grey sky.

***

Once again I found myself both spectator and participant in a society that appeared to be bent on self-destruction. Street violence had become so fierce and frequent that the police more often than not made little or no attempt to intervene. There was a slight improvement in the situation when the government passed a decree banning any groups from wearing uniforms or emblems (a decree obviously aimed at the growing bands of Storm Troopers), but it was already too late. Once again the faces of the people in Munich wore the familiar blank stare; once again they had only one immediate goal — survival.

In addition to the external turbulence, I was struggling to free myself from a personal, existential quagmire. I perceived my life and the lives of my German contemporaries in terms of a series of historically unparalleled crises, with little or no hope for improvement in the future. What could become, I wondered, of an entire generation nurtured on violence and deprivation? What was one to expect from a society that kept itself alive by feeding on hatred and lies? I had read Hitler's vicious, deranged book, and knew that his was not a voice calling in the wilderness. Gradually I began to grasp the truth that had always lurked just beneath the surface of my consciousness: my grandfather had been right from the beginning — there was no place in Germany for a Jew. There was no place there for me. Rather than unburden me, my realization plunged me into an even deeper depression. I felt as if someone had kicked my supports from under me, leaving me helplessly suspended above an abyss. For many weeks I bore the burden of my conclusion alone, unable to communicate it to anyone. I was faced with an impossible dilemma. How could I leave my family behind to cope with the very situation I myself found impossible to bear? Equally remote, though, was the possibility that we could all go off together in search of a new haven. I knew that my father would never agree; to do so he would have had to admit to himself that his own life had been a failure. Finally, no longer able to keep my thoughts and feelings contained, I decided to go to the only person whose opinion I felt would be guided by a degree of objectivity.

Judge Linsdorff listened to me patiently before responding.

"I wish I could tell you that you are wrong," he said, measuring his words carefully, "that your fears are unjustified." We sat across from each other in his study, surrounded by bookshelves crammed full with imposing leather bound volumes. Frustration and anger were evident in his tone. "It would make me feel a lot better if I were able to tell you to be more optimistic, but I cannot, Heinrich. In all honesty I cannot." As they met and held mine, his penetrating blue eyes seemed to grow dull and flicker like lighted candles that have almost burned to their bases. "We are fast becoming a nation of criminals. We use the law as an instrument of power rather than one of restraint..Instead of fostering order, it gives impetus to the growing chaos. The courts have lost any sense of impartiality. They pass judgment on the basis of a person's politics rather than on what the person has done. And those few of us who still attempt to maintain standards of decency and justice grow smaller in number and are increasingly unsuccessful. I am ashamed, Heinrich...very ashamed." He hesitated for a few seconds, staring past me at an invisible spot somewhere in the distance. Suddenly, he pulled back his shoulders and slammed his fist down on the table. "But I'll be damned if I am going to make it easy for those gangsters. They may be riding the crest of the wave right now, but sooner or later they will drown in their own filth." He hesitated again, then added in a subdued voice, "I only hope that they don't pull us all down with them."

There was good reason for his doubt and anxiety. The parliamentary elections in September had been disastrous. The Nazis had picked up 107 seats in the Reichstag, almost nine times the number they had occupied two years earlier. The Communists had also done very well, and now the two enemy parties had joined in a cynical alliance aimed at destroying the tottering Weimar Republic. This is what the judge was referring to in his next response. I had asked if he thought there was any alternative to my plan to leave Germany.

"I am neither a prophet nor a god," he began, sounding very tired. "But one does not have to be either to see what Germany's future is. I do not believe, as do some of the eternal optimists I know, that these elections are just a temporary setback. On the other hand, I can't allow myself to join with the doomsayers who have taken up Heimdall's horn and spend their time warning of a second *Götterdämmerung*, without doing anything to try to prevent it. Probably we will experience a reality somewhere between these two extremes, but that will hardly be a consolation. I'm afraid, Heinrich, that even the median point will prove to be cataclysmic." He removed his glasses and rubbed the bridge of his nose between his thumb and index finger for a few seconds. Then, replacing his glasses, he went on. "You have been like a son to me," he said softly, fixing his eyes on mine. "And for that reason, it is even more difficult for me to tell you this." I tensed, fearing what he would say. "The question, Heinrich, is not whether there is an alternative. There is always an alternative. The question is whether that alternative is one which will give you the chance to live the happy, productive life you deserve. The answer, as odious as it is for me to concede, seems to be no, at least not in the field of justice. Not in Germany." He lowered his eyes. When he looked up again, there was an angry scowl on his face.

"Unless and until we can restore sanity in this country, it will be impossible for decency to survive here. You have lived here your entire life, as have I, and yet there are those who say that only one of us is a true German. Well, if they are the models, I prefer to be excluded too. And I will fight them with my dying breath, because if they are successful in their aims there will come a day when being German is considered a curse."

What little remained of law and order deteriorated almost on a daily basis during the early months of 1931. The Reichstag became as disorderly as the city streets; members of the various parties engaged in shouting matches, sang songs while their opponents spoke, and frequently came to blows with each other on the floor. Finally, recognizing the fact that it had become a parody, the highest legal body in Germany adjourned and did not reconvene for a full seven months.

In spite of it all, I still had not discussed my intentions with my family as spring approached. After my talk with Karl's father, I stopped attending my classes in law and government. Instead, I devoted all of my energy to literature and, for obvious practical reasons, began to study English.

"Hello, Heinrich, and how are you today?" The greeting, spoken in English, startled me momentarily. I was sitting at a rear table in the little student café on Veterinstrasse. I looked up from my book at Uncle Solomon. When he saw the puzzled expression on my face, he grinned and slapped me affectionately on the shoulder. Still grinning, he sat down across from me and picked up the English grammar book I had been studying. "I see we have a common interest," he said, this time in German. "Perhaps we should study together sometime."

"You are studying English too?" I asked uncertainly.

He smiled again and nodded. "Oh yes, certainly," he answered, in accented English. "I someday hope to speak very well in English." Switching back to German he added, "My goal is to be able to seduce women bilingually. Aim for the stars I always say." We were both laughing as he motioned to the waiter to bring him a stein of beer.

"And when do you intend to make your mad dash for freedom?" He leaned back, awaiting my reply.

Ignoring his question, I put one of my own to him. "But how did you know?"

"Now, now Heinchen," he smiled and wagged his index finger at me playfully. "Did you really think that you could fool the great Solomon Vogelsang, who sees all and knows all?" He picked up the large beer stein and took a long swallow. Then, wiping his mouth on his sleeve, he went on. "Actually, what surprises me is that it has taken you so long to decide. In a month you will be twenty-five years old...old enough to leave the nest. As it is, I am probably going to beat you to America. Who knows, we may be the ones to prepare a new family nest." He took another sip of beer and waited for my reaction. The fact was that I was not surprised by his revelation. He had been hinting as much for quite some time now.

"When do you intend to go?" I asked. "And if you knew that I was thinking along the same lines, why didn't you say something to me sooner?"

"We are a lot alike, you and I," he said, touching my arm. "We are both fairly realistic. Basically, we are survivors." He paused again, but only for a moment or two. "As you know, leaving one's country is not the easiest thing to do, no matter how obvious it is that such a move is in one's own best interests. I have always respected your father for having had the courage to do it. But never as much as now. Until recently, I didn't realize how much courage it takes to pack up one's life and transport it to a strange place. Habit is a seductive force. People have the paradoxical ability to adapt to just about anything to maintain the status quo. It is a dangerous ability."

"But does that mean we should run away whenever we sense danger or discomfort?" I blurted out, my frustration growing.

He patted my arm and answered calmly, "I have more questions than answers, and had I an answer it might not even be the correct one for me, let alone for someone else." He lifted the heavy stein again and drained the last of the beer in one long gulp. "What I can say, though," he continued, without breaking stride, "is that danger and discomfort are relative terms. Certainly, it would be wrong to run away if by staying you could reduce the danger or discomfort for others. That would change it to a question of courage, and even then it would become the topic for some very complicated analysis, since too much courage can sometimes be destructive. But when it is clear that you cannot do anything to mitigate the danger and discomfort, when there iş no longer any doubt that your presence will only result in another victim, then retreat seems to be the only intelligent course of action. It is neither heroic nor useful to charge a firing machine gun. That kind of foolishness only adds another corpse to the pile."

Nothing that Uncle Solomon said was really new to me, no matter how prophetic some of his statements were to seem in later years. And yet, the most important question still remained, the one on which all the others hinged. I leaned forward, my eyes locked to his. "What about everyone else? Those we love? How can we go off and leave them behind?"

Uncle Solomon grimaced slightly and breathed a deep sigh. "There is a lot of truth to the old saying that you can lead a horse to water, but you can't make it drink," he began, shifting uncomfortably in his chair. "And it's even harder when you have to deal with a jackass who refuses even to be led to the water in the first place." He smiled, in spite of his obvious exasperation.

"I don't understand," I said. "Do you mean to say that you have already talked to the others about it?"

He spread out his arms to indicate his frustration. "Talked, pleaded, argued, shouted. Believe me, Heinrich, I have tried everything. I have warned that we cannot hide our heads in the sand and wait for all to be well again. This sickness in Germany is more than a common cold that will be gone in a week whether you treat it or not. It is a cancer, fast becoming inoperable."

I did not make an effort to respond. In effect, he was saying exactly what Judge Linsdorff had expressed to me earlier. How tragic, I thought; in another time and place they could have been friends.

"The only reason I didn't say anything to you," he added, his anger suddenly gone, "was that I knew it was unnecessary. Besides that, I didn't want anyone to feel that I was influencing you." He smiled his ironic smile and added, "Now we can both say with complete honesty that you came to your decision independently."

"Do you mean to say that my parents know what I am planning? If so, why haven't they said anything? My father, for one, has never been one to keep his feelings or his ideas to himself."

"I have wondered about that myself," he answered, wrinkling his brow.

"It's just possible that he knows I am right, no matter how much he argues against what I say. Your father may be a stubborn man, Heinrich, but he is far from a stupid one. At any rate, he realizes that if he tries to stop you, you can throw back into his face the fact that he did the very same thing when he was your age, that you inherited a *Wanderlust* gene from him. But I don't think any of that will be necessary. In a way, I think he rather approves, even though he would never admit it."

"I'm not at all sure of that," I replied, as I mulled over his last remark. "But even if you are right about my father, what about the others? They must feel either angry or hurt that I haven't shared my thoughts with them. I wanted to, but..."

Before I could go on, he interrupted. "Not at all, Heinchen, not at all. No more than I do. Give the old folks some credit. They understand some things without explanations. We aren't altogether stupid, even though you probably blame us for botching up the world. And I suppose there is some truth in that." He hesitated for a few seconds and added, "But to answer your question — and here I can only make an educated guess — they are afraid. Just as you and I are. The only difference is that they are afraid to leave and we are afraid to stay. It all amounts to the same thing."

As usual, I was impressed with my uncle's perception, but I was still unsatisfied.

"I can understand my father feeling that way," I said. "And I wouldn't expect my mother to do anything other than support him, just as Aunt Rachel supports you. But for the life of me, I can't see how this applies to Grandfather. It would seem that he would be the first to pack up his things and head for the nearest ship to Palestine. Hasn't he been predicting for years the very things we now see happening?"

Uncle Solomon smiled again, but not in his customary, playful way. This was a strange, new expression, a combination of wonder and melancholy, disbelief and admiration.

"Jacob Feinberg," he said, maintaining that unique smile while he spoke, "is a remarkable man, and the only one I know who is even more of a paradox than I am. I have never doubted that he is 100 percent sincere when he says he believes that the position of the Jew in this country will remain untenable until Palestine is reclaimed. But your grandfather has an alter ego, a *Doppelgänger* of whom he is unaware. This other Jacob Feinberg will not leave Germany for a very elementary reason: in spite of everything, he loves this twisted land."

***

Years later, on a freezing winter night in a Treblinka barracks, I saw that Uncle Solomon had hit upon the truth. A group of us had spent most of the day clearing away the fresh corpses from two Polish transports, piling them onto carts so that they could be dumped into the large ditches just beyond the camp fence. Once we had finished that macabre work, we were assigned the task of sorting out the personal effects of the victims which lay stacked in huge piles in the barracks at the left side of the gas chamber in which their owners had been exterminated on the previous day. Finally, physically and spiritually exhausted from our labor and the constant beating that accompanied it, we were lined up for the dreaded roll call.

That particular evening was even more horrible than usual. Due to some real or invented discrepancy in the count, we were forced to remain standing at attention in the subfreezing weather for more than two hours, while the kapo in charge counted and recounted. Throughout it all, the guards continued to beat us at random with clubs and whips. Finally, when the tally was correct, we were allowed to drag ourselves into the barracks and slump onto the hard wooden bunks for a few hours of rest. I was at the point of slipping into the death-like sleep that had become so familiar in Treblinka, when a voice suddenly snapped me back awake.

"Heinrich, can you hear me?" At first I thought that I had been dreaming; but then I heard it again. "Heinrich, over here. It's me, Arthur." I turned to the side and saw my neighbor's shadowy outline. He was in a sitting position, his legs dangling marionette-like over the side of the bunk.

Arthur Metzbaum had been assigned to the grave detail a week earlier. A German-Jew from Düsseldorf, he had managed to get the bunk next to mine after learning that I was a "fellow German." Because of the arrival of one huge Polish transport after another that week (we estimated one day's total gassed to have been well over 25,000), we had not been able to speak together at any length. At any rate, I had no desire for conversation or friendship. I had learned very quickly not to make emotional attachments in Treblinka; one did not want to become close to the corpse one would have to carry to the pits on the following day or week. Yet, something in his voice that night made me sit upright, some indefinable human quality that I had almost forgotten during my time in that hellhole.

"What is it?" I whispered, leaning across to see him better. Although I couldn't see his face, for some reason I sensed that he was smiling. "What is it?" I repeated, a bit impatiently. I was annoyed that my rest had been interrupted. Another few moments passed in silence.

Then he said, "Have you ever been to Düsseldorf, Heinrich?" His voice was as calm and natural as if he were addressing me across a dinner table, not a lice-infested bunk in a factory of death. "It really is a beautiful city, you know," he continued, almost rapturously. "The old city in particular. Such wonderful guest houses and outdoor cafés. How I miss it!"

For a few seconds, I could scarcely believe my ears. Then I suddenly remembered Uncle Solomon's words about my grandfather — "*In spite of everything, he loves this twisted land.*" As kindly as I could, I replied, "Please,

Arthur, try to get some rest. We will need all of our energy for tomorrow."

"Yes, yes, tomorrow." he said softly. I watched as his silhouette shifted to a prone position.

I stretched out again and within seconds fell into a numb stupor.

The sight I awoke to on the next morning startled and sickened me, although it was not an uncommon one in Treblinka. Arthur Metzbaum's head hung over the side of his bunk. A large, congealing puddle of his blood had formed beneath him on the floor, released from his severed throat by the piece of broken glass he still grasped in fingers already grown stiff with death.

***

"It is different for me, Heinchen," said my father, rubbing the stump of his amputated leg more vigorously than usual. "I won't allow those bastards to force me out. Once in a lifetime is enough."

We were all seated at the dining room table. I had just finished explaining the reasons why we should leave for America. Although they were silent, I knew that my mother and sisters had been listening carefully.

"Besides," he added, "what makes you think that we would be any better off in the United States? According to all the reports I've read, their economic situation is no better than ours. Even Victor has been sending back pessimistic news about the soaring unemployment there. Feinberg's America has been forced to lay off almost half of its employees, in spite of his early successes in securing contracts. At least here I am assured my veteran's disability pension."

"It isn't only a matter of economics," I replied, already sensing that my arguments would be futile. "If that were the case it wouldn't be so bad. The thing that worries me most is that the lunatic fringe is quickly becoming the mainstream in Germany. Like it or not, we have to take Hitler and his kind seriously."

"Goddamn this Hitler!" My father brought his fist down onto the table with considerable force, startling everyone. My sister Ursel cringed visibly, as she usually did during such outbursts, while Jutta, who was much bolder by nature, shook her head reproachfully. "He fancies himself a German Napoleon, but he looks and acts more like Charley Chaplin."

"But he is no comedian, Erich. You know that very well." My mother stood behind him and placed a hand on his shoulder. "Perhaps we should let Heinrich finish what he has to say."

My father pursed his lips angrily. "What can he possibly say that we haven't heard before?" he grunted. Then he added, almost sighing, "I'm sure he and Sol have worked it all out together. We will all go to New York and live happily ever after. Sol will eventually become mayor of the city, and will appoint me commissioner of police, while Heinrich goes on, with

Victor's backing, to become president." His anger seemed to have faded as suddenly as it had flared up. A smile replaced the scowl as he continued. "You can't win a battle with your backside, Heinchen. You have to stand up and confront the enemy, with force if necessary. Defeat is not the worst thing that can happen to a man. It is much worse not to stand up for your convictions." I was impressed by my father's calm response, but had anticipated this approach. As I was about to answer, however, my mother spoke again.

"I am sorry, Erich, but this time you are wrong." My father spun his head around, surprised. Her sad eyes met and held his gaze. "You're wrong," she repeated, now running her hand gently along the side of his face. "It is foolish to remain in a burning building, or to try to put the flames out with a glass of water. You have to get out, even if it means leaving your convictions behind."

My father continued to look up at her, his features suddenly softening as he saw the love and sorrow in her eyes.

"Women don't understand this sort of thing," he muttered, more to himself than aloud.

My mother patted his shoulder and replied, "Women understand very well, Erich, or at least as well as it is possible to understand. After all, we are the ones who bring life into this world. And we are usually the ones who have to bury our sons and husbands along with their dead convictions."

My father's expression of surprise changed to one of confusion as he listened. My sisters and I exchanged meaningful glances.

"And what about your parents?" he asked. "What will they do? Would your father be willing to give up his business?"

There was a note of resignation in that seeming question. I suddenly realized that he had come to the same conclusions as I even before our talk.

"If we were to leave," my mother answered, "they would have no reason to stay here." This statement, simple as it was, seemed to settle our family's future. We would go to America.

***

And yet we waited. It seemed that once we had made the decision to depart it no longer remained urgent to do so. Just as my mother had predicted, my grandfather acquiesced when he saw that we had made up our minds to leave Germany. There were, however, many business matters to settle, and they could not be taken care of overnight. He told us that while he had hoped to keep the main branch of Feinberg's in Germany, that was no longer possible, and he would begin immediate negotiations for its sale. The fact that he had several "interested parties" was proof that he had anticipated our decision.

The months that followed were happy ones for my family. An invisible barrier had been removed. Eagerly, we prepared for our new life. I stopped attending all lectures at the university, and hired a tutor to help me with my English studies. At home my role was reversed; our apartment on Jägerstrasse became a classroom, and I the English teacher for my parents, sisters, and occasionally for my aunt and uncle. To my surprise, my father proved to be my best student. I watched with admiration as he spent hour after hour going over English vocabulary lists and dialogues until he had mastered them. I remember his joking explanation for this unusual dedication. "For once, just once, I want to show your Uncle Sol that someone can talk as much as he does. For another thing, I'll be the only one of us who can speak English with two foreign accents."

The worsening economic situation delayed the sale of Feinberg's Ovenworks. Prospective buyers were finding it more and more difficult to obtain credit from the threatened lending institutions. My grandfather did not attempt to conceal his disappointment when negotiations with one interested party faltered.

"It doesn't look very good, Heinrich," he said, examining the papers on his desk. We were in his office at the plant. My grandfather had requested my opinion, although my knowledge of legal contracts was limited to what little I had learned in the classroom. I nodded my head in agreement. The new offer was ridiculously low, but it was clear that if he decided to reject it, he would have to start from the beginning with a new buyer. "You don't know," he went on, "how many times I've had to bite my tongue while some son of a bitch has run off at the mouth about how unscrupulous Jews are in business. Yet it is perfectly all right for a so-called Aryan to make an offer like this." He slapped at the papers with the back of his hand. "Maybe I should just give them the company as a gift. What do you suggest, Heinrich?"

"It isn't a fair offer," I answered, trying to measure my words carefully. "And I don't think anyone with half a brain would claim that it is. But we have to examine our options before we reject it out of hand. We aren't in the best bargaining position right now, not with production and sales down as far as they are."

"Not everyone is suffering from this damned world depression," he spit out angrily. "Don't be fooled. The cartels are still making large profits, large enough to enable them to gobble up smaller firms like ours for practically nothing. But it can't go on like this forever. You'll see, now that the United States has declared a moratorium on Germany's war debts and reparations, things will start to improve. And there is strong talk to the effect that all of Germany's creditors will agree not to call in any loans for a period of time. We can weather the storm. After all, it isn't as if we have to sell."

"You can't really blame them for taking advantage," I said. "They are in business to make money, not dispense morality. You understand that better than anyone. Besides, we do have other reasons for wanting to liquidate. Isn't that true?"

He looked at me and smiled for the first time that morning. "So, my own grandson is on the other side," he said, grinning even more widely. "You advise then that we take our losses and run as if we were the thieves, and not they. I never thought it would come to this." His smile faded all at once, replaced by a frown.

"It all boils down to how much you want to leave," I said softly. "Or to put it differently, how little you want to stay. You know better than I that the future of Feinberg's Ovenworks is uncertain at best. It is not just idle speculation that the Nazis will eventually challenge President von Hindenburg at the polls. As difficult as it is to accept, they are becoming more powerful every day. Can you imagine what would happen if Hitler were actually to win? Where would we be then? We would be lucky to get an offer like the present one with the Nazis in power."

"The German population would never allow that," he replied in a firm voice. "That is one thing I am sure of." Then, noting my wry smile, he added, "I know what you are thinking, Heinchen — that I am suddenly changing the tune I have played all these years, defending those I've always mistrusted. Well that isn't the case. I still believe that Jews will remain second-class citizens in this country until they have established an independent Jewish homeland. I have never faltered in that belief, and have contributed considerable time and capital to the cause of Jewish independence. What I do not believe is that the people here will be idiotic enough to follow a Pied Piper into the river."

"Just for the sake of argument," I answered, "let us say that the impossible happens. You have read his book..."

"Please, Heinchen," my grandfather chided, shaking his head as one would at a child. "You might as well ask me what I would do if your father suddenly became a Socialist. As for that book, I don't think there are many people masochistic enough to read it through, regardless of how many actually buy it. And even if they did, it wouldn't matter. They would see it for the swill it is. While they may not love or even like Jews, they certainly don't dislike us enough to go out of their way to do us any harm. Their indifference is our protection. So relax. We don't have to pack our bags tonight and take the first train out of Germany. We have time."

"You're probably right," I answered. "Still, the fact that the respectable German burghers have learned how to carry out a *pogrom* doesn't make me feel secure. But they aren't like drunken Cossacks — they'll try to destroy us through official channels. That is the German way. At least that's what Judge Linsdorff says. And if anyone is in a position to know about such things, he is."

"Ah, the good judge," responded my grandfather with interest. "And what does he think of our proposed exodus? Once he told me that he hoped we would meet again someday on a common road. I wonder what he thinks now."

"He is suffering as much as we are, Grandfather," I said. "And for good reason. For one thing, he has had to sit by helplessly and watch as so-called justice becomes more and more perverted. The last time I saw him, about a week ago, he was even speaking about quitting the bench, although I doubt that he would ever do that."

"No, I don't think he would do that either," agreed my grandfather, wrinkling his brow. "If there is to be any hope at all for Germany, more people like him will have to stand up and be counted. But you didn't answer my question. What is his attitude toward our leaving?" From the way he said it, it was obvious that my grandfather placed a great deal of importance on Judge Linsdorff's opinion.

"He's convinced that we have no choice, but he is very sad about it," I replied. "He also feels guilty."

"So, so," said my grandfather softly, shaking his head thoughtfully. "I suppose if I were in his shoes I would feel the same way. But the next time you see him, Heinrich, you must tell him that he is no more guilty for being German than we are for being Jews. On the contrary, he is as much a victim as we. We share a common oppressor."

"It is slightly more complicated than that," I replied, thinking of my last conversation with the judge. "You see, his brother has become an avid follower of your mustached neighbor. The very idea of such a thing is eating away at him."

My grandfather's brow wrinkled again. He let out a deep breath before he answered. "Yes, I know all about Dr. Linsdorff. I have read some of his warped ideas in the Nazi rags. Among other things, he fancies himself an expert in the increasingly popular field of comparative racial physiology. One of his pet theories is that the calibre of a race can be determined by the measurements of the skull. He calls it cranial indexing. He has written articles in which he claims that Jewish skull measurements demonstrate the inferiority of the race. Can you imagine such nonsense coming from a man of medicine?" He shook his head in disbelief and continued. "But Judge Linsdorff should feel embarrassed rather than responsible. After all, he is not his brother's keeper. In fact, it is hard for me to believe that they are really brothers." After he said this he seemed to be lost in thought for a few moments. Then a strange smile played at the corners of his mouth and he asked, "Have you heard from your friend Karl lately? I understand he has followed in his uncle's footsteps in so far as vocation is concerned. Do you think that he also judges people on the basis of their skull measurements?"

"I haven't seen him for about three years," I answered, feeling a bit uncomfortable at my grandfather's implication. "We have corresponded, though," I added quickly, aware that my tone of voice betrayed my discomfort. The fact of the matter was I hadn't heard from Karl for more than a year. If it hadn't been for my continued relationship with his father, we would probably have lost touch completely.

"So where is he now, and what is he up to?" he went on, obviously unwilling to let me off the hook so easily.

"The last I heard, he was serving an internship at a hospital in Berlin. In about a year or so he should be a full-fledged surgeon." There was a trace of bitterness in my voice as I said this — envy that he had been able to follow his star because he had the "correct" heritage.

"Don't worry, Heinchen," my grandfather said, his eyes narrowing. "One day soon you will be able to write to him from America about your accomplishments."

***

"They finally came!" Uncle Solomon held up a brown envelope and smiled broadly. "Poor Victor had to use up a bit of shoe leather to get the final documents in order, but as the English say, 'All's well that ends well.'" He emitted a sound somewhere between a snort and a giggle, obviously impressed by his own bilingual talent.

It was New Year's Day, 1932, the last such occasion, we believed, that any of us would celebrate in Germany. The mood on Prinzregentenstrasse was a mixture of premature nostalgia and excited anticipation.

"Here, let me take a look," said my father, limping over and taking the envelope out of my uncle's hand. He carefully opened the flap and pulled out the documents. "Ten months seems an awfully long time to wait for a few pieces of paper," he muttered, attempting to decipher the bureaucratic language in the letter accompanying my uncle's and aunt's visas to the United States.

"The Americans are tightening up their immigration procedures quite a bit these days," replied Uncle Solomon, "what with a depression of their own to contend with. Victor tells me that there is a lot of pressure on his government to keep foreign labor out; some extremists even demand that immigration be stopped altogether. Fortunately, he was able to convince those in authority that my services were indispensable for the future success of Feinberg's America. Now that he has some practice at this sort of thing, he should be able to do the same for the rest of you much more quickly. As they say in America, 'Practice makes perfect.'" He looked over toward me and winked his eye. "By the way," he added, switching his glance first to my father and then to my grandfather, "what is the status of your visa applications? If I'm not mistaken, you submitted the initial forms several months ago. Have you gotten any response yet?"

There was a short, embarrassed pause. My father was the first to reply. "I'm afraid we ran into a few delays, but within the next few weeks we will have all the proper forms filled out and delivered to the American Consulate. It took me several months just to do the necessary paperwork to assure that my disability pension will be continued when we emigrate. Without Heinrich's help, I would probably still be going from one office to another without getting any results."

"Actually," I interrupted, "it was Judge Linsdorff who cut through all the red tape. He did with one or two phone calls what all of my letters failed to do. No one pays any attention to a university dropout."

Uncle Solomon's expression became very serious as he listened. Addressing himself to my grandfather he asked, "And what about you, Jacob? Do you also have an excuse for procrastinating? And all the while I thought..."

"Calm down, Solomon," chided my grandfather. "Rome wasn't built in a day. You are perfectly aware of all the difficulties we have had with the sale of Feinberg's. After all, didn't you yourself advise that I hold out until a fair offer was presented?"

"Yes, but I was under the impression that you had already taken care of the visas," replied my uncle with irritation. "You would still have had time to complete the transaction, or, if worse came to worst, you could have left it in the hands of your attorneys. I just don't understand what you are all waiting for."

He looked at me as if to indicate that I was to blame for not forcing them to act more quickly. What he did not know was that not only I, but my mother as well, had repeatedly urged both my father and grandfather not to delay. My father, however, had refused to even consider doing anything before settling the matter of the pension he had earned with his flesh and blood. He would never agree, he said, to live on the charity of others. My grandfather blamed the prerequisite sale of his business for his inertia. And so we had waited.

"Take off that sour face, Sol," my grandfather admonished. "And stop worrying so much. You are going to give yourself an ulcer. Before you know it, we will all be sitting around a kitchen in Brooklyn talking about the good old days in Munich. I'll bet Yaffa has already decided not only in which neighborhood we will live, but if I know her she has it narrowed down to the block, if not the house. So you see, we are being well taken care of."

"This is no joking matter," snapped Uncle Solomon. "Don't you realize that Hitler and his henchmen, or some other maniacs with similar ideas, are going to take control of this country eventually, perhaps sooner than any of us would like to believe? I dread the thought of what might happen after that. You can't wait any longer."

A shiver went down my spine as my uncle made this prediction, even though I knew that it was shared by a growing number of people in Germany. I looked at my mother who had come in from the kitchen several minutes before, and saw from the expression on her face that she had been similarly affected.

"Nonsense!" bellowed my father, running his fingers along the side of his face. "Hindenburg will give that Austrian a sound drubbing if he decides to run against him in the next election. What surprises me most, though, is that people can still take him seriously as a candidate for high office after that business with his niece last September. The official version is that she shot herself, but it wouldn't surprise me if he had something to do with it."

"Come now, Erich," said my grandfather. "He wasn't even in Munich at the time. He would have to be more than a magician to perform a trick like that: to give a speech in Nuremberg and commit a murder in Munich at the same time. It was a clear case of suicide. But that doesn't mean that he didn't drive her to it. I saw and heard them arguing more than once during the past few months. You can ask any of his neighbors about it." He walked over to the front window and pulled back the curtain. Then, pointing across the street he said, "I watched them bring Fräulein Raubal's body down from the apartment that Saturday morning. There were police swarming all over the block, poking around and asking questions. She was such a pretty young girl. And polite too. She always said hello when I passed her. I wonder what her uncle would have thought about that."

"And yet there wasn't even an inquest," my father said, still unconvinced. "One or two articles in the newspaper and then the whole thing was hushed up. There was even one article that claimed her body was all bruised and her nose broken. How does that add up to suicide? Do you think she beat herself up before she shot herself in the heart? At any rate, a leader of a country having his niece for a girlfriend... The whole thing stinks to high heaven."

"We don't even know that for sure," replied my grandfather, still gazing out the window at Hitler's building. "According to his followers he is simply a grieving uncle. And from what I saw when he arrived back from Nuremberg that day, he was grieving. Unless, of course, he is not only a magician, but a professional actor."

"If only he were just an actor," observed Uncle Solomon, "we wouldn't have to worry so much. I'm afraid, though, it is more than an act. At any rate, a country that allows men like Hitler to rise to power is a country that will eventually allow many other things. Whether or not he killed his niece will probably never be known, but I have no doubt that given the opportunity he will prove himself to be a first-rate killer." Uncle Solomon wiped his brow with his fingertips. "I hate to sound like an old nag," he concluded, "but you cannot afford to waste any more time."

Uncle Solomon's warning had shaken me. The following week I went to the American Consulate. After I had managed, in my halting English, to answer a series of questions put to me by a pleasant receptionist, I was given a number of preliminary forms.

"This is preposterous," bellowed my father, leafing through the papers

I had handed him a few minutes before. "It looks like they want us to write autobiographies before they will even consider granting us visas. Now I know why they advertise America as the home of the brave. You have to be brave even to try to read through all of this nonsense, let alone answer the questions." He extracted one sheet from the others and held it out at arm's length, reading it with some difficulty. "Look at this," he muttered. "They want each one of us to produce a police certificate attesting to our good conduct for the past five years. Did you ever hear of anything like that? What do they think we are, jailbirds? Not only that, but they want two certified copies of birth certificates. I don't even have a birth certificate, and I managed to get here from Russia without one."

"I'm sure these are only formalities," I answered, although I was also awed by the sheer volume of information and detail demanded. "We'll just have to do our best and hope that it will satisfy them," I added. "The Americans are reasonable people. I don't think they expect the impossible."

"Reasonable people wouldn't concoct something like this," he grumbled, as he began to fill out the first sheet.

With the help of the veteran Uncle Solomon, we eventually completed the initial paperwork, which I immediately brought back to the American Consulate. Once again I was subjected to a miniature interrogation, this time by a young official who frowned and shook his head repeatedly as he examined the forms I had given him. When he had finished, he said something to the effect that there seemed to be some data missing, and added that we would hear from him soon regarding our status. As I left the consulate I felt ill. I realized for the first time that there was a possibility our visas would be denied. By the time the tram reached my stop, however, I had put the depressing notion out of my head, and when my mother asked me if everything had gone well I was able to answer in the affirmative and believe it.

***

Uncle Solomon and Aunt Rachel's departure for America coincided almost to the day with an announcement made by Josef Goebbels, a rising star in the Nazi firmament, that his Führer had decided to run against the eighty-four-year-old president von Hindenburg in the upcoming election. The family had gathered at my grandparents' home.

"*Mazel tov!*" declared my grandfather, lifting his glass ceremoniously. Everyone followed his lead, clinking glasses. Although she was smiling, Aunt Rachel's eyes were rimmed with red. My grandmother surreptitiously wiped at the corner of an eye as she looked at my aunt. "Don't worry about us, Sol," he continued. "We will survive the short interval that we will be deprived of your lively wit. Germany has provided us with a new gimpy comedian to substitute for you while we remain here. And at the risk of offending you, I must say that he is funnier than you could ever hope to be."

Having said that, my grandfather stood up and began to shout in a shrill voice remarkably similar to Goebbels', "Our glorious Führer will deliver us from shame and lead us into a new and glorious future, for he is no mere mortal, but a living god! His steel-blue eyes can pierce the infinite and decipher the secrets of the universe; his moustache is more divine than the halo of an angel!"

"Why do you think I really decided to leave?" said Uncle Solomon once the laughter had subsided. "I can't compete with such a natural clown. And one with a Ph.D. from the University of Heidelberg no less. Let it never be said that Solomon Vogelsang did not know when he was beaten. One thing I must admit, though, is that it does my heart good to see a fellow cripple work his way up in the world to become a leading representative of the Master Race. Don't you feel the same way, Erich?" My father smiled and drained his glass without replying. "The crowning moment for us," continued Uncle Solomon, still directing his words to my father, "would be if the Americans were to elect that fellow Roosevelt president this November. He has you, me, and Goebbels beaten at our own game: while we all have only one lame leg to propel us to glory, he has two."

Two days later we all gathered at the railroad station to see my aunt and uncle off on the first phase of their journey. From Bremen they would make the connection for the port of Bremerhaven where the ship to the United States would be waiting. The women's tears flowed freely and the men's faces tightened as farewells were exchanged. I was particularly touched when, as my father extended his hand for a final handshake, Uncle Solomon pushed it aside and embraced him warmly. As he awkwardly returned the embrace, my father could not conceal the fact that he was deeply moved.

"We'll see you in New York," shouted Uncle Solomon as the train slowly pulled out of the station. Aunt Rachel stood next to him at the open window, sobbing as she waved her handkerchief toward us. My mother, grandmother, and sisters stood with arms linked, repeating their tearful farewells in choked voices. I stood and waved woodenly, feeling as if a hole had been torn in my life.

***

"I'm afraid that we have run into some difficulty." Mr. Raines, the American Vice-Consul, motioned me to take a seat as he examined the document on the desk before him. The nausea I had experienced the last time I was there returned even more powerfully as I listened.

"As you are undoubtedly aware, Mr. Hartstein," he continued, finally looking up to meet my gaze with his tired eyes, "for various reasons my country has had to tighten up its immigration laws quite a bit in recent years." He looked away as he said this. "As a matter of fact, for the entire year of 1931 a grand total of fewer than a hundred thousand American visas were granted. Moreover, this year I expect that there will be even fewer than half that number issued." Before I could respond, he went on. "If you compare this to the million annual immigrants to the States at the beginning of the century, you can begin to see how much more selective the process has become."

"Do you mean to say that our applications have been rejected?" I stammered awkwardly, my composure quickly vanishing.

He shifted uneasily in his chair. "That isn't exactly what I am saying, Mr. Hartstein," he replied. "A final decision has not yet been made with regard to all of the members of your family. There are some serious problems." He picked up a pencil and began to tap it rhythmically on the desk.

I remained silent as he began to speak again, fearing what he would say. "One of most strictly enforced provisions of the United States' immigration policy is the so-called 'Public Charge' restriction. Simply stated, this provision declares that no applicant may be granted a visa to the United States if there is any possibility of that person becoming a public charge at any time in the future."

"I don't understand," I interrupted. "What does that mean?" His eyes met mine again for a moment and then darted away nervously. I noticed beads of perspiration forming on his upper lip.

"What it means," he said softly, "is if my government decides that an applicant might become a burden to society, a visa application is automatically denied."

"But what does that have to do with us?" I blurted out, still wondering if my imperfect knowledge of English had led me to misinterpret his words. "My grandfather is a wealthy man."

"Yes, yes, I know all of that," he answered impatiently. "But in his case there are other factors involved...certain affiliations that must be examined. One can become a burden in areas other than the economic." Tap, tap, tap went the pencil, each sound magnified by my growing sense of panic.

"You mean his ties with Zionism?" I offered, attempting to keep my voice calm and level. "Isn't it true that there are many like-minded American Jews? Surely their desire for a Jewish homeland presents no burden to the United States. All they want is..."

"Mr. Hartstein," he interrupted, his voice now as tired as his eyes. "I am quite aware of what is involved. It may interest you to know that I am not unsympathetic to the reasons behind this desire for a Jewish state. But that does not alter the fact that being a Zionist can have a negative effect on a visa application." He looked up at me again and this time maintained eye contact as he spoke. "I am sorry, but my hands are tied in this matter. Believe me, if I had my way you would all be on the next ship out of Germany. Don't you think I know what is going on here? You must try to understand, though, that I have very limited authority; I have to follow the guidelines set down for me by my State Department, whether or not I agree with them. Let me show you what I am up against." He got up from his chair and walked over to the grey filing cabinet behind him. After rummaging through one of the drawers for a few seconds, he withdrew a manila folder, stepped back to his desk and opened the folder.

"This is just one case history," he said, holding a sheet of paper apart from the rest. "The visa application of a German physician and his wife, both in their early thirties. They have the equivalent of about two thousand American dollars, plus three affidavits of support from relatives in the United States. In addition, the doctor has a sister in America who owns almost one hundred thousand dollars worth of property and has more than ten thousand dollars in additional assets." He looked up from the paper, frowning. "Now you would think that such prospects would be granted visas automatically, as long as there were no criminal records or links with subversive organizations involved. And not very long ago you would have been right in assuming that. The fact of the matter is, though, that because of our present standards their application was denied."

"Denied? On what grounds?" I asked.

"Grounds?" he repeated, emitting a short, bitter laugh. "Let me read you the 'grounds' that the consul involved gave for his decision." He sat back and began to read. "'The funds available to the physician and his wife are insufficient. The greater part of the resources as listed on the affidavits has not been proved, and the number of dependents which the relatives who signed the affidavits have has not been stated. None of the persons mentioned have any direct obligations to the physician. Therefore, the visas are refused on the grounds that the physician and his wife are likely to become public charges.'"

He leaned forward again and looked at me. I felt numb.

"I could cite you case after case like that one," he said, clearly frustrated. "Some even more striking. And even in those cases in which the consulate advises that a visa be granted, there are a good number rejected at the higher levels." His frustration was building as he continued. "I must admit to you...may I call you Heinrich?" I nodded absently. "I must admit to you, Heinrich, that I am not at all satisfied with some of my country's regulations in this particular area, but there is really nothing I can do. You can imagine how difficult it is for me to accept the fact that other countries are more willing than mine to open their borders to those seeking sanctuary."

My shoulders sagged noticeably as he continued to speak. Noting this, he added, without looking me in the eye, "Don't give up hope, though.

As I told you before, the final decision on all of your applications has not been made yet." He got up and came around the desk toward me to indicate that our meeting was over.

I stood up slowly and looked directly into his eyes. "Which means that you have made your final decision on some of us." My voice cracked as I said this.

"You will receive official notification in the mail," he replied, turning his back on me and retreating behind his desk again.

I felt trapped as I left the consulate, wondering what to do next. It was as if a doorless cage had been placed around me, one from which there was no chance of escape.

***

"It is out of the question," I said. "Absolutely out of the question. Either we all go together, or none of us go. I never considered any other possibility."

The letter from the American Consulate lay on the dining room floor where I had angrily thrown it. My mother mechanically stooped over, picked it up and placed it on top of the serving table in the corner.

"Before you make up your mind, think it over carefully," she said, smiling her sad smile. "Your situation is different from that of the rest of us. The consulate's decision is proof of that."

"Like hell it is, Mama," I answered, not knowing at whom to direct my anger. "It makes absolutely no sense whatsoever to single me out. Absolutely no sense." I went over to the serving table, picked up the letter and began to reread it, as if by so doing I might change its contents. Mine was the only visa granted. Visas had been denied to my grandparents, parents, and sisters. There was no explanation given.

"Your grandmother and grandfather are no longer young, Heinrich," she went on, ignoring my outburst. "And to tell the truth, I am not quite sure they really ever wanted to make such a drastic change in their lives. You have to realize that it is a very difficult thing for them to do. They have lived here all of their lives."

"And what about you, Mama?" I choked out, still stunned. "What about you, Papa, and my sisters? Do you really think I could leave you all here? Impossible.'"

"Heinchen, Heinchen," she replied, stepping over to me and grasping my hands. "Isn't it possible that things are not quite as bad as you think they are? Nothing is totally black or white. Perhaps it will not be so bad for us after all. We do have a certain degree of security here. Germany is still our home." She spoke very softly, almost as if trying to convince herself. Then she added a bit louder, "Your situation is very different, though, and if you think about it you will see that I am right. You are at the beginning of your life. You must go where there are the best opportunities for you to develop your full potential. A young man must have the freedom to grow." She squeezed my hands lovingly and looked up into my eyes.

"There is no security here for anyone so long as the possibility exists that the Nazis will take control," I replied, my emotions spilling over into my tone. "And what about Jutta and Ursela? What about them? What about their potential?"

"They are women. It is not the same," she said simply, as if this statement needed no explanation.

I gritted my teeth and let out a sigh. Then, after several seconds I took a deep breath and responded, "No, Mama. I told you before and I will tell you again. I will not go and leave you here. I could never feel free if I were to do that. But I do not intend to give up so easily. There must be a way to convince the Americans that they have made a mistake. There must be a way. And if there isn't, we will just have to go somewhere else."

***

My grandfather patted me on the shoulder and smiled. "So you see, Heinrich," he said, "there are still millions of people in this country who have not lost their minds altogether."

We were in his office going over some of the latest sales figures. Business seemed to be on the upswing again, as the German economy inched forward almost imperceptibly. For the first time in more than two years the company had actually shown a profit, a very small one, but profit nonetheless. This, coupled with the March 13 election results, had lifted my grandfather's spirits considerably.

"Now aren't you glad I decided not to sell, or should I say give away, the company? At least you can be sure of having a steady job with a wonderful employer." He smiled even more broadly and added under his breath, "Soon those thieves will wish that they had offered me twice the amount they did." He laughed out loud and clapped his hands like a happy child.

"Some say that this thing isn't over yet," I said, feeling guilty at my attempt to dampen his mood. "Hitler still has the option of a runoff election, since Hindenburg was unable to get a clear majority. There is a lot of speculation that he will run again."

"Of course he'll run again," my grandfather answered firmly. "He has been flushed down the toilet, but he doesn't know it because he feels at home down there. Let him try. The next time he'll be beaten by even more than seven and a half million votes. Then, hopefully, we will have seen the last of my blustering neighbor, and good riddance to him too. Maybe he will go across the border and become president of his own country. Can you imagine, his Nazi friends in Brunswick had to appoint him to a bogus government position in order to get him German citizenship so that he could run for president. It seems that he had forgotten that little detail until the last minute. At times like this I am doubly glad that I am a Jew and not a Christian. At least I don't have to love my neighbor, especially if he is a miserable son of a bitch." He threw back his head and laughed again. Then, apparently recalling something, he added, "Speaking of miserable sons of bitches, I saw Herr Goebbels on Prinzregentenstrasse this morning. He was probably there to shed a few crocodile tears with his Führer over their defeat. He was limping even more than usual. You know, there is something about that man that makes him look as if he is perpetually constipated." He chuckled.

Although I still had serious misgivings about the true significance of the election results, I was glad to see my grandfather so cheerful.

The runoff election on April 10 left me feeling even more ambivalent than before. President von Hindenburg had won 53 percent of the vote, the majority necessary to retain the presidency, and yet there was an ominous aspect to this important victory, one hailed in the liberal press as a triumph for the forces of moderation. Even my grandfather conceded that things had not turned out as well as appearances indicated. It was late in the afternoon of Monday, April 11. My father, grandfather, and I were in my grandfather's office listening to the latest election results on the radio.

"Damn it," my grandfather said, turning the radio off and shaking his head in disgust. "I don't like it. Not a bit. I didn't think the Nazis would make such a strong showing. They are the largest single party in the Prussian parliament now, and they've also made significant gains in some of the other districts." He looked from my father to me.

My father shrugged his shoulders and responded calmly, "Now don't start crying gloom and doom, Jacob. No matter how they try to distort it, the fact is that Hitler got a good drubbing. And even though they have more representatives than the other parties, the Nazis still don't have a majority in the parliament. Hindenburg will probably give Hitler some insignificant cabinet post to keep him quiet, and things will muddle on just as they always have. Didn't the government outlaw the Nazis' private army of Storm Troopers? That should take the wind out of their sails. The tide is going to turn sooner or later. Wait and see."

"I still don't like it," my grandfather repeated, more to himself than to us. "Thirteen million Germans voted for Hitler. That is a gain of two million since the last election. Hindenburg may have gotten six million more votes than Hitler, but he has one foot in the grave and everyone knows it. He is practically blind and more than a little bit senile. I tell you, I don't like it at all."

I listened in silence, surprised by my grandfather's latest about-face. But I understood. He was afraid. Torn between emotion and intellect, he was the archetypal wandering Jew: at home nowhere, yet longing desperately to belong.

He feared not so much that he would be unable to adapt to a new culture, or that living conditions would not be up to his sophisticated European standards. Those were not the primary reasons. In the last analysis his fear was abstract, psychological — almost metaphysical. He was afraid that by attempting to realize his dream, he would destroy it. He was prepared to continue an uncertain, imperfect and, in many ways, negative existence here in the land of the acknowledged enemy, rather than take the chance that the idealized alternative would also prove defective. Another paradox. He did not go to Palestine because he simultaneously believed very deeply in it and lacked the necessary faith. The classic Jewish dilemma, I thought, realizing how much I missed Uncle Solomon. He was the only one who could understand.

Meanwhile, my efforts to get the American authorities to reverse their decision on my family's visas met with one defeat after another. My telephone calls were never put through to the Consul or Vice-Consul, and in response to my written appeals I received curt form letters repeating that the petition was denied. Eventually, even these responses ceased. My Uncle Victor's attempts to sway his state department were no more successful. At my wits' end, I decided to make one final, personal appeal.

"I'm sorry, Heinrich, but the decision is final. There is really nothing I can do about it. All of the applications have been reviewed carefully." Mr. Raines closed the folder before him in a symbolic gesture and pushed it over to the side of his desk. It was obvious that he had no desire to discuss the matter further. For two weeks I had vainly tried to get an appointment with the Consul. Finally, giving into my persistence, the Vice-Consul had agreed to see me in his place "for a few minutes." I was determined to have an explanation.

"But it makes no sense," I said. "You must see that yourself. Why would I be granted a visa and not the others?"

He clasped and unclasped his fingers nervously as he replied. "I tried to explain to you the last time you were here that there are certain standards that must be met before my country will grant a visa. Apparently you have met these standards while the others have not. That is all there is to it."

"I don't believe it," I shot back, my anger and frustration gaining the upper hand. "You know as well as I do that there are many unfilled places on the immigration quota, and that the quotas for certain countries, like Ireland and England, are much higher than for others. What kind of standards are those?"

"We are just wasting time," he said, rising slowly to dismiss me.

I ignored this and added in a soft voice, "Are you ashamed to tell me the reason that you denied my family visas?"

He sat back again; for an instant his nostrils flared, but he gained control at once. "I did not deny anyone in your family a visa. My recommendation was affirmative for all of you. I was overruled."

As his eyes met mine, I knew that he was telling me the truth. I felt crushed. Weakly I asked, "What reason was given?"

"In your grandfather's case," he began, his voice cracking slightly, "it was just as I told you. His connections with International Zionism were deemed sufficient grounds for denial." He stared silently at his blotter for a few moments before continuing. "As for your parents and sisters, they were rejected under the Public Charge provision." Before I could protest, he added, "I know, Heinrich, I know. It is ridiculous. It was felt that your father's disability would prevent him from making his own way in a new country, and the idea that a sister-in-law or brother-in-law would support him and his family was rejected as unrealistic."

"But the German government has assured his pension," I protested. "And he has a position waiting for him in Feinberg's America."

"I'm afraid my state department does not recognize assurances made by governments it considers unstable. As for his position with your grandfather's firm, that is not allowable under the contract labor provision in the American immigration code."

"Contract labor provision?" I repeated dumbly. "What is that?" The Vice-Consul hesitated, a slight blush coming to his cheeks. "You have to keep in mind that there is a depression in the United States too," he said defensively. "There are millions of Americans unemployed and a lot of pressure on the elected officials to do something about it." He hesitated again before going on. "As a result, this provision was added to the immigration laws. Briefly stated, it says that no alien can enter the United States under an employment contract. The purpose of this restriction is to insure American workers any available employment opportunities, rather than have them filled by immigrants."

"But that's absurd," I said. "On the one hand your government rejects applicants who might be unable to support themselves, and on the other hand it rejects those who can. Can't you see how impossible that is?"

He looked down at the blotter without answering.

"Why was an exception made for me?" I asked finally, barely able to get out the words.

Shrugging his shoulders, he replied, "I don't know, Heinrich. I honestly don't. I guess not everything in this world makes a great deal of sense."

This final meeting with the American Vice-Consul left me feeling as if my family and I were caught in a whirlpool. I knew only that I would not leave without the others; at that point I felt even more hostility toward America than I did toward Germany. The only thing that concerned me was what we should, what we could do next. I recalled what Mr. Raines had said about the liberal French immigration laws, wondering if perhaps our destiny lay there. This question was answered firmly and quickly by my father whose attitude toward France had remained constant.

"Go to France? Why not make it the moon? You can't be serious, Heinchen," he bellowed, jutting out his chin like a prizefighter. Don't you realize that the French are the ones who put us into this miserable situation by insisting on that miserable miscarriage of justice at Versailles? I tell you, if it weren't for those lace-sleeved bastards, Germany wouldn't have become a stomping ground for fanatics. We can thank the French for the likes of Hitler. Their aim from the beginning was to drive us so deeply into the ground that we would never find our way out again."

I knew from experience that it would be fruitless to try to discuss this subject logically with him. To my father, the French were and would always remain the enemy. His attitude toward the English was almost as negative. They were "cowardly bastards" for having thrown in their lot with France in the Great War. And despite his efforts to master the language, I knew that he never was enthusiastic about emigrating to America. Like my grandfather, he seemed to be more relieved than disappointed when he learned that his visa had been denied. The fact of the matter was that as late as 1932 the Russian-born Jew who had changed his name from Szmulski to Hartstein still considered himself first and foremost a German. I, on the other hand, born and raised in Germany as a German whose accidental heritage was Jewish, was no longer sure who or what I was, or where I belonged.

Uncle Solomon continued to write long letters, urging us not to stop trying to secure our visas, and assuring us that Victor was doing everything in his power to assist us. There was an undercurrent of anxiety in these letters, although they were filled with amusing anecdotes about the difficulties of adjusting to life in the new land. And while he refrained from advising me directly to come to the United States alone, I could read this message between the lines. He seemed to sense that Germany was already very close to the abyss.

***

The year 1932 was a political and emotional roller coaster. The eighty-five-year-old president was failing quickly, while Hitler gained strength almost daily. This was the state of things when I next went to see Judge Linsdorff.

"Come in, Heinrich, come in. It is so good to see you." Judge Linsdorff put out his hand and grasped mine firmly. Then, unexpectedly, he embraced me and repeated, "It is so good to see you, Heinrich."

It was almost a year since our last meeting. We had spoken to each other on the telephone several times during that interval, but for one reason or other had not gotten together. As I returned his embrace, I realized how much I had missed him.

"Now," he said, leading me into his study, "tell me what you have been doing."

"So, so," he said thoughtfully, as I finished the detailed account of my efforts to secure American visas for my family. "And I thought that today you would be telling me the date of your departure. I am afraid that this is not very good news...not very good at all. Apparently, bigotry can even cross an ocean." By the disgusted expression on his face, I could see that his attitude toward Hitler's party had not softened. He leaned back in his easy chair and rubbed his chin thoughtfully. "Have you decided what you are going to do now?" he asked.

"I will not leave without my family," I replied softly.

He nodded his head. "That doesn't surprise me at all, Heinrich. If I were in your place I would make the same decision. But that still leaves the question — what will you do? I suppose you have considered other possibilities...other places." His eyes bore into mine.

"I'm afraid it isn't up to me alone," I explained, sensing that there was something he wanted to tell me. "Predictably, my father absolutely refuses to think of settling in France or England. Somehow America seemed the only logical place for us to go. I still can't believe what happened. We should have listened to Uncle Solomon. If only we had acted sooner, we probably would have had no trouble getting visas."

"Don't blame yourself, Heinrich. It isn't your fault that Germany is becoming more of a madhouse every day. Your only sin is that you have held onto your sanity. Sometimes I am not sure whether that is a blessing or a curse." I could see the muscles in his cheeks twitching nervously as he spoke. I nodded agreement and he continued, "But don't give up on the visas yet. You are dealing with a bureaucracy, and all bureaucracies are basically similar. They transcend national boundaries. These petty officials are the same no matter where they come from. You can beat them at their own game if you try. Since they live in a world of paper, you must learn to use this world against them. You must write and write and write. Inundate them with your written pleas, protests, threats, anything you can think of, no matter how trivial it seems to you, write it down. Each piece of paper you send will become a document in your file. The larger the file, the more respect it will command. Perhaps when the file gets too big for a folder they will relent. I am not joking. Sometimes it can all boil down to something that trivial."

From his serious expression, I could see that he meant what he said. He continued, "And have others write on your behalf. Your uncle in America, and anyone else you can think of. I will make my contribution." He was frowning as he went on. "These glorified clerks usually have a blind reverence for titles, not that mine has any real validity anymore. To be a judge in these times is more of a joke than an honor." He frowned and looked down at the floor.

"It has gotten much worse, hasn't it?" I asked, knowing the answer.

"Let's just say that the world Franz Kafka portrayed in his works is not at all farfetched. Now I realize why you recommended I read them." He smiled and pointed to the bookshelf to my left.

I got up and walked over to the shelf. "I never thought you would follow my advice," I said, taking a volume out. It was Kafka's novel, *The Trial.* "And you really like what he had to say?" I asked, leafing through the book.

"I hate it," he replied, his upper lip curled in a sneer. "It strikes much too close to home for that. But there is no doubt in my mind that he was a great writer. I only hope that he doesn't prove to be a prophet. It is a shame that he is so little known. It was not at all easy to find his works in print. I had to send all the way to Berlin for them. An old friend of yours had to locate them for me." Suddenly he was smiling.

"Karl?" I asked, hesitantly. He nodded. "How is he?" My voice quivered a little. Karl and I had not communicated with each other for more than two years; yet I had thought of him often. Lurking somewhere in my mind had been an unexpressed fear that I continued to suppress, a fear that I sensed Judge Linsdorff shared.

"I think he has almost recovered his senses," he replied enigmatically, studying my face to see if I understood. "For a while there I thought there was no hope," he continued. "I believed that my brother had seduced him with his hair-brained ideas. It was a bitter pill to swallow, I can tell you that." He paused and looked me straight in the eye. "But there was a lot more involved than philosophy or politics. You know how much I hate everything the Nazis stand for. No, it was not only a moral dilemma, but also a question of pride. The idea that first my brother and then my son could have embraced the devil was a great blow." He paused again to let his words sink in. Then he went on, "I felt as if they were doing it to spite me. Can you imagine that? And you know, I was actually jealous of the fact that my brother had been able to exert more influence over Karl than I. Forget the fact that the Nazis might plunge the world into a new dark age. I was hurt. Like a child. Funny, isn't it?" He let out a short, bitter laugh.

"I'm afraid you are not the only one who took it personally," I answered. "You know, Karl was not only my best friend." I struggled to find the right words. "To me he has always epitomized hope and freedom, as naive and idealistic as that might sound. He was always so free, so uncontrolled — what I always wanted to be and never could be. When I began to think he might have thrown in his lot with the Nazis I felt personally betrayed. I took it as a personal rejection."

"Very good, Heinrich," he laughed. "Now we've both made our confessions. But perhaps we were both wrong in doubting. Perhaps Karl's ego is the one that should be bruised by our lack of faith. What is it that Mephisto says in the beginning of *Faust* about a good man always knowing the right way?"

"At the risk of finding myself in contempt," I interrupted, laughing, "let me be so bold as to correct Your Honor. It wasn't Mephisto, but God who made that profound observation. He has an advantage over us, though, because He controls the future. The devil, on the other hand, is at its mercy just as we are. Some people find it rather strange that Goethe has the devil and God on such friendly terms. Today it seems to be getting more and more difficult to know the difference between them. I hope you aren't giving into the temper of the times by confusing the two." He threw back his head and laughed more loudly.

"Whatever, whatever," he said finally. "Now I'll have to get out my dusty volumes of Goethe and brush up, or my reputation as a literary scholar will be completely destroyed. To tell you the truth, though, it doesn't really matter to me who said it, so long as it is true. And in Karl's case, I believe...no, I know it is."

"Please tell me about it," I said, feeling better than I had in quite a while.

"No, I don't think I will do that," he replied, assuming a serious expression. "I just don't think I will." He looked at me sternly and then broke out into another broad smile. "I thought I'd let him tell you himself. He will be coming to Munich later this week. Who knows, maybe between you two you can figure out the answers to some of these disturbing metaphysical questions."

***

I had been waiting for about a half hour when the train from Berlin finally rumbled into Munich's main station and glided to a stop. I scanned the faces of the emerging passengers eagerly, but there was still no trace of Karl. I was about to give up when I felt a light tap on my shoulder.

"Hello, Blacktop." The familiar voice was slightly deeper than the one I remembered. I turned and grasped the extended hand firmly. The next thing I knew we had locked each other in a bear hug.

"It's good to see you, Karl," I managed to stammer after we had untangled ourselves. The years between had faded away magically with that embrace.

"It's good to see you, too, Heinrich," he replied, smiling broadly. "Though I can think of some prettier faces I would have preferred to have greet me on my triumphant return to Munich."

"And I can think of some prettier ones I'd have preferred to greet," I retorted. We embraced again briefly, and then, taking one suitcase each, made our way up the stairs to hail a taxi.

During the ride to his parents' house, Karl drank in the various landmarks like an enthusiastic tourist. Finally, we arrived at Brienner

Strasse.

"The Prodigal Son has returned," he remarked gaily, as we jostled each other at the entrance to the apartment house in an attempt to get a favorable position for the race up the stairs, something we hadn't done since we were teenagers.

"Not fair," he shouted when I reached his parents' landing a few steps ahead of him. "You have the lighter suitcase." Both of us were breathing very heavily from the unaccustomed exertion.

Recalling my friend's former athletic ambitions, I said, "I don't think either one of us is in shape to make the Olympics in '36."

After a happy reunion with his parents and brothers, followed by the extravagant dinner his mother had prepared to celebrate the occasion, Karl and I excused ourselves to go out for some fresh air. It was a warm July evening. The calm streets of Munich belied the underlying tensions, and as we strolled along Brienner Strasse, I felt a serenity I had not known for quite some time. It suddenly became quite clear to me just how much I had missed Karl, how much of a gap there had been in my life without his friendship. Neither one of us had spoken since we left the apartment. It was as if we were content merely to be together. As we approached a familiar square, Karl slowed his pace somewhat.

"I guess you remember this place," he said, looking toward Odeonsplatz.

I smiled and nodded. "It seems like only yesterday," I answered, recalling the scene vividly. "That was an historic event." We had reached the approximate spot where a stray bullet had wounded me on that cold November afternoon almost nine years before. "On the whole, though, I would say that Germany gained that day. While she lost a would-be Führer, she gained a future giant of medicine."

Karl didn't answer immediately. I looked over at him out of the corner of my eye; he had a serious look on his face. His eyes, although not quite as deep a blue as his father's, seemed to contain the same power.

"It could just be that neither of those will prove to be true in the long run," he said softly. Then he added, "Come, though, let's go have a nice stein of beer and reminisce like two old fogies. There is quite a bit to catch up on."

A short while later we were sitting at a table in the Hofbräuhaus, sipping full-bodied Bavarian beer and listening to some cheerful folk tunes played by a lively group of musicians in traditional *lederhosen*.

"You know, Heinrich," Karl said, leaning over so that I could hear him over the music, the clinking glasses, and the animated conversation surrounding us, "Berlin cannot match this. Did you know that Munich is famous the world over for its Gemütlichkeit? In North Germany they think that one goes to Bavaria to relax and forget about the cares of the world. It certainly makes one wonder."

"Wonder?" I replied. "You are home. There is nothing to wonder about in that. One is always most comfortable at home."

"No, I didn't mean it in that way," he explained, a thoughtful expression causing his brow to crease. "What I was trying to get at is the great gulf between reality and appearance." He paused, smiled, and added, "Since you are the literary expert, though, tell me the truth: does literature imitate life or is it the other way around? Not that it really makes any difference in the long run." He tapped the side of his beer stein with his fingers.

Unsure what point he was trying to make, I asked what he meant.

He smiled sadly. "As I have gotten older I have tried to understand why we Germans are the way we are. It seems to me sometimes that we are a nation of schizophrenics. Munich is a perfect example." His voice trailed off.

"I think," I responded, leaning toward him to compete with the surrounding din, "you would enjoy talking to my Uncle Solomon. He is an expert on the subject of paradoxes. But we don't seem to do so badly in that area either. After all, didn't we choose the noisiest place in all of Munich to have a nice, quiet talk?"

"You're right, Heinrich," he said, lifting his stein. "Come, drink up and let's get out of here. There is a much more sedate place just three blocks away from here where we can be quietly profound and still get as drunk as we want."

We attempted to sort out the debris of the past years for two hours. As we spoke, it became increasingly clear to me that Karl was as dissatisfied with his situation as I with mine. At first it was difficult for me to believe. After all, he had earned his medical degree and successfully gone on to complete his surgical internship in a major Berlin hospital. I, on the other hand, seemed destined to spend the foreseeable future in the alien world of business. Another paradox.

"I must have had a strong sense early on that I would never become a lawyer," I said, trying to think back. "My true interest was always literature. The great works of literature will be around for a long time; the law is subject to the whims of a bunch of uniformed thugs. As for my business career, that was only supposed to be a temporary situation. My family and I would go to America and live happily ever after. It was the stuff fairy tales are made of."

Karl shook his head sadly and sank back against the upholstered booth. He seemed to be experiencing some discomfort. There was anger in his voice when he replied. "You should know that not all fairy tales have happy endings, particularly German ones. I feel terrible about not having been there when you needed me. The truth is, though, that I didn't only lose contact with you. For a while I lost contact with myself. I found myself being drawn into an invisible trap. Before I knew it, I was a prisoner. Believe me, Heinrich, it scares the hell out of me to think about it. I feel so goddamned guilty."

"Don't be ridiculous," I countered. "We aren't children anymore. I can hardly expect you to protect me from all of the Otto Eberthals in Germany. Anyway, there are too many of them here right now."

His voice suddenly rose. "That is just the point. Not only did I learn to close my ears and eyes to them — something I wouldn't have done when I was young enough not to know better — I began to accept them. And what is worst of all, I almost became one of them. That is what frightens and sickens me." He shook his head again, stared down at the tablecloth for several seconds and added, "But you guessed as much, isn't that so?" He looked up again.

I nodded. "The important thing," I said, "is that you didn't. I never believed you could. As an ex-athlete you know that the score in the beginning of the game doesn't really matter. It's the final score that tells you whether you have won or lost."

"The difference is that this is no game," he answered, refusing to be mollified. "I hardly need to tell you that. It's becoming more and more serious every day. You have no idea just how seductive and dangerous these people are."

"There are some diseases one learns about without going to medical school," I said. "Hatred is one of them. Unfortunately, it is also highly contagious." My stomach had begun to churn, but I remained outwardly calm. "I guess your uncle just never inoculated himself against it, although as a doctor he should have practiced better medicine. I wonder how he feels knowing that his nephew proved to be immune. Or doesn't he know?"

"Oh, he knows all right," Karl blurted out, laughing. "Poor Uncle Rolf. It isn't easy to lose a prospective disciple, you know. I have to give him credit, though, he really had me going for a while. He is a very impressive and persuasive fellow, especially when he is in his milieu. He is considered by many in the medical world to be at least semi-divine. It is hard to describe the effect that a man like that can have on others."

"I know exactly what you mean," I interrupted. "I saw his counterparts in the hallowed halls of academia. One of my literature professors was a devout Nazi, complete with party pin and glazed stare. He had the uncanny knack of proving that all of the great names in German literature, men like Hoffmann, Kleist, Goethe, and even Schiller, would have agreed with the basic ideals of National Socialism. You know, Karl, he was so articulate that at times I almost found myself believing him. So don't think I don't understand how easy it is to be seduced. I wonder sometimes what my reaction would have been were I not Jewish. I wonder if I would have been able to resist. And he wasn't my uncle."

Karl let out another short laugh. "As far as my esteemed uncle is concerned," he said, "I am no longer his relative. But I guess that became true when he disavowed my father — I should say, when he and my father mutually repudiated each other." He laughed again, and then became serious. "I think you might like to hear one of the last conversations I had with my dear ex-uncle," he continued, an amused glint in his eyes. I nodded.

"I had telephoned him," he continued, "to ask his advice on the treatment of a patient. At first he was rather helpful, but in the course of our talk he learned that my patient happened to be Jewish — he usually made a point to find such things out — and his whole tone changed. He advised me curtly not to spend too much time worrying about people like that, but to devote my energies to those who were deserving of them. When I reminded him that a doctor's responsibility was to heal all people, he became very angry. He told me that I was naive, added something about the apple not falling far from the tree and then hung up."

"Your father would have appreciated that," I said, smiling.

"Oh, he did," replied Karl, returning my smile. "When I told him about it he summed it up very succinctly by saying that his brother had always been and probably always would be an asshole."

At first neither one of us noticed the new arrivals. Four young Storm Troopers had seated themselves diagonally across from us at the other end of the tavern. We became aware of their presence only when they began to sing the song they called "The Fighting Song of the SA."

You Storm Troopers,
young and old
Take your weapons in your hands,
Because the Jews are causing
disaster
In the German Fatherland...

We looked across at them; they were obviously even more drunk than we were. They had stood up as they sang, and were now weaving back and forth as if they would all topple over any moment.

When the Storm Trooper treads the flames,
Yes, there will be delight,
For when Jewish blood spurts from the knife,
Then things will be set right...

They continued to sway, their brown shirts accenting their red, black, and white swastika armbands.

"Those dirty bastards," Karl cursed, slurring his words. "They keep coming back like a bad dream. How could Hindenburg have lifted the ban on those vermin?" Karl had gotten up from his seat and was shouting toward the Storm Troopers.

"Take it easy, Karl," I cautioned, my own voice thick with alcohol. "I've heard their songs before. The words might be idiotic, but you have to admit they know how to exploit a catchy tune. Let them gag on their own spit. Besides, you're a doctor now, not a prizefighter."

But Karl refused to be silenced. His light skinned face was flushed a deep red as he shouted even louder, "Idiots! Why don't you wrap up your horseshit and take it home where it belongs? Idiots!"

By then the SA men had stopped singing. For several seconds there was silence; then the tallest of the four took two or three unsteady steps toward us and shouted back, "You'd better keep your goddamned mouth shut if you don't want to wind up in the gutter!" The others, encouraged by their comrade's example, added their profanities.

Before I realized what was happening, Karl had made his way across the room and now stood toe to toe with the obvious leader of the group. A party of middle-aged patrons seated between us and the Brown Shirts saw what was about to happen, got up quickly from their table and hastily retreated to the exit.

"If anyone winds up in the gutter it will be you," Karl hissed. "And I'm sure you'll feel right at home there with the rest of the dogshit."

The Storm Trooper, who was about three inches taller than Karl, looked uncertainly toward his companions who had not yet made a move to support him. Meanwhile, I had risen from my seat and made my way clumsily toward them, my head clouded from the unaccustomed amount of alcohol I had consumed. I automatically picked up an empty beer bottle from the table just vacated and held it threateningly in the air.

"Please, please, gentlemen, no trouble, please." The proprietor of the tavern, an elderly man with a wisp of white hair protruding over each ear, seemed to have materialized from nowhere. "Please, gentlemen," he pleaded, wringing his hands in desperation. For several more seconds the scene was frozen, like a film when the projector malfunctions.

The tall Storm Trooper muttered, "What the hell," turned on his heel, and staggered back to his friends. "These two aren't even worth beating up," he said with false bravado and slumped down in his seat.

Karl continued to glare at him for several seconds. I stood behind him with the bottle dangling foolishly from my hand. Satisfied at last, Karl turned, winked at me and whispered, "Let's get the hell out of here before they figure out that they have us outnumbered two to one."

"I guess we accomplished our mission all right," observed Karl, as we walked along a narrow side street. "Only I think we did a little more drinking than profound philosophizing." Then he stopped suddenly, grasped my arm and blurted out, "You should have seen yourself. Standing there with a beer bottle in your hand like some barroom brawler in an American western film. It was priceless." Karl slapped his thigh and laughed until the tears began to run down the sides of his face. I was laughing too.

"You should talk," I said. "That was an award-winning performance you gave, especially the part where you compared that poor idiot to dogshit. I never knew you were a poet. It was magnificent." We both laughed even harder, doubling over with pain.

We were standing in front of the ornate fountain on Marienplatz, a little winded by our brisk walk from the tavern.

"I think we can take a little rest now. Our friends with the swastikas weren't in any shape to follow us this far," Karl said, seating himself on the edge of the fountain.

I sat down next to him. By that time, the effects of the alcohol had worn off considerably.

"You know, Karl," I said, after a few moments of silence, "it isn't very funny at all. Can you imagine what it would be like if people like those four cretins actually were to come to power in Germany? It makes me shudder just to think about it."

"I don't think that they are the ones to fear the most," he answered, looking up toward the impressive, ornate clock that crowned City Hall. "What worries me are the seemingly intelligent ones, men like my Uncle Rolf and your Nazi literature professor. They are the ones who make the others dance to whatever tune they play. And for however long they play. They will dance right over us if we let them."

"Can anyone stop the music?" I asked, without really expecting an answer.

"Someone will have to," he answered. "Sooner or later someone will have to."

***

The Reichstag election returns at the end of July were ominous. The National Socialist German Workers' Party had 230 deputies elected, almost doubling the Nazi representation. To make things even more chaotic, the Communists also picked up considerable strength, which meant that the two extreme parties of the right and left now held an absolute majority in the Reichstag. Together they could block any proposed legislation which the new chancellor, Franz von Papen, used as an excuse for increasing the use of the dangerous Article 48 of the Weimar Constitution. This provision stated that the president could rule by decree if the "public safety and order were seriously disturbed," and that he could temporarily suspend the fundamental rights of the people if he deemed it necessary. The devious von Papen was destroying what little was left of democracy in Germany.

On the positive side, at least from a personal standpoint, was the fact that Karl was returning to Munich permanently. He had saved that important piece of news for the afternoon following the incident in the tavern. We were in my family's apartment on Jägerstrasse; my mother had invited Karl to dinner.

"That was wonderful, Mrs. Hartstein," Karl said, as he finished the last bit of freshly baked apple pie on his plate and wiped his mouth with the linen napkin he had taken from his lap. "Absolutely wonderful." My mother smiled broadly at the compliment and asked him if he would like another piece. He refused politely and added, "But don't worry. Now that I will be coming back to Munich to stay, I'll have a chance to sample your pies all the time."

"That calls for a good drink," barked my father, who had been very favorably impressed by my friend during the dinner. He got up laboriously, limped over to the wine cabinet and took out a prized bottle of French cognac.

"At least the damned French know how to do one thing right," he said gruffly, returning to the table with the bottle carefully cradled under his arm. A minute or so later we were all drinking to the future, which seemed to have suddenly become at least a little brighter.

Fate continued to favor us in the latter part of 1932. Dr. Griep had taken Karl into his practice, confident that the latter would be an able successor when he retired. My situation at Feinberg's Ovenworks was strikingly similar to Karl's. My grandfather gradually transferred more and more responsibility to me, satisfied that I could assume the helm when he stepped down. As I became more familiar and capable at my work I actually began to find satisfaction in it. By then I had no hope that my family would be granted American visas despite Uncle Sol's encouraging letters. Since everything was going so well, moreover, I no longer felt a pressing need to emigrate.

Another unexpected development further heightened my misleading sense of well-being at that time. True to his word, Karl had become a frequent visitor to Jägerstrasse, his interest aroused more by my sister Jutta than my mother's pies. Karl confided in me about his feelings one day in early October. It was a beautiful autumn afternoon; Karl and I met at his office and walked to the nearby Botanical Gardens.

"I always loved coming here when I was younger," he said, as we reached the main path. He took a deep breath of the aromatic air. "It's hard to believe that we are in the middle of a large city." We strolled along the spotless path at a leisurely pace, on either side of us neat rows of varied flowers. As we turned a corner, we came to a gazebo covered with rose vines. We went in and seated ourselves on the bench inside.

"You know, Heinrich," Karl said, looking down at his shoe tops. "I feel rather silly right now." He let out a short, nervous laugh.

"What do you mean?" I asked, glancing over at him. He continued to look down.

"I mean, I feel like a little child lost in a department store. Can you believe that?" He raised his head; there was a strange, almost foolish smile on his face.

"That's the way it is when you fall in love," I said, returning the smile. "Everyone knows that being in love makes one look and act like a fool."

"Is it that obvious?" he asked, wrinkling his brow and looking even more foolish.

"Let's just say that one doesn't have to be a detective to see the signs," I replied. "But don't look so glum about it. You should be turning cartwheels, not moping around with an idiotic look on your face."

He shrugged off my attempt to make him laugh. "It's just that...well, there are certain problems involved," he said, almost stuttering. "What do you think about the whole thing? After all, she's your sister." He sat back, looking miserable.

"Which one?" I teased. "Or doesn't it matter? I have trouble myself keeping them straight. It must be very confusing to fall in love with a twin. I can think of all kinds of problems that might arise. Suppose, for instance..."

"Come on, Heinrich, I'm serious," he pleaded, before I could go on. I didn't have the heart to prolong his suffering.

"You know what I think about it, Karl," I answered. "I think it's great. And I can tell what Jutta thinks about it every time I see her look at you. We used to call her the quiet twin, but when you are around she can't shut up for a second. She always has a silly look on her face too."

Karl's eyes lit up at my words. "You really think so?" he asked. "I thought so, too, but you never can tell what is going on in a woman's head. Even if you are right, though, what about your parents? How do you think they would react to the idea of your sister getting involved with a...what do you call it...a *goy?*"

"So, you are learning a little Yiddish to get ready for your courtship?" I quipped. "Before we know it, you'll be wearing a *yamulka* and quoting from the *Torah*, although I don't think that will be necessary to win over my parents. In fact, my father would probably like you less if you were to convert. Believe it or not, he still considers himself a loyal German. I know he despises the Nazis, but sometimes I think that he resents his Jewishness even more than he hates them. Strange, isn't it? One thing you can never do is figure out the Jewish mind."

"Oh, I don't know," Karl replied, shaking his head from side to side. "These days my father seems to be just as resentful about being German as yours does about being Jewish. I think this damned country is in the middle of a nervous breakdown." He paused and then added, "What about your mother? I know she likes me personally, but I'm not sure that is enough."

"I think," I said, trying to be as honest as I could, "that she would have certain reservations about you and Jutta. Not because she disapproves of you, but because she is basically a realist. She would worry about the difficulties that others would make for you and my sister."

Karl shook his head. "If you mean my parents," he offered, "I think you can set her mind at ease on that score. My mother and father would never object."

"That isn't what I meant," I said, trying to choose my words carefully. "I'm sure my mother has no doubts about their attitude. But what about the others? You can see what is happening in Germany. Your Uncle Rolf is not exactly a voice in the wilderness any longer. He represents the tip of the iceberg. Getting mixed up with a Jewish woman will not make your life or hers any easier."

"Life is never easy, particularly when you go against yourself, Heinrich. I know that from experience," he replied, in a low, sad voice. Then, almost as an afterthought, he added, "And what do you think your grandfather is going to say about all of this? I suspect he has some strong feelings on the subject of intermarriage."

"I'm not sure," I replied honestly. "I'm really not sure. He admires your father very much. My grandfather has a typically Jewish mind. His essence is contradiction."

"Aren't you describing the German mind as well?" Karl asked, warming to the discussion. "Although I never put as much time and energy into our German literature courses as you did, I still remember that famous line from Goethe where Faust complains about having a dual nature. I can still see our literature teacher screwing up his eyes and looking toward heaven as he quoted them."

Karl stood up and did a comic imitation of the teacher in question, *"Zwei Seelen wohnen ach in meiner Brust."* ("Alas, two souls dwell within my breast.")

"You may have struck on something here," I said, laughing. "I never really thought of it, but now that you mention it, in some ways my grandfather even outdoes my father in being German. For instance, did you know that it took him many years to accept my father — not because my father assumed a German name and sought to assimilate, although for a long time I believed that was the reason — no, it was because he could not stomach the idea that his daughter was marrying a foreigner. Some Zionist. He couldn't reject my father for being a non-Jew, so he refused to accept him on the basis that he was not a fellow German." I paused again in order to see if Karl had followed my train of thought.

"People are confusing, all right," he said, shaking his head. "I have learned a great deal about how their bodies work, but their minds remain a complete mystery to me. I can tell you something, though, and I'm sure it is no revelation to you. If our minds are as similar to each other as our bodies are, and from what we have been saying here it seems there is a strong possibility they are, then there really is no basic difference between a German and a Jew until and unless one or the other decides to create one."

"That sounds very logical, Karl," I replied, "It's only too bad that we can't convince everyone else that it is true."

***

Our spirits rose even higher in late autumn. One evening my father beamed as he walked into the dining room and spread the evening newspaper out before himself on the table.

"You have to hand it to von Papen," he gloated. "He has finally taken some wind out of that crazy Austrian's sails." The newspaper headlines proclaimed the latest election results: Hitler's party had lost almost two and a half million votes from the previous election, and now held a total of thirty-five fewer seats on the Reichstag.

"I knew that sooner or later they would get what was coming to them," my father continued, reading happily. "Those Nazi dogs have been heading for a fall right from the beginning. This is the beginning of the end for them."

It was the beginning of the end, alright, just as my father had predicted, but not for the Nazis. It was the beginning of the end of a civilization based on the concepts of justice and human decency.

How did it happen? How could it possibly have come to pass, especially at the very time when it seemed as if a beacon of light had finally pierced the long gathering darkness? I search and I search for a possible explanation, tearing my mind and soul apart with torturous memories, clinging to the fading, withered hope that I might discover a crucial clue that will give me peace at last. I search, knowing full well that there is no such clue, that there can be no logical, no human explanation for the evil that was about to envelop us all. I lie awake at night, every night, my memories wrapped around me like the burning cloak of Herakles, wondering why and why and why, as whatever little remains of my being is painfully seared away.

How did it happen? One can read and reread the voluminous historical accounts and attend the lectures of experts who impress their audiences with erudite summaries of the complicated political maneuvers involved during that crucial time; one can study the logically thought out explanations of how the entire course of history could have been changed if only this or that person or group would have taken a slightly different approach in a given situation — and in the end one still would not be able to comprehend. Hadn't von Papen been victorious in November? Hadn't the National Socialists been set back for the first time since the beginning of the depression? Wasn't it clear that the German people were finally beginning to tire of the violent tactics of the Storm Troopers and their like? Yet, within two weeks of the election, a whirlwind swept through Germany.

Chaos returned with a vengeance. Suddenly, the aristocratic chancellor was out of office, forced to resign by the man who had been his strongest backer, General Kurt von Schleicher. By the middle of January it became evident that von Schleicher, who neither wanted nor was qualified for the office, had failed, and on January 28 he made it official by resigning. Two days later, President von Hindenburg reluctantly appointed my grandfather's neighbor, Adolf Hitler, the new chancellor of Germany. The whirlwind had spawned a demon.

***

On a cold Saturday, two days before that fateful appointment, the family sat at the large table, painstakingly avoiding the subject that dominated all of our thoughts. It was as if we had all sworn ourselves to silence, as if we believed that to express our fears, to admit to them, would have the effect of justifying them. As I looked around at the others, I could see the apprehension in their downcast eyes, just as I could feel it in mine. My father was the first to break the silence.

"I'll be damned, but I don't believe Hindenburg will do it. That runt Goebbels is probably behind all these rumors. He loves to stir things up. I just can't imagine the president offering the chancellorship to that...that...," he sputtered, unable to find the proper word. "No, I just don't believe it is possible." My father's face flushed with emotion. By force of habit he ran the fingertips of one hand along the side of his face over the faint, white scars there.

"Hindenburg is eighty-five years old," answered my grandfather softly. "I don't think he knows what he is doing any longer. At this point I think he would just as soon close his eyes for good as have to go on with the pretense that he gives a damn about what happens. Still, I am inclined to agree with you, Erich. It is unimaginable. From all I have read and heard he despises Hitler. He calls him the 'Bohemian corporal.'"

"According to Karl and his father, Hitler has a very good chance of being appointed chancellor," interrupted Jutta. "In fact, Judge Linsdorff said that he has already been offered the post of vice-chancellor twice, but turned it down both times." She looked from my father to my grandfather, expecting a loud contradictory response from one or both. Surprisingly, neither responded. They knew that what she said was true. Hitler had refused the vice-chancellorship in a coalition government after the large Nazi showing in August, and again recently when Schleicher offered it to him. He apparently felt confident that before long he would be given the higher post. My father continued to probe his scars absently; my grandfather simply sat with his eyes lowered, absorbed in thought. Seeing their unwillingness to respond, Jutta looked around the table at the others. My mother twisted her napkin nervously between her fingers, then got up and began to help my grandmother clear the dishes from the table. It was Ursela who finally spoke.

"Does it really matter who becomes chancellor? It seems to me that politicians make all kinds of promises and threats, but once they get into office they are the same. Maybe Hitler is no worse than the others. Why, even my piano teacher, old Frau Wenzel, likes him. She has a picture of him on her mantelpiece. She says that he is very sensitive, more like an artist than a politician."

"An artist," bellowed my father. "Frau Wenzel is an imbecile. The only reason he is here in Germany stirring everything up is because he couldn't make the grade as an artist in his own country. As for having a picture of him on her mantelpiece, that only proves that she is a silly old bitch."

Ursela frowned. "Come on, Papa, that isn't fair," she replied. "She doesn't mean any harm by it. She is just a lonely old lady, and she has always been very nice to Jutta and me."

"She doesn't mean any harm by it," he mimicked, scowling. "And I suppose she thinks it is sensitive the way Hitler rants and raves about Jews being parasites...or that all Jewish women are whores. She is a nice old lady, all right, like all the other nice people we have here today. They smile kindly while they plunge the dagger into your throat." He pushed his chair back and began to rub the stump of his leg. Ursel looked as if she were about to burst into tears.

"Your father has touched on something very important, Ursel," intervened my grandfather, nodding his head sadly. "Whether Adolf Hitler is an artist or a politician doesn't really matter. But these so-called 'good' people do. They are much more of a problem than Hitler or his roughneck Storm Troopers."

"You mean Frau Wenzel?" said Ursel, a note of disbelief in her voice.

"I mean exactly Frau Wenzel," replied my grandfather without hesitation. "And the millions of others like her here in Germany and all over the world. They mean well, and would never do anything to harm anyone; but in their blind, submissive stupidity they give Hitler and his kind their greatest source of strength. Acceptance. Without that acceptance they cannot exist. It is their lifeline. They know very well that if they can get the 'good' people to accept them they will win, because the progression from passive acceptance to active approval is as inevitable as the shift of sand in a desert." He sat back, obviously drained of energy.

My grandmother had come back into the dining room. She stepped over to her husband and placed her hands on his shoulders.

"Please, Jacob," she said protectively, "don't get yourself excited. You know that the doctor warned you about that." He reached back and patted one of her hands gently. "It isn't worth getting yourself so upset about," she repeated, kissing him on the top of the head as one might a baby.

Then the unthinkable happened. The question "What if?" which had troubled us for so long was replaced by the question "What next?" and no one knew the answer. At worst, we thought, life would become somewhat more difficult for Jews in Germany now that Hitler was chancellor; we would temporarily suffer some annoying discomfort. Never, never even in my most morbid moments did I suspect the the horrible magnitude of the event that took place in Berlin on that cold January 30, 1933. The Weimar Republic died at the moment Adolf Hitler swore his oath to defend and preserve its constitution. Its death had been so gradual, however, that many, perhaps most Germans, seemed neither to notice nor to care. Some who did realize this — those who were not loudly shouting "*Sieg heil*" with arms outstretched and torches blazing as they marched along Berlin's Wilhelmstrasse — reacted like a family that had gone through the long-drawn-out, excruciating terminal illness of one of its members: they breathed a silent sigh of relief that the suffering was finally over, prayed for better days, and prepared for the funeral. After all, the Nazis had never disguised their intention to bury the old system; their election placards had promised that the Führer would end the chaotic series of elections, that he would restore Germany's pride. And so now they waited and hoped.

Others, I among them, knew that for them there was little reason to rejoice or feel relieved. We felt trapped and helpless as we tried vainly to sort out the meaning and implications of what had happened. Then, because we were rational beings, we began to rationalize.

***

The mood was tense at the Linsdorff's home, although it was the celebration dinner for the engagement of Jutta and Karl. My father swallowed a mouthful of potatoes, wiped his mouth on his napkin and, unable to remain silent any longer, barked, "I would be damned surprised if he lasts another month. He might be able to make the rabble wallow around in his manure, but running a government is a different story."

Jutta looked across the table and frowned. She had made my mother promise to ask my father to "behave" during our dinner visit at the Linsdorff's; if necessary to plead with him not to get carried away in any political discussions. My mother returned Jutta's glance and shrugged her shoulders. She knew it was hopeless to try to change the habits of a lifetime. Noticing Jutta's discomfort, Karl, who was seated next to her, winked and smiled.

"I am afraid I have to disagree," responded Judge Linsdorff, setting his glass down on the table and leaning toward my father amiably. "It is much easier to catch a disease than to find the cure for one. The trouble with most of our countrymen, though," he continued, "is that they waited too long to seek proper treatment, and now that their condition is critical they have put their faith in a quack. They don't want to know that there are no panaceas in this world."

"Don't you think," I asked, "that the fact that there are only three Nazis in the cabinet is a safeguard against any Nazi extremism? The Social Democrats and the Communists will be watching every move he makes, waiting for him to make a mistake so they can throw him out."

My father snorted. "And who will be watching them when they deliver the country over to Russia?" he quipped. "The only difference we would see then would be streets full of Cossacks on horses instead of Storm Troopers on jackasses." He lifted his glass and drained the remaining wine from it with one gulp.

"Horses or jackasses, either way the street cleaners will have their pails full. Not much of a choice for them is it?" observed the judge, laughing. Then, addressing himself to me, he said, "Logically, what you say should be true, but unfortunately we don't live in a logical world. For one thing, the Social Democrats are weak and tired. They do not have the will or the conviction to provide significant opposition to the Nazis. The fact is, many of them are not sure whether to rejoice or lament the demise of the Republican government. They always looked upon the Republic as a stepping stone on the way to socialism, and never really gave it more than half-hearted support. The Nazis will make mincemeat out of them if it comes to a showdown. As for the Communists, they are fools. While they claim to be his greatest enemies they are at least partially to blame for Hitler's success. They cynically and blatantly cooperated with the Nazis to undermine the Republic, didn't they? And now they refuse to cooperate with the more moderate voices on the left. It really doesn't make any sense."

He turned to my father again. "You see, they believe as you do, Herr Hartstein. They think that Hitler is a flash in the pan, that he will fail very quickly and they will then be able to rush in to fill the political vacuum. Believe me, I hope with all of my being that you and they are correct and I am wrong, but I think this is a great miscalculation. After all, Hitler did not get where he is by accident. He is the product of over fifteen years of turmoil and suffering in Germany. He has become the symbol of a mystical longing for a glorious past that never existed. And this longing is felt by people in every area of society: in the universities, the military, the churches, the fields of medicine and business, and I am ashamed to admit, in the judiciary. He is our creation, and if we sit back and wait passively for him to disappear like an autumn storm, we will be swept away like so many dead leaves." His eyes flashed blue fire as he concluded.

For several seconds everyone around the table sat mesmerized. Even my father remained motionless, his brow wrinkled in deep thought. Frau Linsdorff finally broke the silence.

"And so you see what it is to be married to a judge," she said, smiling affectionately at her husband. "One pronouncement after another." He returned her smile with a sheepish grin. Then she turned to Jutta and, still smiling, added, "I certainly hope the wife of a doctor doesn't have to listen to long descriptions of operations at the dinner table." Jutta blushed deeply as Karl bent his head to her and kissed her on the cheek. The tension of the moment had been broken. I took the opportunity to propose a toast to the happy couple, and very quickly the conversation turned to less ominous subjects. It was obvious to all concerned, however, that the mood just beneath the surface was far from lighthearted.

***

As the first days of the Third Reich passed, I began to feel less apprehensive. Life went on in Munich much as it had before. There were a few isolated incidents of Storm Troopers attacking Jews or Communists, but this was no deviation from the norm and caused no undue alarm. A very positive sign of better things to come was that in early February Feinberg's Ovenworks was awarded the contract to supply the new heating equipment for a number of municipal properties. Apparently, Hitler's avowed hatred of Jews was not being translated into practical bias. My grandfather was not quite as sanguine as I, but in retrospect his analysis was still relatively optimistic.

"When it comes to money, they don't make a distinction between Jews and Aryans," he said. "As long as we can provide them with a superior product at a better price, they will not give a damn that we are evil and subhuman."

But we got our first true taste of the future very quickly. In the early hours of the morning of February 28, I was awakened from a sound sleep by a very loud disturbance in our hall. I sat up in bed groggily, believing at first that the building was on fire. But as I hastily put on my bathrobe and stepped out of my bedroom I was reassured not to see any signs of smoke or flames. When I got to the front room I was surprised to see my mother silhouetted against the front window. She was holding the curtains apart and peering down onto Jägerstrasse.

"What is it, Mama?" I whispered as I came up to her.

Startled, she let the curtains fall. "You frightened me, Heinrich," she said, putting her hand to her chest. Then she opened the curtains again and added, "Something terrible is happening. They dragged Herr Feder into that truck. They were beating him with clubs." I went over to her side and looked in the direction she had indicated. A large, black van was parked at the curb directly in front of our building. Two men in Storm Trooper uniforms were standing at the rear of the vehicle; one of them was shouting something into the interior, while the other was gesticulating wildly in the direction of the house, as if trying to wave someone back. Then, apparently finished with whatever they were doing, they both ran to the cab and pulled themselves in. A second or two later the van sped away down the deserted street.

"Are you sure it was Herr Feder?" I asked dully, still not fully awake.

"Yes, I am sure," she replied, letting the curtain fall again. "They were hitting him so hard." Her voice trembled perceptibly. Down below, the front door slammed. Footsteps echoed in the hall for a few seconds, another door clicked shut, and then it became silent.

For the next several days the radio and newspapers supplied a running account of the sensational chain of events that had begun on the evening of February 27. According to the new Minister of the Interior Hermann Göring, Communist fanatics had set fire to the Reichstag. This was, he warned, a signal to their followers that the revolution to overthrow the legal government had begun. This message was repeated and embellished daily by Josef Goebbels, whose shrill voice reached hysterical proportions as he repeated Göring's vow to crush the conspirators without regard to legal procedure; to destroy and exterminate all enemies of the Reich, as Göring bluntly expressed it, in words that would later prove not to have been understated. Night was descending over Germany.

***

"My father has written a protest letter to Hitler himself. I've never seen him this upset." Karl turned the page of *The Munich Post* to find the continuation of the front page article describing the latest government measures to crush the alleged Communist conspiracy.

"And for good reason," I replied. "It is hard to believe that the men who sat down in Weimar to establish a democratic republic meant Article 48 to be used to eliminate all of our civil rights. Just like that they've put us back into the Middle Ages. No one here in Munich, or the rest of Bavaria for that matter, would ever tolerate Berlin taking over the state government in the name of the Reich. Yet when you look at it objectively, you have to admit that Hitler was forced into taking drastic action. And he did it all within the framework of the constitution, with the full approval of his cabinet. Even Vice-Chancellor von Papen went along with him. Whatever else von Papen is, he can never be accused of being a supporter of the Nazis. So maybe things aren't as sinister as they look. It is an emergency and the measures are only temporary. After all, they did burn down the Reichstag."

"I said more or less the same thing to my father," replied Karl. "But it didn't make much of an impression on him. He thinks that the crazy Dutchman who set the fire is just a fanatic who was acting on his own. A high police official in Berlin who actually took part in the initial interrogation told my father that van der Lubbe is somewhat of a simpleton, perhaps even retarded. If that is true, it seems unlikely that the Communists would use him to begin a revolution."

"I certainly hope it isn't what my Uncle Solomon told us," I replied, thinking of the phone call we had received from America on the previous day. "He said the American newspapers are claiming that the Nazis set the Reichstag on fire themselves. They say the conspiracy story is just a ruse to make Hitler dictator of Germany. My uncle was frantic. You should have heard him; he didn't sound at all like himself. He repeated at least five times that we should get out of Germany. I think he believes that Hitler intends to lock us all up along with the Communists." I couldn't help laughing at this thought.

Karl gave me an accompanying chuckle. "I can just see your father in a cell filled with Communists," he said, shaking his head from side to side in amusement. "They wouldn't last an hour. Besides, I would miss your father's dinner table tirades." We laughed again. Then, abruptly changing the subject, Karl asked, "By the way, have you heard anything about your neighbor? Jutta told me that you had a bit of a commotion here the other night."

"You mean Herr Feder," I said, my smile fading. "Yes, it was quite a commotion. They say that he was arrested because he is a member of the Communist Party, but I really don't believe that is true. I only knew him to say hello, but he certainly didn't seem to be a political activist. He is a bank clerk, hardly the kind of position you would expect a revolutionary Communist to have."

Karl shook his head and frowned. "I understand they were pretty violent with him," he said, more as a question than a statement.

"My mother saw that part of it. That is why she is so upset. By the time I got to the window they already had him in their van. We stayed up for about an hour after the Storm Troopers left. The whole time she kept telling me how badly they were beating the poor fellow. It really sickened and frightened her. She has gone downstairs a few times already to see if she can be of any comfort or assistance to Frau Feder, but she says that the poor lady just sits there crying that it is all a terrible mistake. She claims that her husband wasn't interested in politics, that he didn't even vote in the last elections."

"I wonder how many 'mistakes' those brown-shirted morons have made so far," interjected Karl. "They and their SS cronies have been working overtime. According to some estimates, they have arrested more than fifty thousand 'conspirators' during the last five days. At this rate, fairly soon there won't be any place left to put the prisoners."

"I suppose," I said naively, "the answer is that they will just have to start letting them go. As soon as the whole thing cools off things will get back to normal. What alternative do they have?"

But there was an alternative. On March 8, Wilhelm Frick, the minister of the interior, announced on the radio almost matter-of-factly that a new detention center for criminals against the state had become officially operational. This prototype of a human disposal factory was on the outskirts of Munich in a little village named Dachau. It was a name I knew well, a name that until then recalled to me a time of happy youth. But now, now when I hear the name Dachau, I feel despair rather than delight. My mind conjures up the vague outlines of ghosts. Dachau. Birthplace of the Nazi concentration camp.

***

"Good riddance, too!" barked my father, snapping off the radio and limping over to the sofa. "It isn't the worst thing he could have done. Now we can wait for someone else to come along and restore the real flag of Germany, without having that other rag hanging next to it."

We had just been listening to Hitler's radio address from the local Munich station. He had used the occasion to announce that on that day, March 12, 1933, the black-red-gold colors of the Weimar Republic were officially abolished; from then on the black-white-red imperial flag, together with the Nazi swastika banner, would fly side by side as the official national colors.

"Our noisy Austrian seems to have quieted down a bit these days, just as I said he would. Don't you agree, Heinrich?" he asked, smiling smugly. "Now that he has the responsibility for law and order on his shoulders, he has had to put his bully boy Storm Troopers on a tight leash like the gutter dogs they are. Can you imagine how heroic they must feel, reduced to passing around collection boxes and begging for contributions to their glorious party? It isn't at all what they expected. If they had their way they would be out smashing skulls, as long as they had a six-to-one advantage, of course. But the revolution is over, and now our screaming Austrian is settling down to protect the status quo. He knows very well that revolutions always devour their own children, and he knows that he is liable to wind up a tasty meal if he doesn't watch out. It is the same old story. Only the names have changed."

I was not so sure. On the one hand, I found my father's assessment of the situation plausible. The general consensus in the press was that the new chancellor was doing his best to control the radical elements within his party, that his was the voice of reason which would now be raised to protect the traditional middle-class values. However, I found it hard to believe that the man who had written *Mein Kampf* could so suddenly have become mild 'Uncle Adolf,' as he was now being called almost lovingly by the same people who had once condemned him. And yet, like so many others, I continued to hope that my instincts were mistaken.

Judge Linsdorff had no such ambivalence. He did not waver for a second in his conviction that Hitler and the Nazis represented the greatest danger facing Germany, nor did he hesitate to express his opinion openly and repeatedly.

Although I was well aware of his outlook, I was nevertheless shocked at what Karl blurted out excitedly on the telephone one afternoon towards the end of March. He had never called me at the office before, so I knew that it had to be something important.

"My father is going to resign," he said, without any preamble. "At this very minute he is writing a strong protest letter to the newspapers stating his opposition to the present government. Maybe you can make him change his mind, Heinrich. I'm afraid for him." Karl's voice sounded very far away. My stomach began to churn wildly as I put down the phone. Yes, I thought, it had to come to this; it was inevitable.

Karl's father held his eyeglasses up to the light and polished them carefully with his handkerchief.

"I'm sorry, Heinrich," he said, smiling gently. "But there is nothing else I can do. No one knows better than you that this is not something I decided on the spur of the moment. I have thought it all out. Actually, it is long overdue." He replaced his glasses and leaned toward me. We were sitting across from each other in his familiar, book-lined study. "Besides, now I will have time to catch up on my reading. Are you familiar with Thomas Mann's work? He is a marvelous writer and, I might add, an outspoken anti-Nazi. He saw Hitler's true colors as early as 1926. Let me show you what he wrote then." He got up, walked over to the bookshelf on his left and took out a volume.

"Right now I am more interested in you than in Thomas Mann," I said. "Don't you realize that what you plan to do will put you in serious danger? The Nazis don't take very kindly to public criticism." I had just finished reading the letter earmarked for *The Munich Post*. In it, the judge had expressed his horror over the "trend of the present government to systematically destroy civilized law." He cited as the latest "travesty of justice," the legislation labeled the Enabling Act, which had just been passed by the Reichstag.

"The truth can be harsh," he replied, replacing the book in the shelf and turning back to me. "Yesterday's action by the Reichstag virtually turned Germany into a dictatorship, and I want that fact out in the open so no one can say that they weren't warned. This so-called Enabling Act gives Hitler virtually absolute power over the entire legislative process. According to its terms, he can now enact laws or conclude treaties without the President's approval. Even Caesar had more restraints on him. What is wrong with people here? Don't they understand?"

He was referring to the action of the Reichstag two days before. On March 23, by a vote of more than four to one, the delegates of the Reichstag had passed a measure that, in effect, had eliminated themselves as a legislative body.

"He still can't do anything without the approval of the cabinet," I replied, parroting what I had read in the newspapers.

"Any safeguards that exist rely on a rational, legal application of power," he replied, a bit impatiently. "Hitler and the Nazis will strip away all reason and law. The only thing that will be left when they finish is raw power. That is their element. There are things happening in Germany today that cannot and must not be tolerated in a civilized society. Did you know, for instance, that Jewish judges in Prussia are being systematically removed and replaced by Aryans, and that many Jewish lawyers have been barred from the courts? I am sure you remember the discussion we had on this subject right in this room about two or three years ago. At that time I told you that there was no future for you in Germany. Well, Heinrich, now the same holds true for me." He paused and let out a deep breath.

When he took up the train of his thought his voice was softer, almost a whisper. "It was true for me then too, but I refused to admit it to myself." He paused again and probed my face with his powerful eyes.

I sat for several seconds without attempting to respond. He was right, I thought. I had been attempting to hide my head in the sand; but how could I do otherwise? Had I not done all I could to get my family away? Was it my fault that the American government had denied us refuge?

With these and other thoughts spinning through my mind, I said, "You told me then that there were always alternatives, but not always acceptable ones. Tell me, what are the alternatives now?" I felt a weariness in all of my limbs as I waited for his reply.

"They haven't changed," he said, without hesitation. "You and your family must leave Germany, if not for the United States then for some other country where there is still some relative sanity."

"And what about Jutta? What do you think Karl would do if she were to leave?" I asked quietly.

"He would go with her, of course," he answered, as if it were as simple as that. "A doctor can practice his profession anywhere. Contrary to what some believe, my esteemed National Socialist brother included, the human body is more or less the same whether it is Aryan, Jewish, Asian, or anything else. I would say that Sweden or Denmark might be good choices." It was obvious that he had also given this more than a little thought.

"What happens to Feinberg's Ovenworks while we are running to Scandinavia or wherever?" I countered. "I can't just pick up and leave the firm to run by itself. My grandfather depends on me."

"Do you think it is any easier for me to do what I am doing?" he answered softly. Again, it was the simplicity of his response that took me by surprise. His eyes reflected the pain his decision had cost him.

I felt like weeping as I asked, "And what will you do now? Where will you go?"

"Go?" he repeated, an enigmatic grin playing at one corner of his mouth. "For the time being, I don't intend to go anywhere. I will stay right here and fight. When you get to be my age you become somewhat stubborn." He smiled and added, "My resignation and letter to the newspapers are just the opening volleys. The ball is in the other court now. All I can do is wait for it to be hit back."

I read the newspaper very carefully for the next few days, but neither Judge Linsdorff's letter nor his resignation were mentioned. At first I thought that he might have reconsidered after all; perhaps at the last moment he had been unable to abandon the profession that had given definition to his life. When I thought it over more carefully, however, I realized that his very commitment to justice had left him no alternative. Unlike many of his colleagues, he could not allow himself to become a parody by pretending that the rule of law existed in the Third Reich.

About a month after Judge Linsdorff mailed his protest letter, I learned why it had not been published. It was an overcast Saturday afternoon in April. Karl, Jutta, and I sat at the kitchen table.

"There were two of them." Karl said, sipping the tea that Jutta had placed in front of him. "They were well dressed and extremely polite, not typical Nazi thugs. They asked to see my father. From their accents I knew they were from the north, and I mentioned this to them. I was just trying to conceal my anxiety by making small talk. Surprisingly, they seemed to welcome the chance to talk, and soon we were chatting amiably, like three people who had met at a social gathering. They seemed particularly interested in hearing my impressions of Berlin and had many words of praise for my Uncle Rolf. Apparently he has become a celebrity there."

He took another sip of tea before continuing. "They were from the Secret Police, the Gestapo as they are called these days. When they identified themselves I must have appeared nervous, because one of them laughed and told me to relax. He assured me that neither he nor his partner had horns underneath their hats. He was a real joker, that one."

"From what I have heard about them, they aren't usually a very humorous lot," I offered. "What happened next?"

"It was very unexpected, to say the least," Karl replied. "When my father came into the room both of them snapped to attention, like recruits in basic training when an officer appears. After a while, the jovial one reached into his pocket and took out an envelope. Without saying anything, he handed it to my father. There were two letters in it."

"Letters?" I asked, puzzled. "What kind of letters?"

"That was the most startling part of all," he said, looking down at his empty cup. "One of the letters was the one my father had sent to the newspaper, the one you read, Heinrich."

I felt a sudden chill pass over my body when I heard this. Jutta, who was seated next to Karl, put her hand over his and held it tenderly. It had begun to rain; the sound of the drops hitting against the windows and side of the house made me even more uneasy. Karl also looked agitated.

"I could see how upset my father was when he saw his own letter there," he continued. "But he didn't let on to them. He calmly asked if they worked for the post office rather than the Gestapo. They looked uncomfortable after that little remark. Before my father could say anything else, one of the Gestapo agents politely asked him to take a look at the other letter. He seemed embarrassed about the whole thing. This time, though, my father couldn't conceal his reaction. The moment he unfolded the letter and looked down at the signature on the bottom, his head snapped back. It was a letter from Hitler himself!" Karl paused, as if the very mention of Hitler's name had constricted his throat.

After a few moments, he went on. "Needless to say, it was the last thing my father expected: a personal letter from Hitler. I'm sure he would have been less surprised if it had been a warrant for his arrest. In fact, I think that is what he expected. The concentration camps are filling up with Hitler's critics."

"What was in the letter?" I asked, unable to stand the suspense. "Were there any threats?"

"It seems that the Gestapo's visit was considered a strong enough threat in itself. As for what Hitler wrote, it was like the remarks one might make at the retirement party of an esteemed public official. The Führer expressed regret that Germany was losing the services of one of its most eloquent spokesmen and thanked him for his years of exemplary service — that kind of nonsense." Karl shook his head in disgust. "It ended with assurances that Germany's star was rising again, and a call for all true Germans to work together to see that it reached its zenith, the kind of political swill that was written for publication. I'm sure the papers will not ignore such a wonderful, sensitive document." Karl's expression mirrored the sarcasm in his words.

"What was your father's reaction?" asked Jutta, a question that was also on my mind.

Karl frowned as he replied, "He read it through the second time, or at least pretended to, then curtly told the Gestapo agents to inform their Führer that he had received his message and appreciated its significance. That was the end of it. They tipped their hats and left, like old friends who had just stopped in to say hello. Once they had left, my father showed me the letter and told me that he had misjudged Hitler after all."

"He said that?" I blurted out in astonishment and dismay, before Karl could complete his thought.

"Yes, he did," Karl replied. "But he didn't mean it in the way you think. Quite the contrary. He explained that he had made the same mistake that so many others had: he had underestimated Hitler's cunning. He was crushed."

***

"You see! You see!" thundered my father, clapping his hands together like a delighted child as he limped into the office. I smiled, pleasantly surprised to see him. Some weeks before he had unofficially "retired" from Feinberg's Ovenworks, confident, he said, that the company was in good hands.

"They couldn't do it after all," he continued, shaking his head up and down as if in contradiction to the negative statement. "In spite of all of Goebbels' propaganda, they have failed."

For weeks, the Nazi Propaganda Minister and his henchmen had been calling for a nationwide boycott of Jewish shops on the first day of April. It was late afternoon of the targeted day; I was at my grandfather's large desk trying to catch up on some paperwork.

"The great Nazi boycott has come and gone like a fart in a blizzard," he added, when he noticed that I didn't know to what he was referring.

"I guess I've been so involved with work that I forgot all about the boycott," I said, a bit guiltily. "How do you know it wasn't successful? I'm sure Goebbels didn't announce that news on the radio."

"That swine would tell you that the sun was out in the middle of a thunderstorm," he replied. "And he'd probably believe it himself." He scowled and went on. "But the people know the truth. Especially those who were in Ackerman's Department Store this afternoon. It was more crowded than ever. Ackerman picked today to hold an irresistible storewide sale. And from what I've heard, many other Jewish shops in Munich did the same. Except for the few owned by Orthodox Jews. They are closed on Saturdays. Maybe the Nazis think they are accomplishing something by boycotting a closed shop?" His scowl had become a smile. "It was really funny," he continued. "There were two shabby looking Storm Troopers posted in front of Ackerman's, passing out leaflets warning 'all loyal Germans' to take their business elsewhere. I watched for about twenty minutes and didn't see one person turn around and walk out. I guess when it comes down to it, the people of Munich prefer lower prices to patriotism."

"Still, it bothers me to think that they would even try such a thing," I said, unsure that we had won a victory. "These people don't give up so easily."

"It is one thing to get people to vote for you," my father replied, annoyed by my lukewarm reaction. "After all, that doesn't hit them directly in the pocketbook. But it is a horse of another color when they have to hand out their marks and pfennings. Money has no race or religion. The Communists are right when they say that everything boils down to economics. The Nazi bastards know enough not to try something like that again."

***

In June, we had a visitor from America. He was a bit greyer and had gained a few pounds since the last time I saw him, but otherwise my Uncle Victor was unchanged.

"Hello, nephew," he called out in his accented German, as he walked across the office with his hand extended. I got up to shake his hand. After we had exchanged the usual words of greeting, he said, "Come, let's go down to some cozy pub and have a pitcher of genuine German beer. I've been dreaming about it for a week. After all, I didn't come all the way across the ocean to sit in a stuffy office. I could have done that in New York."

"It is hard to believe that eight years have passed," he said, stretching his legs out under the heavy wooden table. "But from what I have seen in the short time since I arrived, it might well have been fifty. Munich has changed quite a bit."

"Oh, I don't know that it is so different," I replied. "The Marienplatz is the same, Feinberg's Ovenworks continues to thrive, and you seem to be enjoying the old-fashioned Bavarian beer."

Uncle Victor ignored my attempt at levity. He leaned across the table conspiratorially and said in a lowered voice, "We have heard reports in the United States about groups of Storm Troopers roaming the streets, looking for Jews to beat up. Just last week there was an article in *The New York Times* that cited several such incidents. In one case, several Americans were knocked around by a gang of those primitive bastards who mistook them for Jews. There is also a lot of talk about a network of concentration camps that have been set up for any opponents of the Nazis. Some claim that Germany is entering a new dark age. What do you think, Heinrich? Is it the truth?" His voice had gotten progressively lower as he went on. By the time he put the question to me, he was whispering.

"Things are always magnified by distance," I answered, unable to keep from smiling at his cloak and dagger mannerism. "Not that there aren't very serious problems here. If I were to say that all is well in Germany I would be lying. Still, I don't think it has reached the point yet where we have to fear that someone will sneak out from under the table and throw us into a concentration camp just for talking."

He looked unconvinced. "Sometimes it is more difficult to see danger when it is right in front of your eyes," he countered, his voice still restrained. "I don't mind telling you that your Aunt Yaffa and I are extremely worried about the situation here. And we aren't the only ones. Your Uncle Sol has become an absolute wreck. He has very little of his famous sense of humor left these days. I really don't blame him for being so upset, even if only a fraction of what we hear is true." He shook his head from side to side slowly.

"What I can't understand," he continued, "is how all of you can be so calm about it. Even your grandfather, who should know better than anyone, told me this morning to stop worrying so much." Uncle Victor shook his head again. "He even seemed to be somewhat defensive about this godforsaken country. Can you believe that? Has retirement made his brain go soft?"

"No, I don't think so," I replied, laughing. "The fact is, though, that he hasn't retired completely. I don't think he ever will, really. Just because I am sitting behind Jacob Feinberg's desk doesn't mean that he isn't watching every move I make. You have already found out that even an ocean isn't wide enough to stop him from making his will felt."

My uncle smiled. "I won't disagree with you there," he said. "So perhaps we should get back to the office and take care of the business matters at hand...that is, unless we want to get a tongue-lashing from the Commander-in-Chief when he makes us report to him later. To be honest, I don't feel all that comfortable here right now anyway. Since I arrived in Germany, I have felt a bit paranoid."

"And Hitler actually lived right there across the street?" Uncle Victor shook his head in disbelief as he stood by the window looking out across Prinzregentenstrasse.

"As far as I know, he still has the apartment there," replied my grandfather. "Although I haven't seen him around lately. I suppose he has outgrown Munich now that he is chancellor. And good riddance!"

"Let's hope the swine doesn't decide to come back when he is thrown out of office," added my father, who sat comfortably in the large sofa at the other side of the living room. I will be glad to chip in for his one-way ticket back to Austria."

"What makes you so sure that he will be thrown out of office?" countered my uncle. "It seems to me that if anything, the Nazis are getting more powerful every day. Could it be, Erich, that you are falling victim to wishful thinking? That seems to be a contagious disease around here these days. There are some very astute thinkers in America who aren't quite as optimistic as you about the situation here."

"America! Don't tell us about America!" my father bellowed, grasping his thigh roughly and beginning to rub it with the heel of his hand. "We have learned first hand about the great sanctuary across the ocean. Those hypocrites!" My father's face had flushed as he leaned forward and spit out his charge.

"The Nazis are saying the same thing," I added, hoping to avoid a serious argument between my uncle and father. "Hitler issued a statement a few months ago in answer to American charges of discrimination in Germany. He said that the United States had no right to protest his anti-Semitic policies, since their own immigration laws are clearly aimed against the Jews. And as much as I hate to agree with him, I think he has a point there. Let's face it, Germany isn't the only bigoted country in the world today."

"It is not the same thing." My uncle's face mirrored deep frustration. "There are no boycotts of Jewish businesses there, no discriminatory laws to compare with the one passed here a few months ago."

"Oh yes, tell us that you Americans have a society based on equality," shot back my father. "And that there aren't any fanatics in your south who hang people simply because they are a different color. You see, we have reports too."

"I can't believe this!" shouted my uncle, looking from one of us to the other. "You are like prisoners defending their jailer. It is beyond belief. When will you people realize that the situation here is becoming critical?" As his eyes met mine, I looked away, embarrassed. I knew he was right. In addition to the anti-Jewish legislation he had mentioned, there had been other serious developments. The Social Democratic Party, the largest organized opposition to the Nazis, had been banned in May. And just three weeks before, the Nazi leadership had supervised book burning ceremonies at many of the leading universities throughout Germany. The works of Jewish and other "objectionable" authors were thrown into large heaps and ceremoniously set on fire, in many instances under the auspices of professors. I knew he was right, but...

***

By the end of the summer, Hitler was the undisputed dictator of the Third Reich. All opposition parties and labor unions had been eliminated. As I review the events of the year 1933 in my mind, it is clear to me that I should have seen the coming cataclysm. I should have known that for a Jew in Germany the only rational course of action would have been to get away as quickly as possible, to settle in some neutral haven, at least until the storm passed. Yet I and many other intelligent people remained in the magic circle even as the flames began to lick at its edges. Some, like my grandfather, did so because they were too old or too tired to break out. A second group, and here I would include my father, obstinately refused to be driven away; they maintained a paradoxical combination of patriotism and faith, and they rejected the notion that they were in any danger just as vigorously as they denied the charge that they were aliens. They were firmly convinced that the "Austrian Corporal and his gang" did not belong. And then there were those such as I who remained in spite of the fact that we saw the approaching flames. We were held back neither by age, nor exhaustion, nor faith in eventual victory. Why were we unable to break out of the circle? Why, and why, and why? There are many reasons, but no answers...

***

As impossible as it sounds, I was happy in spite of the impending disaster. I was in love again! While not exactly monastic, my social life during the preceding few years had been almost nonexistent. Between my considerable responsibilities at Feinberg's Ovenworks, and my continued, insatiable passion for literature, I had had little time to play. In addition to my extensive reading, I had begun to set my ideas down on paper in the form of poetry and short stories, which provided me the freedom that I was denied in the external world — an escape from the ugliness of reality. The few casual relationships I had established during my years as a student in the university had not withstood the test of separation, and my grandfather's sporadic attempts to pair me with a "suitable" partner from within his circle of acquaintances had come to nothing. While my parents seemed resigned to my bachelor status, Karl often chided me good-naturedly and offered his services as a matchmaker, even more so now that he and Jutta had settled on an early autumn date for their wedding. And so my life continued until one Saturday afternoon in late September. I was working alone in my office on some correspondence when the phone rang.

"Hello again, Heinrich."

I knew her voice at once. "Birgit?" I said, more than slightly nonplused. "Is that really you?" There was a pause. For a moment or two I thought I might have been mistaken. But then I heard the familiar voice again.

"How are you?" she asked calmly, as if we spoke to each other on the telephone every day.

My pulse raced wildly. "Is something wrong? Where are you?" I asked, a bit tongue-tied.

"Here in Munich," she answered, ignoring my first question. "As a matter of fact, I am just a few blocks away from you." There was another pause. Then she added, this time with a trace of nervousness in her voice, "Would it be possible for me to see you today?"

Later, as we strolled aimlessly along the impressive Residenzstrasse, surrounded by a breathtaking mix of architectural styles, I said, "It seems so long ago since we saw each other last." We had reached the Max-Joseph Platz.

"Let's sit for a while and talk," she suggested, pointing to a sidewalk café a few meters ahead. I nodded a silent assent, my emotions swirling.

"I have missed you, Heinrich," she said, lifting the cool drink the retreating waiter had just set in front of her. She lowered her eyes for a moment, then looked up again, smiling shyly.

I felt a pleasant weakness in my limbs, a sensation I remembered from so long ago.

"I don't blame you for wondering what this is all about," she said, setting the glass down and leaning forward toward me. "To tell you the truth, I am just as bewildered by it all as you are."

I reached out and placed my hand over hers. Then, to my own surprise, I whispered, "I have missed you, too...very much." As I squeezed her hand gently, I became aware of something digging into my palm. I relaxed my grip, withdrew my hand gently, and stared foolishly at the diamond ring on her finger, and the plain gold wedding band beneath it.

"It's all right...all right," she repeated, her face and throat reddening. Then she reached across and placed her hand in mine again.

"I suppose I never was the best judge of character...with one exception," she said, leaning her head against my shoulder. I held my arm around her tightly, content just to sit there without speaking. We had left the café some time before and made our way to the familiar Hofgarten. Now we were sitting on the very same bench we had occupied during our last meeting some three years before.

"So your husband has become an officer in the SS, and you will be living in Munich," I said at last, trying to digest what she had been telling me. "It all seems so hard to believe." I stared out at the people passing by on the narrow walkways without really seeing them.

"Yes," she replied, her voice a bit distant. "We are looking for an apartment in the city. We will be moving here in the late fall. Dieter has been assigned to the staff at Party Headquarters here in Munich. I don't really know what that means. He never talks about his work. In fact, we seldom talk at all these days. My father used his influence to get him the appointment. In fact, it was he who convinced Dieter to join the SS in the first place, 'to insure a good future for himself and his family.' As you know, my father is a very persuasive individual." Her voice trailed off. We sat silently for several minutes.

Finally, I summoned up my courage and asked, "Do you love Dieter?"

She buried her face deeply against my chest. Her long brown hair was draped softly over my shoulder and arm.

"No," she replied. "Do you think I would be here if I did?" She turned her face upward and looked into my eyes. Tears were making their way down both sides of her face, and yet she was smiling.

I bent my head down and kissed her gently on the lips. "I love you," I whispered, feeling as if I would burst from the intensity of my emotion.

"And I you," she whispered back, returning my kiss. "That has never changed."

***

"I thought it was something like that when she called me," Karl said, as he peered into the mirror above the bathroom sink and carefully trimmed his full, blonde moustache. "I hadn't seen her for more than a year. I didn't think you would mind my giving her your office number." He put the small scissors down on the edge of the sink and turned to me. "My final clue that something extraordinary was happening was when you followed me into the bathroom. It's a good thing I only came in here to shave."

I had to join him in a laugh over that. In my enthusiasm to tell him about Birgit, I had been following him around like a puppy.

"So her husband is an SS man," Karl repeated, shaking his head and rubbing his freshly trimmed moustache between his thumb and index finger. "My Uncle Rolf must be very proud to have such a fine son-in-law, especially now that the SS are the new heroes of the Party. They are supposed to be the models of the Nordic super race. If nothing else, their uniforms are a big improvement over those drab ones the SA strut around in. The latter always look like they have a load in their pants. I'm sure that if my uncle didn't consider me a lost cause politically, he would be trying to get me to join up with the SS too. He always used to tell me that I was a superb example of German racial purity: the blonde-haired, blue-eyed Aryan. It is quite ironic, you know, when you think that Hitler doesn't quite fit the bill himself, not to mention some of those miscreants around him. What a Master Race they are!" Smiling a bit oafishly, he added, "But you have to admit that old Uncle Rolf was right about one thing...I *am* quite a handsome devil."

"A regular Sigfried," I scoffed, waving my hand at him in mock disgust. "But I didn't come here to feed your huge ego."

Karl jutted out his chin comically. "And how about this for ego. Does it ring a bell?" He tilted his head upward and put both his hands to his sides.

"Duce," I laughed, amused by his comic imitation of Mussolini. Not to be outdone, I took my black comb out of my pocket, combed a few strands of hair down over one eye, and placed the comb on my upper lip. With my free hand I gave the Nazi salute, clicking my heels together as I did so. Almost doubling over with laughter, the two of us practically stumbled out of the bathroom.

Minutes later, we sat at the kitchen table, two steaming cups of coffee in front of us.

"I'm sorry it didn't work out differently for you and my cousin," Karl said, no longer in a jesting tone. "The two of you belong together. I knew that from the first. Birgit was right about one thing though. Her father is a very persuasive man. I can vouch for that." He stirred his coffee aimlessly. "You will have to be careful, Heinrich," he added. "Becoming involved with the wife of an SS officer is a very dangerous business, especially for you."

"Are you trying to tell me that we should forget about each other?" I shot back testily.

"No, not at all," he replied. "All I am saying is that you are going to have to be more cautious. You can't be sitting around in the Hofgarten like two young lovers. Even under normal circumstances one would have to be discreet."

"Please, Karl, don't reduce this to a common affair. You of all people should know better."

"And you should know better than to think I would even hint at something like that," he answered, looking up at me with a hurt expression. "What I do want you to keep in mind is that the people you are dealing with are merciless."

"Especially to Jews," I said disgustedly, biting my upper lip in frustration.

"I hate it as much as you do," he answered. "But I'm not speaking abstractly. I have already had some first-hand experience with relationships between Aryans and Jews."

"In what way?" I asked, my curiosity aroused.

"In a very direct way," came the swift reply. "I have already had two 'interviews' with an official of the National Socialist Party; a pompous little ass who wouldn't qualify for a position as a floor sweeper in a grocery store if he didn't have a party pin. It seemed that he was quite upset about the marriage application Jutta and I filed. He did his best to convince me that such a union would not be in my own, or Germany's best interests."

"Those dirty bastards!" I muttered through clenched teeth. "Did he actually threaten you?"

"Do wasps sting?" he rejoined. "Of course there were no direct threats *per se*. He simply appealed to my patriotism, and gave me the standard quasi-scientific lecture on how intermarriage pollutes the purity of the blood and undermines the glorious future of our country. It was really sickening. He was lucky I didn't puke all over him, the little turd."

"What kind of a response did you give?" I asked.

Karl smiled broadly, his white teeth gleaming, "I reminded him that I was a doctor and had a bit of first-hand knowledge about blood. And I couldn't resist playing a little joke on the poor idiot. I leaned over and pretended to be studying his eyes. Then I put on a very serious expression and asked him whether he had ever suffered from hepatitis. When he said he hadn't, I advised him to have a medical examination as quickly as possible. By the time I left he looked pale and worried." Once again, the two of us had a hearty laugh. When we had calmed down, Karl reached in his pocket and took out a key.

"It's to the apartment adjoining my office," he said, grinning. Jutta and I won't be needing it after December. And I think she would be happy to know that we are keeping it in the family."

In early December, Karl and Jutta were married in a short civil ceremony. The occasion was marred by the absence of my grandparents; my grandmother, whose health was failing, was confined to bed. Karl's brothers were also absent, as they were completing their studies in Switzerland. After the meal, Karl and Jutta left to visit my grandparents briefly. Then they went on to the railroad station to catch an evening train for Italy where they were to spend a honeymoon week.

As I kissed my sister good-bye and shook Karl's hand, I felt simultaneously happy for them and depressed that Birgit and I could not share a similar experience. My only consolation was that I would be seeing her again within a few short weeks.

***

There was no traditional family gathering to celebrate the arrival of 1934. In spite of Dr. Griep's best efforts, my grandmother's condition worsened quickly; on New Year's Day she lay in the hospital in a coma. I can still feel the pain and emptiness that her death evoked, still hear my mother's unrestrained weeping, and see my grandfather's hollow, red-rimmed, lifeless eyes. Had we known what was ahead, however, so soon ahead, we would probably have felt relief rather than sorrow at her passing.

***

The year had begun with personal tragedy, but general conditions in the country seemed to have passed their nadir. The economic situation showed continued evidence of improvement, and in spite of the increasing propaganda and sporadic legislation aimed against Jews, Feinberg's Ovenworks did not suffer. Thus, while it was now virtually impossible for a Jew to enter the academic profession, the civil service, or the field of law, and while many Jewish employees were summarily dismissed from Aryan firms, in some instances the Hitler government actually intervened to prevent Jewish businessmen from liquidating their enterprises. This was not done out of any sudden change of heart on the part of the Nazis, but rather as an expedient means of achieving their stated goal: the eradication of unemployment in the Third Reich.

In the following months, Birgit and I met regularly in our sanctuary behind Karl's office. We made love, listened to music, and many times just sat quietly and spoke of our plans for the future.

The news during the beginning of July was electrifying. We were sitting in the living room listening to the latest reports.

"They have finally begun to turn on each other," my father shouted, as the radio announcer finished reading an official statement about the suppression of an anti-government revolt undertaken by leaders of the SA. "And if we are lucky, they'll all kill each other and leave the rest of us in peace."

The details of the sweeping purge of the SA leadership were beginning to emerge, a purge that, according to the government accounts, had been both lightning-swift and merciless.

"Why would they be doing such things to their own Storm Troopers?" my mother asked, a perplexed look on her face. "It doesn't make any sense."

"It all boils down to power and politics," responded my father in a knowing voice, as if what had happened needed no real explanation. "Now that Hitler is on top of the heap, he wants to make sure that no one will knock him off. The Storm Troopers were becoming too powerful, too independent. There is very little room on a mountain peak. Whatever he is, our chancellor is not politically naive."

"How will any of the others who follow him ever be able to trust him?" she asked simply, unconvinced by my father's explanation. "Don't they realize that any one of them could be next?"

My father smiled condescendingly. "You just don't understand the political world, Esi," he said, shaking his head. "Trust has nothing to do with it. Respect is what counts in politics. Our Austrian corporal is now looking for respectability to go along with his authority. Ernst Röhm and his brown-shirted bullies had become an embarrassment to him. Herr Hitler likes to go around in a top hat and tails these days, and rub elbows with the high and the mighty."

"What kind of people murder each other just to avoid embarrassment?" my mother asked, looking even more confused and upset.

"They are all scum!" bellowed my father, his patience giving way to emotion. "But don't feel sorry for any of them. Try to understand and appreciate the fact that from our point of view this bloody farce is a very good sign. It means that Hitler has decided that it is time to cast off the extremes and move toward moderation." He smiled again, looking extremely satisfied that he had reduced the events of the past week to their essence.

My mother, however, sighed and said, "It seems crazy to think that murder is a sign of moderation. It doesn't make any sense when you think about it. Why can't men just live in peace with each other?" She looked over at me as she spoke, hoping perhaps that I would have a better answer than the ones my father had given. I shrugged my shoulders. The fact was, I understood it just as little as she.

In August, the circle was closed. On the second of the month a grieving Chancellor Hitler led the country in mourning the death of the aged President von Hindenburg. Then, with the blessings of the military, he promptly combined the office of president with that of chancellor. On August 19 he called for a plebiscite and received the endorsement of 88 percent of the voting public. No one could doubt any longer that Adolf Hitler was the Führer of the Third German Reich. Not even his enemies.

"He's hoodwinked them all again. I never thought he would be able to do it," marveled my father with grudging admiration as the radio announcer gleefully reported the final results of the plebiscite. "But sooner or later they will put a tighter leash on him. Don't you think so, Karl?" He turned his head to face Karl who was busily chewing on a piece of bratwurst.

"For goodness sake, let him eat," admonished my mother, frowning. "You will have plenty of time to discuss politics after the meal. There are happier things to think about right now. After all, it isn't every day that we get such good news." She smiled broadly at Jutta and Karl.

My father, realizing that this was one of those times when my mother was prepared to stand firm, did not press the issue. He silently picked up a roll and took a large bite from the end.

"I suppose I should be happy, too," chimed in my grandfather, who sat at the other end of the table. "But somehow the idea of becoming a great-grandfather leaves me with mixed emotions. I still like to think of myself as a dashing young fellow. Nonetheless, *mazel tov!*" He lifted his glass toward the happy couple; we all followed suit and repeated the blessing. I was very pleased to see this indication that he was beginning to regain his old spirit. Since my grandmother's death, he had aged perceptibly. On those rare occasions when he came to the office at Feinberg's, he sat silently while I attempted to review the latest transactions, nodding now and then, but showing no genuine interest. The only time he displayed any real signs of life during that period was when, a few months earlier, my mother suggested to him that his apartment on Prinzregentenstrasse was much too big for one person, and that perhaps he should think of coming to live with us. He had answered with unaccustomed rancor, making it plain that he did not feel alone in the home he had so happily shared with his wife, and that he was perfectly able to take care of himself.

Even my father was concerned about his well-being; he went out of his way to engage my grandfather in conversation on the various events of the day, but met with no success. Statements that formerly would have triggered a lively exchange of opinions were met with an indifferent shrug of the shoulders or, at best, a monosyllabic response. The only one who seemed able to communicate with him to any degree was my sister Ursela. They would sometimes sit together in his large living room and speak quietly. In recent weeks, moreover, she had begun to visit him on her own, something she had never done in the past.

"And what about you, Ursel," my grandfather added, turning to her with a mischievous smile. "How is your young man doing these days?"

Ursela feigned a frown and replied, "Since you see him more often than I do, you shouldn't have to ask."

"Your young man?" Jutta exclaimed, wagging a finger at her sister. "And you didn't even let your twin know about this development? Pray tell, what other secrets are you keeping?" She placed her hand over her heart dramatically and screwed up her face into a pained expression.

"Oh, stop being so silly," Ursela laughed, amused by Jutta's mock theatrics. "You don't tell me everything that you do these days either. But from the announcement you and Karl made today it isn't very hard to guess at least part of it." So saying, she wagged her finger back at her sister, who responded with a hearty laugh. The others at the table joined in the laughter.

"Come, come, Ursel," I admonished playfully, getting into the spirit of the conversation. "Tell us all about it. Don't keep us in suspense."

Ursel smiled at me knowingly. "And in return, big brother, will you tell me your secrets?"

I felt myself blush, and wondered how much she knew about Birgit. Mercifully, Karl came to my rescue.

"I'm a bit curious too. Who is this mystery man anyway, dear sister-in-law?" he asked, in the teasing tone he sometimes used with Ursela. "I am beginning to think all kinds of fantastic things. Could it be that you are carrying on a secret affair with one of your grandfather's neighbors? Perhaps it is the Führer himself? That would explain your visits to Prinzregentenstrasse. Could it be possible that Jacob Feinberg has a leading role in this intrigue? I wouldn't be surprised to learn that he was the matchmaker who brought you and his famous neighbor together." Another wave of laughter swept across the table; this time even my father could not restrain a vigorous belly laugh.

"I hope you are still able to keep your sense of humor when you meet your future son-in-law, Erich," offered my grandfather, once the laughter had died down. "Actually, I think it is about time we had a rabbi in the family."

Ursela frowned and waved him away.

"Well, he certainly looks and acts like a rabbi," complained my grandfather jokingly. "You should hear the sermons he gives me. Why, you would think that I was his errant disciple, the way he carries on." He smiled at Ursela, who had just given a short description of her "young man." His name was Joshua Adler and he was, she explained, not a rabbi, but an editorial writer for the newspaper *Jüdische Rundschau*.

My father's ears perked up when she mentioned his occupation. He fixed his daughter with his most intimidating stare and said gruffly, "So, you have gotten yourself mixed up with a Zionist fanatic, have you? Now I understand why you wanted to keep it to yourself." Wincing, he reached down under the table and roughly grasped the stump of his leg, as if he had suddenly felt a sharp pain there.

To my surprise, Ursela was not intimidated; she met my father's gaze without blinking and said sharply, "He is no more a fanatic than you are, Papa. And we are not mixed up with each other. As for keeping it to myself, you can't blame me for wanting to avoid scenes like this." Then she added more softly, "You should meet him before you make up your mind about him. I think you and he have more in common than you imagine."

My father, taken off guard by her mixture of defiance and conciliation, simply sat back, perplexed, while my mother skillfully changed the subject back to the less controversial topic of Jutta's pregnancy.

***

It seems incomprehensible now that we were able to continue our lives normally; but how could I have known then that a time was coming when I would soon see human brains dashed from a skull by an SS officer's rifle butt? A time when I would witness the bloody spectacle of a man's genitals torn apart by a dog trained specifically for that gruesome function? A time in which I would help to build mountains of corpses, and watch the dead flesh burst apart and melt like wax under the relentless flames of a cremation grid. How could I have known that *their* faces would forever struggle within my tortured mind, the faces that were not, are not, can never become the faces of the enemy, although it would be so much easier to remember or think of *them* as such. How can I ever comprehend or accept the fact that *they*, too, are the faces of my loved ones?

***

The Hartstein family met Joshua Adler several weeks later. My mother used her powers of persuasion to convince my reluctant father that it would be only proper to meet Ursela's friend.

Joshua arrived at Jägerstrasse punctually. I liked him right from the first moment I saw him. One could sense an aura of intelligence about him, a strength that came from within. He appeared to be in his mid-thirties, which surprised me slightly. For some reason, I had expected him to be younger. His yellowish-brown eyes, while not as striking as Karl's or Judge Linsdorff's, were equally intense and seemed to change color, chameleon-like, from one moment to another.

In contrast to Ursela, who was nervous as she introduced him to my father, Joshua seemed relaxed. Before dinner was over he had won my father over completely with his nearly encyclopedic discourse on the various campaigns of the Great War. As he described the strategies and counterstrategies employed by both sides, my father sat back and listened intently, interrupting every now and then to add an observation of his own, or more uncharacteristically, to ask a question. My grandfather had not been far off the mark when he likened Joshua to a rabbi. Listening to him speak, one got the distinct impression that one was in the presence of a true teacher.

Later, my father, Joshua, and I sat in my father's study and continued the conversation begun at dinner.

"We have no real difference with regard to our deep attachment to Germany, Herr Hartstein," Joshua responded at one point, after my father had expressed the opinion that it was unfair to condemn an entire country for the insanity of a relatively few misfits. "Many German Zionists are not very different from the assimilationists in the Central Association when it comes to identifying with Germany. We realize that it is very difficult to dissolve century-old ties."

"But isn't it true," I interrupted, believing I had caught him in a glaring inconsistency, "that your primary stress is on the fact that Jews are a separate people, that their true home is not in the Diaspora, but in Palestine? It seems to me that there is a contradiction between this and what you just said."

"Because we declare our Jewish peoplehood does not mean that we disavow our debt to the German spirit," he replied, as if he had anticipated this observation. "In fact, it is the German culture itself that has molded the thinking of Zionist-minded Jews. Your grandfather and I have discussed this topic at great length and are pretty much in agreement on that point. And I know that I don't have to tell you, Heinrich, how important the literature of this country has been in delivering the message of human potential, love, and freedom. We can't disavow those messages anymore than we can reject our Jewishness."

"I'm afraid that literature is not always the best standard of measurement for a people," I replied. "Great writers, in fact great artists in all areas, reflect the human condition rather than a national point of view. That is one of the prerequisites of greatness. And the greatest of them are often at odds with the societies in which they live. The same will probably hold true of Israel and her artists should you ever achieve your goal of reestablishing a Jewish homeland."

"I can't argue with you there," he said, smiling. "We all know from experience how difficult it is to get Jews to agree on anything. But the fact that such ideas did and do exist here in Germany is reason for at least a modicum of hope. Now don't misunderstand me," he looked from me to my father. "I have no great illusions. I don't expect to ever see the day when Hitler invites a Jew to Berchtesgaden for a vacation weekend. No, tomorrow will not bring us happiness. I fear that there are bad times ahead for us all." He paused. His smile had faded.

"I don't think that we can exist on hope alone," he continued. "But it would be a serious mistake to automatically turn tail and scamper off like beaten puppies. Perhaps it was possible in ancient times to escape our enemies by parting a sea. Today, unfortunately, we are faced with an ocean."

"You're damned right we shouldn't run!" bellowed my father, who seemed to have been waiting for some opportunity to offer his views. "Just who the hell do these sons of bitches think they are? Cossacks in jack boots, that's what they are! If we let them push us out, why would any other country hesitate to do the same thing? And we would deserve it." He rubbed the side of his face angrily with his thumb.

Before he could reply to my father, I turned to Joshua and asked, "Have I misunderstood, or are you saying that you are against Jewish emigration, even to Palestine? If so, I completely misunderstand what Zionism is all about. "

"The answer to both of your questions is no, Heinrich," he said softly. Then, turning to my father he added, "And I agree with you, Herr Hartstein, that some of us must stay and fight. The only question is how? And where?" He took a deep breath before going on. "The decision to emigrate is not entirely in our hands, as you well know," he continued, directing his remarks to me again. "As for emigration to Palestine, that is certainly the answer for some of us, but realistically, not for all. Even if there were no quotas, there would be many Jews who would find it impossible to adjust to life there. Perhaps Moses was one of them. I don't think he could have adjusted to The Promised Land even if he had been permitted to enter. In fact, I sometimes wonder if it wasn't his own decision to stay out and view it from a distance. There is nothing more painful to a revolutionary than winning the revolution."

"Is that why you stay in Germany?" I asked, fascinated by his analogy. "To start a revolution?"

"I honestly can't say it isn't at least a part of the reason," he replied without hesitation. "Like you, I have more than one reason for staying in Germany." He nodded his head to me conspiratorially.

"And we are not alone," he continued, satisfied that he had made his point. "Many of our fellow Jews who emigrated in panic when the Nazis came to power have returned. They believe that Hitler's purge of the Storm Troopers means that he has become a moderate. Nothing could be further from the truth. If anything, he simply wants to strengthen his control. You see, Röhm and his men were much like Moses — revolutionary warriors who were not ready for their promised land either." He paused to see if his analogy had been understood. Satisfied that it had, he went on. "But the fact that so many have returned from exile demonstrates what I have been saying here today. In spite of everything, they feel that Germany is their home."

"Home," I said wistfully. "Can a land that rejects us ever be our home?" I felt myself caught in the familiar whirlpool, spun around in a circle that was drawing me further and further down.

"How could it be otherwise?" he replied, his voice once again rabbinical. "How can we expect others to accept us when we reject ourselves? The Nazis castigate us. They accuse us of betraying Germany, but they are wrong. We have betrayed no one but ourselves. By refusing to be Jews we opened the way for others to degrade us. It is up to us to begin the process of closing that road, and we can only do that by affirming ourselves. We cannot expect to feel at home in Germany if we don't feel at home within ourselves." He looked at my father with an intensity that was frightening. To my amazement the latter, not one to back down from a confrontation, offered no rebuttal.

"In practical terms," I asked, seeing that my father would remain silent, "what can we do to remedy our situation? It seems to me that we are relatively helpless."

As if he had anticipated my question he responded, "The Zionist Union has petitioned the government to recognize it as the logical and proper group with which to work out an agreement vis-a-vis the Jews. The strategy is to get the Nazis to recognize Jewish status on the basis of a group, rather than attempt to get them to correct the wrongs in the area of individual rights."

"I don't understand what the purpose of such a strategy is," I said, puzzled. I could see from my father's expression that he, too, was unable to follow the thinking involved.

"It is a technical legal point," he explained patiently. "You see, according to the terms of the Geneva Convention, national minorities are placed under international protection for a limited period. This has already been tested in Upper Silesia with the Jewish population there. When this territory was given to Germany on the basis of the 1922 plebiscite, Germany signed the Convention. As a result, Jews in that region are still permitted to hold office and work in the professions. We simply want this status expanded to all Jews in Germany." He paused to see if we were following his explanation.

"But why would they go along with it?" I asked. "What do they have to gain if they agree?"

"A very good question, Heinrich," he replied, like a teacher who is proud that his student is beginning to think. "There are two things we have offered in return. First, we indicated that in return for their agreement to grant us minority status we would be willing to use our influence to call a halt to the boycott of German goods abroad. And as a sweetener, we also offered to encourage Jewish emigration, and asked for their assistance in that area. We have tried to point out that it is to their benefit as well as ours to have a regulated emigration policy."

"And what kind of a response have you gotten?" I asked, impressed by the boldness of the plan.

"As of yet, nothing official," he answered. "But we will not give up so easily. We are also encouraging the program of 'occupational restructuring' for Jews. We have to open up new areas of the labor market for ourselves, and dispel once and for all the charge that Jews always seek to gain a monopoly in certain professions and businesses. It is also easy to understand that if we are ever going to establish a new homeland, we will need people trained in all fields."

"What will you do if all of your proposals are either ignored or rejected?" I asked. Although impressed, I was far from convinced that the Nazis would be inclined to soften their approach.

He put his head to one side. "In that event, we will have to find a different way to fight them." He spoke softly, through clenched teeth. "We have to try to concentrate on the positive elements that still exist here and build on them. We have to continue to hope."

"Sometimes I wonder," I said, thinking of my own situation, "whether it wouldn't be better were there no such positive elements to hold us here, whether hope might be our most dangerous enemy. Sometimes I have the sinking fear that we may be like moths seeking to conquer a flame. We are unable to resist it, so we fly straight at it, flapping our wings wildly as if the wind we create with our feeble effort will extinguish it...but in the end, it consumes us." Even as I said this, though, I realized that while there was a Quixotic ring to Joshua's entire approach to the dilemma, at least he was not sitting back passively, as I and so many others like me were.

Later, it was clear that my father had been more than a little impressed by our guest. When Ursela asked him timidly what he thought of her friend, my father said simply that he was a very interesting and thoughtful young man, which from him was tantamount to a ringing endorsement.

***

The action of the Nazis at the end of the summer of 1935 should not have come as the shock it did. After all, the groundwork had been well prepared. We should have known; the new legislation that was announced during the Reich's Party Day in Nuremberg on September 15, 1935 should not have struck many of us like a bolt from the blue. We should have known...

"The filthy bastards!" shouted my father, flinging the newspaper across the room. Then he limped over to the sofa and collapsed into it heavily, his chest heaving. My mother rushed into the kitchen to get a glass of water, but when she offered it to him he shook his head and waved her away. He sat there silently for several seconds. Then, as if suddenly stung by a bee, he grasped his head and cried out my mother's name. She was barely able to turn back and prevent him from pitching face downward onto the floor.

As soon as I saw Jutta's face that evening I knew something serious had happened.

"Papa had a stroke," she told me, before I had even crossed the threshold; her voice shook perceptibly. "Dr. Griep left only a few minutes ago. Karl and Mama are inside with him right now." I kissed her on the cheek and walked swiftly to my parents' bedroom without saying a word.

Karl put his index finger to his lips as I entered, and motioned with his head toward my father. My mother was sitting on one of the kitchen chairs at the side of the bed, holding my father's hand. I tiptoed over to the bed and looked down at him. His face had a greyish hue which made his scars more visible than usual. One corner of his mouth seemed to droop abnormally, but otherwise he looked perfectly serene.

"Let's go inside," Karl whispered, motioning with his head toward the door. "He'll be asleep for a while yet." I stepped over to my mother, kissed her on the forehead, and then mechanically followed Karl into the kitchen.

"Is he going to be all right?" I asked, looking from him to Jutta, who had just finished picking up the scattered pages of the newspaper.

"It will take a little time before we know for sure, but I think he is going to pull through," he answered. "There might be some permanent damage. It's just too early to tell. Neither your mother nor I thought it would do any good to call you at the office."

"They did this to him," hissed Jutta, who had poured us each a cup of coffee and sat down next to Karl at the small kitchen table." She pushed the newspaper over to me and pointed to the obscene headlines. As I read, I began to feel the strength drain from my limbs.

"Easy, Heinrich," cautioned Karl, as he watched me carefully. "It won't do us any good if you work yourself up to a stroke too. I don't need patients that badly." His voice had a hollow ring to it. I looked up into his eyes and saw the anger in them.

"No wonder he had a stroke," I said quietly, looking back down at the newspaper. "Listen to this," I added, reading aloud, "'Jews are no longer citizens of the Reich, but as of this day, September 15, are to be designated subjects...'"

"So," Karl said, "just like that Jews are no longer entitled to the rights guaranteed by German citizenship." He gave a short, bitter laugh. "Now isn't that the height of absurdity? Any German or, as they put it, 'any person of cognate blood,' would be able to see the sick humor in that. The idea of rights became a joke in Germany from the moment Herr Hitler stopped being one. We have the right to assent, and if we don't exercise that right vigorously, we have the right to go to a concentration camp. But you are leaving out the juiciest parts." He grasped the paper and leafed to the second page. "'Law for the Protection of German Honor and German Blood,'" he read, with an accent that sounded familiar, but which I was unable to identify at first. "'Number one: Marriages between Jews and citizens of German or cognate blood are forbidden. Any marriages of this kind that are entered into in spite of this decree are void, even when they are contracted abroad with the intention of circumventing this law.'" He looked up and added, now in his normal voice, "Herr Kulp must be a very happy man today, don't you think?" As soon as he mentioned our old teacher's name I recognized the accent he had been simulating.

"Aren't you glad, Jutta," he added, placing his hand over hers, "that we decided not to have a long engagement?" Jutta, whose face had paled as he read, looked as if she would burst out into tears at any second.

"The second provision was written just for us," he added, looking from me to Jutta. His bitterness and anger seemed to increase with each word. "'Extramarital relations between Jews and citizens of German and cognate blood are forbidden.' Now I know why your father threw the goddamned newspaper across the room. He should have tossed it out the window." For what seemed like several minutes we all sat silently. I thought of Birgit, and recalled our lovemaking of the previous day.

"The worst provisions are yet to come, though. Listen to number three. 'Jews may not employ female citizens of German or cognate blood under the age of forty-five in their households.' Now you will have to fire all of your Aryan maids, Heinrich. How will your mother ever get along without them? Even worse, provision number four forbids you to fly the Reich's flag or the national colors. What are we going to do with all of our treasured swastika flags and armbands?" Karl and I looked at each other and suddenly began to giggle like little children. "But since the Nazis are afraid they might be hurting the feelings of some Jews with this last law," he added, now finding it more difficult to restrain his laughter, "they are going to permit the flying of Jewish colors, and they even offer the protection of the state to see that no one interferes." The table shook with our laughter now; the coffee spilled from the cups onto the tablecloth.

Jutta sat in amazement and pulled her hand away from Karl's. Glaring first at him and then at me, she shouted, "What is wrong with you two? Have you both gone crazy? Papa has just had a stroke. We have practically been outlawed, yet you sit here laughing like lunatics. I don't understand it."

Her outbreak instantly sobered us. We looked sheepishly at each other and then at my sister. What she had failed to understand was that, under the circumstances, there was not much else we could do but laugh.

***

But our talent for self-deception was far more developed than our sense of humor during those years. I suppose that should not be very surprising, since, as the old adage goes, "practice makes perfect." The manner in which the hateful September legislation was greeted in some Jewish quarters demonstrated the extent of our mastery. A particular conversation I had with one of Feinberg's suppliers was a striking example of this. It was mid-November; Herr Mendel and I were discussing an order for copper we had placed with his firm. In the course of our conversation, the subject of the laws that had been announced at Nuremberg two months earlier arose. Gradually, we graduated to the wider question: the plight of Jews in the Third Reich. Although I had known and dealt with him for at least two years, this was the first time we had ever spoken together of anything other than business.

"Do not worry, Herr Hartstein," he drawled, rubbing his palm over an almost completely bald head. "These so-called Nuremberg Laws will turn out to be beneficial to us for one very good reason — they will help to reestablish stability in Germany, at least insofar as we Jews are concerned. The most important thing right now is to get these crazy *goyim* to calm down and moderate their behavior. I think the action taken at Nuremberg is the first step on the road back to law and order in Germany. It seems to me that the higher-ups in the government are as appalled as we are by the senseless violence. It is hardly to their benefit to have reports in the foreign press about old Jews being beaten up by their thugs, or photographs of Jews being forced to clean the streets with a toothbrush. It does not fit the image of a modern, enlightened world power."

"That certainly is a novel way to look at it," I said, interested to learn how he could justify such a conclusion. "Are you sure, though, that the opposite isn't more likely?"

"As sure as one can be," he replied in a confident voice. "I have seen evidence with my own eyes that supports my view."

I indicated with a slight nod that he should go on.

"Yes," he said. "I have actually seen the police in Tübingen, which is where I live, supervising the removal of an anti-Jewish sign that had been erected in the market place. When I asked an acquaintance in the police department about this, he told me that they had received an official order from Berlin forbidding any placards that advocated illegal acts against the Jews. Not so long ago the government encouraged such things." He sat back with a satisfied look on his face.

"And yet," I countered, "we still see signs, some right here in Munich, that make it very clear that Jews are unwanted. Signs in shop windows that say 'Jews Out' are not very comforting to me."

"Herr Hartstein, Herr Hartstein," he replied, looking up to the ceiling and smiling at what he obviously considered my naivete. "You know as well as I do that it is perfectly legal to disapprove of someone. No law can force a person to like or want another. Besides, from the practical point of view it doesn't matter whether they want us or not. Tell me one country that really wants Jews. The only important thing is that they need what we can provide for them. The Führer is not an absolute fool, you know. If he really wanted to run the Jews out of Germany the way he says he does, don't you think that he could easily use the same method he used to purge his own Storm Troopers? Or, even if we suppose that he wants it to look more civilized, couldn't he easily cook up some economic legislation to strip us bare?" He paused for emphasis and then went on. "Look at your own business. I assume from the size of your present order that you are doing well these days, not so?" He smiled a sly smile and nodded his head up and down.

"But how do we know that they will still need us tomorrow?" I asked, still fighting my nagging doubts. "How can we be sure that at this very moment they aren't preparing the legislation you just mentioned?"

"Armaments!" he barked out, leaning forward over my desk so that the glow from the lamp illuminated his hairless head. "Armaments," he repeated. "It's that simple. Have you forgotten that military conscription was reinstated this spring? The army is growing daily. In addition, Germany is building a new air force. Do you believe for even an instant that all of this is just for show?" He smiled knowingly.

"And even if it were," he continued, "there would still be the necessity for equipment. That means such ancillary items as uniforms, housing, and yes, Herr Hartstein, heating equipment. So you see, although you are a Jew, Hitler needs you." He slapped his palm against the end of my desk and laughed. "And since you need me, that means that Hitler also needs me." He sat back and blinked his eyes in satisfaction.

I thought about what Herr Mendel had said for the remainder of the day and was unable to find any glaring flaw in his reasoning. It was both true and logical. There was no doubt that certain essential products were produced only by Jewish firms, and that any actions against these firms would work to the detriment of the New Reich. My own experience was evidence that this was so. Feinberg's Ovenworks seemed headed for its most successful year since the early depression. Another positive sign had been mentioned by my Uncle Victor in a recent letter. Through a colleague, he wrote, he had learned that the new Reich's Minister of Economics, Dr. Schacht, was exerting pressure to call a halt to the repeated demands made in some quarters of the Nazi Party that Aryan German firms with branches abroad get rid of all of their Jewish management personnel. Such a policy was bad for business, Schacht had concluded, in that it often resulted in the loss of profitable markets to other countries. Herr Mendel was correct: Hitler needed his Jews.

The Nazi's economic miracle continued. Unemployment dwindled swiftly, the currency was stable, and almost through his demonic force of will alone, Hitler had restored the country's sense of national honor. His decision to have German troops reoccupy the Rhineland in March, which most of his advisors had cautioned him to reconsider, had been as successful as it was daring. France and England had complained but backed down, unaware that even a token resistance on their part would have sent the meager forces of the Führer scampering back across the Rhine.

As absurd as it sounds now, even those of us who had been so unjustly scorned and disinherited shared the triumphs of the country we still considered our homeland. Things were getting better. Even the most critical observers were forced to admit that a turning point had been reached, that extremism was no longer the order of the day.

Karl, always ultra cynical when it came to the Nazis, was not immune to the infectious optimism. It was early spring; he had stopped over at Jägerstrasse to examine my father, who, aside from an occasional slurring of his speech, was making good progress in his recovery from the stroke of the previous summer.

"I don't think you are going to be competing in the Berlin Olympics this year, but you keep up the good work and you may well qualify four years from now." Karl smiled and removed the sphygmomanometer cuff from my father's arm. The latter grunted and rolled his sleeve back down.

"What will I qualify for, the marathon?" he replied bitterly, turning the corners of his mouth down in a frown. "And which country will I represent? Since Jews are only permitted to fly the Jewish colors these days, I suppose I should apply to the Jewish team. The only problem is that I don't know what the hell the Jewish colors are, and there is no Jewish team." He grunted again and turned his face away.

"Let's hope that all that nonsense will be over by then," Karl said, carefully arranging his equipment back in the black leather doctor's case. "I have heard from a friend of mine in Berlin that some positive things are happening there recently."

"The only positive thing I would like to hear would be that Hitler and his friends had been flushed down the toilet like the shit they are!" shot back my father, slurring his words slightly.

Karl looked over to me and indicated with a nod that we should leave.

Later, as we walked along Jägerstrasse in the direction of the tram station, Karl said to me, "It isn't good for him to get all worked up like that, but he is perfectly justified in feeling the way he does. Most of the time I am just as angry and depressed as he is. Sometimes I think that if one of those goose-stepping sons of bitches ever came into my office bleeding to death, I would advise him to go home and soak in a bathtub filled with warm water. It was good enough for the ancient Romans." He kicked angrily at a small stone and set it clattering against the hubcap of a parked car. We walked on for several steps without speaking. Finally, I broke the silence.

"Now what about this friend of yours in Berlin?" I asked, curious to know what cheerful news for us could have come from the nesting place of our enemies. "Just what did he have to say that could possibly have made my father stop grunting? Or was it another one of your clever doctor tricks? Sometimes I think they give all of you a course in medical school on how to smile while you tell a patient he is totally kaput."

"You mean like this," he said, turning to face me and smiling oafishly. "No, I didn't learn that in school. It's just a natural talent." He rolled his eyes and smiled even more broadly, trying to make the most comical face he could.

"Is that the way for a man of medicine to act?" I asked, laughing at his antics. "And one who is going to be a father any day now? What will your son or daughter say when they see you behaving like a clown?"

Karl's features changed immediately. What had been a smile a moment before was transformed as if by magic into an almost somber expression.

"What is it?" I asked, not sure whether he was joking or in earnest.

"Do you realize, Heinrich, that they even control that part of our lives?"

"I don't follow you," I replied. "What do you mean?"

"Well," he explained, "most couples expecting a baby wonder if it will be a boy or a girl, and they enjoy the suspense. At least that is the way it happens in the civilized world. In our case, there is no suspense. Thanks to our Führer, we know exactly what to expect." He slammed his medical bag against the side of his leg in obvious exasperation.

"I still don't understand," I said, shaking my head. "What the hell do the Nazis have to do with whether your child is a boy or a girl?"

"Don't you see, it doesn't matter," he said sharply. He had grasped my arm tightly and pulled us both to an abrupt halt. "Whether it is a boy or girl is a mere technicality in the Third Reich, at least in our particular case. They already know what our child will be. It has been determined by law. It will be a *Mischling* of the First Degree, with all of the handicaps that accompany exclusion from the Master Race."

We walked along for another block without speaking. My mood had sunk considerably. I began to think of my own life, how unfair it was that my relationship with Birgit was a criminal offense punishable by imprisonment in a concentration camp. I thought of my neighbor, Herr Feder, who had spent several months in Dachau simply because a clerk had mistaken him for someone by the same name who happened to be on the Nazi list of Communists. Those months had apparently been time enough to leave him with a permanent look of terror on his face. As for adultery, SS Captain Dieter Hoppe was Birgit's husband in name only. He seemed, she had told me, content with this arrangement. So long as she attended the important party functions with him and smiled politely at his superiors, he did not complain. The subject of divorce, which she had attempted to discuss on more than one occasion, had been rejected out of hand. She had a duty to her Fatherland to remain with him.

"In answer to your earlier question, though," he said suddenly, as if there had been no interruption in our conversation, "it seems as if international sports and world opinion are having some influence on the situation here." It was a few seconds before I could focus clearly on what he was saying. "For one thing," he continued, "my friend informed me that all of the anti-Jewish signs along the highways leading to Olympic Village have been removed. The same thing is true in other areas as well. If nothing else, we now have racially unbiased autobahns. And speaking of the Olympic Village, did you know that the architect who designed it is Jewish?"

"That is interesting," I said, gradually emerging from my semi-stupor. "Maybe you weren't too far off the mark about my father being in the next Olympics, that is, if they decide to make debating one of the events. I read recently that the government is under pressure to allow Jews on the team, and that they might actually give in. To tell you the truth, though, if I were one of the athletes in question I wouldn't pack my bags and buy a ticket to Berlin."

Three days after this conversation, my sister Jutta gave birth to a healthy, blonde baby boy.

Ursela's wedding late that summer was the last really joyous family event I can remember. The ceremony took place in the Bahnhof district of Munich, in the synagogue which, like so many others in Germany, would be reduced to rubble by marauding SA and SS men little more than two years later. The reception celebration following the wedding was as elegant as any in the best of times. My grandfather had rented a large hall and hired musicians and caterers in order to, as he put it, "show the Nazis that while they might be able to drive Jews out of the drug stores, they cannot stop us from singing and dancing." For the first time since my grandmother's death he looked like his old self; his spirits had been lifted by Ursela's and Joshua's happiness. He was also cheered by the fact that a number of German acquaintances had shown the courage to come, thus defying the threats and exhortations of the Propaganda Ministry not to have social contact with any "Jewish vermin."

The mood beyond the wedding hall was no less festive. With the exception of those thousands locked behind barbwire and electrified fences in an increasing number of concentration camps, the German people were basking in national glory. The Olympic Games had been an unqualified triumph, both from the competitive and the propaganda standpoints. The athletes of the Third Reich had won more gold, silver, and bronze medals than those of any other country, and everywhere one looked one saw evidence of the miraculous metamorphosis in German society. Even many who opposed the Nazi state, including some members of the foreign press, were unable to conceal their admiration. Those who looked more objectively at what was taking place, however, found it difficult to conceal their growing fears.

***

"I don't know if I can go on like this, Heinrich. Whenever I leave you I have this terrifying feeling that we will never see each other again. You don't know the things I have heard. I am so afraid." It was a cool day in late autumn. Birgit buried her face against my chest as we lay next to each other under the soft feather quilt. I felt a warm, tickling sensation as a tear fell from her eye and made its way slowly down my side.

"I believe the worst of it is over for us," I said, turning her face upward gently with my free hand and kissing her moist eyes. "Sooner or later," I added, "this bad dream will end and we will be able to be together as we should." I kissed her again, this time on the lips.

"I don't know," she said, pulling away gently. "It just doesn't seem as if we will ever be free again. I want to believe that we will, but I can't." As she returned my kiss, I could feel her fresh tears on my face. Involuntarily, my own eyes began to fill and brim over.

***

The "good" times continued into 1937. In the last months of 1936, Hitler skillfully concluded the Axis Pact with Italy, as well as the anti-Soviet Comintern Agreement with Japan. Preoccupied with the goal of building Germany into a major military power, the Nazis seemed to have decided that the hated Jews were no longer important enough to persecute with any increased intensity or regularity. It also looked as if more rational minds were beginning to win out in Berlin. To achieve the goal of self-sufficiency put forward in the Four Year Plan announced by Goering that August, the Nazi government needed a smoothly functioning economy. Jewish entrepreneurs who ran enterprises like Feinberg's Ovenworks were safe, at least for the moment. Or so we wanted to believe...even when there was reason to question this conclusion.

***

"I agree with you wholeheartedly that it is a most unpleasant thing to have to put up with, but perhaps not as ominous as it appears," Joshua assured me, smoothing back a strand of hair that had fallen over one eye. "They haven't singled out Feinberg's Ovenworks for special persecution. They are doing the same thing all over the country, and not only in Jewish-owned concerns. It's the old story of the victors collecting their spoils."

I had just finished telling Joshua about an applicant who had appeared in my office that morning to apply for a nonexistent managerial position. In his hand he held a letter of recommendation from some official in Nazi Headquarters, a letter whose tone made it quite obvious that I was not being given a choice about hiring him.

"That may be true," I replied. "But it doesn't make me feel any better. I never did agree with the thinking involved in that so-called piece of wisdom: 'I felt terrible because I had no shoes until I saw a man who had no feet.' To me, that is a perverse viewpoint. There is no way in the world that seeing a man with no feet could cheer me up. If one carries through such a line of thought, one should feel even better to see someone without legs. And just think how much brighter the day might be if one had the good fortune to come across someone without arms or legs. Ecstasy. No, misery may love company, but miserable company is not my idea of fun." I put my hands behind my head, leaned back in the stiff leather chair, and let my eyes wander around the little room.

Joshua's working quarters at the *Jüdische Rundschau* looked more like a large closet than an editor's office. The disproportionately large desk was covered with open books and loose papers of all sizes, shapes, and colors. Some of the latter were little more than uneven pieces ripped from paper bags or package wrapping, and all were covered with seemingly illegible scribbles. A black typewriter sat in the center of the desk, almost completely concealed by the litter around it.

"Come now, brother-in-law," he said, amused by my observation. "You know very well that the author of those lines didn't really expect you to derive pleasure from other people's suffering. If that were the case, we would all be deliriously happy most of the time." He paused to brush back a few more strands of hair from his eye. "Maybe," he continued, "Hitler wants to have a war so that more people can be happy when they see the soldiers coming back without arms and legs. I would love to print that in the next issue of our paper, but I don't think it is worth the risk of being put into a concentration camp." His smile faded as he said this. He pushed a few books and papers to the side and leaned forward. "And I don't think rejecting this fellow they sent to you is worth it either. We have heard some terrible things about the camps. If he is incompetent you can always stick him somewhere where he won't be able to do too much harm. On the other hand, he may be qualified for the job in spite of the sordid company he keeps, and prove to be an asset to Feinberg's. Either way, it will not be a catastrophe. As for the extra salary outlay involved, you might even think of padding the next government contract you get just enough to make up for it, with a bit added for good measure. If the Nazis want their people to work, it is only fitting that they subsidize them." He looked at me slyly, and then broke out into a wide grin. "You see, Heinrich, there are ways to deal with the Master Race after all." Then, becoming serious again he added, "But one must always remain extremely cautious, just as a lion trainer should never believe that he has actually tamed the beasts in his act, no matter how obediently they follow his every command. We always have to keep in mind that we, too, are dealing with wild animals. We must never underestimate their savagery and destructive potential."

I nodded my agreement and was about to respond, but before I could, he spoke again.

"Nor should we underestimate their ability to uncover even the most closely guarded secrets, our most intimate secrets." He looked at me and raised his eyebrows to see if he had made himself clear. I looked at him searchingly for a moment or two and shook my head. "So you know about Birgit and me?" I said, continuing to study his face, which was etched with concern.

"There are a few basic rules of human nature, Heinrich, rules which are as infallible as any Papal dogma. Rule number one states that a husband has no secrets from his wife, except those which might compromise him with her. Then there is rule number two, which states that a wife has no secrets from her sister, particularly a twin sister. And finally, the third rule: a wife has no secrets from her husband, except those which would compromise her with him. A very neat system, not so? And symmetrical. It is much easier to understand than the *Talmud* or the *Cabala*, and one does not need a learned rabbi to explain its essence."

"I see," I said weakly, relieved rather than upset by his revelation. "Passing along a secret is almost like a game of soccer, like passing a ball from one member of your team to another. From Karl to Jutta, then on to Ursel, and finally to Joshua. Quite neat. Where does the ball go from here?"

"I think you forgot the very first pass," he replied, smiling. "The one from you to Karl. Where it goes from here is your decision. I have just passed it back to you. The cycle is complete. My only worry is that there will be another series of passes which will involve members of another team." Once more, his smile faded suddenly; there was a palpable tension in his eyes.

"There is no cause to worry about Birgit telling anyone about us," I replied, slightly annoyed. "For one thing," she wouldn't tell her husband, since that would compromise her with him and violate your rule number three. And since she has no sister, twin or otherwise, we can forget rule number two. Rule number one, moreover, does not apply here either, so I would have to conclude that you are worrying for nothing." I made no attempt to camouflage my annoyance. Before he could respond, I added, "Could it be, though, that I've misinterpreted what you are saying? Perhaps it isn't so much that you are worried, but rather that you disapprove?" I looked at his face to see if I had hit the mark.

He sat there impassively and returned my gaze. Then, in a low voice he said, "You mean am I against your relationship because Birgit is not a Jew?" He shook his head. "No, that isn't it at all. Contrary to what you may think, Heinrich, all Zionists are not fanatics. We are not Jewish counterparts of the Nazis. In my case, for instance, the belief that Jews must acquire an independent homeland was not the result of a sudden, divinely inspired flash of insight, or a mysterious calling from above. It is merely a pragmatic application of the basic law of self-preservation."

"So you don't look at yourself as one of the Chosen People?" I asked.

He gave a short, somewhat bitter laugh. "Oh yes, we are chosen all right," he replied. "The important question, though, is what have we been chosen for? Wherever we go we are made quite aware of our singular status, whether by means of random *pogroms* or specific legislation. Our Christian neighbors choose us every time they need an outlet for their hatred or frustration. Don't you think that it is about time we started choosing for ourselves?" His voice rose to sermon level. "And we can never do that until we have our independence, and we cannot have our independence so long as we remain a people without a country. It is really elementary."

"And when we finally have this country of our own," I countered, "will we all pack our bags and take the first ship that sails for it?" I shook my head slowly for emphasis and added, "The answer is obvious. If it weren't, every Jew in Germany would already be in Palestine. But here we are. Why? Why do we stay here? Why the hell do we stay?"

My question was directed as much to myself as to Joshua, and he seemed to realize this at once. He threw his head back and stared at the ceiling for a few seconds. Then, leaning back to face me, he answered enigmatically, "Perhaps some of us have been chosen to stay in order to work for the time when all of us will be able to stay or leave as we please. And with whomever we please. Perhaps we stay because we must."

I studied his face; there was a trace of uncertainty in his eyes. "Do you really believe that?" I asked.

"Sometimes I do," he replied. "But at other times I want to rush down to the steamship line and book passage on that ship you spoke about. It is always in my mind. You might say that our situation is similar to that of someone attending a performance at an unfamiliar theater. It is a good idea for such a person to acquaint himself with the emergency exits just in case there should be a fire. Those of us who are very cautious always make sure that we have a seat very close to one of those exits."

Following his analogy, I countered, "Wouldn't it be better to simply walk out without waiting to see the performance if we suspect that the building has serious fire hazards?"

"Perhaps," he said thoughtfully. "But it would be very difficult to do that, particularly if we had paid a great deal for the tickets. After all, we are only human." He smiled and held his hands out in front of himself.

I returned his smile and leaned back in my chair.

"I suppose then," I replied, "as my Uncle Solomon would say, the bottom line is that I should hire my Nazi and keep my eyes on the door."

"Not exactly," he countered. "My advice is to keep only one eye on the door. Keep the other one glued to the Nazi." He smiled his sly smile again. "And be very careful. Remember, he will be watching you at least as closely as you are watching him. And he will be able to use both eyes."

I did not dislike Wilhelm Kröner. He was polite, unobtrusive, and as I was to learn, capable if not exceptional at his work. Had I not known who he was, I would have taken him for an average, middle-level bureaucrat, certainly not an emissary of the devil. Our second meeting had been awkward for both of us; Herr Kröner seemed embarrassed as he entered my office. He bowed formally and shook my extended hand. As we discussed the managerial position he would be filling in the sales department, I noticed how his eyes swept across the room methodically, much as those of a prospective buyer inspecting a home that is up for sale. With Joshua's advice in mind, I reasoned to myself that his contacts with the "correct" people in the field could only work to our benefit, and the more I thought about it, the more it seemed to me that the addition of this mild mannered Nazi to our staff was going to turn out to be a stroke of good fortune for Feinberg's Ovenworks.

I expressed this idea to Karl one evening later in that same week. I had stopped in after work to deliver a present to my nephew. Karl and I were seated on the living room floor enjoying little Franz' fascinated expression as the wind-up tin figure raised and lowered two tiny drumsticks and tapped a steady rat-a-tat-tat on the lacquered drum it held balanced on its knees. Jutta stood at the other side of the room with hands on hips. Finally, she walked over to us and said, "I hate to interrupt your fun, but I am afraid I am going to have to take the baby into the kitchen for his evening meal. We will only be a few minutes, so you little boys can continue to play if you want." She stepped over and scooped her son up in her arms; for a second or two he struggled to get free, reaching out for the tin drummer and squalling.

"So they have put their spy in with you, have they," Karl remarked, as we stood up and brushed ourselves off. I had already given him a very brief account of my new manager. "What do you think of this...Kröger?" he added, a slight smile playing at the corner of his mouth.

"Kröner," I corrected, stooping down to pick up the toy so that no one would step on it. "The only thing I can say about him is that he isn't what I expected. He looks like a typical Munich burgher; the kind of person you meet, chat with for a while about the weather, and forget ten minutes later."

"Don't let that fool you," he said, frowning. "Most of these Nazis are nondescript. Sometimes I think that is what makes them join up in the first place. If they didn't have something to shout about they would bore themselves to death. Look at Heinrich Himmler, for instance. I'll be damned if he looks like the leader of the feared SS. Take off his sinister black uniform and we have a gentle school teacher or poultry farmer, take your pick. Their ordinary appearance is the most frightening thing about them. We expect our villains to be easily identifiable, like Cain. And just think how much less intimidating Dracula would be without piercing eyes and sharp, bloodstained teeth. But even if he were dressed in *lederhosen* he would still be Dracula, and you would be very foolish to expose your jugular to him." Karl bared his teeth and made as frightening a face as he could.

"I think you picked the wrong example, at least as far as I am concerned," I replied, smiling. "I would be at a distinct disadvantage if I ever came across a vampire, since I am not in the habit of carrying a crucifix around with me. I would be a goner, unless it were a Nazi vampire. I could chase one of those away by waving a Star of David in front of its face."

Karl laughed and said, "At least a vampire gives you something in return for just a few pints of blood."

"What exactly is that?" I asked.

"Immortality," he replied in a deep, drawling voice. "I never did understand why that idea frightens people so much. On the one hand everyone wants to live forever, but when they have a chance to do it at the cost of a little bite or two on the neck they are scared shitless. The Nazis, on the other hand, drain away freedom and decency, offering only some vague promises of future glory. And millions eagerly expose their throats."

"You know," I replied, unaware of how ironic my words would eventually prove to be, "I think maybe it wouldn't be such a bad idea to wear a Jewish star. Just in case."

***

There was a mood of dejection on Prinzregentenstrasse as the new year began. A week earlier my grandfather had received official notice that his apartment was being requisitioned by the Reich for "suitable occupancy," therefore he would have to vacate by the end of the month. Hedged in quasi-legal language, the eviction notice merely stated that it was against the best interests of the state to allow one individual to occupy such a large dwelling. The true reason, however, was obvious.

"Can they really do this? This is illegal, isn't it?" my grandfather asked, as I read the document he had just handed me. He paced back and forth in front of his former desk, a bit more slowly than in previous years, but with the same nervous energy.

I finished reading and looked at the Nazi seal stamped in black ink at the bottom of the page: an eagle grasping a globe with a swastika in its center.

"It seems official," I answered quietly, the growling sounds from the pit of my stomach betrayed my agitation. "And as you know, in the Third Reich what is official is legal."

He stepped over and grasped the side of the desk with both hands. His shoulders arched forward, his head drooped down onto his chest. Fearing he was about to slump to the floor, I sprang up from my seat and hurried around the desk to support him, but when I got to his side he pushed me away with an elbow and shook his head.

"It's all right, Heinchen," he said, almost in a whisper. "I'm all right." I continued to stand by him for several moments. Finally, he straightened up and said through clenched teeth, "I've been a fool, a damned old fool." Without explaining what he meant, he added, "God only knows what will become of us now."

***

"Then I am right in thinking that there is nothing we can do about it?"

Judge Linsdorff's somber expression was answer enough to my question. He shook his head slowly and motioned me to sit down. He had just finished reading the notice evicting my grandfather from his apartment.

"The thing I find most grotesque about it all is that these Nazi dogs continue to pretend that there is such a thing as law here," he said bitterly. "I really don't know why they bother. Anyone with the slightest intelligence can see Germany slipping, perhaps I should say marching, steadily back to a period of precivilization." He sat down across from me and stared vacantly at his hands which trembled visibly. His face seemed much thinner. Lines I had never seen there before ran from the corners of his eyes down past his cheekbones. When he looked up, however, I saw the familiar, piercing, steel-blue eyes; if anything, they were even more striking than ever. He continued his train of thought.

"Tell your grandfather that it would not only be fruitless, but dangerous to seek redress. Justice is dead in the Third Reich. Obscene anti-Jewish legislation is streaming out of Berlin daily, like dung from a cow. The executioner's axe has never been sharper."

I shrugged to indicate that I was unsure of exactly what he meant.

In a tone similar to that he had used with me when I was an eager law student and he my mentor, he said, "For one thing, there are now forty-six categories of crime that are punishable by death. Forty-six!" I involuntarily let out a low gasp at this; formerly there had been but three. Before I could comment, he went on. "As for any hope of a fair trial, that is history. In many instances the verdict is in before the accused ever steps into the courtroom. The state censors all mail sent or received by the defendant, including that between him and his defense attorney. And to top it all off, the prosecutors and judges often determine the final sentence before the trial. This is law? This is justice?" He sat back to let his words sink in. All I could do was shake my head in disbelief. His voice had risen as he spoke. Now he leaned back and lowered his voice to a normal conversational level.

"And it is getting worse almost daily. One cannot even count on the status quo, as horrible as it is. New laws are issued arbitrarily and then enforced retroactively. What is legal today can become a crime next week, a crime for which you will be prosecuted...that is, if you are an enemy of their Reich. And everyone is a potential enemy. In this way, no one is ever safe. No one." He sat back again and waited for my reaction. By this time I was numb. It had not occurred to me that things could have gone so far.

Seeing that I had nothing to say, he went on. "Do you remember, Heinrich, how I always used to emphasize to you that the law must be impartial in order to be effective, that one must judge what a person does objectively, and not be concerned with who a person is?" I nodded. "Well that is not the case today in the Third Reich. You see, there is no longer uniform punishment for crimes. The judges now base their judgments on what they call pictorial image, which means that the punishment varies. Thus, while one person may receive a small fine or even a warning for a particular offense, another might very well wind up in a concentration camp. It all depends on who the offender is, and/or who the prosecutor happens to be. They are even beginning to dispense with trials altogether when it suits their fancy. You are accused and sentenced. It is very swift and very simple. And don't think that a sentence means anything these days either," he continued. "It is happening more and more frequently that instead of being released after serving his term, a prisoner is transferred to an insane asylum or a concentration camp and left to rot away there for an indeterminate period." He took a handkerchief from his trouser pocket and wiped the perspiration that had formed on his upper lip.

"But there must be others like yourself, others who find all of this intolerable," I said. "The friends you spoke of before. Surely they can use their moral influence to stop this." I realized how foolish I sounded even before I finished my sentence.

Judge Linsdorff noted my embarrassment and smiled.

"I understand your dilemma, Heinrich," he said softly. "When one is caught up in a whirlpool, spun around violently and pulled further and further down into an abyss, it is impossible to keep a balanced perspective. You are hardly alone when it comes to that. Sometimes when I look around me, I think that this country has become a wonderland like the one Lewis Carroll wrote about. People see things as if in a magic mirror. Even my friends, more accurately my former colleagues, have succumbed to the distortions. While a few still dare to whisper among themselves about the desecrations I have just described to you, they validate the new order by not refusing to be part of it. They rationalize, make excuses, and sometimes even defend what is happening as a necessary, if temporary evil." He paused, removed his glasses and began to rub the bridge of his nose. "No," he said finally. "There is no hope from that quarter. Those men are as dead as the law they claim to serve."

"Then in your opinion there is no hope at all?" I ventured timidly, dreading his answer.

He leaned forward again; his eyes flashed momentarily with their old fire as he replied. "Without hope there is no life. Or at least no reason for life," he said sharply. "And I can assure you that unlike those whom I have just been speaking about, this old judge is still very much alive." He stood up suddenly, walked across the room, and picked up a thick brown folder from his desk. "And when Herr Hitler and his toadies see this, they will know it too." He held the folder in his hand for a few seconds, then stepped back across the room to where I was sitting and handed it to me. I looked at the front cover. There, in bold letters, were the words *Evil on Trial*. I opened the folder and began to read the manuscript inside. It was written in the judge's neat hand. I felt a chill go down my spine as the first sentence leaped out at me:

> *Between January 1933 and the present, German freedom, justice, and decency have been systematically murdered in cold blood. It is now time for those who were and are responsible for this premeditated crime to be made to pay...*

I sat transfixed, captivated by the flow of words which were at one moment as cool and objective as a legal brief, and the next as ardent as any love poem. One by one the misdeeds of the present regime were exposed and condemned, as well as those responsible for them. One by one the layers of mendacity and duplicity were stripped away, gradually lifting a clear portrait of evil to the surface. It was all there, documented in the meticulous style that had made the legal writings of Judge Paul Linsdorff so highly regarded in his field that even those law professors with National Socialist sympathies continued to use them as textbooks. I read without pause, devouring the pages greedily. When I had finished, I sat for several minutes staring at the concluding statements in the monograph:

> *At whatever cost, we Germans must rid ourselves of the evil that has already cast a shadow over our spirits. Life itself would not be an unreasonable price to pay for the attainment of this goal.*

When I finished reading, I looked over at Judge Linsdorff who had sat down again just a few feet from me. He had apparently been watching me carefully the entire time.

"This is frightening," I said in an unsteady voice. My mouth felt dry, my throat constricted. "But," I hesitated momentarily, afraid that my question might be misinterpreted. "What do you intend to do with it?" I held the manuscript out, almost like a religious offering. He got up and stepped over to me.

"I intend to make it public," he replied, taking it gently from my hands and carrying it back to his desk. "It is high time that everyone gets a good whiff of this Nazi cesspool. Perhaps when they have, they will begin to clean it out."

"How will you be able to do it, though?" I asked, recalling the unsuccessful attempt to have his letter of resignation published. "Controls are much stricter now then they have ever been. All of the newspapers and publishing houses are under the absolute control of the government. You point that out in your manuscript. You must realize that they would never allow your manuscript to appear in print."

"Not in Germany," he said, a sly smile playing in his eyes. "Thank God we haven't reached the point yet where Germany is the entire world."

I straightened up in my chair and looked into his eyes, which were no longer smiling. In that instant I knew that he had made an inalterable decision. In a resigned voice I asked, "What will they do to you?" My voice cracked and faded.

"I suppose that is up to them," he replied calmly. "We all do what we must in this short, troubled life. Perhaps...perhaps their options will be limited as a result of my efforts. It is late in the day, but the day is not over yet. Who can tell, we may even witness a few resurrections along the way."

The final words in his manuscript echoed in my mind as he spoke: *"Life itself would not be an unreasonable price to pay..."*

What I had feared happened two weeks later. I was in bed in a semi-sleep when the phone rang. Heart pounding, I groped my way through the dark to the kitchen, picked up the receiver, and was shocked awake by Jutta's frantic voice.

"Karl's mother just called to tell us that his father has been arrested!" she blurted out. "Karl has gone to Gestapo Headquarters to make inquiries. I am frightened, Heinrich. I don't know what to do." She was sobbing; in the background I could hear my nephew crying loudly. For a second or two I felt so light-headed that I thought I might lose consciousness.

"I'll be right over," I said weakly, leaning against the wall for support. Regaining control, I gently replaced the receiver in its cradle and turned to go back to my room. As I reached the doorway I almost bumped into my mother who was standing there silently. She held her hands clasped in front of her face; in the dim light I could see her shoulders trembling.

"What is it, Heinrich?" she asked fearfully. "What has happened?" I quickly recounted what Jutta had told me, and made my way back to my room. Even though it was a bitter cold winter night, perspiration poured from my body as I dressed.

I purposely avoided all of the main avenues, instinctively keeping to the side streets and alleys. Never, not even during the years of greatest turmoil, had I felt so vulnerable as I did then, trudging along with my head bowed against the biting wind. By the time I reached my sister's apartment house, my hands and feet were numb from the cold. Snow had begun to fall lightly, further magnifying the silence.

"What will they do to him?" Jutta asked, as she poured steaming coffee into the cup before me. Her face was lined from worry and lack of sleep.

"I don't know," I replied, taking a large gulp of the hot liquid and shuddering as it seared its way down to my stomach.

"Karl was frantic," she added. "I have never seen him so upset. I'm afraid he will do something rash." She put her hands to her face and began to sob again. I got up and embraced her, my head spinning.

"Karl is no fool. He will be all right," I assured her, although I was just as worried as she.

As we waited for Karl, Jutta and I sat and talked quietly far into the night. We discussed many things: Judge Linsdorff, the situation of the Jews in Germany, our family, Karl...and Birgit.

Karl returned early the following morning. His face was drawn and pale; there was a faraway stare in his bloodshot eyes as he embraced my sister and then extended his hand to me.

"They wouldn't let me see him," he said in a tired voice. "The only thing they would tell me was that he was being held for questioning." He walked unsteadily over to the kitchen sink, turned on the cold water and splashed some on his face. "I am going to go back later this afternoon with my mother. Maybe we can get to talk to him then." Although he tried to keep his voice steady, the uncertainty and worry were evident.

"How is your mother?" Jutta asked, handing him a dish towel so that he could wipe his dripping face.

"Very shaken up," he replied. "But standing firm like a model German wife. I stopped off to see her before coming home. She was still trying to straighten up the mess the Gestapo made in the apartment. She didn't want my father to be too upset when he comes home."

"Did they say he would be released today?" I felt my hopes rising in spite of the fact that I knew what his answer would be.

"They found the manuscript," he answered, almost in a whisper. Then he punched his fist into his open palm and added in a loud, angry voice, "They found the goddamned manuscript before he could get it out of the country. The bastards seemed to know exactly what they were looking for."

It was several days before Karl and his mother were allowed a very brief visit with Judge Linsdorff. Karl stopped in at Jägerstrasse to describe the meeting to me.

"They were actually civil," he said, his deep frustration indicated by clenched fists. "It was almost as if they were trying to torment us with their good manners. It would have been much easier to bear if they had called us names or mistreated us. They even offered us coffee and pastries while we were waiting."

"And how was your father?" I asked, a bit confused. In my mind, I had conjured up quite a different scene.

"He looked very tired, but otherwise seemed to be none the worse for wear. He even joked to my mother about getting the recipe for the prison soup so she could prepare it for him when he came home. Obviously he was putting on a show for whomever was listening in."

"You mean they didn't have a guard with you while you were together?"

"What for?" he replied, giving a short, bitter laugh. "I'm sure they didn't expect us to slip him a hacksaw blade to cut his way out with. And I'm just as sure that they monitored our every word and gesture quite thoroughly. The Gestapo is very efficient."

"What do they intend to do with him?" I asked hesitantly. "Did they tell you anything?"

"Nothing at all," Karl hissed. "I'm not even sure they know themselves. The Nazis are very propaganda conscious, that much is certain. At this point I don't think they would like to publicize the fact that a man of my father's international stature has come out against them, although they are very unpredictable. They have already woven such a tangled bureaucracy that it must be difficult even for them to determine which end is up." He paused and looked at me with his worried, bloodshot eyes. "I have to admit though, I have a bad feeling about it. They aren't going to sit back and ignore what he wrote about them."

Karl's pessimism proved to be realistic; several days later, Judge Paul Linsdorff was transferred to the concentration camp at Dachau.

"Do you think your father will try to help him? No matter what their differences, they are still brothers. He can't just sit back and let his brother rot away in a concentration camp." Bursts of steam shot out from my mouth as I spoke. The cold February wind bit through our coats and gloves as Birgit and I stood side by side on the unsheltered S-Bahn platform. I had called her from a pay phone earlier in the week to ask that she meet me there instead of at our room. I was afraid that Karl or I might be under surveillance. As a further precaution, I had taken two different busses, gotten off several blocks from the station, and followed a circuitous route up and down side streets, looking over my shoulder continuously to make sure that I was not being followed. Birgit had been equally careful.

"I really don't know," she answered softly, hunching her shoulders against the cold. "He really seems to hate Uncle Paul. He never speaks of him, and has done everything he can to disassociate himself from him. Considering what has happened, I am afraid that, if anything, his feelings are even more negative. You would never believe how unreasonable and violent he is when it comes to politics. It is impossible to try to talk to him about certain things." She paused for a couple of seconds and looked around nervously. "If he were to find out about us, for example, I believe he might be capable of doing something terrible to us. If he were to even suspect..." Her voice broke off and she shuddered. I put my arm around her shoulders protectively and drew her against me.

"Perhaps you could get your husband to intercede," I ventured, my mind spinning in an attempt to find some way to help.

"Dieter?" she said, in a voice filled with disgust. "He would torture his mother if he was ordered to do it. He is like a puppet on a string — a model SS man, dedicated not to a political philosophy, but to his Führer and Reich. He is not as intelligent as my father, but just as dangerous. No, I wouldn't think of asking him to intercede for Uncle Paul." Her voice trailed off and she shuddered again.

"I'm sorry that I have added to your difficulties," I said, at that moment feeling a wave of such tender love and anguish that I thought my chest would burst. "If only we had met in a different place, at a different time. Perhaps it would be best if we..."

She raised her face up to mine and kissed my lips before I could finish.

"Don't, Heinrich," she said. "You know I can't conceive of life without you. I could never stand to lose you again." She kissed me again as the train glided smoothly into the station and came to a stop.

***

By 1938, the momentum of tragedy picked up to the point that it could no longer be stopped. We were drawn along in the events like leaves in a swift moving stream. A numbness spread through our psyches, rendering us incapable of action. While we went through the motions of living, we seemed to be waiting for something we sensed rather than understood. We waited. The extent to which we lost our ability to react to the world around us can be illustrated by the event that took place on the twelfth of March: the long rumored annexation of Austria. Had something so momentous occurred in previous years, it would have provided the material for continuous conversation and debate around the family dinner table for weeks; but now it was met with such indifference that it might just as well have happened on another planet.

"So the dogs have started collecting bones," muttered my father, as the radio commentator described the triumphant entry of German troops into Austria. "But any fool knows that you can never give a hungry dog enough to eat," he added, slurring his words slightly. "It will always want more." Other than that, he gave no other sign that he was either interested in or upset by the news. He had not fully recovered from the stroke. He never left the apartment anymore, spoke very little, and from time to time would break off a sentence in the middle of a thought and stare vacantly into space, oblivious to his surroundings. More often than not, the evening newspaper I brought to him remained unread.

"I suppose now we can't call Hitler an Austrian," replied my grandfather matter-of-factly. "Since now there is no more Austria."

From the time he had moved in with us the previous month, my grandfather had aged perceptibly. More and more he looked and acted like a man approaching his eightieth year; both his eyesight and hearing were beginning to fail, and although he still took his customary evening walk, it was obvious from the pain and effort it cost him simply to rise from his chair that before long this would cease. He had not visited Feinberg's Ovenworks in months, and when I attempted to discuss business matters with him he listened absently. It was increasingly obvious that my grandfather, Jacob Feinberg, had already begun to dissolve his ties with a world grown increasingly unpalatable to him.

If anything, I was even more dazed than the others. I felt as if I were caught in a giant web where any attempt to struggle free would simply entangle me more hopelessly. And at the same time I knew that acquiescence could only result in disaster. Instead of easing, my dilemma became more acute with the passing months and years. Questions. Always the same tormenting questions. How could I remain in a land that was steadily robbing me of my humanity? On the other hand, how could I leave my parents, now that they needed me most? How could I continue to function in a land where my neighbors rejected me because I happened to have been born a Jew? People like Frau Wenzel, who now shut her door loudly when I or any other member of my family walked by; the same kind spinster who for years had patiently taught my sisters to play piano and sent plates of fresh baked cookies back with them. How could I remain in such a place? But how, oh God, how could I leave the only woman I had ever loved, the one whose presence was the only effective antidote to the poisoned universe? How? Paralyzed by these conflicts, I gave in to inertia and waited.

I waited until April when a law was passed which made it mandatory for all Jews to report to the government any financial holdings exceeding five thousand marks. I waited and submitted my statement in accordance with the law. I waited until the Third Decree of the Reich Citizenship Law demanded the registry of all Jewish business enterprises; I waited and registered Feinberg's Ovenworks in accordance with the law. In that same month, June, the synagogue in Munich was destroyed by an angry mob. I waited until August, when it was decreed that as of New Year's Day, 1939, all Jews would have to add the surnames of Sarah or Israel to their identity papers. I waited and added the surname Israel to my papers in accordance with the law. In that same month, the synagogue in Nuremberg was put to the torch. I waited until October when the law also made it mandatory for all Jews to have their passports stamped with a large J. I waited and had my passport stamped in accordance with the law. In the meanwhile, Jews had been banned from public parks, sports grounds, swimming pools, and Jewish children were excluded from the state school system. And yet, I waited. I waited and watched in horror as the world drifted toward war in September, and breathed a sigh of relief along with the rest of the world when agreement to avoid conflict was reached in Munich, even though this agreement to secure "peace in our time" cost Czechoslovakia its right to exist, and further strengthened Hitler's outlaw government. I waited.

***

History books refer to the night of November 9-10, 1938 as *Kristallnacht* (Crystal Night) although some translators find it impossible to use such a pacific, almost poetic designation, and choose to call it The Night of Broken Glass. It is hardly surprising that the Nazis, masters of euphemism that they were, should have given such a benign name to one of the worst *pogroms* the world has ever seen, certainly the worst in modern times. What the historians do not say, what they cannot possibly describe, is the terror the victims of that horrendous night experienced, that night in which along with glass, so many human lives were broken. While words are inadequate, however, those who remain as witnesses need no medium of communication other than their continued existence. The sights and sounds are burned forever into their beings. They are the living, shattered mirrors of Crystal Night, and the more dreadful days and nights which followed.

It was Karl who first recognized the extent of the danger. He and Jutta were at our Jägerstrasse apartment when I arrived home from work on the evening of November 8.

"Have you heard the news?" He put the question to me in the foyer; before I had even finished taking off my overcoat.

"What happened?" I asked, alarmed by his grave expression. My initial thought was that something had happened to my father. "Was it another stroke?"

"No, nothing like that," he replied, giving me a helping hand as I struggled out of my coat. "I was talking about the news from Paris — the assassination attempt." I shrugged my shoulders to indicate that I didn't know what he was talking about.

"A Jewish boy shot one of the secretaries from the German embassy there. Now there is all kinds of wild talk about reprisals. This is serious business, Heinrich. An ugly mood is building."

I threw my coat over the rack and the two of us went into the living room. My mother and Jutta were standing by the radio listening to the shrill voice detailing the latest developments.

"There have already been some unpleasant incidents reported from small towns," Karl explained. "Reports of mobs setting Jewish businesses and synagogues on fire, with no interference from the authorities. Let's hope it doesn't spread to Munich." The radio report had ended, and now loud strains of martial music began to play.

"Shut off that noise, will you!" barked my grandfather from his seat on the sofa. My mother reached over and did as he had asked. "Those warmongers in Berlin will give us the real thing soon enough, and that won't be as easy to turn off," he added, nodding a greeting to me.

I walked over and kissed my mother and Jutta.

"Your father is inside resting. He isn't feeling too well today," explained my mother without my asking. I nodded. In recent days his health had declined markedly.

"Franz is taking a nap too," added Jutta, anticipating my next question. She knew how much I always looked forward to seeing and playing with him.

"Your father's blood pressure is way up," interrupted Karl. "He either refuses or forgets to take his medication. He is not exactly what I would call the model patient." I spread out my hands and shook my head in frustration. Whatever else, my father was as stubborn as ever.

Then, getting back to the original topic, I asked Karl, "What do you think will happen now? Is there any chance that this will blow over without any serious repercussions?"

"It all depends on what Hitler and his gangsters decide to orchestrate. Goebbels has already begun to scream for Jewish blood. I wish the dumb kid had shot *that* son of a bitch." He clenched his fist and gritted his teeth menacingly. "To be on the safe side, we should prepare for the worst. I would suggest that you stay home from work for the next few days. Close the business until the hysteria passes."

"I can't do that," I replied. "There are too many others involved. One doesn't shut down a plant just like that." Since his father's arrest, Karl had become increasingly protective of those around him. As a result, I tended to view his latest suggestion as an overreaction.

"Well then, be very careful for the next few days," he cautioned. "We know what these bastards are capable of."

We thought we knew, but we were mistaken.

My trip to Feinberg's the following morning seemed to confirm the fact that Karl had been overly apprehensive. I could see no signs of anything extraordinary on the faces of the other tram passengers, nor did the clean, quiet streets of Munich indicate that a volcano was about to erupt. At the office, the day ran much as any other. In order to test the situation somewhat, I sought out Herr Kröner and pretended that I wanted to discuss a minor business matter with him. His polite, deferential manner calmed my fears, and as the day went on I almost forgot the incident in Paris that had caused us so much concern.

The conversation at the dinner table got off to a lively start, reminiscent of former years. The latest bulletin from Paris had just been announced: the assassin, vom Rath, had died from his wounds. My father, who appeared to be having one of his better days, showed some of his old flare when my grandfather brought up the subject of the assassination.

"Those windbags have been bragging about how they can conquer the continent with their fancy new planes and tanks," he began, his voice loud and steady. "And yet they whine like frightened puppies over one dead diplomat." He rubbed his thigh and added, "I wonder how long any of them would last in the trenches today."

"And I suppose being able to sit in a mud-filled hole in the ground for weeks at a time makes one a better human being," injected my grandfather, smiling. I looked over at him and he winked slyly; it was obvious that he was playing devil's advocate in order to stimulate further response from my father. The latter, however, already seemed to have lost his train of thought; he stared into his dish and made no attempt to answer the provocation. My grandfather shrugged his shoulders as if to indicate that he had tried, and also became silent.

After dinner, I excused myself and retired to my study to read. For the previous few days I had been reintroducing myself to the work of Heinrich Heine, a poet to whom I felt an increasing affinity. I read the words over and over, feeling a combination of pain and pleasure:

> *Once I had a beautiful fatherland,*
> *The oak tree,*
> *Grew there, so high, the violets*
> *nodded gently;*
> *It was a dream.*

> *That kissed me in German and spoke*
> *German*
> *(one can scarcely believe how good*
> *that sounded)*
> *The words: 'I love you!'*
> *It was a dream.*

As I read the beautifully modulated cadences of Heine's lyric, the distant sounds of shouting voices and breaking glass failed to register in my consciousness. I clearly remember thinking that even had Heine not been a Jew, he would still have been banned by the Nazis because of his irreverence and love of truth. Suddenly, a cry from the other room snapped me out of my meditation.

"Heinrich!" My mother's usually soft voice was so shrill that it set the hair on my arms bristling. I dropped my book and ran to the living room.

"What is the matter?" I asked.

"Your grandfather!" she blurted out. "He never came back!"

"Came back?" I repeated, like an automaton. My mind was somewhat unfocused. I shook myself to gain my bearings. "Have you checked his room?" I turned and was about to go to his room in the rear of the apartment.

"I just looked there," she replied, growing more agitated. "I thought he was in there the whole time. He said that he was only going for a short walk. That was almost two hours ago. He isn't at Jutta's or Ursel's either." She wrung her hands as she spoke; her eyes were opened very wide, like those of a frightened animal.

"I'll go out and look for him," I said, already in the foyer putting on my coat. I took the stairs two at a time and raced out onto the sidewalk, trying to suppress my panic. For the first time I became aware of the unusual sounds that seemed to be coming from at least two directions. Short bursts of shouting voices, like those made by a crowd at a sporting event when their team scores a point, were mixed with the almost continuous, high-pitched sounds of breaking glass. Interspersed with these were the wailing of fire engine sirens. I searched the block for any trace of my grandfather, but it was deserted. My attention was caught by a portion of the sky in the direction of the railroad station; it was aglow, as if lit up by a huge torch. Turning, I saw a similar illumination a bit to the left of the first one, and then a third at a point much closer, possibly not more than several blocks to the south, in the vicinity of Marienplatz. I began to walk swiftly up Jägerstrasse toward the main street, Oskar-von-Miller-Ring. As I got to the corner I saw several people running along the sidewalk a few hundred feet ahead and heard scattered shouts. But before I was able to make out what was happening, they disappeared around the next corner. For some reason I started to trot, swiveling my head right and left and straining my eyes to make sure that I didn't overlook any doorways in which a person might be concealed. Nothing. As I turned onto Brienner Strasse, I almost crashed head on into a figure running in the opposite direction. We both stopped momentarily and peered at each other.

"Karl?" I managed to blurt out, uncertain I was seeing correctly in the dim light.

"Heinrich," he answered, reaching out to grasp me by both arms. His breathing was even more labored than mine. He stood there for several moments trying to catch his breath.

"What the hell is going on?" I asked, as he continued to hold my arms in a tight grip.

Finally, his chest no longer heaving, he replied, "We can't stay here. Let's get back to your apartment right away." He let go of me and started to run again.

"But my grandfather is out here somewhere," I shouted to him as I ran alongside. "I have to find him."

"It's too late for that," he replied. "Hurry." I kept up with him as best I could, my lungs straining from the unaccustomed exertion. The words "too late" kept repeating in my mind as my feet hit the pavement in steady, rapid succession.

"I looked everywhere within a ten block radius," Karl explained, his face still bright red from running. "He must have been picked up by the SS." My mother's knees began to buckle; she grasped the chair in front of her to steady herself. "We can't do anything tonight, but tomorrow I will make inquiries," he added, stepping over to her and leading her around the chair so that she could seat herself in it.

"I telephoned Jutta and Ursel," she said, in a weak, tired voice. "They said they hadn't seen him." She paused, her eyes fixed on a point in space. "Joshua got on the phone to tell me that there were terrible things happening throughout the country, terrible things. He said that Jewish businesses and synagogues are being destroyed and Jews taken away to concentration camps. Can it be true? My God. My God." I stepped over to her and put my arm around her heaving shoulders.

"Joshua called me first," explained Karl. "I didn't say anything to you, Mama, because I didn't want you to get more upset than you already were." Then he turned to me and said, "That was a terrible mistake. It was stupid of me to keep silent. I should have realized that you would go out looking for your grandfather. They might have gotten you too." His quavering voice betrayed the strain. "I think the safest thing to do is for all of you to go to my parents' place, at least for the night. We don't know what the intentions of the SS are." I nodded my agreement.

Surprisingly, my father did not protest when my mother told him to get ready to leave. At first I thought that he didn't understand what was· happening, an impression that was strengthened when he emerged from his room some twenty-odd minutes later, dressed in his old army uniform, complete with his Iron Cross First Class pinned over his heart. With Karl in the lead, we made our way down to the street.

The noise outside seemed closer than it had been earlier. The illumination in the sky to the south had been reduced to a dull, flickering glow; there was a stale odor of smoke in the air, and in the distance the almost musical sound of breaking glass. I listened in fascination, wondering if there could really be that much glass in the entire city.

The four of us walked slowly along the still empty Jägerstrasse toward the Linsdorff apartment. With the aid of the cane my mother had fished out of the hall closet, my father hobbled along at a steady if not swift pace, my mother and I on each side to support him if necessary. Karl walked a few paces ahead, turning around every few seconds to see if we were keeping up with him. The first sign of life we saw was in Wittelsbacherplatz. Up ahead of us, on the far side of the square, I could make out the outlines of several figures milling about. Karl stopped momentarily and then signalled us to follow. Apparently, however, we had already been seen; several members of the group in the square had broken off from the rest and were hurrying toward us, shouting something as they ran.

"Let me do the talking," Karl whispered, as he stepped back alongside us. In the light of the street lamp I could see my mother's frightened face.

My father put his arm around her and bent over to say something in her ear; then he straightened his shoulders and stood at attention, like a soldier during an inspection.

"Hey, you there!" shouted the first one to approach, a short, stocky individual. He bobbed his head up and down and from side to side, apparently looking us over without being quite able to decide what he was seeing. "What are you people doing out here tonight?" Two of his companions had joined him, and now they, too, studied us curiously.

"We were just out for a walk," answered Karl calmly, taking a few paces toward the three. "What is all the racket tonight? What's going on anyway?"

The short fellow laughed out loud and turned to the others. "Can you imagine that? Nobody has told them that we are finally giving it to the Jews." The other two mimicked his laughter. "You wouldn't happen to know where we could find any around here, would you?" asked one of the others in a mocking, suspicious voice. Karl smiled and moved even closer to them. His blonde hair contrasted sharply to the dark jacket he was wearing, and apparently had not gone unnoticed.

"I am a doctor," he said calmly. "These are members of my family." He made a sweeping gesture in our direction with the back of his hand.

He was about to add something when my father, cane raised, limped forward shouting, "Since when do the likes of you own the streets of Munich? Get out of our way or I'll show you what I think of you." The three of them stepped back in unison when they saw the upraised cane and heard my father's stern voice. He was now directly under the street lamp; he stopped and thrust out his chest so that the Iron Cross could be clearly seen.

It had the desired effect; the short fellow nodded to his friends and said, more to us than them, "Come, let's go. We are wasting time. There are still a few stores to take care of before we call it a night." Then he turned back to Karl and said over his shoulder, "You had better get your family home, Herr Doctor. Tonight is not a good night for a stroll." With that, they walked briskly back across the square to the larger group. I let out a loud sigh and released my grip on the handle of the kitchen knife I had put into my pocket before we left our apartment, relieved that I had not had to use it.

Several minutes later, we were greeted warmly by Karl's anxious mother, who had already gotten our sleeping quarters ready.

Kristallnacht and the days following it completely eradicated any final doubts I had about our future in Germany. The shattered panes of imported Belgian glass that littered streets from Schleswig Holstein in the north to Bavaria in the south were symbolic of the shattered hopes and dreams of those who had believed sanity would return to Germany. These optimists had believed that conditions would improve; they had repeated again and again, as much to convince themselves as others, "tomorrow will be better, just wait and see." One night of savage madness, however, had made it as clear as the ubiquitous shards of glass that littered Germany that tomorrow was today, and that the future did not exist for us.

Our attempts to locate my grandfather were futile. It was as if Jacob Feinberg had been snatched from the earth by an invisible hand. On the following day, my mother phoned one government office after the other, begging for information. The responses she received ranged from indifference to open hostility.

Although the intensity diminished, the *pogrom* continued for several days. Government-sanctioned vandals systematically destroyed those few shops and small businesses that had escaped the initial attacks, while the police often stood by either helplessly or indifferently. The latter did not dare disobey the orders from above which instructed them only to prevent damage to Aryan establishments.

We dared not leave Frau Linsdorff's apartment for the next few days. I telephoned my key managers, including Herr Kröner, to inform them that the plant would remain closed until the situation returned to normal. I feared that in spite of the fact that most of the employees were gentiles (my grandfather had consciously limited the number of Jewish employees in the firm), Feinberg's would meet the same fate as so many other Jewish-owned establishments.

As it turned out, my fears were unjustified. For reasons that soon became apparent, Feinberg's was spared by the rampaging mobs. In fact, when we reopened on the following Monday, it was almost as if *Kristallnacht* had been nothing more than a bad dream. The efficient German sanitation crews had cleaned up virtually all the debris, and the windows of hundreds of shops had already been boarded up neatly. For many of us, however, things would never be the same, not for our family or the others whose loved ones had been swept away by that Nazi *pogrom*.

According to the official reports, fewer than one hundred Jews were killed in all of the Reich during that night and the two or three days following, a minuscule number compared to what was to come before very long. Will future generations remember or care that seven thousand Jewish business establishments were wantonly destroyed; that a quantity of plate glass was shattered that by some estimates equaled six month's production of the entire plate glass industry of Belgium? Will they gasp at the depraved decrees the Nazi government passed three days after *Kristallnacht*, one of which held the Jews responsible for the scandalous event which had "aroused the indignation of the people over the agitation of the international Jews against National Socialist Germany?" Will the world remember that the Nazi government forced the Jews to relinquish any insurance claims? And will later generations smile and shake their heads admiringly when they hear that on November 12, 1938, Göring diabolically levied a collective fine of one billion marks on the Jewish population of Germany to punish them for the material destruction inflicted during *Kristallnacht*? To punish them for being victimized! How were we to respond to such perversity? If we had been able to accept the truth, we would have concluded that *Kristallnacht* was merely a dress rehearsal, not an aberration, never to be repeated. But we could not accept a truth so terrible. We could not.

***

It was all accomplished according to the letter of the law. Yet another decree had been issued by the flamboyant Hermann Göring, on November 12: The Decree Eliminating Jews from Economic Life aimed to accomplish exactly what its name said. And it did. With stunning speed and simplicity, Jews were effectively expelled from the working economy of the Third Reich: Jewish management of retail stores and mail order houses was banned, nor would Jews be permitted in the future to offer goods or services in any market, fair, or exhibition, or to advertise them or accept orders for them. For those who thought they could use their sales skills to survive, there was another article, one which prohibited Jews from exercising independent trade. The Jew in Germany (it was only logical that we were no longer permitted to call ourselves German-Jews, since we were not citizens), had virtually ceased to exist as a person.

Article 2, Section 2 of the Decree dealt specifically with me and those in my particular circumstances. It stated: "If a Jew is a leading employee in a business concern he may be dismissed at six weeks' notice..."

***

"It's from him! It's a letter from your grandfather!" my mother shouted, waving an envelope in the air happily. I rushed over to her as she tore open the envelope and took out a single sheet of paper. Her hands trembled visibly as she unfolded the letter and spread it out on the table in front of her. My father had limped out from his bedroom and now stood silently in the doorway of the dining room.

"'Dear Family,'" she read, "'I am in the concentration camp Buchenwald.'" her faced paled, but she went on. "'Do not write to me until I send you further information. I am in good health.' Oh my God," she whispered, letting the letter slip between her fingers and flutter to the floor. I bent over, picked it up, and stared at my grandfather's familiar, but shaky handwriting. Underneath the scant, obviously forced message, he had written, "Love, Jacob."

A wave of nausea swept through me. In the meantime, my father had made his way to my mother's side and was now holding her head against his chest as she sobbed.

"At least he is alive. He is alive," she said. Then, in a voice that sounded like a little girl's, she added, "Erich, what will happen to my poor papa? Why are they doing this to him?" He cradled her clumsily in his arms and looked over at me pleadingly, as if expecting me to supply the answer he lacked.

Buchenwald. Once again the flurry of desperate phone calls to various government offices. My mother had convinced herself that it was all an error. What could an old man like Jacob Feinberg possibly have done to warrant being taken to a concentration camp? Surely it was a case of mistaken identity; these things happened all the time. Had we not seen proof of this in the past, right in our own building? Had not Herr Feder been taken to Dachau because of a clerical mistake? Buchenwald, a new name in the lexicon of hell. Later that week Joshua stopped into my office to tell me what he had learned.

"Buchenwald is a large camp in the vicinity of Weimar," he explained. "About the same size as Dachau. I've been told that thousands of Jews were taken there during the three or four days of the *pogrom.*"

I shook my head in disgust as I listened. It was characteristic of Nazi perversity: to erect a concentration camp near the city in which Germany's greatest poet had written some of the most humanly sensitive works the world had ever seen.

"We don't know what they're up to," he continued, his voice reflecting the strain of the past few days. "But there are indications that the great majority of those who have been interned are wealthy. We think there may be a ransom demand for their release."

"Ransom?" I repeated, hardly able to believe my ears. "Since when are nations in the business of kidnapping?"

"A nation that punishes victims for the crimes it commits against them cannot be judged by any known standards of civilized behavior," he replied. "The Third Reich is a moral cemetery, populated by millions of people whose sense of decency has died and rotted away." He spit out his words as if they were too bitter to hold in his mouth. "Did you ever imagine that the good burghers of Munich would stand by as they have without lifting a finger to stop the carnage against their innocent neighbors? And it was the same story throughout Germany and Austria. Honest, God-fearing, law-abiding citizens watched with indifference as hundreds of synagogues were desecrated and burned. In many instances they stood by and laughed as Jews were publicly beaten and humiliated. I have read reports of incidents from Berlin and elsewhere that would turn your stomach." Joshua's face twisted in disgust.

"Can you use any of your contacts to help my grandfather?" I asked. "Perhaps your newspaper..."

His sharp, bitter laugh cut me short. "Jewish contacts do not exist in

Germany these days," he said. "And as for the newspaper, it and all other Jewish publications have been officially banned. The *Jüdische Rundschau*, like the Jewish shops and synagogues, is kaput. Just like that." He lifted his hand and snapped his fingers.

"Many of us were surprised that it didn't happen sooner," he continued, his face reddening. "What those bastards don't realize, though, is that it is much easier to smash a printing press than to hide the truth. We have already begun to set up our new offices in Paris." He said this nonchalantly, but I could see the tension in his eyes.

"Will you be leaving then?" I asked hesitantly, feeling more lost than ever.

"If I am able to," he replied. "One never knows whether one's name is on their lists. Several of my colleagues were arrested in the general roundup. To tell the truth, Heinrich, I am getting a bit tired of waiting for the Gestapo to knock on my door in the middle of the night." He put his hand on my forearm and added, "You and the rest of your family have to get out of here, too. You must." He squeezed my arm so hard that I let out an involuntary gasp.

"I wish it were that easy," I replied, my temples throbbing. Added to the impediments that had already immobilized me was my grandfather's uncertain fate.

"You have no choice," came his abrupt reply. "The time for discussion is over. I've already begun making the arrangements for all of you to emigrate to Palestine."

My mouth dropped open and I was about to respond, but before I could he held his hand up and shook his head vigorously from side to side.

"Please, Heinrich, don't say anything. You know as well as I that it is crazy to delay any longer. Believe me, it wasn't easy to get places for your parents on the Palestine quotas. The preference is understandably for younger people. I had to pull quite a few strings at the Palestine Bureau to bend the restrictions." His voice betrayed exasperation. I felt a sudden panic as I realized that the time for a firm decision had come; there could be no more procrastination. And yet, how could I go? Joshua was watching me carefully. Suddenly, his expression softened and he reached out again to touch my arm, this time gently.

"You can't help your grandfather by staying. Don't you realize that you and every other Jew remaining in Germany are prisoners, just as he is? You will have to free yourself before you can help him. I have already spoken to your parents, and they understand."

"My father has agreed to go to Palestine?" I blurted out. "If you managed to convince him of that, you truly are a sorcerer." I smiled, but only for a moment. Again, Joshua noted my agitation.

"She will understand too," he said, almost in a whisper. "If she loves you a fraction as much as you her, she will want what is best for you...for both of you."

"And Feinberg's Ovenworks?" I asked after several seconds of silence. I was mentally drained. "Do we simply leave it for the Nazis to gobble up like a midday snack?" I let my eyes wander around the familiar office, sensing my grandfather's presence there.

"I don't think you are going to have much choice in the matter," he replied. "Whether you want to admit it to yourself or not, a takeover of Feinberg's is inevitable. I would expect them to begin proceedings within a year. My newspaper has been publishing Aryanization statistics for quite some time now, although we have had to be very careful not to condemn the Nazi bastards for their blatant thievery. Until now they have tried to maintain the appearance of legality...to make it look as if the Jews were willingly liquidating or transferring their businesses to acceptable Aryans. But they are going to pick up the pace from this point on, and I don't think they will concern themselves too much with legality. After all, what or who is going to stop them? Certainly not the great German people I spoke of before. Why should they? They have been told repeatedly that they will benefit from the expulsion of Jews from the economic life of Germany. Many of them are sitting there anxiously, like hungry dogs under a dinner table waiting for some scraps to drop their way. The pharmacists, professors, doctors, and lawyers did the same when their Jewish competition was eliminated." He stopped for a few seconds to catch his breath. He had raised his voice considerably. I looked nervously at the door, wondering if anyone in the outer offices could hear. Joshua noted this and let out a long sigh.

"And don't expect help from abroad," he went on, his voice now lowered. "The foreign press writes emotional articles condemning Nazi barbarism, and the politicians make impressive, humanitarian speeches, but the world dozes on. No one really gives a damn. One almost gets the feeling that they admire Hitler for doing what they would like to do themselves." He took out his handkerchief and dabbed the perspiration that had formed on his brow.

"Are you sure you aren't being unfair?" I asked. "My Uncle Solomon writes that there are many people in the United States who are quite concerned over what is happening here and are putting pressure on their government to intercede."

"To intercede, that's a laugh," he snapped back, his eyes narrowing to slits. "I've seen some of that concern first hand. I read an article recently that told how members of the medical associations from both England and the United States have expressed publicly, and in no uncertain terms, that they don't want 'alien' physicians to be permitted to practice medicine in their countries. They are afraid that the latter will charge lower fees and cut into their practices. Yes, they want their governments to intercede. Not on our behalf, but on their own. And they call themselves men of healing." His voice had risen again. Catching himself, he paused, gave his brow a final dab, and stuffed the damp handkerchief back into his trouser pocket. Then, once more at a normal conversational level he added, "The Nazis are pragmatists. They know that appeals to racism don't always work. People are either too lazy or too obstinate to hate on command. On the other hand, they have seen through experience that an appeal based on human greed is almost always effective. They understood that right from the beginning. Greed and hatred are the cornerstones of the heralded Thousand Year Reich. Caught between these two forces, the Jew in Germany is slowly being crushed to death. Our only hope is to escape so that we can fight from a distance. You must go to Palestine, Heinrich. You must. And, the Lord willing, before long your sister and I will be there too."

His words moved me greatly. Before he finished speaking I had made my decision to go to Palestine. I owed it not only to my family and myself, but to Birgit as well. Joshua was right — the time for talking was long past. Perhaps one day Birgit would be able to join me there; perhaps Karl and Jutta would also.

"But what is the sense of telling you what you already know," he said. Before he could continue, I turned to look him directly in the eye, nodded my head, and smiled. With a mixed expression of relief and sadness, he put out his hand and returned my smile.

My father's health took a turn for the worse during the next weeks. No doubt the prospect of going to Palestine was partially responsible. Although I had not really discussed it with him in detail, I could see that he looked upon our impending exile as a crushing defeat. He did not try to hide the fact that he was not looking forward to life on the "desert." My mother, on the other hand, appeared to be anxious to leave even before the early March departure date Joshua had arranged. That is not to say that she did not feel any ambivalence. My grandfather's situation continued to torment her, but she seemed to know that he would never return, and so she now directed her entire energy to the safety of her family. Her concern for Jutta was allayed somewhat by the fact that Karl was planning to "visit" his brothers in Switzerland in the near future.

The most difficult part for me was to tell Birgit of my decision as swiftly as possible. For obvious reasons, we no longer met in Karl's apartment, but thanks to a chance encounter with an old friend several months before, we now had a new refuge for our increasingly irregular meetings. I literally bumped into Carla Schupp one afternoon in the Schwabin district, still the preferred section of Munich for the dwindling number of artists who had not yet fled the increasingly restrictive creative atmosphere of the Third Reich. I had just come out of the little bookshop on Wernherstrasse, one I had frequented since my student days. My head was bent against the cool autumn wind; tucked under my jacket was a slender volume of Franz Werfel's poetry, banned by the Nazi regime. I felt a sudden, light jolt as we collided. The book slipped out and fell to the ground at my feet. I bent down quickly to retrieve it, muttering a frightened apology without looking up. I could already feel a cold sweat breaking out on my upper lip.

"Heinrich?" At the unexpected sound of my name, my head jerked up. A familiar pair of eyes met mine. Although her hair was shorter and beginning to grey a bit in one area, I recognized her immediately.

"Carla," I gasped, instinctively spreading my arms out. She responded in kind, and for several seconds we stood there embracing silently. Finally, I released my grip and held her at arm's length. "My God, it is so good to see you! You look fantastic!" I said emotionally. It was true; if anything, the years had worked to her advantage.

"You don't look so bad yourself," she replied in that familiar mischievous tone of hers. "How long has it been?"

I tried to think back on our last meeting, calculating as quickly as I could. "At least eight years," I said at last, still holding her hands in mine. "Eight years," I repeated slowly, awed by the incredibly swift passage of time. She shook her head from side to side in disbelief. For the first time I noticed the thin lines curving downward from the corners of her eyes and mouth.

"Come," she said, wiggling her hands free from mine and gesturing for me to follow her. "We can't stay here blocking the door all day. Put your forbidden book back under your jacket and we'll go to my new 'studio' to catch up on the news." She linked her arm to mine and led me down the street almost as one would a blind man.

"And so, here I am, back in Munich again. But I can assure you that it won't be a very long stay this time," she explained, as she cleared some papers off the sofa so that I could sit.

"What made you come back in the first place?" I asked, studying the half-finished modernistic painting resting on the easel at the corner of the small attic room.

"Oh, I don't know," she answered. "To see old friends... curiosity...perhaps a bit of naivete." She stepped over next to me, cocked her head to one side and studied the painting. "I'm afraid the Führer would not approve," she said after a few seconds. "He fancies himself an artist, you know. Can you imagine that? An artist. Yet he hates anything that smacks of individualism. Calls it decadent. His idea of great art is a painting of some huge government building. I'll bet, though, that somewhere he has a secret collection of smutty little nudes to excite himself with. Men with little moustaches always do." She laughed her familiar, throaty laugh, throwing back her head like a frisky mare.

"But let's not talk about him," she said. "Come inside and sit down for a few minutes. We can have a glass of wine and reminisce about our lost youth."

"And has your curiosity about the German Fatherland been satisfied?"

I asked, leaning back onto the soft cushion I had placed behind my head, and sipping the cool, white wine Carla had poured for me. We had been chatting pleasantly for almost an hour.

"Indeed it has," she replied. "It is much worse than I imagined. You hear things, you know, but you tend to believe that they are exaggerated." She hesitated, and then in a very serious voice asked, "Is it true that Judge Linsdorff is in a concentration camp?"

I nodded slowly. "My grandfather is also a guest of the state," I added. "Along with God knows how many thousands of others. He is in the concentration camp at Buchenwald, near Weimar."

She sighed loudly. "Right from the beginning I felt that there was going to be a disaster, but I never thought it could be like this. I just assumed that my morbid artistic imagination was getting the best of me. Then, too, living in Italy leads one to believe that nothing in this world is really serious, that it's all one big operatic comedy."

"What do you mean?" I asked, a bit puzzled by her remark.

"Well," she explained, "you actually have to be there while Mussolini is giving one of his speeches to understand. The way he holds his hands on his hips, the way he tilts his head to the side like a curious dog looking into a mirror. But that isn't even what I mean." She paused for a second, obviously trying to find the right words. I had to smile as I thought of Karl's comical imitation of Il Duce. She continued, "It's more the way the Italians react to him that makes it into a farce, how they smile and wink at each other as if to indicate that they are proud of the way their leader is playing his stage role. It isn't the same way in Germany. The people here see Hitler as a god."

We talked for quite a while. I learned that Carla and her husband were no longer together. She told me without apparent regret about the Spanish dancer he had met and followed to Barcelona or Seville, she wasn't sure which. As for herself, she had lived with an Italian painter for almost a year, but had had to break off the affair when his wife came to her to beg, on behalf of her nine children, for the return of her husband.

She listened with interest as I gave her a synopsis of my life during the years we had not seen each other, and seemed genuinely happy to hear that Karl had married my sister. On the whole, however, our conversation was colored by an undercurrent of gloom. She was convinced, as was I, that there would soon be another war, one which would bring untold destruction to the entire world.

It was at that point that I told her of my personal dilemma. Emotionally I explained how difficult it was going to be for me to leave Birgit. She smiled softly, took my face between her hands and, looking deeply into my eyes said, "As banal as it sounds, Heinrich, you must always remember that most people in this world are never fortunate enough to really love and be loved. You are one of the lucky ones. You must hold onto that thought, no matter where life brings you." Then she made the suggestion that Birgit and I use her apartment as a meeting place in the future, as she would be leaving for Paris within the next few weeks. I could, she explained, simply continue to pay the rent in her name and no one would be the wiser. Unorthodox arrangements were fairly common in the artists' quarter. When I asked her why she was leaving Munich, she reminded me that according to the racial laws of the Third Reich she, too, was racially impure: a *Mischling*. "Besides," she quipped, "Paris is the city of love." As I was leaving, she pulled my face down to hers and, after kissing me tenderly on the lips, smiled sadly and said, "We did have some good times, didn't we, Heinrich?" Then, with a mischievous glint in her eye, she whispered, "Birgit or no Birgit, I still have hopes of getting you to pose in the nude for me someday. And Karl too. You tell him that for me, will you?"

***

It happened even more quickly than Joshua had predicted. In early December I received official notice that the National Socialist Government had placed Feinberg's Ovenworks under the trusteeship of Party member Wilhelm Kröner, effective immediately. Herr Kröner, the note went on, would discuss with me my further, temporary services to said firm during the transferal process agreed to by its owner, Jacob Feinberg.

I clearly recall the surprising indifference with which I read that document up to the very last sentence. If anything, I experienced a sense of relief, the feeling that another weight had been lifted from my shoulders. As I reread the final words, however, I broke out into a cold sweat. The idea that my grandfather had simply agreed to "transfer" his company was preposterous. It was obvious that either their assertion was a blatant lie, or that coercion was involved. At first, I did not mention it to either of my parents. In view of my father's precarious physical condition and my mother's equally fragile mental state, I decided to remain silent until I could get some definite information.

The day following receipt of the Aryanization notice, I arrived at Feinberg's Ovenworks at my usual time and went straight to what had previously been my office. My mood was a mixture of anger, curiosity, and fear as I reached the threshold and looked inside.

"Come in, Herr Hartstein." Wilhelm Kröner sat comfortably behind my grandfather's desk and beckoned me forward with the sharply pointed pencil he held between his thumb and index finger. Like an obedient schoolchild, I allowed myself to be drawn forward by the hypnotic pencil.

"Sit down," he said, turning the point of the pencil to his right and downward to indicate the chair at the side of the desk. Without saying a word, I seated myself and waited for him to speak again. It took all the will power I could muster to conceal my growing irritation and anxiety. I smiled blandly and looked across at Herr Kröner as if our reversed positions were perfectly normal. This seemed to unnerve him somewhat; he sat up straighter and began to tap the pencil nervously on the desk blotter.

"I think that we can dispense with trivialities, Herr Hartstein," he began, measuring his words carefully. "We both are well aware of what this is all about." He leaned back imperiously in the familiar black leather swivel chair so that the springs groaned loudly. Surprised by the unexpected sound, he leaned forward quickly, again to the accompaniment of the noisy springs. Unable to maintain my benign expression in such an absurd situation, I let out a short laugh. Herr Kröner's face instantly turned a bright red. He snapped the pencil he was holding in two and threw both pieces onto the desk in embarrassment and disgust.

"It is very strange to me that you find this so amusing," he hissed, his teeth clenched as he spoke. "Or is that just an example of the fabled Jewish sense of humor?"

I felt I had been slapped across the face. It was not so much the words he used as the way he spoke them; there was unconcealed, deep hatred in his voice. For a split second my mind played tricks on me; I imagined I was back in a familiar classroom being reprimanded by my old teacher, Herr Kulp. I felt the blood draining from my face as I shifted nervously in my chair.

Apparently satisfied that he had regained the upper hand, Herr Kröner continued. "Until the transferal procedure is completed, I have been appointed to take charge of Feinberg's Ovenworks." His expression was simultaneously smug and defiant. Once more I had to exert all of my self-control, this time so as not to push my fist right into the middle of his hateful face. "Naturally, the name of the firm will be changed to a more suitable one," he continued, as if this was so obvious that it needed no explanation. The process of eliminating any firms with Jewish sounding names had been going on for quite some time already. "And there will be certain changes in personnel. But for the time being at least, we will be making no major changes in operating procedure."

I sat silently, biting my tongue to keep from screaming back my response to this pompous little ass who was able to speak so nonchalantly about the destruction of my grandfather's life's work.

"I would like to see the papers signed by my grandfather," I finally said.

He narrowed his eyes and gave me what I'm sure was intended to be an intimidating look. I returned his stare without flinching, growing angrier by the second. He seemed to sense my change of mood.

"I can assure you that everything is perfectly in order, Herr Hartstein," he replied, in the polite manner he had always used with me. "In due time you will be able to see for yourself. I can insure that personally." The sudden change of tone caught me slightly off balance, but I learned what was behind it very quickly. Before I could make any further comments he added, "Until then, I would appreciate it if you would stay on at Feinberg's as a consultant so that the transition can take place as smoothly as possible. You will be provided with an appropriate office and will receive commensurate compensation."

The hard glint in his eyes made it clear that I was not being given a choice in the matter. Again I resisted the temptation to smash my fist into his face. I sat there and tried to compose myself. It really made no difference, I decided. In a few months my parents and I would be far away from this prison. I could not afford to do anything to jeopardize our escape. Finally, I looked up and nodded. His face broke out into a mocking smile.

"Excellent," he declared. "I knew that you would be reasonable." He stood up and came around the desk. "Now come with me. I will show you to your new working quarters." Like an obedient pet, I followed him out of the office.

***

It was the holiday season. I feared the worst when Karl telephoned early one morning to tell me that Birgit had contacted him and wanted to see me as soon as possible. We had been together in Carla's apartment only two days earlier, and while both she and I had become very emotional when I told her of my decision to leave Germany in March, the fact that we would still have three months together had made it bearable.

As I walked through the door and saw her face, I knew that my fears were justified. Before greeting me she blurted out what had happened: Dieter had been promoted to Hitler's personal staff with the rank of colonel and would be transferred to Berlin within the month. All of her efforts to stall her own departure had been futile; he had insisted that she accompany him to the capital immediately after Christmas in order to set up their home there.

"If only I could go with you, Heinrich. If only this nightmare would end," she sobbed, her face streaked with tears. We clung to each other, almost afraid to let go. Her skin molded itself to mine so tightly that it was difficult to tell where hers ended and mine began. "You must not forget me...never forget me," she pleaded, releasing a fresh stream of tears. I buried my face in her soft hair, breathing in the familiar fragrance. A giant fist seemed to twist violently inside my chest.

"We will manage to keep in touch," I promised, fighting back the terrible despair that had welled up in me. "We will find a way. And someday soon we will be together again."

We continued to hold one another for a long time without speaking. "We will be together again." As melodramatic and trite as my promise might have sounded, there was not a single night in Treblinka that I did not repeat it to myself again and again, even as I listened to the agonized screams of the dead and dying...

***

My mother turned the envelope over in her hand and began to tear open the flap nervously. It was the typical dull, brownish-grey kind that streamed endlessly from the ubiquitous offices throughout Nazi Germany. She took out the single, thin sheet of paper, unfolded it, and read. Aside from a slight trembling at the corner of her mouth, her expression did not change. When she had finished, she walked over to the table where I was seated and handed it to me without saying a word. It was short and to the point:

Dear Mrs. Hartstein,

Your father, Jacob Feinberg, died in the Camp
Hospital on January 5, 1938. May I express my
sincere sympathy on your bereavement. Mr. Feinberg
was admitted to the hospital on January 4, with
severe symptoms of exhaustion, complaining of
difficulty breathing and of pains in the chest.
Despite competent medication and devoted medical
attention it proved impossible, unfortunately, to
keep the patient alive. Should you want his ashes,
you may request them and they will be shipped to you
for a fee of three marks.
The patient voiced no final requests.

That was all. The stamp of a government office and the signature of the camp commandant made it official. Such was the cruel, unfeeling eulogy Jacob Feinberg received from the Third Reich. The unwritten message the letter contained was clear: the remains of a human life were worth less than the price of a medium quality hat.

Yitgadal veyitkadach schyme raba, May his name be blessed and exalted. Again the words of *kaddish*; words that I heard so frequently in that kingdom of death called Treblinka; words that became commonplace because of the frequency of their repetition; commonplace, because where death rules it is life that is the alien force. These words assault my senses now even though I cannot force my lips to say them; and in their silent persistence, they have sharpened themselves to daggers, cutting into my mind, piercing my heart.

My grandfather's death appeared to affect my father more adversely than it did my mother. His face mirrored an inner, uncomprehending grief.

But she seemed almost serene in the face of this tragedy. It was as if she had reached deep within herself and found some final reserve of strength. And when my grandfather's ashes were interred alongside my grandmother's in a short, traditional ceremony, the tears she shed were less due to grief over his death, than from relief that his ordeal had finally ended.

***

In early February, I was informed via a succinct memo that at the end of the week my services would no longer be required at Munich Heating, the name my grandfather's former company would bear once the final legal problems had been worked out to sever any remaining connection with the American subsidiary run by my Uncle Victor. The inevitable message left me unmoved. Moreover, I felt nothing but emptiness as I left the familiar building for the last time. Herr Kröner, either out of embarrassment or disdain, had arranged my final day there to take place while he was away on a business trip to Stuttgart.

From all appearances, he was doing his job well. To meet the new government contracts and increased private sales to enterprises with National Socialist Party affiliations, it had been necessary to almost double the work force. With the exception of one or two who could not be dismissed immediately because of the highly specialized nature of their work, virtually all Jews had been eliminated from the payroll. Those who remained were already training their Aryan successors and would have to step aside as soon as they were no longer needed.

On Jägerstrasse we lived in limbo. My grandparents were gone, and the reminder of my circle of family and friends was growing smaller and smaller. Uncle Solomon, Aunt Rachel, Aunt Yaffa, Judge Linsdorff, Ursel, Birgit...scattered to the winds: America, Paris, Dachau, Berlin. Those of us who remained, moreover, were merely biding our time before we would join the forced exodus. Karl and Jutta spoke more and more about their desire to leave for Switzerland with Karl's mother, while each day brought my parents and me closer to our appointed date of emigration to Palestine. It was overwhelming. Had life really been so much different just five or six years before? How had it happened? How?

Joshua had taken every precaution to make certain that there would be no last minute roadblocks placed in our path. He feverishly checked and rechecked our documents, and scattered liberal bribes among the many officials he thought could be of any use to us in the event of some unforeseen problem. When he and Ursel left for Paris at the end of January, he was quite convinced that he had left no stone unturned.

With two weeks remaining, I found myself mechanically counting the hours. Palestine. The thought made me uncomfortable, in spite of my attempts to rationalize. After all, we were not setting out like explorers willingly pursuing their destiny; on the contrary, we were more like hound-pursued rabbits running in the only direction open to us to escape. I tried to comfort myself with the thought that my grandfather would have been happy to have his flesh and blood finally enter The Promised Land, but there was no solace in the thought. I walked the cold, deserted streets of Munich during the day, drinking in the familiar sights: the cinema, museums, concert halls, amusement areas, lecture halls, public parks, all denied to me now because I had been born a Jew. I sat alone on my familiar bench in the Hofgarten, defiantly expressing, by my illegal presence, the refusal to submit totally to such injustice. The bitter cold February wind, unsympathetic to my plight, numbed my face and limbs. Helpless anger, coupled with an indescribable sadness and longing, flooded my being. Heine's words echoed again and again through my mind: "*Once I had a beautiful fatherland...*" Heine was correct. It was a dream.

***

It was more the type of grunting sound an animal would make than one you would expect to have come from a human mouth. The pen I was holding slipped between my fingers and fell onto the letter I had been writing to my Uncle Solomon, leaving an ugly blot in its center. The sound was repeated a second time, followed by a series of loud crashes. I jumped up from my chair and rushed to the kitchen.

My father lay in a twisted mass on the kitchen floor, broken pieces of pottery scattered around him. One of his hands still tightly gripped the overturned chair that he had taken down with him as he fell, while the other was flung outward, fist clenched. A strap from his artificial leg had come loose, leaving the foot pointing grotesquely in the opposite direction from his thigh. He groaned once or twice more as I entered the room, then his eyes rolled upward and he became silent. A thin trickle of saliva bubbled from the corner of his mouth and ran down onto his chin and shirtfront. In a state of panic, I bent over and inexpertly took his wrist in my hand, feeling for a trace of pulse. After a few empty seconds, I was relieved to perceive a faint, irregular beat. He was still alive! I loosened his collar and covered him with my bathrobe; then I ran to the telephone.

"He's resting comfortably now." Karl made the announcement as he rolled his sleeves down slowly and entered the kitchen.

My mother was picking up the last pieces of the dish my father had been holding when he collapsed. "Shouldn't he be in a hospital?" my mother asked, worry lines creasing her face.

Karl looked at me out of the corner of his eye and shrugged his shoulders almost imperceptibly. "We'll take care of him here," he replied, avoiding any direct response to her question. The stress had made her forget that Jews were no longer accepted as patients in the hospitals. "I'll stay here with him for a few hours. Later on, I'll get Dr. Griep to come over and take my place. The first twenty-four hours or so after a heart attack are the most critical. If he makes it through the night, we have a very good chance of saving him."

My mother threw the final pieces of pottery noisily into the garbage receptacle under the sink and turned around wearily. "It is that bad, Karl?" she said, more as a statement than a question. She turned on the kitchen faucet and began to move the washcloth around in the sink in a practiced, circular motion.

"It was a major attack," answered Karl softly, stepping over to her and placing his hand on her shoulder. "There is no way of knowing how much damage was done to his heart. The one thing in his favor is that he has a very strong constitution. He is a fighter, and that is important now." He paused for a moment and added, "Would you like me to call Jutta now and tell her what has happened, or would you rather do it yourself?"

"I'll call her," my mother replied, putting her hand on top of his and patting it affectionately. "You and Heinrich go inside and rest for a little while. You must both be very tired."

For the first time I became aware of the pain in my arms, the result of the effort it had taken to help Karl carry my father into the bedroom.

"Come, Karl," I said, taking hold of his arm. "Let's find my father's secret stock of brandy and have a few drinks." My mother was already speaking to Jutta on the telephone as we left the kitchen.

"I think you should leave as scheduled," Karl advised. "I can take care of your parents until they are able to join you. There really isn't much you can do here." He took a sip of the gold-colored brandy and waited for my response.

"You know I can't do that now," I answered, draining my glass at a single gulp and wincing as the liquor burned its way down to my stomach.

He was silent for a few moments. Then, punching his hand down onto the arm of the sofa, he said angrily, "What kind of tricks is God playing on us all these days, Heinrich?"

I exhaled deeply and replied, "It is pretty obvious that there is no God in Hitler's Reich. Perhaps He didn't measure up to the high racial standards here." Then I smiled and added, "I just hope that He didn't have any trouble getting a visa for wherever He decided to go."

My father hovered between life and death for the next several days, but Karl's assessment of his constitution turned out to be accurate. Less than two weeks after the heart attack he had regained enough strength to spend an hour or two each day on the living room sofa; he even managed to muster up enough of his natural stubbornness to hobble there unassisted, though it exhausted him. In spite of this seemingly miraculous improvement, however, both Karl and Dr. Griep agreed that the coronary infarction he had suffered had been a massive one, and even under the best conditions it would be quite some time, if ever, before he would be able to make a journey as long and physically demanding as the one to Palestine. And so, our planned date of departure came and went, and we remained in Munich, prisoners of both fate and the Third Reich, one more perverse than the other.

***

For the next few months it seemed as if the Nazis had finally had their fill of persecuting Jews and were now going to devote their efforts to more grandiose projects. We mistakenly attributed this change of focus to the fact that they had achieved all of their racial goals, and had now decided that it was about time to stop beating an already dead horse. After all, the economy was already virtually "Jew free." Those Jews who remained were restricted from all but the most menial jobs. The future was decidedly Aryan. What useful purpose would further persecutions serve?

During the first weeks of March, the Goebbels' propaganda machine found a new scapegoat to occupy the Nazi's insatiable hatred: the battered remains of Czechoslovakia. The promises made by Hitler in his heralded Munich meeting with British Prime Minister Chamberlain were about to be trampled into the dust. The helpless little country was portrayed in glaring headlines as the abode of evil incarnate. Lurid accounts of murders, rapes, and other mistreatment of innocent Germans by evil Czechs were published daily in every major newspaper and broadcast incessantly on the radio. Using the bullying techniques that had proved so successful in the recent past, Hitler pressed for the total capitulation of his small neighbor. Finally, on March 15, the President of Czechoslovakia agreed to lay the "fate of the Czech people and country in the hands of the Führer of the German Reich." One could clearly read the mammoth pride and joy on the faces of Munich's citizens. Their pride was magnified by the fact that the greatest German in history, as they now called their Führer, had begun his meteoric climb to the stars in their very city. The popular greeting "*Sieg heil*" took on greater meaning than ever.

By the end of March, I was convinced that Hitler was leading the world to another war. All of the signs were there. The German Luftwaffe had already undergone a successful dress rehearsal in Spain. Thanks to the skill and power of the glorious German pilots, Franco's fascist forces now ruled there. Further, Hitler and Mussolini concluded a military alliance, calling it provocatively the Pact of Steel. Mussolini, eager not to be outdone by his increasingly successful German ally, signalled Italy's return to glory by conquering minuscule Albania. Those of us who had not lost touch with reality waited for the next dangerous move in what sometimes appeared to be little more than an overblown children's game. Perhaps for this reason, we were still able to laugh at the absurdity around us.

The news in late August stunned us all: Germany and the Soviet Union had signed a nonaggression pact. Even Goebbels, master rabble-rouser that he was, was finding it impossible to convince the German populace that the country which had been portrayed as evil incarnate had suddenly sprouted wings. The citizens of Munich walked around with expressions of bewilderment on their faces.

Karl and I sat on the large living room sofa, speaking quietly so as not to disturb my father who snored intermittently from his perch on the easy chair across from us.

"They really do take us all for fools, don't they?" he began, shaking his head and making a clicking sound with his tongue. "If we are to believe the latest news, our gifted foreign minister, von Ribbentrop, has outdone Jesus Christ. While the latter merely converted a few barrels of water into wine, the former was able to turn hundreds of millions of devils into angels with the stroke of a pen. I tell you, it has gotten to the stage of absurdity. That limping cadaver Goebbels must think that the German people are all idiots. It should be clear to anyone who has the slightest ability to think that this is just a move to untie Hitler's hands for some new international intrigue. All of this hysteria about the atrocities committed against us by Poland has a very familiar ring."

"I know you're right," I replied. "But in one sense it is reason for hope, at least from a personal standpoint."

"How so?" he asked, looking at me quizzically.

"If the Nazis were able to change their minds so drastically about the Russians," I explained, "isn't it possible that they might also eventually do the same with regard to the Jews? After all, we are much less of a threat than Stalin and his battalions. And besides that, even if they were to get rid of every single Jew in Germany, that won't give them an inch more of the living space Hitler has talked about since *Mein Kampf*."

"What makes you think they have changed their minds?" countered Karl. "Tactics, yes, but that is all. You never have been able to accept the fact that these bastards are consistent when it comes to hatred. The trouble with you, Heinrich, is that you still believe that reason has a rightful place in a discussion about Nazis. Believe me, it doesn't. I have seen them very close up, and I can assure you that they operate on a principle that leaves no room for such extravagances." He paused, let out a deep breath and looked up at the ceiling. "My father understood that right from the beginning." He lowered his head and added so softly that I barely heard, "God, how I miss him."

I swallowed hard, choking back the surge of emotion that Karl's sudden shift in the conversation had evoked. "I do too," I said, picturing Judge Linsdorff's steel-blue eyes, and attempting to recall his resonant voice. At that very moment, my father's eyes opened wide. I don't really know for certain if he was speaking in his sleep or if he had been following our conversation. Whatever the case, his words had a chilling effect.

"It is too late! We are trapped!" he bellowed. "Too goddamned late!" Then his eyes closed again, and within a few seconds his loud, rasping snore echoed through the room.

One week later, the German army invaded Poland and plunged the world into the bloodiest war it had ever seen.

Trapped. Is this what my father had meant in that moment of semi-conscious prophecy? Too late. Although we did not know it immediately, the outbreak of the war took away the luxury of ambivalence and indecision. Too late. Now there would be no escape for us; not to America, which continued to hold doggedly to its rigid immigration quotas in spite of the well publicized persecutions across the ocean, and not to British-administered Palestine, which had become enemy territory on the third of September, the moment Britain fulfilled its treaty obligations to Poland by declaring war on Germany. Too late. In those first days, however, my mother's main concern was not with our missed opportunity to emigrate, but with what she considered a more urgent matter: my sister's precarious situation in Paris.

"We will be able to communicate with Ursel and Joshua by way of America," I explained, trying to calm her as much as possible. The war was entering its second week and her anxiety grew steadily as the days passed. The announcement that Germany and Poland were at war had not been a great surprise to anyone, but few had expected the swift action of Britain and France. We had assumed that they would issue the customary loud protests, as they had when Czechoslovakia was swallowed up by the Reich, perhaps even make a few face-saving threats about intervention, and then acquiesce. France's declaration of war on Germany, made only hours after England's, placed my sister and Joshua in "enemy" territory.

My answer did not comfort my mother. Her eyes mirrored her fear as the radio blared out the news of the lightning-swift German advances into Poland.

"But what will happen if France is defeated?" she asked simply. What will happen to Joshua and Ursel?" It was not an idle question. Joshua had told us before he left for Paris that he intended to expend every effort to expose the full truth about the Nazis to the world, and I was certain that he had carried out this intention.

A bit uncertainly, I replied, "I am sure that Joshua has an escape plan. But France will be quite a different story than Poland. In addition to their superior army, they have the Maginot Line to protect them from invasion. Hitler has bitten off more than he can chew this time."

"I don't understand it," Karl told me on the day that Warsaw capitulated. "If anything, I should feel terrible about what has happened, and I do, I really do. But somewhere inside of me there is something else, something I find frightening. Could it be, Heinrich, that I feel a sense of pride?" He let his face sink down into his hands and held it cupped there for several seconds. Then, looking at me with pain-filled eyes, he added, "How can that be possible? You know how much I hate everything the Nazis stand for."

Karl's revelation unnerved me, not because I did not understand what he meant, but because it forced me to admit something I had been repressing from myself.

"I suppose," I replied, more to explain this phenomenon to myself than to him, "you haven't been fully able to make the crucial separation in your mind."

"Separation?" he repeated, puzzled.

"What I mean is," I explained, "you can't quite accept the fact that you are able to despise the Nazis and yet at the same time have positive feelings toward Germany, or more specifically, toward the German people. You haven't made the distinction between the two." I became silent, aware that I was guilty of the very same failure.

He continued to stare at me, as if searching for some hidden message. Finally, he looked away and said sadly, "Are you sure there is any real difference between the two? Are you sure?" I shook my hand to indicate that I wasn't. Two days later, Karl received notice that he was to report for compulsory service in the Wehrmacht. Germany would need all of the skilled doctors it could get for the coming campaigns against the Western powers, even those doctors with Jewish wives.

By the end of September, Poland had ceased to exist, gobbled up by Hitler and Stalin like a rotting carcass by starving hyenas. According to Hitler himself, however, the victory had not come cheaply: more than ten thousand Germans had died, and over thirty thousand had spilled their blood for the Reich. As one walked through the Marienplatz and along the shopping streets of Munich, there was little overt celebration. Occasionally, one could see the familiar signs of grief on the face of a passerby. My stomach constricted as I thought that my friend would soon be in the midst of the carnage.

A few days before Karl's designated date of departure, the two of us went to the Hofbräuhaus together. I had hesitated at first, but Karl insisted we attempt to pretend to ourselves this one last time that all was well with the world.

"Don't worry, Blacktop," he said, using the affectionate nickname from our youth. "You are now under the protection of a future officer of the German Wehrmacht. Soon I will be all decked out in my fancy new lieutenant's uniform, and then all of these lowly privates, corporals and sergeants will have to jump up off their backsides to salute me." He snickered loudly, indicating with a sweep of his arm the small groups of enlisted men scattered at the tables surrounding us. I was too depressed to return his smile.

A few weeks had passed. Karl and I sat in a small booth in the darkened little inn and spoke quietly. "It's going to be all right, Heinrich," Karl said, reading my mind. "I will be back before you know it and we'll come here again for a few more steins of this incomparable Munich beer." He lifted his stein and took a long swallow.

"How will you get through it, Karl?" I asked, amazed at his levity. It was clear to me that he was not putting on an act for my benefit. Since he had received his induction notice his mood seemed to have risen. I voiced this observation to him haltingly. "I don't understand it. You seem almost happy about going."

He smiled and put his hand gently on my arm. "Believe it or not, I'm relieved. It's a lot easier to go than to sit here passively and wait for God knows what," he replied, without any trace of self-consciousness. "You are the philosopher, so you should know that when one has no choice there is no conflict. I have no choice. It is my duty to go."

"Duty?" I interrupted loudly. "How can you say such a thing?" I felt my lower lip quivering. His grasp on my forearm tightened.

"Yes, duty," he said, scanning the room with his eyes and lowering his voice so that only I could hear him. "Not my duty to them, but to myself. You must understand, Heinrich, that I am a doctor. It may sound rather theatrical, but I have taken an oath to save lives." He paused briefly, then added, "I know that oaths don't mean very much these days in Germany, but I can assure you that when I vowed to devote myself to healing, I did not do it blindly like these starry-eyed fanatics who have signed over their souls to a power crazy maniac. And I will try to save some of these misguided kids who will be shot to pieces if this war with England and France becomes a reality. Don't you see?" He moved his face close to mine and held my eyes with his, which at that moment were as steely as his father's.

I looked away, suddenly ashamed at having questioned him, even for a moment.

"I'm sorry, Karl," I stuttered, wishing I could sink into the ground and disappear.

He leaned back again and replied faintly,"So am I, Heinrich, so am I."

***

Another farewell. How many there had been over the years. How very many. Each like a death within me; each a reminder that destiny shows no respect for love or friendship or hope. I held little Franz tightly in my arms as I watched the train slowly begin to make its way out of the station. Such a familiar scene. Karl kissed Jutta one last time, bounded up the steps, and gave a final wave in our direction before disappearing into the interior. Another farewell. Another death within me.

***

During the next weeks it was difficult to believe that we were at war. If anything, the atmosphere in Munich seemed more relaxed than it had been during the period of tension leading up to the conflict. The shelves in the stores were adequately, if not elaborately, stocked for the eager shoppers, and music echoed from the bustling cafés of the city. The radio broadcasts and the newspapers reflected a strange paradox: the Nazi government, responsible for starting the war, had mounted a new propaganda campaign in which they presented themselves as the champions of peace. In one speech after another, Hitler repeated the claim that he had made and would continue to make every effort humanly possible to restore tranquility to Europe now that the villainous Poles had been dealt with. And although the other so-called belligerents, England and France, were not fooled by his rhetoric, they seemed content to sit back and wait for events to unfold. The so-called *Sitzkrieg* had become the subject of derisive cartoons in all of the newspapers. There was a general attitude that the war had, in fact, already ended, and lacked only the formality of a written document.

In a rare moment of animation, my father expressed the opinion many others in Munich shared. "The French are craven cowards. They have no will to fight. They abandoned what was left of their courage in the bloody trenches of Verdun, and now they sit along the Maginot Line like fat-assed roosters, waiting for the sun to rise even though they have forgotten how to crow. And the English are no better. They would much rather carry an umbrella than a rifle."

My mother was noticeably less anxious than she had been at the outset of the war. Unable to face the alternatives, she convinced herself that my father would soon be well enough to travel, and that this, combined with an early peace treaty with England, would enable us to carry out our plan to emigrate to Palestine. She was somewhat cheered by a letter from Aunt Yaffa. The latter relayed greetings and love from Rachel and Joshua who had written that all was going well for them in Paris. The situation in America, my aunt added, was one of optimism; it was the firm conviction of most Americans that the "silly" war would be over shortly.

The fact that no further outstanding punitive measures were taken against the German-Jewish population was another reason for my mother's change in mood. In spite of the persistent rumors that the government was considering the proposal to segregate Jews from the rest of the population in so-called "Jewish Houses," nothing of the sort had yet been done. Materially, too, we were not suffering unduly. Our financial condition was actually relatively good considering all that had happened. My father's pension continued to arrive on schedule, and I had accumulated a fairly respectable savings during my tenure at Feinberg's Ovenworks, a good portion of which I had not reported to the government in spite of the recent decree demanding that every Jew submit a written summary of his or her total worth. In addition, even though as yet there had been no payment, my mother had received written assurances that the legal details connected with the sale of the family firm were being finalized, and that it would not be long before she received her rightful share. In their typically bizarre fashion, the Nazis continued the illusion that they presided over a government ruled by law.

By the time the holiday season arrived, however, the mood had begun to deteriorate. The fast end to the war that everyone had hoped for had not come about. The steadfast burghers of Munich no longer attempted to conceal their dwindling patience and their dissatisfaction with worsening living conditions. They complained about the senseless blackouts which, as far as they were concerned, protected them only from imaginary bombers, and they spoke disdainfully of the phoney war that kept so many of their men away from home. They griped about the reduced selection of foodstuffs available at the markets; even the winter cold was indirectly blamed on the military and political situation.

It was a few days before Christmas. As I sat on my favorite bench in the Hofgarten, hat turned down and collar up against the December wind, I didn't notice the approaching figure until he stopped and stood directly in front of me. His highly polished military boots reflected and magnified the weak rays of the afternoon winter sun. Startled, I let my eyes travel nervously upward, past the spotless grey uniform to the familiar, smiling face.

"Karl!" I blurted out, momentarily confused.

"Is that any way to greet a brave, loyal defender of the Führer and the Reich?" he replied, jerking out his arm at a ninety degree angle to his body and clicking his heels together loudly.

"*Drei Liter!*" he barked, standing rigidly at attention as he parodied the Nazi greeting.

"*Drei Liter!*" I responded, jumping up from my seat with arm outstretched. Then, laughing loudly, we lowered our arms and clasped each other's hand tightly.

"One can look at it in two ways," Karl said, when I expressed my surprise that he had been granted a leave so quickly. "Either it means that the persistent rumors are right, or that they are wrong." He smiled and waited for me to react.

"Which rumors?" I asked, taking the bait.

"Well," he began, "there are those who believe that we are getting ready to invade Belgium and the Netherlands, and that we were granted leaves so that we could have one last taste of normal life before all hell breaks loose, a kind of Christmas present from Uncle Dolf." He smiled broadly, warming to the topic. "Then there are others, the cynics, who also believe that the invasion of the low countries is imminent, but claim that our leaves are a clever ploy to deceive the Belgians and Dutch into thinking that we have no such intentions."

"You mean," I asked, "everyone is convinced that this war is going to heat up? I had thought there was a good chance that there might be an early armistice."

"No, not everyone," he answered. "There is yet another group, even more cynical than those I just mentioned. They believe that there will be no invasion. They say that we are stationed in such force along the borders just to put political pressure on our enemies, and that we were granted leaves because the government wants to save the money it would cost to feed us decently during the holidays. Either way, I am home, so they won't get any complaints from me." He put his arm affectionately around my shoulder and, in a serious voice, added, "I hope to God the latter theory turns out to be correct. I've been up in the Berlin area, in a military hospital there. I have seen some of the results of our glorious victory in the East. Believe me, Heinrich, it is horrible." He released his grip on me and let his arm fall limply down to his side. "Many of them are just kids," he sighed. "Just kids torn apart like meat in a butcher's shop." He brought his hand up and wiped roughly at the corner of one eye. "I've had to remove their shattered legs and arms, take hunks of metal out of their skulls, and stand helplessly by while some of them took their last breath. I have even seen some of them die with an angelic smile on their faces, their final words dedicated neither to God, nor lover, nor family, but to the lunatic bastard who is responsible for all of the butchery." There was a degree of fury in his eyes. A full minute passed before we resumed speaking. His voice shook with anger.

"There is one fellow in particular that I can't get out of my mind, an SS officer. He must have been just about our age, Heinrich." The anger had faded. His voice now sounded tired. "He had been wounded by an exploding shell during the assault on Warsaw, terribly wounded. The prognosis was very grave." He took a deep breath and ran the back of one hand over his mouth. "I had operated on him the night before, but I was unable to remove all of the shrapnel lodged in his mutilated body. He was just too weak." Karl paused again, his eyes downcast. "During the night he began to hemorrhage internally. By the time I got to him the whole front of his hospital gown was soaked with blood, and a thin stream trickled down the sides of his mouth. His skin was already turning grey. I immediately ordered blood and got ready to give him a transfusion." At this point, Karl paused and gritted his teeth. He was obviously struggling to keep his voice level. "Don't ask me why he wasn't unconscious," he said, when he had regained control. "By all rights he should have been, judging from the amount of blood he had lost. At any rate, as I was about to insert the needle in his arm he opened his eyes and spoke to me. Calmly. As if he were asking me the time of day." He fixed his eyes on mine; his breath was shooting out short puffs of smoke. "Do you know what he said to me, Heinrich? Do you know what that crazy son of a bitch was worried about even as his life poured out of his mouth?" Before I could react in any way he gave me the answer. "He wanted to know if the blood I was going to give him was pure Aryan blood! He told me to make sure I didn't put any contaminated Jewish blood into his body! And his eyes...they looked absolutely serene. One would have thought that he had seen a vision of God. Can you imagine such a thing? He was more worried about being racially polluted than he was about dying!"

"Easy, Karl," I said, feeling a weakening in my legs. Karl's shoulders were heaving slightly. He took a step back to the bench and sat down heavily. For a moment I thought he might be weeping.

"Do you know what I thought of at that moment, Heinrich?" he asked, his voice cracking. I shook my head dumbly, also overcome by emotion. "I thought of my beautiful, little Franz...and what was in store for him in such a hateful world. He is too young to understand right now, but soon they will make him aware of his 'tainted' blood. They will taunt him about it and punish him for it, the filthy scum. Believe me, I wanted to kill that dying fanatic with my bare hands, to rip the tubes from his body and watch him slowly bleed to death." He clenched his fists and held them up in front of his face for a second or two. Then, letting them drop back onto his lap, he looked up into my eyes and added, "Of course, I didn't do it. Instead, I went ahead with the transfusion without answering him. There was really no need to answer; he had lapsed into unconsciousness. At any rate, he needn't have worried. He should have realized that Jews are prohibited from giving blood in the Third Reich."

I sat down next to my friend, as thoroughly drained as he was.

"I guess you must be sorry you ever met me," I said, childishly indulging my twisted sense of guilt. I regretted my words even before they were out.

Karl frowned. "So they have gotten through to you, too, have they?" he hissed, shaking his head.

"What do you mean?" I asked, stung by his angry tone.

"I mean," he explained, "they have convinced you that the victim is the one at fault and not the criminal who persecutes him. If you really accept that, then you are little better than they are. In fact, if you feel that way you have become one of them."

In all of the years I had known him, Karl had never spoken to me so harshly. I felt as if ice-cold water had been thrown into my face. Slightly dazed by his attack, I tried to test its validity. I wondered if it could be true.

Yes, I finally had to admit to myself, there was some truth in it, enough to make my head begin to pound. I wondered how many other Jews had finally come to believe in their own worthlessness? How many had turned their hatred from those at whom it should have been directed and focused it onto themselves? I sat there for a full minute, letting this realization sink in.

We walked in silence from the Hofgarten, each lost in thought. I was still smarting, not so much from what Karl had said as from the fact that he had not been entirely off the mark. As we came to the busy Ludwigstrasse and stood waiting for the traffic light to change, he turned to me and said, "I'm sorry, Heinrich, but I just can't stand what is happening to all of us. I didn't mean..."

"No," I shot back, before he could finish. "Please don't apologize for the truth. I'm just surprised that I wasn't able to see it myself. Where have I been?"

"In hell," he replied quietly. "We have all been there for quite some time now, drifting slowly but surely toward the seventh circle."

"The only difference," I said, "is that we did not abandon all hope when we first entered. It might have been better for us if we had. Hope may very well prove to have been our worst enemy in the Third Reich."

"We are coming very close to the point where we will have to give it up," he replied, becoming agitated again. He took a deep breath in an obvious attempt to calm himself, then continued. "That SS officer and all those other wounded boys I spoke about before are only the tip of a very bloody iceberg." His voice trembled slightly, but remained firm. He tilted his head back and seemed to search for something in the cloudy Munich sky. "The extent of suffering in Poland is many, many times greater. We have done terrible things there."

"I know," I replied sadly. "I've read and heard the glowing accounts of the heroic Luftwaffe bombing city after city. It makes me ill just to think about it."

"That isn't exactly what I meant", he said. "If what I heard is true, that is only a fraction of the horror we have inflicted on them. And it seems to be only the beginning. In spite of the fact that the war with Poland is officially over, the worst may be yet to come."

"The worst?" I asked, wondering what could be worse than screaming bombers raining death and destruction onto helpless people. We continued to stand at the corner, semi-oblivious to our surroundings. A fine, wet snow began to fall, melting as soon as it made contact with the concrete sidewalk. A convoy of trucks and light armored vehicles began to rattle past us in the direction of the university.

"The Nazis are determined to destroy Poland," he went on, ignoring the impromptu military parade. "If what I have heard is even partially true, there has already been a monstrous bloodbath."

"I still don't understand," I said, shrugging my shoulders.

"There was a general," he replied, a faraway look again in his eyes. "An old line soldier like your father." He smiled at the thought, but only for a moment. "He had been passing by while a team of anti-demolitions men was trying to defuse an unexploded bomb that had landed at the side of a government building in the center of the city. Just a case of being in the wrong place at the wrong time." He paused and wiped a few wet snowflakes from his face.

"In addition to the anti-demolitions team, several people in his entourage were killed instantly, and to tell the truth, he would have been better off if he had been too. When I saw him he had already been operated on three times, and it was clear that he would not survive for more than a few days. Unlike the SS officer I told you about before, who, by the way, actually recovered from his wounds, the general was beyond the point where he would have had to worry about receiving polluted blood." Karl frowned and shook his head.

"I was on duty the night his body gave out. By the time I got to his room he was convulsing. His liver had failed; his eyes and skin were already a bright yellow. There was nothing I could do to save him." Karl spoke in a low monotone. From time to time I had to strain to hear him as a truck rumbled past. "I managed to stop his convulsions by giving him a heavy dose of morphine, but it was obvious that he was almost gone." Karl looked up at the sky again. Larger snowflakes fell now and began to stick to the pavement. He turned back to me and continued, "I was just about to leave the room when he called out to me in a faint voice. Surprised, I went back over to his bed and leaned over him. His lips were moving rapidly. At first I couldn't make out what he was saying. I thought he might be hallucinating from the morphine, but as I began to piece his words together I decided that he wasn't. I had the strangest feeling. It was as if I was listening to his final confession. I think...I think that in a way he actually was asking for absolution, even if he didn't know it himself."

"What did he have to tell you that was so urgent?" I asked, my curiosity piqued. The thought of a German general with a guilty conscience seemed almost beyond the realm of possibility.

"He repeated several times that we were killing thousands of innocent people. At first I misunderstood. I thought the same thing you did just a few minutes ago, that he was referring to the so-called normal casualties of war. When I indicated as much he became agitated, but by that time, even though he continued to slip in and out of a semi-sleep because of the morphine, his pain had eased. He was able to speak a little more easily during his lucid moments. He told me of unprovoked killings, murders numbering in the tens of thousands. I assumed he was exaggerating to make a point. He said that the Gestapo and SS were rounding up as many of the rich and educated Poles as they could and summarily executing them. He also spoke of mass deportations to ghettos and concentration camps, and although he didn't give any details, I surmised that he meant the Jewish population of Nazi Poland. There have been rumors circulating in Berlin..."

My stomach turned over wildly as I listened to Karl's story. I found myself wishing he would stop, while at the same time I was riveted to every word.

"As his voice began to fade, he told me of women who had been the cream of Polish society only months before selling themselves openly to German soldiers for a loaf of army bread, and of hungry children begging for food in the streets. And do you know what he said right before he died, Heinrich? This general in the greatest army the world has ever seen? Do you know what he told me?" Karl had grasped my sleeve and was tugging at it. His eyes were simultaneously pleading and furious. I shook my head slowly without answering, scarcely able to endure watching my friend suffer so deeply.

"He told me that he was ashamed to be a German, that he was glad he was not going to live to see the German people bring a disgrace onto themselves from which they might never recover. Can you imagine a general of the Wehrmacht saying such a thing?"

That evening, our depleted families gathered together at Jägerstrasse to celebrate Karl's return, temporary though it was. Karl seemed to have shaken the bleak mood of the afternoon. With little Franz perched happily on his shoulders, he followed his mother and Jutta into the apartment, bending carefully to maneuver his precious burden through the doorway. My mother and Mrs. Linsdorff embraced warmly, while my father managed an awkward bow to the latter, followed by a smart Prussian salute to Karl. Karl gently handed his son to me, smiled, and returned the salute.

At dinner, the two grandmothers fussed over their only grandson, admonished every once in a while by my sister who complained good-naturedly that they were spoiling him too much. Neither Karl nor I made any reference to our earlier conversation, although when the topic of the war came up we exchanged knowing looks. My father limited himself to one or two sharp comments about the "cowardly" French and then lapsed into his usual silence. Before the meal was concluded, he had fallen sound asleep and had to be assisted into the living room where he could rest more comfortably. Later, just before Karl, Jutta, and Franz were getting ready to leave (Jutta and Franz had moved in with Frau Linsdorff on Brienner Strasse when Karl was inducted), Karl indicated that he had some personal news he had not told me that afternoon. We excused ourselves and went to my study.

"I had intended to tell you this afternoon in the Hofgarten," he began. "But I let myself get sidetracked. I saw Birgit last week."

At the sound of her name, my heart skipped a beat. While almost a year had passed since I last saw her, there had not been a day that passed, scarcely an hour, that I did not think of her.

"How is she?" I blurted out eagerly.

"Surviving, just like the rest of us," he replied. "She misses you very much, Heinrich."

I felt my composure melting. There was a lump in my throat as I pleaded, "Tell me what she said. Tell me everything."

"I called her right after I arrived in Berlin," he replied. "But we didn't have a chance to meet until last week. Her freedom of movement is rather limited. It seems as if SS Colonel Dieter Hoppe is a steadily rising star in the Nazi firmament, with many important social commitments. He is said to have the ear of Himmler himself. I find that as ironic as it is dangerous. Can you imagine what would happen if he were to find out about you?"

I nodded impatiently, anxious for him to go on.

"Almost from the moment I saw her," he continued, "she spoke of nothing but you. She was a nervous wreck until I was able to convince her that you were alive and well. She told me that she hadn't had a good night's sleep since she left Munich. And she gave me this to bring to you when I got home on leave." He reached into his shirt pocket and brought out a white envelope. I reached for it with a trembling hand. I stood there dumbly and stared at my name, written in Birgit's familiar handwriting on the front of the envelope. "I only wish," he added, as he turned to leave the room, "that I could have brought you back more than just a letter from Berlin."

I read and reread her letter that night and in the days that followed, devouring each word greedily like a starving man who had suddenly had a banquet set before him. She had not written to me sooner, she explained, because she had been terrified, not for herself, but for me and my family. Any moderation or sensitivity her husband may have formerly displayed had been replaced by a harshness and cruelty that defied belief.

I suffered anew each time I reread that portion, wondering how much had been left unsaid and imagining the worst. It was possible, Birgit wrote, that she would be in Munich in the near future. Perhaps we would be able to see each other, if only briefly. My life began to revolve around that "perhaps."

I saw Karl almost every day for the two weeks of his leave. We laughed and joked together as we always had and enjoyed outings in the crisp December air with Jutta and Franz. Karl got particular pleasure out of teaching his son how to kick a soccer ball; the little fellow clapped his hands with glee every time he was able to send the ball past his father who pretended to fall down in a vain attempt to block it. Watching them, one would never have known that the world was about to explode.

We exchanged the customary toasts and good wishes for the New Year as 1940 began, but our mood was more apprehensive than joyful. As the time approached for him to return to his division, Karl became increasingly distant; it was as if he were trying to prepare himself and us in advance for the renewed separation. The two of us said our good-byes on the day before his departure; by mutual agreement we had decided not to indulge in another melodramatic parting scene at the railroad station. As Karl put it, "It is very difficult to be sentimental at five-thirty in the morning." I gave him the long letter I had written to Birgit, which he promised to deliver at the first opportunity. Then we shook hands and almost believed it ourselves when we said that we would see each other again very soon.

That evening, a light tapping at the door startled me. For a moment I feared the worst. I knew from experience that the Gestapo often paid their dreaded calls in the middle of the night, the time when their victims were most likely to be at home and also when they were most vulnerable. I suppressed that thought immediately, however, reasoning to myself that the Gestapo would not be likely to knock so tentatively. I put down the book I had been reading and went over to unlatch the door. It was Karl. For several seconds we stood there on opposite sides of the doorway without speaking.

"Well, aren't you going to invite me in?" he finally asked, grinning weakly. "Or have you forgotten who I am already?"

"I had to talk to you again, Heinrich," he said, leaning across the table and keeping his voice at a level just slightly above a whisper. "I don't want to make things more difficult for you, but there are some burdens that I simply can't carry alone." We had gone into the kitchen to avoid disturbing my sleeping parents. Even in the dim light I could see the bluish-black rings under his eyes, evidence that he had not been sleeping well these past days.

"There are other things I heard about in Berlin that I didn't mention to you," he began. "I had intended not to say anything about it to you because I didn't want to add to your worries."

"I thought there was something you were holding back," I replied, growing apprehensive. "Besides, I can't imagine anything even a fraction as terrible as what you told me in the Hofgarten the other day."

"Murder is murder," he countered, looking up at me through tired eyes. "But like anything else, there always seems to be a difference when it strikes close to home, particularly when the guilty parties are supposed to be saving lives instead of snuffing them out. After all, one expects a physician to be a healer, not a murderer."

"Physician?" I asked, puzzled. "I don't understand."

"Understand?" he shot back. "Don't even try to. This is one of those times when understanding cannot help." He sat for several seconds without saying anything. Then he leaned forward again and whispered, "Right here in Germany, right under the people's noses, they are systematically killing human beings. Gassing them."

"What?" I gasped, my mind automatically rejecting the idea. "Where did you hear such a thing?"

"There is an office in Berlin," he replied, measuring his words carefully. "I don't know exactly where, but I know it exists because I met one of the men who was involved in its work. Like myself, he is a surgeon stationed at the army hospital in Berlin. I knew him slightly from my student days in the capital. He is really a very nice fellow." He paused for emphasis. "One evening he became loose-tongued after having a few drinks too many. Once he started talking there was no way to stop him. It was clear to me that he was being eaten alive by guilt."

I tried to follow what he was saying, but my mind still refused to register properly. An office for killing, staffed by surgeons? It didn't make any sense. I knew the Nazis were capable of many things, but this...

"They call it mercy killing," Karl continued, his voice laden with sarcasm. "As if they have any notion of mercy. On the other hand, they are very quickly becoming expert at killing."

Karl then proceeded to describe what he had heard. The Nazis were gassing deformed and retarded children, mentally ill adults, and the aged, and chronically ill inmates of nursing homes. As he spoke, his face alternately contorted and reddened; his voice, although subdued, was harsh and unrelenting. I had to hold onto the edge of the table as he concluded with a final, astonishing revelation. "And one of the men in charge of the program is none other than my dear Uncle Rolf."

"My God," I gasped, grasping my head between my hands, as if I were afraid it would burst apart. "Does Birgit have any idea?"

"We didn't talk about it directly," he replied. "But from certain things she said when I mentioned her father, I was fairly convinced that she knew something. I am sure that his prized son-in-law, Dieter, is also involved in the rotten mess."

I let out an involuntary groan. "Poor Birgit," I said, shaking my head. "What she must be going through. It must be unbearable for her. How could anyone do such things?"

"It doesn't really surprise me all that much," he replied. "There were many clues I should have picked up on when I was a medical student under my uncle's wing. I should have known what he was leading up to. He had this planned a long time ago. The trouble with me, though, was that I never thought all of his talk would amount to anything...all of those theories about a Master Race and survival of the fittest. I can't believe that I almost let myself be drawn into the slime." He shook his head. Then he added in a disgusted voice, "I should have done something."

"It doesn't make sense to blame yourself," I said. "There isn't a thing you could have done about it. Look what happened to your father for trying."

He raised his head. There was a mixture of anguish and pleading in his eyes. "At least he had the courage to try," he said softly. "If enough others had done as much, who knows what the results might have been."

As he spoke, I was struck by an unnerving realization: Karl had not come to me simply to tell me of the euthanasia program and his uncle's involvement in it. Although he did not realize it, like the dying general in Berlin, he felt the need to offer up a confession. How ironic it was. A blonde, blue-eyed Aryan, the outward model of Nazi perfection, had come to a Jew to ask forgiveness for a sin of omission. The final irony was, I was just as guilty as he.

***

Winter passed, and except for a number of remote battles at sea, war continued to be a word rather than an experience for the great majority of Germans. Our personal lives had settled into a difficult, but not impossible routine. My mother, schooled in the art of survival by the previous war and the chaotic peace that had followed, maintained a remarkable stability in our home, doing her chores and tending to my father's needs without complaint. The latter's condition had neither improved nor deteriorated. The only noticeable change was that now from time to time he might pick up the newspaper and read for several minutes before dozing off on the sofa, or, occasionally, turn on the radio and listen to the news with a faraway look on his face.

My own life continued to be dominated by waiting, waiting for a future I could not clearly visualize. For the most part my days were uneventful. To combat my growing depression, I had developed the routine of visiting my sister and nephew daily. Some days, when the weather was good, I took little Franz with me for a walk, or, hand-in-hand, we would board a tram and ride comfortably along the spotless Munich streets. I would point out the interesting sites to the fascinated three-year-old and tell him stories of my childhood experiences there, many of which included his father. In a certain way, I suppose, I was attempting to reassure myself that there had actually been a better past. One time I even took him to see the building that housed the firm now called Munich Heating, and tried to explain to him that his great-grandfather had been its founder. As I stood with him on the sidewalk and looked at the familiar structure, however, I felt only a strange emptiness; it was as if all of that had happened to someone else in another lifetime. I also showed him my other favorite places, such as the Botanical Gardens and the Hofgarten. I stood by smiling sadly as he chased after the little groups of stray pigeons, or laughed at a squirrel that happened to scamper by. I could not help worrying over the kind of tomorrows he was destined to have.

Spring approached, and with it came the clear indication that the *Sitzkrieg* was rapidly drawing to a close. The headlines in *The Munich Post* one day in early April seemed even larger and more frenetic than usual. German troops had landed in Scandinavia. With the swift conquest of Norway and Denmark (the Propaganda Ministry explained cynically that soldiers of the Reich now occupied the two Scandinavian countries to protect their neutrality), the Third Reich had been extended all the way up to the Arctic Circle.

One month later, the long expected thrust through the low countries began. In less than a week, Holland was added to the growing Nazi empire; eleven days later, Belgium. I began to wonder if Hitler had not been telling the truth in *Mein Kampf* when he stated that he was "...acting in the spirit of the Almighty Creator." As I pursued this line of thinking, another of his claims merged with the first one, namely, that he was doing the Lord's work by attacking the Jews. Always the Jews. Deep within me I had known from the beginning. This war was more than an attempt to gain power or territory, more that a quest for revenge. I knew, without having been aware of it, that in some enigmatic, twisted way, the Jews were and always had been directly involved. Always the Jews, I thought, tormented by doubt and self-hatred. Always the Jews. My time of waiting was swiftly coming to an end.

***

My father leaned toward the forbidden radio on the little end table, straining to hear the announcer. I stepped over and also put my ear close to the speaker. The announcement had just been made that the French had abandoned Paris; France had capitulated. The disgrace of 1918 had been avenged at last. The ecstatic voice became silent and the strains of the Imperial National Anthem "Deutschland, Deutschland, Über Alles" burst forth. I studied my father's expression as he shifted his weight against the high sofa back and absent-mindedly rubbed the stump of his leg. For a moment I thought I saw a faint smile flicker across his face, but it faded at once and was replaced by a perplexed frown. He closed his eyes and retreated into a troubled sleep.

***

In spite of spectacular military successes, the atmosphere in Munich was subdued. Isolated from virtually everyone but my family and Frau Linsdorff, I could only guess the reason for so little enthusiasm. Dr. Griep summed up the general attitude one afternoon during his weekly house visit to my father. He had just finished his examination and was getting ready to leave. As I accompanied him to the door, he turned and said, "You should try to get him to exercise a bit. The worst thing for his heart is for him to lie around all day and vegetate. Stir him up a bit if you can. Get his blood moving. I tried, but I couldn't even get him to argue with me. Maybe you will have more success."

"I'm afraid it's hopeless," I replied. "He won't even strap on his artificial leg anymore. I don't think he ever wants to leave the apartment again. Most of the time he acts as if he isn't even here."

Dr. Griep nodded his head. "I don't blame him for that," he said, shifting his medical bag from one hand to the other. "This isn't exactly the best place in the world to be at this point in history, particularly for him and the rest of you." He shook his head sadly and stepped toward the foyer. "I don't understand a bit of it. Everything has been turned topsy-turvy." We had reached the door. "By the way," he added, turning to face me. "Have you heard from Karl lately? The last letter I received from him was over three weeks ago. The postmark had been snipped out, so I can't be sure where he was writing from. He really didn't say much of anything. The censors are very strict these days."

"Jutta did get a letter last week," I replied. "But it was pretty much the same as yours. If I had to bet, I would say that he was sent along with the invasion force to the low countries. The last time I talked to him he told me that he expected to be sent there. Hitler is providing doctors with bigger and better injuries to patch up. All for the glorious Fatherland, of course."

"Don't worry, Heinrich," he replied, patting my shoulder affectionately. "They aren't fooling everyone with their propaganda. No matter how gloriously they try to paint the war, I think most of the people are against it. Whether they say it or not, they would rather keep their sons and brothers alive and healthy than have them blown apart for some meaningless military victory. I'm sure the British won't knuckle under so easily, the way the French did. Hitler has finally met his match in Churchill. He is not the kind of fellow to be frightened by threats or deceived by sweet talk. I fear, my young friend, that before this thing is over, the German people will pay the price for this madness."

Dr. Griep's prophecy began to come true in August as British bombers launched retaliatory bombing raids on major German cities. Now we had more than the dreaded knock on the door to worry about. With increasing frequency, the silence of the night was broken by the terrifying wail of air raid sirens, and the explosions of anti-aircraft shells and bombs. War had arrived in Munich.

***

"Don't worry," I assured my worried sister as I took Franz by the hand and opened the door. "It is very unlikely that the English will attack a flower garden." It was a bright summer day; I had decided to take advantage of the weather and bring my nephew to the Botanical Gardens. So far, the British bombing raids had only been on military and industrial targets. And so, with Franz' hand securely in mine, I set out in the direction of Sophienstrasse.

I stood next to my nephew at the edge of the little pond as he giggled and pointed at the large goldfish clearly visible just below the surface of the water.

"Gofish," he shrieked happily, turning to me and clapping his hands together. Then he looked beyond me, smiled even more broadly and cried out, "Oma, see the gofish!"

I swiveled my head around and for a split second thought I was hallucinating. Frau Linsdorff was standing on the pathway several yards away, next to her a younger woman. I blinked once or twice to make sure I was not mistaken. There was no mistake.

"Birgit," I gasped, rooted to the spot for several seconds.

"There is so little time," she said, her eyes still filled with tears. "I would have gotten to you earlier today, but I had to make sure that no one was following me. I'm sure I am worrying for nothing, but the only thing I could think of was what would happen if we were seen together." She squeezed my hand, looked around nervously and added, "If he ever found out..."

We were sitting in a gazebo in a relatively remote section of the garden. Several strollers made their way along the paths on both sides without paying particular attention to us. I reached out and drew her to me. The fragrance of the dark red roses that clung to the trellis surrounding us was replaced by the familiar scent of her skin and hair.

"I would have left him long ago if I weren't so afraid for all of us," she said, her lips drawn tightly around her teeth in an angry scowl. "I hate myself for being such a coward. But you just can't imagine how it is...the unspoken threats. Oh, Heinrich, they are capable of doing terrible things. I feel so lost." She trembled as she spoke.

"You don't have to explain. I know about your father," I replied, stroking her soft hair gently. She pulled back suddenly and put her hand to her mouth.

"How?" she asked in a choked voice. "How did you find out?"

"From Karl," I answered. "He didn't really want to tell me, but it was eating away at him. Anyway, it won't remain secret for very long. Sooner or later, it is bound to become public."

"I am so ashamed," she whispered, her shoulders sagging. "And I have been so afraid of what you would think of me, afraid you might hate me. To think that my father could do such things."

"I would sooner hate my life," I said, kissing her hair. "You are no more to blame for what is happening than I am. The Nazis are the ones who believe in genetic guilt. If evil were inherited, people like your Uncle Paul, Karl, and you would not exist."

We sat and talked quietly for another hour or so, less interested in the content of our conversation than in the fact that we were finally together again. When the time came for us to separate, we renewed our promise to keep in contact, no matter what the price, but our eyes betrayed our words.

***

As 1940 drew on there was no end to the war in sight, despite the Führer's promise of an early victory. By late autumn, bombs fell with increasing frequency on many German cities. Few people were comforted by the reports that London was being systematically leveled by the Luftwaffe. There were no cheers in the movie theaters when the German newsreels showed the English capital in flames. Even the Nazi-controlled press indirectly expressed impatience. For the first time questions were raised and guilt assigned. No one seemed to have a satisfactory answer.

In October, a frightening incident forced me to end my outdoor excursions. Twice within the space of a week I was stopped on the street and asked for identification. On the first such occasion I was not unduly alarmed; the policeman routinely examined my papers and returned them to me without comment. The second time, however, it was quite a different story.

I had taken Franz to the Marienplatz. We were walking to the tram station to return home when I was suddenly confronted by a burly fellow who identified himself as Gestapo and demanded my papers. While he waited for me to comply, he asked me gruffly why I was not in uniform, eyeing me suspiciously the whole time. I explained that I was Jewish.

"You have the nerve to come out and mix with decent people, do you?" he hissed, a malicious expression on his bloated face. "And what are you doing with that child?" he added, pointing at my nephew. He was obviously puzzled by the boy's Aryan appearance. Franz clung tightly to my hand as I explained that he was my sister's son and that his father was a German officer at the front. Instead of softening his attitude, however, this information sent the Gestapo agent into a rage. He literally threw my papers back at me. Then he unleashed a stream of profanities directed not only at me, but also at the "traitor to his blood," who had dishonored his country just to "get between a filthy Jewish bitch's legs." The veins in his neck bulged out so far that I thought they would burst. At one point he raised his hand to strike me, and probably would have had Franz not cried out in fright and huddled more closely against me.

I stood there in a state of shock, waiting for his tirade to run its course. People walked hurriedly by us, their eyes averted. After what seemed like an eternity, he dismissed me with a final flurry of abuse. Shaken and humiliated, I made my way quickly back to Frau Linsdorff's. At one point Franz tugged on my hand and asked, "What did you do bad?"

I felt a lump rise in my throat as I answered, quite honestly, "I'm not sure, Franz. I'm really not sure."

How could I have told him that my crime was having been born a Jew?

***

We had a surprise visitor one morning in late November. Maurice Benoit was a tall, intense looking man in his early forties. His bright orange hair, although thinning slightly in front and greying at the temples, was still very striking, as was his lean, muscular frame.

"Good day," he said, as I opened the door and looked up into his pleasant face, towering some five or six inches above mine. "My name is Maurice. And you must be Heinrich." He extended his hand and without waiting for me to confirm his deduction added, "I am a friend of your sister and Joshua." His German was clear and correct, but spoken with a clearly discernible French accent.

"And so you must not worry, Frau Hartstein," he concluded, wiping the remaining egg from his plate with a thick hunk of bread. "Ursel and Joshua are doing well. They have many friends in Paris. Besides, they are not exactly unfamiliar with living in a country temporarily occupied by the Nazis." He smiled ironically and delicately deposited the dripping bread into his mouth. After he had swallowed his mouthful, he leaned toward my mother and added, "Before too long we will drive those roaches back into the woodwork where they belong." Then he looked at his wristwatch, got up with extreme agility for a man his size, and stepped over to the window overlooking the street. Standing to the side, he swept his eyes from one side to the other. Satisfied with his findings, he stepped back to us.

"I must leave now," he said. "It wouldn't do to keep my punctual German colleagues at Party Headquarters waiting." He took my mother's hand and kissed it gallantly. Then he and I walked over to the hall door. As we got there, he turned to me and said very quietly, "There is a very difficult time ahead for us, Heinrich, a very difficult time. I will do all I can to take care of your sister." Then he embraced me, opened the door and hurried away.

"I am glad Ursel and Joshua have such friends," my mother said, as she gathered the lunch dishes and silverware together. "It was kind of him to try to spare me worry, but not at all necessary. If I were there I would join them." She had stopped what she was doing and turned to face me. I returned her gaze and nodded, envious of my sister and brother-in-law. Apparently, they had found the opportunity to fight back, while here in Munich we were virtual prisoners.

Maurice Benoit's visit raised our spirits, at least temporarily. We became aware that there were defects in the supposedly flawless Nazi machine. How active or widespread the resistance movement was, or what role this tall, red-haired Frenchman played in it, I could only guess. What mattered most was that we were not alone.

***

The winter seemed colder and greyer that year. Food and fuel were scarce, and yet we endured. Incredible as it sounds, I found myself more bored than frightened during this period. Each day was the same as the one before it, with no incentives, and little reason to hope that the situation would change. I began to withdraw into myself, just as my father had, not in imitation of him, but out of some primitive survival instinct. Even my visits with Franz, now less frequent, failed to penetrate the gloom. I felt increasingly isolated.

The radio was our only reliable link to the outside world, but it was also becoming a source of anxiety. After my unpleasant experience with the Gestapo, I became more cautious. Although I had known all along that if we were reported by a zealous neighbor the result might be a heavy fine and possible arrest, I had never really believed it could happen to us. But I was no longer so sure. As a precaution against this possibility, I now kept the radio hidden far in the back of the study closet. On most evenings I took it out and listened to the latest reports from the BBC and the local German stations, the volume set at a level barely audible. This routine ended one afternoon in late January. I was sitting in the living room, writing in my daily journal, when my mother came in. I knew that she could not have finished shopping for the day's rations, since it had been less than an hour since she left (a fraction of the usual time necessary). When I saw the frightened expression on her face I knew something was very wrong.

"We must get rid of the radio, Heinrich," she said frantically. "We must get rid of it at once." I put down my pen and looked up at her quizzically. "I met Frau Feder on my way to the grocer's. She told me that someone has reported us. She didn't say who it was, but I think it was Frau Wenzel. Who else could it have been?"

I stood up quickly, my mind racing. My first inclination was to try to find a better hiding place, but I quickly rejected that. The Gestapo, I reasoned, or whoever else handled such matters, was probably expert at finding hidden radios. There was only one solution: I would bring it to the Linsdorff's.

I quickly wrapped the bulky radio in some plain brown paper and set out for Brienner Strasse. I tiptoed past Frau Wenzel's floor like a burglar, feeling both fearful and foolish as the stairs creaked in spite of my caution. My heart racing, I finally reached the street, quite relieved to find it practically deserted. With my head down, I battled my way through the bitter cold January wind. My arms ached and my breath came in short gasps by the time I reached the Linsdorff's apartment building. In spite of the freezing temperatures, I was coated with perspiration. I quickly ducked into the house and closed the hall door behind me, feeling an incredible sense of victory.

In the days that immediately followed, I waited for the Gestapo to come and search our apartment for the illegal apparatus. But no one came. The absurdity of that episode only became clear to me sometime later when I learned that the Nazis had that very month begun the process of "resettlement" of Jews, Poles and any others of the conquered peoples of Europe who were not "racially valuable." Thus, while this massive shifting of human cargo was taking place, one which was a rehearsal for terrible things to come, I had been expending my energies to move a radio the distance of scarcely more than a kilometer.

***

Karl came home on his second leave in late February. As soon as I saw him, I sensed a profound change. His eyes were sunken and devoid of life; there were deep lines running down from the corners of his eyes and mouth.

"Greetings, Heinrich," he said, as I stepped into the foyer, shaking the snowflakes from my head and brushing my sleeves with the backs of my hands. I returned his greeting and we embraced silently. The sentimental scene was suddenly interrupted by little Franz who came running into the foyer.

"See, Unca Heinrich," he chirped. "My daddy is home! My daddy is home!" Karl turned and scooped his son up into his arms, a weary but happy smile creasing his face even more.

"I have to report back in a week," he said, rubbing his eyes as if to rid them of an unpleasant image. It was about eight o'clock in the evening. We were sitting in Judge Linsdorff's study.

"You look like you have been through hell," I observed, taking the glass of wine he held out to me. "It was terrible, wasn't it?"

"It seems like a distant nightmare," he replied softly. "It's hard to believe that little more than a year has gone by since I was last home. It seems so much longer."

"You were at the front during the heavy fighting, weren't you?" I asked, as he began to rub his eyes again. "You didn't say very much in your letters. We were worried."

"I thought I would save the censors some work," he replied. "But you needn't have worried. Doctors are not like infantrymen. They don't have to go out into the field and fight hand-to-hand with some other poor slobs who also happen to have been born in the wrong place at the wrong time. Our job is simply to put the pieces back together." He shook his head sadly and went on. "To answer your question, though, I was in Belgium and France, but one country looks just like another when you're in a field hospital. Torn up stomachs, crushed skulls, bloody entrails...they don't differ with the location." His voice trailed off momentarily. When he began to speak again there was bitterness in his tone.

"But I must admit that it was invaluable practice for me. While it took some of those young heroes at least eighteen years to grow a leg or an arm, I learned how to cut one off very neatly in just a few minutes. And sometimes, when we had no anesthesia, I did it even faster. But we shouldn't feel depressed about things like that. As the Führer has often said, 'Pain purifies man for his higher task.' A true German warrior should accept pain as a sublime duty to Führer and Fatherland. *Sieg heil!*" He threw his head back and drained his glass with a single gulp. Then, frowning, he snapped, "The dirty bastards! They really have screwed up our lives. In some ways it really is easier to be on the battlefield than it is to be here. At least there I can fool myself into thinking that I make a difference, that I am balancing things out a bit by saving a life here and there. I have even managed to piece together a few Belgian and Dutch bodies. All I can do here, though, is stand by helplessly and watch like everyone else." He leaned back and let his eyes wander across his father's neatly ordered bookshelves.

"You have read most of this," he continued, sweeping his hand out in an arc. "What do you suppose the great thinkers would say about what is happening in Germany today? Socrates, Shakespeare, Goethe? What solutions would they offer?"

"Great thinkers don't offer solutions," I said, wishing I could break through the suffocating gloom. "At best, they present the problems and wait for those who are more practical to come along and act out the solutions. Thinkers are cursed with the inability to act. While they are examining the various alternatives, many times alternatives that don't even really exist, the pragmatists sweep them aside as swiftly and easily as a charwoman wipes dust from the woodwork."

I had no sooner finished saying this when the wail of an air raid siren began in the distance. Minutes later, there was the frighteningly familiar thud of bombs. From time to time the windowpanes rattled, and a flash of light penetrated the thick curtains.

"The sights and sounds of pragmatism," Karl quipped, motioning with his head toward the window. I managed a weak smile and nodded. We sat there without speaking until long after the all clear had sounded.

***

The number of casualties continued to mount as the British bombing raids gained intensity. Conveniently forgetting Warsaw, Rotterdam, and London, the Munich newspapers continuously condemned the "savage enemy" for their indiscriminate slaughter of innocent civilians in Berlin and other German cities. Munich also suffered. Our nerves were strained to the breaking point because we were so vulnerable to attack. More than one residential area had already been struck; the sirens were no longer always in the distance. In spite of this, the Nazi juggernaut continued to crush everything and everyone in its path. By spring we read that German troops had moved into Greece and Yugoslavia. And then, in June, Hitler again demonstrated that the vows he had made in *Mein Kampf* were not intended as rhetoric as he unleashed the armies of the Reich on Soviet Russia. I read the screaming headlines of *The Munich Post* with fascination and disbelief: the feared Second Front had exploded under a wilting barrage of Nazi bombs and shells.

The people of Munich were bewildered. Their Soviet ally became a treacherous enemy overnight. For me and my family, though, the news had a very personal meaning. Karl was being sent to the Eastern Front.

"It arrived this morning," Jutta said, reaching into her pocketbook and withdrawing the letter. "I am really worried, Heinrich. He avoids saying anything that will upset me, but I can tell from his tone that it must be terrible there."

I skimmed the short letter quickly. There were the usual inquiries about everyone's health, assurance that he was doing well, and then the almost offhand sentence that he would be visiting the Szmulskis very soon.

"He guessed that the censors would overlook that," I commented, anticipating Jutta's question. "He'll be all right," I added, giving her back the letter with a slightly unsteady hand. "They don't put doctors up on the front lines." I said this with conviction, although I feared that the war in the Soviet Union would not follow any conventional order.

***

There was one bright spot that summer. In mid-July Frau Linsdorff received unexpected news about her husband. She told me excitedly of the phone call she had gotten from a man identifying himself as a friend of Judge Linsdorff, and how, in response to his request, she had agreed to meet with him in the main court building to discuss a matter of "importance."

The caller was an attorney from Karlsruhe who had known Karl's father some years before. Speaking very quickly, he explained to Frau Linsdorff that, although he had been a staunch conservative and an early supporter of Hitler, his support quickly changed to criticism in the aftermath of the Reichstag fire. When he openly protested the "illegal" jailing of the opposition, the Nazis demonstrated their appreciation for irony by arresting him as well, and shipping him off to Dachau. He had made it a point to seek out Judge Linsdorff when the latter arrived in the camp, and eventually was able to have the judge placed in the camp laundry with himself and other trusted "politicals."

Frau Linsdorff was unable to answer any of my questions about the general conditions in the camp. She explained that there simply had not been enough time to discuss any of these details; the former attorney, who had either inadvertently or intentionally not given his name, was quite nervous during their meeting and seemed eager to deliver his short message and leave. At any rate, her main concern was that her husband was well and was not being mistreated.

My initial reaction to what Frau Linsdorff told me was also a feeling of relief. As I thought about it during the next days, however, I became increasingly depressed. I realized how pathetic we had all become. A brilliant, eloquent jurist, a man whose only crime was that he desired justice and truth, had been consigned to the laundry of a notorious concentration camp, and we regarded this as a stroke of good fortune.

From then on there would be no more "strokes of good fortune" for us in the Third Reich. The growing frustration of the people was becoming more and more overt as another winter approached with no end to the war in sight. For the most part, this feeling was not expressed directly; nevertheless, from the tone and content of the reports in the newspapers I was able to piece together a fairly good picture of the true state of public opinion. In addition to the daily reports of spectacular victories in the east, and close-up photographs of the extensive destruction done by the Luftwaffe to London and other English cities, there was an ongoing undercurrent of rebuke directed at the German people for their growing cynicism and doubt. The authors of these didactic pieces chided those who dared suggest that victory was not inevitable, reminding them with thinly veiled threats that to doubt this would be to doubt their Führer.

As much as the people might have been growing sceptical about their leaders, however, there was little reaction when the announcement of the latest anti-Jewish measure was made. My stomach churned and my head began to pound as I read the details in the newspaper on that early September morning: Jews over six years of age would have to wear a Jewish star when they appeared in public. In keeping with their mania for detail, they gave exact stipulations for their pseudolegal mark of Cain:

> *The Jewish star is a yellow piece of cloth with*
> *a black border, in the form of a six-pointed star*
> *of the size of the palm of the hand. The inscription*
> *reads 'Jew,' in black letters. It shall be worn*
> *visibly, sewn on the left chest of the garment.*

I dropped the paper onto the table and gasped. The tension of the past years seemed to reach its culmination in this latest profanity. Cradling my head between my hands, I began to weep. My body rocked back and forth as if under the control of an external force, and deep guttural sounds burst forth from my throat. And yet, through all of this a part of my mind remained unnaturally clear; I felt as if I had suddenly been split into two separate beings, one a calm spectator to the disintegration of the other. I remember being struck by a strange idea as I rocked rhythmically: I am praying, I thought; for the first time in my life I am praying as only a Jew can. With tears.

My mother reacted to the new decree with outward calm, but I could see that it also affected her deeply.

"We are marked already," she told me when I brought the subject up that evening. "This does not change anything. We know very well who we are."

She was right, of course, but for some reason the visual reminder of my subjugation was the most difficult of all for me to endure. Some weeks before, I had put my fears aside and begun to emerge from our apartment more frequently. This came to a halt in September. I could almost feel the yellow star burning into my flesh when I donned my jacket to go out; I began to take a briefcase with me each time I went, holding it high against my chest to conceal what I considered a badge of shame. I found myself envying the people I saw in the street, those who were able to walk wherever they pleased without any trace of self-consciousness, their hands dangling smugly at their sides. My disorientation was so complete that I even began to feel estranged from my sister Jutta, who was excluded from the decree because she was "living in a mixed marriage."

My father's reaction was quite different from mine. His fighting spirit, dormant for some time, was aroused. His anger reached a high point on the day my mother began the task of sewing the neat, six-pointed stars to our clothing, cut carefully from the swatch of yellow material she had secured for that purpose. My father sat across from her without saying a word, watching as she swiftly and masterfully raised and lowered the needle.

"Those filthy sons of bitches!" he bellowed, shaking his fist at the air. Then he lapsed into silence, but he did not fall asleep. His eyes kept following my mother's needle as if it were a magic wand.

Later that afternoon we learned what he had been thinking as he sat there. Neither my mother nor I took much notice when he disappeared into his bedroom; we assumed that he was going to take his usual nap. A short time later, however, he emerged again, dressed in his old army uniform, which although wrinkled and smelling strongly of camphor, still fit him passingly well. Instead of the yellow star demanded by law, however, he wore on his chest the Iron Cross First Class, a clear violation of Article Two of the decree forbidding Jews to wear "medals, decorations or other insignia."

My mother paled as he stood there shakily, a strange smile on his face. At first she tried to reason with him not to carry out his act of defiance, and when this did not work she pleaded, pointing out that his heart was not strong enough to withstand such stress. But she knew that he had made his decision and that nothing would deter him from carrying it out.

"I must do this," he said with uncharacteristic gentleness. "Try to understand, Esi, I have no choice."

I stood quietly at the side of the room and watched the drama unfold. My father looked from my mother to me and in the same soft tone added, "You understand, don't you, Heinchen?"

I nodded, feeling a mixture of pride, anxiety, and futility. My mother had also turned to me. When she saw that I would not help her to dissuade him, she turned back to my father.

"Very well then, Erich, we will go together," she said firmly. To my surprise, he did not protest. Minutes later I watched from the window as my parents slowly walked arm-in-arm along the sidewalk in the direction of the busy Ludwigstrasse.

An hour later the doorbell began to ring insistently. I threw down the book I had been unsuccessfully trying to concentrate on and rushed down the stairs to the lower hall. My father was leaning against the wall breathing heavily; my mother stood at his side, struggling to support him. Except for the thin, white scars that crisscrossed it, his face was red and covered with perspiration.

"Help me to bring him upstairs," my mother said. She was clearly exhausted. I stepped quickly over to them and grasped my father around the waist, placing one of his arms around my shoulder. He offered no resistance. With my mother on the other side, we slowly managed to get him back to our apartment and over to the living room sofa. He slumped heavily onto the soft cushions, his breath coming in short, labored gasps.

"I'm all right, stop your fussing," he said, resisting weakly as my mother handed him a glass of brandy and then began to loosen his collar while he sipped from it. She ignored his protests and began to unstrap his artificial leg.

"We showed them, didn't we, Esi?" he mumbled, rubbing the stump of his leg with the heel of his hand. "We showed the sons of bitches a thing or two."

She smiled. I could see both love and sorrow in her eyes as she replied, "Yes we did, Captain Hartstein. We showed them."

My mother's voice strained as she recounted their experience of the afternoon to Dr. Griep and me. The doctor had just given my father a sedative; the latter was resting comfortably.

"And when the shopkeeper saw the yellow star on my sweater he refused to let us come in to rest for a few minutes. He told me that he was sorry, but it was bad for business to have someone die in his store. He eventually did bring a cup of water out to us, but your father threw it down onto the sidewalk and cursed him. People just walked by as if they hadn't heard or seen anything. I don't know how we managed to make it back home."

Dr. Griep patted my mother's arm and said reassuringly. "He is all right, Frau Hartstein. He is a very strong man. He just isn't used to so much walking anymore. He overdid it."

My mother shook her head slowly from side to side. "Can you imagine?" she asked in amazement. "They would have let him die right there on the sidewalk."

"Try to forgive them," the doctor replied. "They are just as confused and afraid as you are. It has gotten to the point where they cannot even trust their own children. I have heard stories from some of my patients that make my skin crawl."

"How you can defend them?" I interrupted. "From what I have seen, they just don't care what happens to Jews, as long as it doesn't affect their lives. If you were anything like them you wouldn't be here right now risking yourself."

He smiled sadly. "Not everyone is as cantankerous as I am. I'm a lot like your father in that way. Besides, I am too old to frighten. No, I am not a valid measurement for comparison. If I were younger, just starting out, who knows how I would react?" His voice trailed off; there was a thoughtful expression on his face.

"So then it is perfectly all right to stand by and watch as human beings are treated worse than animals," I countered angrily. "As long as one has something to lose by being decent."

Dr. Griep shook his head and lowered his eyes. Finally, he looked up and said, "No, Heinrich, it is not all right. I guess I really am getting to be an old fool. There is really no excuse for any of it."

***

A new, terrifying word entered the Nazi lexicon: resettlement. Now the Aryans were not alone in dreading the arrival of the mail each day, fearing the standard grey envelope containing official condolences and heartfelt thanks from the Führer and Reich to the family of a warrior who had fallen heroically while fighting for his country. For the Jews of Nazi Germany the sight of the letter carrier was as much, if not more, a cause for trepidation. While the letter they unfolded with trembling fingers could not possibly announce the loss of an heroic loved one on the field of battle, it could, as we ourselves would soon learn, evoke an equal measure of grief.

My mother heard about it first. Although she rarely complained, I knew from our meager meals that it was becoming increasingly difficult for her to secure even the severely restricted rations allotted to Jews. Had it not been for Jutta and Frau Linsdorff, who shared their ration cards with us, we would never have enjoyed the rare "prohibited" items such as fruit, meat and coffee from time to time. One day in late November, she returned from a particularly gruelling effort to acquire some staples.

"I met Frau Grünfeld today at Sabatini's," she said, as she stepped into the foyer. I took the shopping bag from her hand and led the way into the kitchen. "You know who I mean, don't you?" She wiggled out of her jacket, folded it neatly over the kitchen chair in such a way that the large yellow star no longer showed, and then began to carefully empty the homemade canvas bag of the few items she had managed to get. As I tried to place the familiar name in my mind, she added, "Her son was your schoolmate years ago. You remember, don't you? His name is Hirsch."

"Of course," I said, as the memory of Herr Kulp's class flooded back into my mind. "I didn't even know that Hirsch Grünfeld was still in Munich."

"He isn't," she replied. "Not any longer." There was a nervous edge to her voice that I hadn't noticed at first, a hint of inner panic.

"How did she know who you were?" I asked, afraid to ask the obvious question. I noticed her hand shaking slightly as she began to cut some thin slices off a loaf of black bread.

"We meet at Herr Sabatini's store now and then," she replied, as if relieved to have been temporarily distracted from her main point. "Many Jewish women shop there. He is one of the few who still serves Jewish customers. He is originally from Florence, Italy." Her words did not flow freely. She was obviously struggling to maintain her composure. Suddenly, she threw the bread knife down onto the table and looked up into my face. My stomach knotted as I saw the fear in her eyes.

"What is it, Mama?" I asked, not really wanting to hear the answer.

She took a deep breath and grasped the edge of the table. Her voice faltered as she replied, "She told me that her son was taken away last week to work to serve in a labor battalion somewhere in the north. She doesn't even know where he is. It happened just last week. He had to report to the railroad station with many others. Heinrich, I am so terribly frightened."

The knot in my stomach had tightened as she spoke. A sudden picture of Hirsch standing up to Otto Eberthal with flailing arms and a bleeding lip so many, many years before came into my mind.

"And the rest of the family, she, her husband, and a daughter who still lives with them received notice two days ago that they are to report to the railroad station three weeks from now for 'resettlement' in the east. She told me that she knew of others who have gotten similar notification. Can it be possible? They are taking people away, Heinrich, taking them away. What can we do?"

I felt the strength drain from my legs at the ominous words "resettlement in the east." What did that mean, I wondered, thinking of the coded message Karl had written for me in one of his recent letters to Jutta: "Tell Heinrich that the exploits of the glorious German forces in Russia far surpass those in Poland." I thought of the dying general and what he had told Karl about Nazi atrocities in Poland. But I quickly suppressed the thought, afraid to draw the logical conclusion.

***

I could scarcely believe it: Hitler had declared war on the United States. Jutta and Frau Linsdorff stood in the doorway, listening intently as the Nazi commentator launched a scathing attack on this latest enemy of the Reich who had "provoked the Führer beyond human endurance, and would now feel the might of German arms." I put my fingers to my lips to shush Franz who had begun to whine because I had inadvertently knocked over the house of blocks we had been building together. He looked to his mother and grandmother for support, and when he saw that none was forthcoming, he sat still and pretended to listen to the radio along with us.

I felt numb; it was as if my brain had been suddenly immersed in a vat of ice water. I thought of Uncle Solomon and the others in New York, and wondered how they were reacting to this latest news. As the voice on the radio launched a vicious attack on American President Roosevelt, my concentration slipped.

"They are madmen," hissed my sister. "As if they haven't caused enough heartache." She looked from me to her mother-in-law for some response. I looked away, still unable to put my thoughts together coherently. Frau Linsdorff stood next to her, silently wringing her hands. Her hair, which had turned almost totally white during the past two or three years, framed a drawn, pale face.

"Come," she said softly to Jutta, as she turned to go back into the kitchen. "We must finish our package for Karl and get it to the post office."

I sat there for several more minutes, although by then I could no longer focus my attention on the avalanche of words from the radio. To Franz' delight, I numbly picked up a few blocks and began to rebuild our broken structure.

***

Although the reports from the front continued to describe overwhelming victories over the Soviet armies, it was clear to all but the most fanatical Nazi followers that the campaign in Russia was not going as expected. The Russians had held. It was more than a month since we had received any word from Karl; the few short notes he had sent had been almost entirely limited to expressions of concern and love for his family. And now even that had ceased. We comforted each other and ourselves with rationalizations: we repeated numbly that no news was good news, that a doctor at the front probably had no time to think, let alone write, and that the packages of food and other small items that Jutta and Karl's mother managed to scrape together regularly to send to him seemed to be getting through. Just beneath the surface of our words, however, was an unspoken fear.

***

To say that it happened suddenly would be more than absurd in view of all I have already written, and yet when the bottom did finally fall out of our world in early 1942, it still seemed to hit like a bolt from the blue. How could that be possible? I had read Hitler's writings and seen them translated into action in the form of the Nuremberg Laws and the many other anti-Jewish measures that followed; I had stood by helplessly while my grandfather's life and the fruits of his labor were devoured by the insatiable Nazi machinery; I knew from Judge Linsdorff's example what their response to opposition of any kind could be; I had heard of the terrible atrocities in Poland and imagined their intensification in Russia. How then could I have been shocked by what followed? And yet it was so. And yet it was so.

The first major jolt came in late January. After almost two months of silence, we finally received word about Karl. In a terse, official form letter the army informed Jutta that her husband was missing in action.

"Is my daddy dead?" Franz tugged at my sleeve as he spoke, his face turned up questioningly.

I patted his head and bent down. "No, Franz, of course not. Your daddy is not dead," I said, feeling as if my heart was being torn from my chest. I gathered him in my arms and held him close to me, afraid that I would break down completely were I to say more. The muffled sounds of Jutta's and Frau Linsdorff's weeping were faintly audible from the kitchen.

I spent the next weeks in a daze. Each day I checked with my sister to see if there had been any further word on Karl, but there was none. My sleep was troubled by horrible nightmares. Scenes of exploding bombs and raging fire alternated with those of vast wastelands of ice and snow. One dream in particular repeated itself night after night: I saw my friend's face, now smiling, now twisted with pain and bleeding. He was reaching out his arms. And then I saw myself standing across a huge, burning pit, straining, but unable to reach him. Blocking my path was a huge, grotesque, yellow and black object that seemed to be continually changing from a six-pointed star into a twisted cross.

***

The letter carrier brought tragedy to Jägerstrasse in mid-March. Our turn had finally come.

"Here, let me see that," my father bellowed, reaching out from his chair and snatching the sheet of paper from my mother's hand. She stood there for several seconds with a haunted expression on her face, her eyes strangely empty. I moved behind my father and attempted to read over his shoulder, but because of his failing eyesight he held the letter too far out in front of himself for me to be able to see it clearly. He must have reread the letter several times. A good five minutes or so passed before he roughly folded it together and crammed it into his bathrobe pocket. He was extremely agitated. When he tried to lift himself from the sofa, though, he lost his balance and fell back down onto his side, causing the springs to groan loudly beneath his weight. I hurried around to help him, but he pushed me away with surprising force, and after a short struggle managed to right himself again. Then, with an expression on his face that I shall never forget — an expression of helpless pleading mixed with disbelief — he looked over to my mother and said in a broken, scarcely recognizable voice, "What are we going to do, Esi? My God, what are we going to do now?"

She bent over him and kissed him on the top of the head the way one might kiss a child. "We will be all right as long as we are together," she replied, directing her gaze at me as she choked back her tears. But her voice was as devoid of conviction as her eyes were of life.

Unlike Hirsch Grünfeld's parents, mine were supplied a destination in their notice of resettlement. On April 3, they were to report to the main railroad station at the civilized hour of nine-thirty in the morning. From there they would be taken to a place called Theresienstadt. What was it? A concentration camp? A city? None of us had ever heard the name. And if my parents were to be sent there, what was my fate to be? The letter had named only them and had been very specific, listing exact details as to how much luggage they would be permitted to take with them, as well as a clear warning not to pass on any of their movable belongings to a third party. Their dwelling was now, it declared, property of the Reich. Through a woman whose husband had been a friend and admirer of Judge Linsdorff, Karl's mother was able to get us a partial answer to our first question. Within days, the answer to the second question came from the offices of the Reich Labor Bureau. In both cases, there was some slight cause for hope.

"Theresienstadt is an old Czech garrison town south of Dresden, right about here." Karl's mother indicated a location somewhere between Prague and Dresden on the large map of Europe she had spread out on the table in front of us. "Frau Meyer assured me that it is not a concentration camp in the normal sense. I believe she used the term 'ghetto' to describe it."

My throat constricted involuntarily as I listened. It was ludicrous. "'In the normal sense?'" I repeated, hardly believing my ears. The fact that a concentration camp could be described as normal clearly demonstrated how far Germany had sunk during the past eight years. I swallowed hard and waited for her to continue.

"It seems," she went on explaining, her voice trembling slightly, "as if it was established specifically for the resettlement of certain privileged categories. Jewish war veterans are one such group. That is why your father..."

"Privileged categories," I spit out scornfully, unable to restrain my anger any longer. "Privileged in what way? Privileged to have their lives turned upside down because they committed the terrible crime of being born Jewish? I suppose my father should be grateful to his German masters for rewarding him so richly. Privileged categories indeed." I was shouting by this time.

Karl's mother stood impassively, waiting for me to finish venting my spleen. When she was finally satisfied that I had, she replied, "I can't blame you for feeling the way you do, Heinrich. No day passes that I do not want to shout out my anger too. First my Paul and then Karl. These are the rich rewards we have gotten, the privileges those monsters have given us."

I was too mentally drained to reply. As I stared down at the map I could not help but notice that, at least on paper, Dachau and Theresienstadt were not all that far from each other. Not very far at all.

For several days after the arrival of my parents' notice of resettlement, we were unable to fully believe what was happening. I tried to convince myself that an error had been made. There was always that possibility, remote as it might have been. This idea was strengthened two days later when my father's pension check arrived on schedule. Surely they would not have continued his pension if they intended to deport him. The fact that my name had not appeared on the document was another straw to clutch at. After all, I was officially registered as an inhabitant of the apartment. Perhaps there was another couple named Hartstein. Perhaps I should make inquiries at the appropriate government offices. Perhaps...

Any speculation about a bureaucratic error was brought to an abrupt halt less than a week later. This time the letter in the drab, grey envelope was addressed to me. They had not forgotten me; nor was I going to Theresienstadt with my parents. Above the detested swastika seal and the signature of some petty official was a terse form letter informing me that I was to report to the railroad station on the twenty-third of March for transport to the site of my Reich labor assignment. In three days, my waiting would finally be over.

***

It is very early in the morning. My mother is weeping as she hugs me tightly to herself. We promise to write to each other as soon as Jutta can give us the respective addresses. My father appears in the doorway, supported on the crutches he has always hated so much. We have already said our farewells, but I step over to him and extend my hand one more time. We shake hands almost formally, each of us unable to speak. We are crying too. I feel as if my lungs will burst unless I get out into the fresh air. I pick up my suitcases and head for the door, bumping the suitcases painfully against my legs as I try to squeeze through. Finally, I am in the hall making my way to the staircase. I descend the familiar stairs for the last time. As I pass Frau Wenzel's door I give in to a sudden whim, step over to it and kick it two or three times with considerable force. I turn back to the stairs and go down the final flight without looking back. As I step out into the street I feel a sense of relief. I head for the tram station, making no effort to cover the large yellow star on my coat. I manage to find a free spot at the rear of the tram, and now stand straddling my cases. It is only as we approach the familiar station that I begin to feel ill. By chance my eyes meet those of a young woman who is standing across from me near the exit. The star on her light green spring coat seems very small in keeping with her diminutive size. Her face is frozen in an expression of despair.

Then we are at our destination and I struggle out with my suitcases, almost falling down the steps as others, similarly burdened, push from behind. I enter the station and head for the assigned track. It is not yet six o'clock, but the station is already crowded. The people all appear to be wearing the distinguishing star. I gaze around, confused by the turmoil. Men and women, some alone, some in small knots, stand there speaking quietly to each other. Uniformed Munich police are positioned at various points along the whole length of the platform, watching lazily as more people arrive. I step over to the wall and set my luggage down, my arms aching.

***

"Herr Hartstein, is that you?" Startled by the unexpected sound of my name, I snapped my head to the side. My expression must have betrayed my puzzlement. "You remember me, don't you?" asked the vaguely familiar stranger, a trace of disappointment in his voice. Then, without waiting for my reply, he supplied the answer. "Martin Rosenzweig." He set the large suitcase down at his feet and extended his hand. "I used to be the manager of a machine shop in Ulm. We did quite a bit of work for Feinberg's. I personally took you on a tour of our operation a few years ago. We also met here in Munich at one of the industrial fairs." He adjusted his eyeglasses and shifted from one foot to the other as he waited for my response.

"Yes, of course," I said, recognizing him. He was slightly heavier than I recalled and had acquired a touch of grey to his sideburns and moustache. "I'm sorry that we have to meet again under such...unpleasant circumstances," I added, speaking a bit louder to compete with the rising noise level of the station. People continued to file in steadily from the stairways, and now animated discussions were taking place in every area of the platform. One could feel the atmosphere of tension building with each minute.

"Do you have any idea where they are sending us?" he asked, his nervous eyes scanning the growing crowd. I shrugged my shoulders and spread out my hands to indicate that I had no answer to his question, the very same question that had been on the tip of my tongue. "The train should be arriving very soon," he continued, craning his neck slightly toward the tracks. "German trains are as predictable as the seasons."

I smiled, although the strain was taking its toll on my digestive system. At almost the same moment I heard first one voice and then another announce the approach of the train. A number of people moved toward the edge of the platform and leaned forward to peer down the tracks. Presently, there was a chugging sound that became louder each second until finally the large, black engine entered the station. I could see those standing at the edge step quickly back as it approached, although my view was somewhat obstructed by the shifting crowd in front of me. Suddenly a woman screamed out, and another, followed by a series of lower pitched shouts. Then there was the shrill screech of metal on metal as the motorman hastily applied the brakes. There were more shouts. Several policeman who had been standing to the side of us began to elbow their way roughly through the throng toward a point diagonally across from us. Even though I stood on tiptoe, it was impossible to see anything more.

"If you will watch our luggage, I'll try to find out what happened," I said, turning to my companion, who was also craning his neck to learn the cause of the uproar. He nodded, his expression even more apprehensive than it had been a few minutes earlier. I inched forward through the crowd to the spot where the policemen had disappeared, but all I could see was a wall of backs.

"What is all the commotion about?" I asked loudly, not directing my question to anyone in particular.

"A woman threw herself in front of the train," came back the excited reply from further up front.

I continued to stand there for several more moments. Just as I was about to leave, a loud shout rang out from somewhere behind me, and before I could turn I was pushed to the side with such force that I lost my balance and almost fell to the floor.

"Out of the way, damned Jewish swine!" barked a heavyset fellow in a porter's uniform. He plunged forward like a miniature bulldozer, propelling a large luggage cart before him with no regard for those who happened to be in the way. The crowd parted almost magically and then closed again as he entered the gap, creating the optical illusion that he had been swallowed up by it. A minute or two later a chorus of gasps erupted from close ahead. Once more there was a rift in the crowd; two policemen emerged, waving us aside with their menacing wooden truncheons. Behind them was the porter, perspiration dripping from his face as he pushed his cart along the avenue that had been created for him by his police escort. As it drew closer to me I was puzzled by the horrified expressions on the faces of those whom it had already passed. I could see something lying on the luggage cart; but from my vantage point it seemed to be only a small pile of red and green rags. It was only when it finally came up alongside me that I saw what was really there: crumpled together in a twisted heap, her arms and legs contorted grotesquely at impossible angles, was the woman I had seen earlier on the bus. I did not recognize her from her face, which was so mutilated that it no longer resembled anything human, but rather from the small twisted star affixed to the torn, green, blood-soaked coat. It was only with a great effort that I kept myself from retching as she was pushed past me, her pitifully broken body wriggling like an earthworm that has been prodded by a schoolboy's stick.

My head was pounding violently by the time I fought my way back to my former place at the wall. Martin Rosenzweig was standing in the same position I had left him.

"Well, what is it?" he asked, moving to the side a bit to allow me to squeeze myself in between him and our cases.

I gave him a succinct description of what I had seen, still fighting back my nausea. He shook his head from side to side sadly.

"Suicide is no stranger to the Jews these days," he said. "Particularly to the elderly. I know personally of at least three cases..." But before he could finish what he was saying, there was a loud sound of static from the speaker above our heads, followed by a shrill announcement.

"Attention! Attention Jews!" the shrill voice began, pausing momentarily. There was an immediate hush all along the platform. Many heads turned up toward the source of the electronic voice, as if this would aid their hearing. After another short burst of static the announcer continued. "Form orderly lines in front of the train doors and have your identification papers and your labor notices ready for examination!"

"We must try to stay together. We must try." Martin Rosenzweig said. He had already grasped his two cases and taken a few steps forward as the message on the loudspeaker was repeated. People scurried this way and that, as if the particular car they chose would alter their ultimate fate. One policemen had stationed himself in front of each door, and now each was shouting out orders to the frightened people in the lines before them. A number of their comrades moved about from one line to another, also shouting loudly and waving their truncheons which they used more as instruments of threat than of punishment. In this way they very quickly and efficiently distributed the people to even out the lines. With Prussian precision, the policeman at each train door now began to inspect the papers handed to him by those in his line. If he found them in order, with a short jerk of his head he motioned the individual to enter the train. Every so often, however, a problem arose. The person involved was waved to the side as the next person's papers were examined, and after a few minutes a policeman led the one whose papers were not in order into the ticket office at the front of the station.

"This isn't at all as bad as I thought it would be," whispered Martin Rosenzweig conspiratorially as we took our place in the line nearest us.

In spite of my headache, I nodded in agreement. Although I had tried not to think about it consciously, I realized that I had also been prepared for a much more unpleasant experience. My thoughts wandered to my parents. I wished I could talk to them, quiet their fears a bit. I could not forget how worried my mother had looked. I wondered if Jutta was with them at that moment.

"Papers." The policeman's large, black, handlebar moustache moved from side to side in synchronization with his eyes, as he casually studied the documents Martin Rosenzweig had just handed him. The latter watched anxiously, and when his papers were handed back to him and he was given the nod to board the train, he turned to me and smiled as if in triumph. Then I was also motioned on without incident. Seconds later the two of us made our way along the corridor in search of a place to settle ourselves.

Anyone who had not known otherwise could well have thought that this was just another German train getting ready to leave on a normal journey. In the compartments was the typical bustle preceding any train departure as each traveler went about the business of staking a claim to a particular seat and carefully arranged suitcases on the luggage nets above. The general mood had become perceptibly better than that on the platform only minutes before. Here and there one could even hear a burst of laughter.

"Here is a free one." Rosenzweig, who was a few steps ahead of me, set his suitcase down and opened the door to the empty compartment, motioning me to enter first. "We can take the seats by the window," he said, as he followed me inside.

We put our cases in the overhead racks and settled ourselves in our seats. Several minutes later the door to the compartment slid open again. A broad, sturdily built fellow leaned his head through the glass door.

"Are these seats free?" he asked, maneuvering his cases through the door without awaiting a reply. I nodded. He stepped inside and in an effortless motion, swung his large suitcase onto the rack. Then he let himself down into the seat next to me and stared down at the carpeted floor. After a short pause he looked up and said, "Arnold Blum," without making an effort to extend his hand. He dropped his gaze even before Martin and I had finished giving our names.

"I wonder when we will be setting out," offered Martin after several more minutes of silence. I glanced through the window across the corridor; the only thing in my line of vision was a small cluster of policemen. The lines of Jews were no longer there. "I think I'll take a closer look," he added, rising and making his way over to the door. He pulled the door open and stepped across the corridor to the outer window overlooking the platform.

I was totally exhausted. My headache had become a dull throbbing pain, and yet at the same time I felt strangely light-headed. I had not slept very well during the past days. I closed my eyes and leaned my head against the soft cushion behind it.

"Stay in your damned seat, Jew, do you understand? You will not leave your compartment until and unless you are told so. From now on we will even tell you if and when you can take a shit. Understood?"

For a split second I thought that the harsh command was part of my disjointed dream. I opened my eyes just as Arnold Blum jumped up from his seat to catch hold of our third compartment mate. In my state of semi-sleep, it almost seemed as if the latter were leaping back into the compartment at us.

"You are not going on a pleasure trip, you worthless scum. And that goes for all of you, understood?" A tall, lean figure clad in the frightening jet-black uniform of the SS stood framed in the doorway. As he spoke, he slapped his thigh sharply with the short swagger stick he held clenched tightly in his hand. Martin Rosenzweig slumped down into the seat by the window and cupped both hands over one of his cheeks. I stared at the SS officer in a kind of stupefied terror. Satisfied that he had gotten his point across, the latter pushed the door closed with such force that the windows in the compartment rattled.

"Are you all right?" I asked, now fully awake.

"Yes, don't worry. I am fine," he replied, still holding his cheek. Blum had not moved from the center of the compartment. He stood there as if weighing what to do next. "I am fine," Rosenzweig repeated, letting his hands fall to his lap. Across his cheek was an angry, red welt.

"The dirty bastards," Blum muttered, balling his hands to fists. "One day they will pay dearly for all of this." He sat back down next to me and became silent again.

The three of us sat in silence for many minutes. Martin Rosenzweig continued to dab at his injured face from time to time, but made no effort to describe his experience. I concluded that he was more embarrassed than hurt, and left him alone. Blum, who was taking advantage of the fact that no one else had entered our compartment, removed his shoes and stretched his legs onto the seat opposite him. Soon he was snoring quietly. At about nine o'clock, our papers were checked again, this time by two nondescript men in civilian clothes who did not bother to identify themselves. Rosenzweig's spirits began to bound back a bit after they left.

"Let's hope there aren't too many like that first one," he said. "These two seemed like decent enough fellows, don't you think? All business."

"Don't bet on it," snarled Blum, stuffing his papers back into the inside pocket of his worn leather jacket. "Any one of them would rip out our guts just as soon as look at us. Don't ever let yourself be fooled into thinking that they have any human feelings." Rosenzweig's face dropped a bit; he looked over at me for support, but I pretended not to notice. My mind was focused on other matters: my parents, Karl, Birgit...

At exactly ten-thirty, the train began to move, starting and stopping for several minutes as it was shunted from one track to another, wheels squealing shrilly. Finally we were out of the station and beginning to pick up speed. Unable to resist, I stood up, opened the window wide and put my head out to get one last glance at Munich now bathed in the morning sunlight. I wondered if I would ever be back, if I would ever see my mother and father again. When I finally sat down I felt more lost and lonely than I ever had before.

For the first hour or so of our journey I sat as if in a hypnotic trance. The rhythmic clatter of the wheels formed words in my mind, but at the same time blotted out any cohesive thoughts: "Birgit...Birgit...Birgit," I heard, over and over again. "Birgit...Birgit...Birgit." And as I stared down at the grey track bed below, an image of her soft hair and smooth skin floated up to me like velvet mist. "Birgit...Birgit...Birgit."

Martin Rosenzweig had fallen asleep; his head was slumped forward and bobbed up and down and from side to side in rhythm to the movement of the train. From time to time he lurched forward, seeming to awaken for a moment to prevent himself from falling out of his seat, then he sank back into sleep.

"We're heading north." Arnold Blum's deep voice snapped me out of my reverie. "Regensburg," he said, pointing toward the window. As the train sped along, I became aware of the neat houses and busy streets of the city flashing by as if they were the moving objects and we the stationary one. "It doesn't look as if we are going to stop here," he added. "We would have slowed down by now if we were. The station is just up ahead." The train's whistle sounded three or four times to confirm his assertion, and seconds later we whizzed past the station signs announcing our location.

"You seem to know this area fairly well," I observed, surprised by his sudden willingness to speak.

"My wife's parents lived here," he replied. "We used to visit them often."

God knows where they are now."

We continued to speak quietly as the train made its way inexorably northward, whistling past the small stations so swiftly that the names were a blur: Irrenlohe, Nabburg, Weiden, Neustadt. In the meanwhile, Martin Rosenzweig had awakened and presently joined in the conversation. We spoke of our families, our friends, the difficulties we'd had to face during these last years under Nazi domination. Soon, even the mild mannered Rosenzweig was giving vent to his anger over the injustices we had all suffered. Time had gained a new dimension. After little more than an hour I felt as if I knew these two men better than many with whom I had lived and worked for years. For the time being, at least, they had become my world.

In addition to the personal fear we felt, each of us was consumed by anxiety over the fates of our loved ones. Blum's eyes filled with tears as he spoke of his wife and the two children she now had to care for virtually alone. His concern was well founded: the small amount of money that he had managed to save from his work as an auto mechanic would last his family for a month or two at best, and since her parents were gone — they had been resettled several weeks before somewhere in Poland — there was no one he could think of who would assist her. Until then he had been luckier than most Jews. Because of his mechanical skills and the fact that the garage at which he worked did a great deal of repair work on the vehicles of local Nazi party officials, his employer had managed to have a few rules bent to keep him on at his position. But only temporarily. One day he, too, received the summons to forced labor.

Rosenzweig's story was equally touching and at least in part very familiar. The Jewish-owned machine shop he managed in Ulm had been Aryanized almost a year earlier. For several months his new employer kept him on — naturally, at a greatly reduced salary — during which time he was ordered to train the properly blooded person who had been selected to replace him. And then one morning he was informed succinctly by his employer that his services were no longer required. Just like that. As for family, his parents were both dead and his only sibling, a brother, had emigrated to Argentina soon after Hitler came to power. He sighed as he recounted his failure to leave Germany as his brother had repeatedly requested. If he had followed the latter's advice, he would now be a partner in a successful meat processing plant and not on some train heading who knew where.

When asked if he was married, he became evasive. Under Blum's prodding, however, he finally admitted that his wife of seventeen years had recently left him. She was, he explained in a choking, embarrassed voice, a gentile. And though she had resisted at first, ultimately she gave in to the pressure exerted by the Reich and her family alike and divorced him. Fortunately, they had had no children.

Early in the afternoon, the three of us shared the food Arnold Blum and I had brought along. My mother had packed a loaf of her homemade black bread and a large piece of cheese into my case, and this, together with the bottle of red wine and the large wurst Blum supplied, made our lunch into a feast. Rosenzweig was apologetic that he had nothing to contribute to our luncheon, and assured us half-seriously that he would make up for it by taking us both out to a fancy restaurant as soon as we reached our destination.

The bathroom problem was solved very soon thereafter. Rosenzweig indicated that he was experiencing a call to nature, but was hesitant to move from his seat because of the SS officer's graphic warning. When he asked our advice, Blum answered by getting up and leaving the compartment. A few minutes later he returned, and with a sly smile on his face announced that even the SS had to acknowledge a call to nature. Certainly, he reasoned, the Minister of Transport did not want to see the compartments of his trains converted into Jewish toilets. When he saw that Rosenzweig was still uncertain, Blum assured him that there were no black uniforms in sight. Ultimately, nature conquered fear and Martin heroically plodded off to the toilet.

Remarkably then, except for the circumstances under which it was being taken, and the short, violent episode at the very outset, our journey up to that point had been almost enjoyable. This changed abruptly when we made our first stop.

"Leipzig," Rosenzweig said, as the train ground to a screeching halt in front of the large black and white sign. It was late afternoon. The three of us stood by the window of our compartment looking down at the frenzied activity on the platform below. There was a small cluster of people to one side. As far as I could see, all were wearing the yellow identifying star. The atmosphere seemed much more electric than that of the morning in Munich; there was an urgency to the commands barked out by scurrying policemen in the unfamiliar dialect of the region. Doors clanged open and shut, followed by the tramping of heavy feet in the corridor. We all turned suddenly as the door to our compartment was noisily pulled open.

A short fellow with a pockmarked face peered in at us. He was wearing a loose-fitting uniform that looked like a cross between a conductor's and a policeman's.

"Get your things together and get out," he snapped, motioning angrily with his hand. For a few seconds we all stood there as if frozen in our places. His face reddening, our visitor took a step into the compartment and shouted, "Are all of you Jew bastards deaf as well as stupid? You heard what I said. Now get your goddamned asses out! On the double!" Apparently satisfied that he had made himself understood, he stepped back out into the corridor and went on to repeat his orders to those in the other compartments in our car.

Mechanically, we helped each other drag our cases down from the racks and started out. Since he was closest to the door, Blum was the first to leave.

"We'll meet down on the platform," he said over his shoulder, as he jostled his way out between those who were already shuffling down the corridor. I was the next to leave, followed by Martin Rosenzweig who stayed so close behind me that his suitcases kept digging into the backs of my legs.

"Quickly. Quickly," came the command from below, as I awkwardly descended the steps, trying vainly to keep my suitcases from smashing into the person in front of me. Apparently, I did not move fast enough. I felt a sharp pain in my side as my first foot made contact with the concrete floor, and was only able to keep from tumbling over by using one of my cases to break the fall. The policeman who had poked his truncheon into my side swung again, this time catching me a glancing blow on the shoulder. I moved quickly out of his range before he could correct his aim.

"Keep moving, you worthless bastard!" he snarled, his anger now directed at Martin Rosenzweig who had witnessed what happened to me and stood frozen in the doorway. When he saw that his words were not having the desired effect, the policeman reached up, grabbed hold of one of Rosenzweig's arms, and gave a violent tug. The latter tumbled down the two metal steps and landed heavily at the policeman's feet. Amazingly, he still held onto his two suitcases as he lay there stunned. I put my luggage down and ran back over to him; with my assistance he was able to scramble to the side, away from the steps. By the time I got him to his feet, the policeman, who was solely concerned with keeping a steady flow of traffic, had already forgotten us.

"Are you sure you're all right?" I asked, as we reached the large waiting room to which we had been directed by a series of shouts and pushes. Rosenzweig nodded his head.

"I think I twisted my ankle, but otherwise I seem to be in one piece," he said, flexing his foot back and forth several times. "But where is Blum? He was right in front of us."

I looked around to see if I could locate the missing member of our triumvirate, but the crowd was so dense it was impossible to get a clear field of vision in any direction. It seemed as if they had gathered the passengers from the train into several groups at different locations throughout the station; I feared that Blum had been sent to one of the other collection points.

We stood there crammed together, waiting for further instructions. In spite of the large number of people involved (there must have been at least two hundred of us), it was very quiet in the room to which we had been directed. Many stood silently or sat on their suitcases, staring straight ahead. In addition to the fatigue from the long train ride, everyone seemed stunned by the sudden brutality we had just experienced. A few men held bloodied handkerchiefs to their heads or faces; others, myself included, still felt the dull ache where the truncheons had struck.

As the minutes ticked by, a low murmur arose, gradually picking up volume. Why had we been herded here so frenziedly? It did not make sense; a half hour had already passed since our arrival in the station and we had been told nothing. Where were we going? Why had we left the train in the first place? These and other questions were repeated and various theories offered. The pessimists concluded that we were waiting for another train, one which would take us to the east. The optimists decided that Leipzig was our final destination, and that shortly we would be taken in busses to the place where we would work. But where had they taken the women? Until someone mentioned this, I had not even noticed that there were only men in the room. Someone suggested that we had been separated because we were going to work as laborers, clearing bomb rubble from the streets and doing other heavy work. Others saw it as a practical measure; they surmised that we would be housed in barracks during our work assignment and could hardly expect the Nazis to consider our biological needs. None of us was yet familiar with the psychological tactic that the Nazis had already perfected — the juxtaposition of fear and hope — the art of keeping their victims totally off balance so that they would be all the more malleable.

The uncertainty continued after the voice on the loudspeaker ordered us brusquely to have our papers ready for yet another inspection. Once again the lines were formed; once again the inspection by some official or other. And then more waiting.

"They would save us all a lot of time and effort if they tattooed our names to our foreheads," quipped someone from a point to my left, without realizing how ironic his words were.

"They want to make sure that we aren't English spies," replied another, although his trembling voice belied the bantering tone.

In the meantime, some changes were taking place; it seemed as if new divisions were being made in our group. In some instances, after his papers were examined, an individual was given the order to report to another location in the station, while others were told curtly to stay where they were until further instructions were given. Martin Rosenzweig and I were relieved when it turned out that we would remain together in the waiting room, even though we had no way of knowing what that meant. Our spirits were lifted even further some minutes later when we heard a familiar voice calling our names from across the room.

"The three musketeers are together again," I joked, as Arnold Blum elbowed his way over to us. Martin and I shook hands with him as if he were an old friend whom we hadn't seen in years.

"And so," began the excited mechanic, "we stood there by the tracks like horses in their stalls, while that nasty SS shithead we met earlier and a few of his comrades screamed their idiotic heads off and slashed out at anyone near them. I can't tell you how relieved I was when they told me to report to the waiting room. I had a very bad feeling while I was out there. They had pulled up a freight train and were opening up the boxcars just as I left."

"Boxcars?" said Martin, incredulously. "You don't suppose they were going to put people in boxcars like cattle, do you?" He had a look of disbelief on his face.

"There were rumors," replied Arnold, lowering his voice so that others around us would not hear. "Terrible rumors. I only hope they are not true." He pulled a handkerchief from his back pocket and dabbed at the drops of perspiration on his upper lip.

"What kind of rumors?" I asked, unnerved by his frightened expression, which stood in marked contrast to his anger earlier in the day.

"That we would be taken to a concentration camp in Poland. They said that the Nazis have set up camps there where they exterminate people. Jews." He dabbed at his upper lip again. His face had paled as he spoke. I felt the familiar emptiness in the pit of my stomach, along with a fluttering sensation in my chest.

"That's preposterous," Martin Rosenzweig said in a loud voice, shaking his head back and forth. "Such a thing is impossible. Idle gossip. As if things aren't bad enough." He continued to shake his head.

My eyes met Arnold's for a moment; it was evident that neither of us discounted the possibility that such camps existed. I thought of the atrocities that Karl had detailed to me and the message he had sent through Jutta. Could it be true? Death camps. My fear was compounded as the loudspeaker began to blare out a new series of commands directing us to assemble at another track. We quickly picked up our luggage and made our way to the new location, wondering if boxcars would be waiting there for us too.

"It's a regular train." Martin's voice expressed the relief we all felt as we moved onto the platform and saw the waiting train.

"It's a short one, only about four cars," Arnold observed, striding along briskly. I was out of breath by the time we got to the first car. A conductor motioned us to keep moving forward. When we reached the second car another conductor told us to get in. I looked around. There were no police or SS in sight, only a few railroad personnel. Hope began to replace fear once again. I boarded the train almost eagerly.

Unlike the previous one, this was an ordinary commuter train. Instead of compartments there were rows of seats. The car was filling up quickly. Since the luggage racks above our heads were inadequate to accommodate all of the baggage, we were directed to leave it in the space between cars.

"Don't worry," I assured Martin, who was reluctant to part with his suitcases. "If they had wanted to steal our luggage from us they would have done it already. Besides, what could you possibly have that they want?"

Even as I spoke, however, I realized the sad truth of our situation. All we had left in the world were the few meager possessions we had in our cases. They had already stolen everything else from us: our jobs, our homes, our families, our freedom.

I lost track of time as we sat there waiting for the train's engine to be fired up. The rumor mill was working at full speed. Depending on who was speaking, we were going to Poland, Russia, Denmark.

There was yet another inspection of our papers which were beginning to look frayed. More waiting. And then, finally, we were moving. It was already dark. All I could see were the indistinct outlines of the city, blacked out because of the bombing raids. Leipzig. I recalled Mephisto's lines: "The people would never recognize the devil, even if he had hold of them by the collar." If anything, Goethe had understated his idea, I thought, as I looked down the aisle at the others. Many of us had not recognized the devil until he had us by the throats.

"Wake up, Heinrich. I think we are stopping."

I opened my eyes reluctantly, unwilling to leave the pleasant dream I had been enjoying. In the dream I was a child again, sitting with my family at the large table on Schwanthalerstrasse. It was our annual New Year's celebration. Uncle Solomon was telling a humorous story, and everyone was smiling: my aunts, my grandparents, my parents, my sisters...

"We've been moving very slowly for the past twenty minutes or so. I believe we are coming into a station." As he leaned across the aisle toward me, Arnold Blum's face was barely visible. The car was illuminated only by the weak glow of the moon. I shook myself awake and glanced to my right. Martin was also stirring.

"Do you have any idea where we are?" I asked, straining my eyes to see if I could distinguish any of the dark shapes beyond the dirty windows. The train had come to a full stop. All of the other passengers were awake by this time, asking each other the same question.

"I'm not sure, but I heard someone say that we were on the outskirts of Berlin. There is the smell of industry in the air." Even before he mentioned it, I had noticed the pungent odor of coal gas mixed with a strong, unfamiliar scent.

"Berlin," repeated Martin Rosenzweig. "What on earth are we doing here?" He pressed his forehead against the window but was unable to confirm our location.

"I think we will find that out very quickly," I offered, as we heard the train doors being opened, followed by a number of indistinguishable thudding sounds.

"Everyone find your baggage and assemble on the station!" came a loud voice from the front of the car. We all scrambled to our feet and headed for the end of the car. When I reached the empty space where we had stored our luggage I became aware that the noise we had heard was that of our cases being thrown down onto the platform below. We quickly exited the car and began searching for our property in the darkness.

I don't know how many of us there were — one hundred, possibly two. A small contingent of uniformed police had apparently been awaiting our arrival; now they lined us up on the small platform of what seemed to be a deserted station and marched us out in chaotic fashion. We stumbled across the tracks onto a ramp that led downward to a tunnel. The echo of our footsteps and our rustling clothing lent an eerie atmosphere to the scene. As we entered the pitch-dark tunnel, I thought of Dante's hell, and the solemn warning over the gate: "Abandon hope all ye who enter here..."

The policemen at the front had flashlights, the thin, bobbing beams of light adding to the spectral nature of the scene. For a moment or two I contemplated bolting from the group, or simply falling down to the side and remaining motionless until everyone had passed; it would have been easy to lose myself in the darkness. But where could I have gone — a Jew wandering the streets of a strange German city, Berlin or whatever it was, in the middle of the night? And so I trudged on with the others, my imagination spinning out various scenarios of what awaited us.

We proceeded along the dark streets for a good twenty minutes or more, turning into one side street and then another. From time to time our guides took us on an obvious detour as piles of rubble blocked our path. The smell of stale smoke hung thickly in the air.

"Bomb damage," remarked Arnold, who was directly in front of Martin and me as we wove our way awkwardly around a high mountain of debris. "You can still smell the powder."

I was too tired to respond. My arms felt as if they were being yanked out of their sockets by the increasingly heavy suitcases. Loud, strained breathing and an occasional low groan from behind me indicated that Martin was also reaching the end of his strength.

Finally we were given the command to halt. I set down my luggage and began to rub my arms which still felt as if they had weights tied to them. We had stopped in front of a building that looked like a huge warehouse. It was still too dark to see clearly, but the structure seemed to extend for at least the length of a normal city block. After a few moments a large door was swung open up ahead, emitting a weak shaft of light onto the cobblestone street.

"Hurry, inside! Quickly! Don't waste any time!" came the commands, in a heavy Berlin dialect. Within seconds, we were inside and the door was slammed shut. At first my eyes smarted slightly from the unaccustomed light, weak as it was.

"It's a good thing we stayed together," remarked Martin. "They must have taken the rest of our group on to another location. I don't think I could have walked another minute." I nodded agreement as I looked around. Approximately twenty of us stood in what appeared to be a long corridor illuminated by small electric bulbs spaced at intervals of a few meters. "Where is Blum?" he added, craning his neck to see past me.

"He was here a minute ago," I replied, also scanning the faces of those closest to us. "He was right in front of me, so he must be close by." As I spoke I caught sight of him up ahead, speaking to one of the policeman who had led us in. A few seconds later he was making his way back to us.

"Whoever said this was Berlin was correct," he announced. "We are somewhere in the southern part of the Tempelhof district. The place we are in right now is a munitions factory. That's all my friend over there could or would tell me." Immediately the word was passed around to all of the others. Before there could be any discussion, however, a door I had not even noticed opened at the side, almost directly opposite me. A tall, bearded fellow clad in a spotless white smock stepped out past us without giving us so much as a glance. Limping noticeably, he made his way over to our police escort. After they had conferred quietly for several seconds he returned.

"All of you, follow me!" he barked, in a clipped, military voice. We picked up our cases and, single file, followed him through the door.

We trailed our limping leader along another long corridor. As I watched his head rise and fall with each uneven step, I could not help thinking of my Uncle Solomon; I recalled how he had always joked with my father about cripples becoming the future leaders of the world. Perhaps, I thought, there was more than a little truth behind the jest, if not in the physical, then certainly in the moral sense.

"Easy, Heinrich. You'll have to keep your eyes open at all times from now on," cautioned Arnold Blum, steadying me with his strong mechanic's hands as I lurched into him and almost toppled sideways. I had been so engrossed in my thoughts that I had failed to notice our little column come to a halt.

"In here." Our white-smocked leader had opened another door and now stood to the side to let us pass through into the large room beyond it. The room was even more dimly lit than the corridors. The first things that struck me as I entered were a strong, stale odor of perspiration and a low rumbling sound, almost like the buzzing of a beehive. As I looked more carefully, I saw movement in the rows of rectangular forms that lined the floor.

"This is where you will sleep," he declared, his voice tinged with disdain. "There are shelves at the rear for your luggage and toilet facilities through the door to your left. You may use any cot that is free. Tomorrow morning, you will be given your work assignments." Without another word he turned and limped from the room. We shuffled to the rear and deposited our cases on the wooden shelves lining a section of the wall, trying to be as quiet as possible so as not to wake those already asleep.

"Come, let's find some cots near each other," whispered Arnold, as he, Martin, and I placed our cases next to each other's on one of the shelves. I was dog-tired. I held my watch up close to my eyes; it was two-thirty in the morning.

By a stroke of good fortune, we managed to find three free cots fairly close to each other over at one side. Without even taking off my coat, I sank down onto the thin mattress which smelled even more strongly of body odor than the air surrounding it. Was it possible, I thought, that less than twenty-four hours earlier I had been in our apartment in Munich? Before I could think any further, I was asleep.

The shrill sound of military music jolted me awake. I sat up and looked around dazedly, my eyes burning from the bright, unshielded electric lights that hung down from the ceiling. Many of the other workers were up and out of their cots. Some had already pulled on their clothing and were standing around in small clusters by the shelves at the rear of the room. Others stood in line at the door leading to the toilets. I heard bits and pieces of conversation in varied languages: German, French, Slavic. I rubbed my eyes and glanced down at my watch; it was just a few minutes past five. They had allowed us less than three hours sleep. I turned my head to look at the bunk next to mine; a young, dark-haired fellow stood there getting dressed. As he pulled on his trousers, he studied me with amusement. When our eyes met, he smiled.

"Welcome to Berlin," he said, with a heavy French accent. "You have been given the opportunity to work diligently for the Third Reich. If you do your work, you will have nothing to fear. If you shirk, you will learn what true suffering is." He smiled again, stood up, and plodded toward the line for the toilet.

"Attention, attention new arrivals! You will wait for work assignments in your dormitories after the others have gone to their work!" The military music had given way to a high-pitched voice that sounded like a poor imitation of the Reich's Propaganda Minister. Still not fully awake, I glanced to the side where Martin Rosenzweig had found a place. He, too, was sitting quietly, watching the activity around him. Turning again, I tried to locate Arnold Blum, but his cot was empty. I recognized several others who had arrived with us in the train from Leipzig. Most, like myself, had not even bothered to remove their coats, and now sat there with the large yellow stars prominently displayed. The room was quickly emptying as those who had finished their morning routine filed out through the door leading to the corridor.

After a few minutes, I stood up groggily and plodded over to the toilet. It was a narrow room; at one side there was a line of about seven or eight open stalls, and opposite them an equal number of sinks. Arnold Blum, who was shaving at one of the latter, nodded to me as I walked past him. I found an empty stall and obeyed my call to nature, wiping myself with the rough strips of newspaper that had been placed there for that purpose. Then I stepped over to greet Arnold.

"You must make yourself presentable, Heinrich," he cautioned, as he held his razor under the faucet and brought it back up to his chin. "One thing I learned in my trade is that looks are very important. The Nazis are no different from anyone else when it comes to that; in fact, I found that they are more fanatical about appearance than about how things really work. In their minds, for example, a clean automobile runs a lot better than one that has mud on it." He winked, put the razor under the thin stream of water again, and then handed it to me. The full significance of this practical observation was to become known to me at a later time. In the camps, one's appearance often meant the difference between life and death.

As I stepped out a few minutes later, my attention was attracted by a commotion at a point in front of the luggage shelves. I immediately recognized Martin Rosenzweig's voice; he was shouting loudly at someone, his arms waving up and down like broken wings.

"You were stealing from my suitcase. I saw you!" he shouted, his face bright red from excitement. The fellow he was confronting was a good fifteen years younger than Martin and quite a bit larger. He stood there with a smirk on his face and ignored the tirade. Suddenly, I saw an arm shoot out and grasp the latter's hand.

"Give it back! Do you hear me? I said give it back right now!" Arnold Blum's face froze to a frightening stare. The other fellow hesitated for a few seconds, then shook his head and let something drop onto the floor. Martin quickly stooped over and retrieved it.

"Aren't things bad enough?" admonished the still glaring mechanic as he released the other's hand. "Are we going to steal from each other too? Is that what we have come to?" The young man lowered his head and walked away without saying a word.

"It's just a few personal things;" Martin explained as I stepped over to him. He held a small leather pouch in the palm of his hand and peered down at it. "A pen, some cuff links, my wedding ring — personal things." He looked up at me almost apologetically and added, "I haven't worn the ring since the divorce, but all the same..."

At that moment the door burst open and two men in white smocks entered. The first one was heavyset. His face had a fierce, leathery look to it. When he started to speak I recognized the voice as the one we had heard earlier on the loudspeaker.

"Pay close attention, Jews," he began, hands on hips and legs spread apart. For a split second the image of Karl doing his imitation of Mussolini flashed through my mind. "You have," he continued, "been given the opportunity to work diligently for the Third Reich. If you do your work, you will have nothing to fear. If you shirk, you will learn what true suffering is."

As terrified as I was, I almost smiled as I heard the words the young Frenchman had uttered to me earlier. But this was no imitation, no joke. And as his voice droned on, I no longer felt any inclination to smile.

***

Our routine was as tedious as it was taxing. During the rest of the spring and well into the summer, we toiled under the watchful eyes of the white-robed overseers. For sixteen hours a day we assembled anti-tank shells, machine guns, grenades, rifles, and other items of war necessary to destroy the enemies of the Third Reich. On Sunday, the Christian sabbath, our Nazi masters indulged their penchant for irony by allowing us the luxury of only a ten-hour workday. Although we were not ringed by barbwire or surrounded by armed guards, it was evident that we were prisoners. Any thoughts we might have had about escape were discouraged by the constantly repeated threat that any such attempt would result in swift recapture and transfer to a concentration camp, where we would come to view our present situation as luxurious. Those who attempted to show their opposition to the government by malingering also ran the risk of reassignment, while the penalty for sabotage was death. I learned very quickly that these were not idle threats. It was common for the Gestapo to appear at any time of the day or night in order to forcibly remove an individual for a real or fabricated infraction of the rules.

Other, more subtle tactics were also employed to thwart any organized opposition. I learned this one afternoon approximately a month after my arrival. I was at my place on the grenade assembly line when the overseer called out my name and ordered me to follow him. As I walked behind him along the now familiar corridors I could feel the perspiration dripping down my sides.

"Sit down, Herr Hartstein. Please." The man who stood behind the ornate, glass topped desk looked like the model industrialist. He was impeccably dressed in a dark, English-style suit. His hair, thinning and streaked with silver, had a razor-sharp part at one side and was matched by the wire rimmed glasses that framed his cool, blue eyes. I was totally disoriented. As I seated myself in the soft, leather chair at the side of the desk, I suddenly realized that I could not remember the last time I had heard the word please. "We live in a very difficult time, Herr Hartstein. A very difficult time," he began, the springs in his swivel chair creaking tiredly as he leaned his weight against its back.

I sat there tensely, still fearing the worst. I had learned too much over the years to be misled by a benign appearance and gentle words.

"You must be wondering why I summoned you here," he continued, appraising my mental state correctly. I nodded. He paused for a moment and then, in a matter-of-fact tone, said, "I knew your grandfather fairly well.

He was a fine businessman, one of the old school. Not like some of these young upstarts today who think they can become a success overnight. Feinberg's Ovenworks was a credit to his entrepreneurial skill."

He paused again, this time to let his words sink in. The unexpected revelation had increased my sense of disorientation. I wondered if this were some kind of trap. For what purpose? One does not have to resort to guile when dealing with slaves. Since it was obvious to me that he did not expect any reply, I remained silent.

"I know, too, that you did a splendid job at the head of the firm during the last years of its existence as such. Much better, I might add, than the incompetents who are there today." He said this as if I were as aware of it as he. Before I could react, he went on. "That is what brings me to the point of our meeting here today." His chair groaned again as he leaned forward and peered at me over the top of his eyeglasses. "Very simply stated, I would like to see your talents better utilized than they have been during these past weeks, unless, of course, you are satisfied with what you are doing."

"No...I mean to say, what did you have in mind, Herr...?" My voice cracked as I stammered out my inane response. In spite of his friendly, almost fatherly tone, I was still skeptical.

"Schramm. Helmut Schramm," he replied, bowing his head formally, although he made no effort to stand or shake hands. "I do not need to tell you how difficult it is to direct an enterprise like this with any degree of efficiency, particularly under the unusual circumstances we have here. And I am sure you also understand how critical it is that everything run smoothly. You do understand, don't you?" As he said this there was an edge to his voice that had not been there before.

"Yes," I replied, nodding my head again.

"You know," he said almost wistfully, "I was not always in the armaments industry. Before the war I owned a plant that produced home appliances — washing machines, refrigerators — that kind of thing. I didn't even know what a Panzerfaust was." He smiled his paternal smile as he spoke, but his eyes remained cold and distant.

"What caused you to come here?" I asked, my curiosity aroused.

"To put it bluntly, and I think you can appreciate this, the sole object of business is profit," he replied, winking conspiratorially. "And what better business in war time than armaments? So you see it was a stroke of good luck that I was conscripted by the Minister of Armaments to do my patriotic duty in this vital area, since it just happened to coincide with my professional goals." He leaned back again, his smile now exuding self-satisfaction.

I felt the blood rush to my face as I listened. Who was worse, I thought. Those who were evil out of twisted, fanatical belief, or opportunists like Schramm, whose evil was a direct result of greed and was better camouflaged. He had made it perfectly clear that both his patriotism and his estimation of human beings were measured by profit. Also very evident was the fact that he was not a Nazi racist. That my grandfather had been taken to Buchenwald to die simply because he was a Jew (and I am certain now that Schramm knew this), was not as important as the fact that the firm was no longer efficiently run. Following this line of logic, I deduced that I was not sitting across the desk from him because he felt sympathy for my personal plight. I was his slave and he accepted that the way one accepts the weather: one adjusts in order to make the best of it. I clenched my teeth and waited to see what sort of adjustment he had made that involved me.

"Simply put, Herr Hartstein," he offered, "I believe that we can come to a mutually beneficial arrangement that will insure your comfort while you remain here." He emphasized the last words to make certain that the inherent threat was understood. Satisfied of that, he went on. "I need someone who can serve as a buffer between the workers and some of those Party buffoons they have foisted on me, misfits who wouldn't even be considered for any position of authority during normal times." He shook his head disdainfully for emphasis. "That fellow Schroeder is a good example of what I mean. He does not understand that the carrot is just as important as the stick in dealing with people. An inferior mind in a mediocre body. His brother-in-law just happens to be a Gauleiter, and so I must put up with him."

I smiled in spite of myself as I thought of the leathery faced overseer he was referring to, although there was really nothing funny about him. More than once I had seen him punch a man viciously in the face or body for not working fast enough, or simply to satisfy his whim of the moment. And it was generally known that his recommendation alone was enough to have one transferred to the east. Soon enough I would learn what men like Schroeder were capable of when given the ultimate power over others. Taking my smile as a signal of agreement, he continued.

"People like Schroeder are incapable of realizing that total reliance on the stick can sometimes produce negative results — a grenade with a shorter fuse, shells with inadequate powder — that kind of thing." His face grew hard for a moment or two, and then relaxed again. My expression must have betrayed my inner tension, because he added, "Don't worry, Herr Hartstein, I know that you would not be guilty of such folly."

I could feel the hair on my arms and neck bristling. I had heard whispering about such small acts of sabotage.

"What I need," he said, "are a few key people whom I can trust, and who are also trusted by their fellow workers. In a sense you might say that they would be buffers. It would be their responsibility to see to it that peak efficiency was achieved and maintained, that such incidents as those I spoke of a moment ago did not occur. And in return for their cooperation, they would be granted certain privileges."

I could feel his eyes studying my face. So that was it, I thought, feeling foolish that I had not understood at once. What he wanted was someone who would spy for him. I wondered how many others he had approached in this manner, how many he had succeeded in recruiting. Or was it simply that this was all a sham, that his true aim was to create uncertainty and suspicion among his slaves so that they would remain divided? These thoughts raced through my mind as I sat there uneasily for several seconds.

"Privileges?" I finally asked, in an attempt to buy some time to order my thoughts.

He smiled broadly, like a fisherman who has felt a strong nibble. "Of course there could be nothing conspicuous," he replied, lowering his voice for effect. "It would defeat the whole purpose if anyone were to suspect that you were receiving special treatment. That is self-evident. But a letter to or from one's family now and then, something like that could be managed with the necessary discretion. I am sure that your parents would be delighted to hear from you. They would be very relieved to know that you are well."

"You know something of my parents?" I blurted out, completely surprised by what he had said.

"Oh, I am sorry, Herr Hartstein. I meant to mention that right at the outset. They are both doing fine, but naturally they are worried about their only son. From what I have heard, Theresienstadt is far from terrible. In fact, it is undoubtedly a lot safer to be there than in Berlin these days. They do not have to dodge enemy bombs at night as we do." He smiled amiably. Then, as if on cue, he looked at his watch and added, "But it is getting late, and I have a mountain of paperwork to complete. Wars are not only fought on the battlefield. They create their own bureaucracies. You think over what I have told you and I am sure you will make a prudent decision."

I wish I could say that my immediate and only thought had been to reject Schramm's offer, that I did not even briefly consider at least pretending to agree to his terms. But I was consumed by worry. My mother's face floated before me, her frightened eyes pleading for something undefined. How had my father managed the difficult journey? Were they truly alive and well, or was that simply a piece of poisoned bait he had dangled in front of me to snare me? If only I could hear from them one time. Just one more time.

By evening, I was more mentally than physically drained. After our scant meal I dragged myself to the dormitory, seeking to escape the dilemma in sleep.

"Is something wrong, Heinrich?" Arnold Blum looked down at me as I sat on the edge of the bunk I had claimed for the night. Arnold and I had become very close during those early weeks in Berlin. Fortunately, we had been assigned the same work shift, and often worked side by side on the same line. This was not the case with Martin Rosenzweig. To his great dismay he had been put on a different rotation when, due to the rising needs of the Wehrmacht, the factory was forced to go on a round-the-clock work schedule. The number of new laborers had increased, while the food rations had been decreased accordingly; now one could tell how long someone had been there by the relatively loose fit of his clothing. Often Arnold and I had to share a mattress, or simply stretch a blanket on the hard, cold floor and attempt to sleep on that.

"What happened? Did you have a run-in with Herr Goebbels?" he joked, letting himself down next to me with a yawn.

"Even worse," I replied, lowering my voice so that only he could hear. "Would you believe that I was offered a carrot by the director of this place?"

"A carrot? I don't understand," he replied, a puzzled look on his strong face.

"His terminology for a bribe," I explained, shaking my head in disgust. "He hinted at the possibility of allowing me to contact my parents."

For several seconds Arnold made no response. Then he wrinkled his brow and asked, "A favor from the devil always has to be paid for. What is the price for this one?"

"Nothing very important," I said, as sarcastically as I could. "All I have to do is become his spy. You know, give the names of a few fellow slaves who are involved in sabotage, that kind of thing." I sank down on the thin mattress and cradled my head in my hands.

"What was your answer?" he whispered, suddenly looking very tired.

"That is the whole point," I replied. "I didn't say no. I didn't tell the son of a bitch to go to hell. I wanted to, but I didn't. What is wrong with me? Naturally I would never agree to do what he wants, but I didn't tell him that outright. And it wasn't because I was afraid. I actually had to think it over."

He smiled sadly and shook his head from side to side. Then, in a remarkably gentle voice he said, "I am only a mechanic, my friend, not a judge. But if you want my opinion, I can only advise you not to be too hard on yourself. Your only guilt is that you are human, and that is the exception rather than the rule these days."

I waited fearfully for Schramm to put more pressure on me, but as the weeks passed and I heard nothing from him, I concluded that he had either decided I was unreliable, or he was too preoccupied with other concerns to bother with such insignificant matters. The bombing raids reached such an intensity during late summer that our sleeping quarters were transferred to an unused storage area below ground. In order to accommodate the larger slave population, crude, two-tiered wooden bunks were erected. The laborers' health began to break under the combined strain of the work, the Allied bombing raids, the heat, the increasingly unsanitary working conditions, and the insufficient rations. These factors, compounded by the psychological pain of separation from loved ones, gradually gave men who had been robust when they arrived a zombie-like appearance. Those who did not have the strength to continue were removed (ostensibly for medical assistance), and replaced by others, many of whom quickly followed in the footsteps of their predecessors. A few, unable to cope with the situation, chose to terminate their suffering with a crudely fashioned noose or whatever other means of self-destruction were at their disposal. We, and others like us, became isolated colonies of human moles, forced to work for an enemy who considered us subhuman, and seemed bent on our destruction.

The constant influx of new conscripts was our only line of communication from the outside world. Through them we learned that the Russian armies were still holding their own, despite the continuous declarations of the Nazi government that their defeat was imminent. As for the war in the west, the invasion of England had still not taken place, and with American industry now in full gear it seemed as if the handwriting was on the wall. The optimists among us were convinced that victory for the Allies lay in the near future, and concluded that this would mean our liberation. The pessimists concentrated on the horrifying rumors of mass murder in Russia, and repeated the reports of new concentration camp complexes in Poland, horrible places whose primary purpose was the destruction of Jews. And although details were lacking, and most listeners discounted them, these rumors persisted. For my part, I had long since reached the point where I believed the Nazis capable of anything.

The newcomers also brought us news of the latest anti-Jewish measures taking place in Germany itself. Instead of deepening everyone's fears, however, these reports resulted in a convoluted reasoning pattern that deluded some into rejecting the belief that the alleged death camps did, in fact, exist. Why, they reasoned, would it be necessary for the Nazis to enact laws banning Jews from public transport and restaurants, to formally forbid them to buy newspapers or periodicals, to use public telephones, or keep domestic pets, if they were simultaneously killing them by the hundreds of thousands in death camps?

More frequently than not, however, we were too tired to think at all, or simply chose not to. Our skin became yellowish-grey because of the poor lighting and the constant irritation from the fine gunpowder that saturated the stale, putrid air. At the end of the workday our limbs felt as if they were separate from our bodies, and our stomachs churned from the constant hunger that could not be stilled by the meager rations allotted us. At times it seemed to me that we would go on like this forever, that like the Greek sinner Sisyphus we, too, had angered the gods, and were doomed to begin each new day with our stone at the bottom of the mountain. In early September, however, our routine was suddenly disturbed.

I had just fallen asleep when the first bombs began to strike. The impact was so powerful that the ground beneath us rolled violently. Some of those in the upper bunks clung desperately to the wooden frames to keep from being thrown out by the shock waves. I managed to roll out of my place in a lower bunk, hurriedly put on my shoes and struggle to my feet. In the ensuing pandemonium I heard my name called out.

"This way, Heinrich." I was barely able to make out Arnold Blum's silhouette standing across from me in the hazy room. For the first time I became aware of the strong smell of smoke. Apparently, I was not the only one to make this discovery; shouts of panic rang out all around me as others began to leap from their bunks and make a wild dash to the stairwells at the far ends of the room. One concussion after another almost shook me off my feet as I hurried up the stairs directly behind Arnold, jostled by those who were running blindly in the same direction.

"Quickly, we have to get away from the building before it blows sky high!" shouted Arnold, as we reached the ground level and groped our way on all fours along the smoke-filled main corridor. "There is an exit up ahead."

By this time I had lost all sense of direction; the smoke was so thick I could scarcely see him. I was beginning to cough as I crawled; my lungs burned painfully and my head pounded. Suddenly, there was a powerful explosion. The entire building trembled for a moment, and then I felt myself propelled forward like a leaf in a windstorm. I heard a loud, grating sound directly behind me and felt a rush of heat. This was followed by the agonized screams of those buried alive by the collapsing walls. Another explosion followed, not quite as strong as the previous one, yet adequate to lift me from the ground a second time. For a moment there was a bright flash of light; immediately after this I experienced a sharp pain in my shoulder and back and felt myself sinking into a black void.

The next thing I remember is opening my eyes and seeing Arnold's worried face hovering above me, as if suspended in an undulating sea of flames. His features were surrealistically highlighted by dancing points of light that moved across them.

"Can you hear me, Heinrich?" he asked, cradling my head in his arms as one might do with a sick infant. I nodded weakly, uncertain where I was or what had happened. I continued to stare up at his face, fascinated by the way his eyes sparkled from the reflection of the surrounding flames. "I want you to try to get up," he said finally. "We have to get as far as possible from what is left of the factory. I'm afraid there might still be some stores of munitions that haven't exploded yet. There are fires everywhere."

He grasped me under the arms and pulled me to my feet. To my surprise, I was able to take a few steps without difficulty; aside from a soreness in one shoulder and a strange ringing in one ear, I did not seem to be seriously injured. Miraculously, there were no further explosions as we staggered down the rubble-strewn street through the smoke and flames.

There were only a few survivors from the bombing raid on the factory complex, and out of these an even smaller number who had not been severely injured. Arnold and I were among the fortunate few who had escaped relatively intact. Those of us who were able to walk were directed to gather in an open area at the side of a canal, located about half a kilometer from the remains of our factory. Gradually survivors from other plants began to stagger in and mill about, some still in a state of deep shock. From where we were we could still clearly hear the loud, wailing fire engine sirens. Shouting firemen worked feverishly to salvage those few structures that had not been totally destroyed during the massive raid. Every now and then the sky lit up brilliantly, and soon after that we heard the sound of an explosion, followed by yet more sirens. After searching unsuccessfully for our other friend, Arnold and I joined a small group of men who were sitting on some large wooden beams that had been discarded by the edge of the canal.

"I don't think there is much of a chance that Martin made it. He would be here if he had," I said, amazed at how little emotion I felt as I made my observation.

"The sector where he was working was pulverized. Most of the powder kegs were stored there. Poor Martin didn't have a chance," Arnold replied, in an equally calm voice. "How about you, though. How are you feeling? You took a very nasty jolt."

"I guess I am tougher than I look," I replied, attempting a smile. "I have you to thank that I can feel at all." I looked down at my tattered clothes. The constant ringing in my ear had become lower, and although my shoulder still throbbed, the pain was not unbearable. I had survived yet another circle of hell.

The next few days were chaotic. At night, wave after wave of Allied bombers pounded the district incessantly, even after several blocks of munitions factories there had been totally demolished. Those of us who had survived were given the task of salvaging any materials and equipment that could be transferred to a new location. Often we worked ten hours at a stretch, dismantling and carrying out large machines and unexploded munitions to the waiting army trucks. When it became dark and the sirens began to announce the approach of Allied aircraft, we were led to an old tunnel by the canal where we slept fitfully on the hard, damp ground as the city exploded around us.

Finally they moved us out in the same trucks they had used for the transport of the machines and munitions. We were packed tightly together in the dark interiors. Leather flaps had been drawn across the rear sections of the vehicles and armed guards situated at the end of the wooden benches along the sides. We rumbled along the cobblestone streets to our new work site.

The first munitions factory had been like a vacation resort in comparison to its successor. I didn't realize it at the time, of course, but I was being given a mild preview of what was to come later. Again, the work consisted of manufacturing and assembling small arms, but whereas before there had been a modicum of civilized human behavior, now there was unbridled savagery. What I remember best, even more vividly than the actual physical mistreatment that often accompanied it, was the constant verbal abuse dealt out by the overseers. From morning until night we were subjected to an uninterrupted barrage of threats and invective. It was as if we were being held responsible for the terror the city was experiencing in the night — we the victims. I worked like an automaton, attempting to block out the obscenities ringing in my ears by making my mind a complete blank, and when that proved unsuccessful I found myself forming violent mental images: I pictured myself loading the rifle I was assembling and proceeding to pump one bullet after another into the hateful heads and bodies of my persecutors. At night, as tired as I was, I could not fall asleep for a long time. I lay on my bunk trembling, not from fear of the bombs, but from the humiliations of the day. Every day. I no longer thought of my family or my former life, nor did I delude myself that better days were ahead or that reason and civilization would soon return to Germany. Something had snapped within me; not only my body, but my spirit had hardened during these months of terror. I learned an important lesson in Berlin, one that would help to sustain me in the terrible days ahead. I learned how to hate.

Winter arrived, bringing with it new torments for the slave army in Berlin. Added to the hunger and exhaustion was the biting cold. The used winter clothing we were given (which, I learned later, was shipped directly from the concentration camps), hampered our movements and did little to fend off the effects of the dropping temperature. Numbed fingers stuck to the metal tools and gun barrels, making it impossible to work efficiently. The moods of the slave masters deteriorated even further as production dropped. Outbursts of violence became more frequent and severe. One of these episodes brought about my separation from Arnold Blum.

It was an exceptionally cold morning in late December; Arnold and I were working on the machine gun assembly line along with a group of French and Polish prisoners of war. A sudden clattering sound to my left startled me. The heavy metal barrel of a gun had slipped from the hands of the Pole working next to me and fallen to the concrete floor. Instantly, the line overseer swooped down on the hapless fellow and, screaming at the top of his lungs, began to viciously punch and kick the latter. Not satisfied with the damage he was inflicting in this way, he stooped over, picked up the gun barrel that had fallen and swung it full force into the Polish worker's face. There was a sickening thud as flesh and bone were crushed from the impact of the blow. The Polish worker let out a short, low-pitched groan and sank to the floor like a sack of sand, his hands cradling what had once been a human face. The overseer, maddened even further by the sight of the devastation he had inflicted, swung the barrel again and again at the prone figure, which ceased to move after the second or third blow.

I stood and stared at the broken body on the floor as if it were some strange object from another planet. Suddenly, a bright flash of light blinded me for a moment; my knees gave way, and I felt myself collapsing in slow motion. Dazed, I looked up; the brutal overseer was standing over me, his eyes rolling wildly. Fortunately, he had only used his fist on me. Now, however, he reached down to retrieve the murderous gun barrel from where he had thrown it after bludgeoning his previous victim. I watched almost disinterestedly, convinced that within seconds I, too, would be a corpse. Before this thought could take hold, however, a foot appeared in my line of vision on the floor and kicked the gun barrel to the side. I looked up; Arnold Blum was standing next to the overseer looking straight into the latter's eyes. There was a strange smile on his face as he spoke in his usual strong, even voice.

"If you kill us all, who will do the work necessary for the final victory of the Reich?" He continued to smile and stare.

The overseer's expression changed almost instantaneously from fury to surprise. For several seconds he seemed undecided what course to follow; finally, he stepped back and barked out, "All right, back to work you scum! And get that load of filth out of here!" he added, indicating the dead body with a jerk of his head. Then, without looking back at me or Arnold, he turned and went down the line to see if any other discipline was needed.

Some time during that night, Arnold Blum was taken away.

***

January, 1943. In the ten years of his dictatorship, Hitler had transformed not only Germany, but the entire civilized world. Millions had already died, and millions more were to follow before the nightmare ended. The slave factories continued to produce armaments and corpses, the latter in increasing numbers. Our rations were barely adequate to sustain life, let alone keep us fit enough to perform the gruelling work demanded of us. Many of the new workers, particularly those Jews from various East European ghettos, arrived in such a pitiful condition that it was obvious they would last for a few weeks at best. I concluded that Schramm's description of war as nothing more than a huge bureaucracy was the only explanation for why they had been sent to work in the first place. Certainly, the Nazis knew that weak, starving people did not make the most efficient slaves. Why and how I was able to survive even then, let alone later, remains a complete mystery to me. I saw many stronger and younger men than I deteriorate in no time at all, their health and spirits broken like dry twigs that have been stepped upon by a heavy foot. January, 1943. I was about to enter the seventh and final circle of hell.

A loud, rasping voice woke me suddenly from a troubled sleep.

"All Jews get up! Quickly!" Confusion filled the factory barracks as the command was repeated, this time punctuated with a few choice obscenities. I pulled on my shoes and staggered out with the others behind the bellowing overseer. What was happening? The question went back and forth but remained unanswered. I pulled my coat collar more tightly about my neck, but it did little to mitigate the effects of the frigid air as we were led out of the building onto the dark street. At the curb was a row of army trucks, motors running.

"Into the trucks, you miserable Jew bastards!" shouted a new voice just ahead of me. Even in the darkness I was able to distinguish the uniforms of the SS. Mechanically, I made my way to the edge of the vehicle and was practically thrown into its interior by the two brutish fellows who were loading us on like so many bags of garbage. Stifled cries of pain echoed through the stygian blackness as we crashed into each other and attempted to regain our balance. Finally, satisfied that we were packed together as tightly as possible, the two SS men raised the tailgate and the truck immediately began to move. Again, the questions were repeated. What was happening? Where were we being taken? Why had the Jews been singled out? For my part, I no longer cared. What more could they do to me, I thought. At worst, they could kill me. I didn't know that very shortly death would become the lesser evil.

We drove haltingly along the deserted streets of the capital, swerving around piles of rubble and bumping noisily through incompletely filled bomb craters. There was an eerie silence in the truck, much like that which one might find in a theater as the drama on stage reaches the final moments before the climax. Soon we would all know whether the resolution for us would be in keeping with Greek tragedy, or whether like in American films there would be a happy ending. I smiled bitterly to myself as I followed this train of thought. A happy ending indeed. Hitler would suddenly realize the error of his ways and call a halt to the war. All of the weapons of the world would be beaten into plowshares, and former enemies would embrace. Jews and SS officers, Poles and Russians would work together to bring about an era of world brotherhood. A happy ending. The Greeks knew better.

"Out! Out! Get your lazy Jew asses out of the trucks!" We obeyed the strident command mechanically, accustomed as we were by that time to constant shouting. We had arrived at what appeared to be a small field somewhere on the outskirts of the city. As I jumped down from the truck, my coat fluttering like a cape over my thin body, the chill air shocked my senses. In comparison it had been so warm in the truck; one might even have described it as comfortable had we not been packed together like sardines.

"Quickly! Quickly!" This order was repeated all along the line as one truck after another pulled up and discharged its human cargo. SS men brandishing automatic weapons menacingly herded the swelling number of Jews toward a growing throng at the far end of the field. The first thought that ran through my mind as I allowed myself to be carried along with the others was that they were going to kill us all right then and there, that they would slaughter us like animals and bury us in this obscure place. We had all heard of similar atrocities.

Apparently I was not the only one to have reached this conclusion. Some of the men prayed loudly, rocking back and forth while they recited the words of *kaddish*; others spoke defiantly, urging those around them not to allow themselves to be butchered without a fight. For all their talk, however, they made no move to put their words into action. I felt strangely aloof from it all; it was as if I were a spectator to some strange, fascinating, but incomprehensible ceremony.

The mood changed abruptly as a loud, rumbling sound became audible and steadily increased in intensity. The ground under our feet began to vibrate as the sound came closer. I squinted and peered into the darkness beyond the thin cordon of armed SS; at that very moment a huge, dark, wall-like object burst into view. A train. As I watched the spectral machine slowly grind to a halt, I became strangely calm, almost serene. A mystical silence once again swept over the mass of assembled Jews. Even those who had been praying grew still and craned their necks to see. There was no surprise, only a kind of reverent awe. It was as if the appearance of the train in that unknown place had been anticipated by all of us all our lives, indeed, since the beginning of time itself. So this is how the Messiah has chosen to reveal himself, I thought, intoxicated from lack of sleep and infused with a growing sense of irony. The Chosen People. So this is what we Jews have been chosen for.

Again the shouting began, this time with even more urgency. We were driven forward by the SS to the gaping boxcars like a herd of cattle, kicked and prodded with the butts of the automatic weapons. I was in one of the first groups to reach the cars. As I scrambled through the open door into the musty interior, roughly pushed along by those entering behind me, I noticed that it was not entirely empty. Huddled in the rear corner were several human shapes. Within minutes, the boxcar was filled to the brim with at least fifty or sixty more people jammed into it. Then the doors were pulled shut with a metallic clang and we were left in the pitch blackness. For several more minutes the train remained motionless. Outside, we could hear the muffled shouts of the SS guards and the sounds of other cars being loaded. Once again there was the low murmur of prayers, but for the most part everyone remained still, as if listening carefully for some clue as to where we were going.

Finally, the train lurched forward with a screeching sound and began to move slowly, picking up momentum with each click of its heavy, metal wheels as they passed over one section of track after another. The strange sensation I had experienced in the clearing earlier returned with even greater intensity; I felt as if I were floating weightlessly in the darkness, a disembodied spirit drifting through the void of time and space. It is almost over, I thought, almost over. The famous lines of Goethe's short poem echoed through my mind:

Over all the mountain tops
Is calm,
In all the tree tops
You can scarcely perceive
A breath:
The little birds are quiet in the forest.
Just wait! Soon
You too, will be at rest.

Peace. Peace. Finally I was going to find peace. The rhythmic clicking of the metal wheels echoed my thought as I closed my eyes and let myself slide to the floor.

I don't know how many hours passed while I drifted in and out of that narcosis-like state. Varied dream images appeared and disappeared in rhythm with the movement and sound of the train. Karl's face appeared at one point; he was smiling at me while he tossed a volley ball into the air and adroitly caught it behind his back. After several more tricks, he winked and gestured with his head toward the other side of the car. I turned in the direction of his gesture and saw Birgit, my Birgit, also smiling. She held out her arms toward me and came closer, but before I could respond, a terrified look came over her face and she disappeared. In the place where she had been was a small, yellow flame which began to grow quickly. As it grew it came closer and closer to my face and began to emit a harsh, crackling sound. When it was directly in front of me, so close that I could actually feel the intense heat searing my skin, it began to take the shape of a six-pointed, twisted star. My lungs began to burn painfully. I flailed out with my arms, choking from lack of oxygen.

"What are you doing? Stop that," came a voice from the side. I awoke with a start as a number of hard blows struck my arms and upper torso. I opened my eyes. A small amount of light was streaming in through a few small openings toward the top of the boxcar. It was early morning. I was lying on the floor of the car, crowded together in a compressed mass with those who had also been sleeping. Apparently, someone had either shifted position or slumped down across me and cut off my air supply. I managed to free a space so that I could sit up and look around me. Soon there was a general stirring as others began to wake and reorient themselves. One young man — he must have been no more than eighteen or nineteen —

managed to hoist himself up along the side of the car to one of the openings and peer out.

"What do you see? Where are we?" questioned those around him as he let himself back down.

"Nothing but flat marsh lands," he replied. "A lot of pine trees in the distance, but nothing else. It looks like we're in the middle of nowhere." He scrambled back up to make a further inspection.

"We seem to have slowed down," observed someone at the other end of the car. It was true. The clicking was coming at longer intervals than before.

"Maybe we're switching tracks again," responded another voice. "During the night we even stopped several times." I was surprised that I had been able to sleep through it all.

"We've come to a station of some kind," announced the young fellow whose eyes were still glued to the opening at the top of the boxcar. "Here, take a look." He jumped down and boosted one of the others up as the train came to a complete halt.

"It is a station," confirmed the second fellow. "There's a sign. It says Obermajdan Station. It also says something about changing for Bialystok and Wolkowysk, wherever they are."

"We must be in Poland," chimed in someone else. "They are probably going to use us for some labor project here. The situation on the Eastern Front has been deteriorating. They must need us here." This explanation met with widespread agreement. Some now began to speculate about the nature of our new work assignment. Meanwhile, the train started up again and inched forward for a minute or so before coming to another grinding halt. This was repeated several more times until finally we heard the engine hiss loudly for a final time and become silent.

The sudden flash of light blinded me momentarily as the door to the car was thrown open. A cold blast of wind immediately set me shivering. I stood up with the others to see what was going on.

"Climb out, please. Climb out." came the polite, but firm command from the gaunt fellow who stood before the open door of the boxcar. He had a blue insignia of some sort on his worn trousers. Within seconds we had all climbed out onto the platform. About two hundred meters or so directly across from us was what seemed to be a long, wooden wall with pleasantly colored doors and windows, the latter sporting bright curtains and neat, green blinds. On each door there was a different name stenciled in clear, bold letters: INFIRMARY, TOILET, STATIONMASTER. There were also a first- and second-class waiting room over to the side, as well as a ticket window and a large timetable a bit further down along the wall. A large station clock caught my eye. Its hands incorrectly indicated the time to be three o'clock.

My suspicions were aroused right from the outset. There was

something about this station that did not ring true. For one thing, the floor where we stood (what was supposed to be the platform) was gravel, and as I looked more carefully at the doors and windows, they seemed strangely one dimensional. It was as if they were painted onto the wall. Permeating the air was a foul odor, like a mixture of rotting garbage and burning feathers; an odor that seemed out of place in these cheerful surroundings. Before I could follow through on these thoughts, however, a new series of orders began to echo through the chilly morning air. Several German SS men and Ukrainian guards appeared and motioned us to follow those from the other cars to a point a few hundred meters to the left in front of a large, wooden structure. There was a group of men there, some already beginning to disrobe in keeping with the harsh commands of the guards who brandished ugly horsewhips and rifles. My heart sank as I looked at the scene before me. To the side, in a large open area that I later learned was the sorting square, there were huge piles of clothing and shoes collected from previous transports. On the top of the buildings were more Ukrainians armed with machine guns that pointed down at the growing crowd in the square below.

"Women and children to the left! Men to the Right!" For the first time I became aware that there were women and children present along the platform, either unloaded from the other cars or from another train. I heard high-pitched screams and pleading; families that had made the journey together were objecting to the order to separate, hanging onto each other in fear. The guards reacted forcefully, tearing people from each other's arms and lashing out with their whips and rifle butts at those who continued to hesitate.

Before widespread panic set in, however, another series of directives restored a modicum of hope.

"Tie your shoelaces together and remember where you have left your things so that you can retrieve them after you have been disinfected." Then, "Anyone who is ill, report to the infirmary." The majority did not suspect that there would be no later for them, that by tying their shoes together and neatly stacking their clothing they were unwittingly aiding their Aryan masters who even committed mass murder in an orderly fashion. Nevertheless, there was a great deal of shouting, crying, pushing, and shoving by the guards and by some of the more skeptical victims.

The women and children were led away to the barracks on the left to undress; the men were told to do so out in the open square. Many were already naked. They stood shivering, their arms folded in front of their chests, eager not to upset the guards even if it meant freezing to death in the sub-zero weather. But there were others, those suspecting the true nature of the fate being prepared for them, who simply stood where they were without making an effort to comply. As I reached the square called the disrobing area, any doubt as to what kind of a place we had come to disappeared instantly. Out of the corner of my eye, just two or three meters to the side of me, I noticed the young man from my boxcar who had been the first to describe what was going on outside. He was standing defiantly, hands on hips, while a Ukrainian guard shouted at him in broken German to undress. All of a sudden, probably as a result of something the youngster said in response, the Ukrainian raised his rifle. Two quick shots rang out, not much louder than firecrackers. The young man's head exploded, sending blood, brains, and bone over those around him. Panic broke out in the square. The prisoners began to run around wildly; some of those who were in the process of undressing hurriedly began to put their clothing back on. More rifle shots rang out, and from a point on top of the barracks a machine gun began to rattle, cutting down many as they sought cover.

I had fallen to the ground instinctively when the shooting began. As I lay there I could see little clouds of dust kicking up across the square in the spots where the machine gun bullets struck. Many others also lay about, some, like the young man from the train, having cheated the gas chamber, and others, like myself, fearfully waiting for the shooting to stop. Time seemed to stand still and then reverse as I watched the macabre spectacle. I remembered a similar experience in the Odeonsplatz in Munich many years before and wondered if it had been a dream, a premonition of the present. I let my eyes wander to my hand, which was flattened against the ground directly in front of my face. The scar from that earlier stray bullet was still there; it had not been a dream.

The shooting stopped as suddenly as it had started. An SS officer in a resplendent black uniform, defying the bullets that whizzed about him, ran to the center of the square and began shouting to the totally panicked Ukrainians to cease fire. To emphasize his order, he drew his luger from its holster and squeezed off several shots in the direction of the machine gunner on the barracks' roof. Almost instantly, the gun became silent and order began to return. Now, mingled with a new series of orders could be heard the moans of the wounded. Several men with the same blue markings on their clothing that I had noticed on the train platform, and others with similar pink and red insignias appeared and began to drag the dead bodies from the square, lashed on by the SS and Ukrainians. I pulled myself up onto my feet, but before I could decide which way to move someone roughly grasped my arm from behind. I turned, expecting to feel the sting of a horsewhip. Instead, I found myself looking into the familiar face of Arnold Blum who silently handed me a bundle and motioned me to follow him.

"I have been watching for you for the last few days, but I really never expected to find you," he said, closing the large door behind us. He had led me to a large, square building back down by the bogus railway station. Inside were a number of trucks and automobiles; the smell of gasoline and oil hung in the air.

"This is the camp garage," he said, leading me toward the rear. "You'll have to stay here until I get back. If it hadn't been for the riot, you would probably be coming out of your final 'shower' just about now. Our commandant has it down to a science, three quarters of an hour from start to finish."

"I don't understand," I muttered feebly, moving along in between the large trucks, a pace behind him.

"I'll explain it all to you later if I can. Right now there will be quite a bit of work to do, and after that I have to take care of a bribe or two to make sure that you don't wind up in the cremation ditches with the others. At least not today. For now, just stay at the back of the garage here and try not to even breathe too loud before I come back." He turned and started back to the door, but after a few steps he stopped and looked back toward me again. "By the way, Heinrich," he said. "Welcome to Treblinka."

For hours I cowered in the corner of the garage between two large trucks, plagued by hunger, thirst, and cold, my mind in such turmoil that I could scarcely put together any connected thoughts. Showers, cremation ditches, Treblinka. Could this all be real?

Initially, I could hear the high-pitched sounds of women's and children's voices, but before very long they became silent. What I was unaware of at the time was that just a few meters in front of the garage was the area where the women from the transports, already nude, were gathered. There they waited to have their hair shorn before being led with the children along the winding path surrounded by pine trees and barbwire fences that had been designated The Tube by the inmates. The Germans, however, with their typical gallows humor often referred to it as the *Himmelstrasse* (The Road To Heaven), since at its end were the thirteen gas chambers. Their warped humor was also evident in the name they had given to the last journey of their victims. They called it the *Himmelfahrt* (The Ascension). In the first hour or so I also heard sporadic rifle shots very close by to my left. After that, except for an occasional loud voice and the constant whining sound of an engine of some kind in the distance, it became quiet. I began to wonder if Arnold would ever return, whether I had hallucinated him in the first place. How could it be possible? What would he be doing in this place, and how could he have been looking for me here? The more I thought about it, the more convinced I became that my mind had played a trick on me. But if that were so, what was I doing in this garage? How had I gotten here? And what was I to do next? Numbed to inertia by the frigid air and these conflicting thoughts, I let my head sink between my knees and continued to wait for what I now believed to be a phantom Arnold Blum.

I felt a sudden rush of fear as I heard the door at the front of the garage creak open, followed by the muted sound of voices. A moment later an electric light at the front clicked on. I hunched myself into even more of a ball, as if hoping in this way to become invisible. As cold as I was, I began to perspire heavily.

"It's all right, Heinrich. It's me." Arnold's voice echoed eerily off the wall in front of me. I jumped to my feet and almost fell down again as the blood rushed from my head. I grasped the sturdy bumper of the truck in front of me to steady myself. My legs felt rubbery from having been cramped in a sitting position for so many hours. So it was true after all, I thought. I had not imagined it. By the time my friend reached my side, I was shaking uncontrollably.

We sat on the edge of the wooden bunk in the dimly lit barrack. While Arnold recounted the story of his arrival in Treblinka, I greedily devoured the entire loaf of bread and two tins of sardines he had brought to me. That we were there together was a miracle of sorts, if one can use such a term to describe anything that might happen in such a malignant place. Unlike myself, he had not been on a transport consisting primarily of Jewish laborers from the munitions factories. For some reason, he said, he had been placed on what seemed to be an ordinary passenger train, just like the one on which we had first met when we were taken to Berlin. The other passengers were, as far as he could tell, all well-to-do German-Jews from the north; there were even entire families dressed in their holiday best, as if on a vacation journey. They had been told that they were being sent east in order to colonize the great plains there. That it was not an ordinary train, however, was evident as soon as it arrived in Treblinka. Once disembarked, he and the others were subjected to the same procedure I had witnessed that morning, although in their case no riot had disturbed the order.

"The day I arrived must have been a very slow day," he observed, reaching under the bunk and withdrawing a corked bottle of wine which he extended to me. I uncorked it and took a long drink. "They went to extra pains to convince us that we were respected guests rather than sacrificial victims. It is a part of the madness here, almost like a game. I hate to admit it, Heinrich, but they nearly had me fooled too. I found myself believing what they said."

He paused, shook his head sadly and then went on, "I was on my way to the disrobing square when a passing SS officer called me over to him. At first I didn't recognize him, but then I remembered who he was — one of my old employer's customers in Munich. I had actually worked on his automobile several times. He acted as though he had discovered an old friend. Can you imagine such a thing?" He shook his head again, as if he could not even believe what he was saying. Then he went on, "To make a long story short, I owe my life to my ability to replace a carburetor. For the time being, I am the favorite of the Deputy Commandant, the one they call Lalka, and should remain so as long as I keep his automobile in tiptop shape, or until he decides to shoot me in the back of the neck or hack me into pieces with a shovel. I am the master mechanic of Treblinka, and you, dear friend, are my assistant, at least as long as your luck holds out."

"Do they really kill everyone?" I whispered, already knowing the answer but refusing to accept it.

"Yes, with very few exceptions," he replied, sighing. "Even those few of us who are still alive have been destroyed by the bastards. You will understand what I mean very soon." Suddenly, he grasped my arm so tightly that I uttered a cry of pain. "But we have to survive this, Heinrich. We have to let the world know what is going on here. We have to." His eyes had a wild look in them, a mixture of hatred and despair such as I had never seen in human eyes before, a look that I still see today each time I gaze into the mirror.

That night I asked him, "You said that you were watching for me. How could that be? How did you know that I would be coming here?" We had continued to speak quietly, so as not to disturb the other prisoners, many of whom were already asleep after their strenuous and appalling labors of the day.

"There were rumors that a transport was coming in from Berlin, that the German factories were going to be swept clean of their remaining Jews. You would be surprised at how few secrets there are in this place. But I didn't really believe that I would be able to find you. The odds were against it."

The hatred in his eyes had disappeared; he patted my arm gently, as one might do with a child. Then, in a voice so low that I could scarcely hear it, he added, "I only hope that you never curse me for having saved you."

I quickly learned why Arnold could have expressed such a thought. Had it not been for him, I would have already been a corpse, that much was certain. Curse him? How could such a thing be possible? And yet it was. He had kept me alive, but the world in which I found myself as a result of his intervention was not one of life, but one of suffering and death. *Treblinka*. Were I asked to sum up in one word all of the evils that have ever existed on earth, all of the pain and sorrow and cruelty that mankind has endured and can endure, I would offer that single word: *Treblinka*. And yet, no word or words can really begin to describe what happened there. Not even that word itself. *Treblinka*.

***

Even hell has its rules. In Treblinka, the basic rule for survival was to remain inconspicuous. In order to live for another hour or day, one learned to become invisible. To incite one of the guards (and one need just attract notice to do this), could mean death. A bruise on one's face, no matter how it had been caused, removed one's invisibility and meant an almost certain bullet in the neck. So we shielded our faces as best we could from the blows that rained down on us indiscriminately. The same SS man who at one moment might speak to you almost as if he considered you a human being, would beat you like an animal seconds later, for no apparent provocation. To appear to be shirking was also punishable by death, and so one learned to live literally on the run. But even then there was no guarantee; one needed simply to be in the vicinity of someone else's "transgression" to be selected for the final punishment. In the last analysis, the primary determining factor was whim. The Nazis had supplanted nature and God as the supreme arbiters and dispensers of fate.

My first few days in Treblinka were only a mild preview of the horrors in store for me. As a result of Arnold's well-placed bribes, I was assigned to the garage as his assistant. I spent much of the day in the relative security of the garage, vainly attempting to understand the mysterious workings of the various vehicles under his care. It was immediately obvious, however, that no amount of training, especially under the distorted conditions in the camp, could make me even remotely resemble a mechanic. Thus, reluctantly deciding that it would be too dangerous to attempt to keep me on there, Arnold used his influence with the *Lagerälteste* to have me placed in one of the other labor details, or *Kommandos*: the sorting commando.

***

It has been said that the mythology of a people provides the most authentic portrait of its intrinsic philosophical and psychological makeup, one more accurate and objective than the biased accounts we regard as history. Treblinka convinced me that this is so. Numbed and horrified by my first day's experience on the sorting detail, I remained awake in my bunk almost the entire night, attempting to retain my slipping sanity. I recalled a particular lecture I had heard at the University of Munich during those early years when Germany first began to peel off its veneer of civilization one thin layer at a time, revealing the savage essence beneath. The speaker was a visiting professor of Classicism from the University of Heidelberg, a charter member of the fledgling National Socialist Party who had come to share his vision of a new heroic age, an age already being heralded in by the nation's future leader, Adolf Hitler. I recall clearly how he proudly repeated his major thesis over and over again, namely, that the Aryan race possessed a divine strength and purity, one inherited from its glorious, mythic past. To prove his thesis, he gave a dramatic rendition of one of the most famous of the ancient Germanic myths, the strange and cruel creation myth of the ancient Norsemen. He revealed to his enthralled audience how, in the vast expanse of nothingness called the Ginnunga Gap, the first life appeared in the likeness of a man — the mighty Ymir, fierce ancestor of the succeeding races of frost giants. As fierce and barbarous as Ymir was, however, he was no match for the next race of beings to appear — the human forerunners of today's Aryan race. These early Aryans were far more ferocious than the frost giants, and in the inevitable battle for supremacy they brutally killed the giant Ymir. So horrible and numerous were the latter's wounds that the other giants drowned in the torrent of blood that flowed from them. Not satisfied with the simple act of murder, moreover, the victors proceeded to dismember the fallen giant, using the salvaged parts of his body to form their future world. His blood became the sea, his flesh the earth, his bones the mountains, his teeth the rocks and pebbles. But that was not all. From his skull they fashioned the sky, and as a final touch, they used his eyebrows to build an impenetrable fence around the world.

As I lay in my hard bunk in the stench of the barrack (the few wooden buckets supplied us at night were pitifully inadequate for our physical needs) thinking of this ancient myth, I was struck by the macabre similarities between it and the world the Nazis had created in Treblinka. Creation through annihilation — this was the essence of the Thousand Year Reich. The new race of heroes had already begun to drown the world in blood, just as their mythic predecessors had drowned the giants. Creation through annihilation. Their future world would also be built from the remains of their victims. Nothing would go to waste. The German fields would be fertilized from the bones of the dead; from their fat, soap would be produced, and their hair would be woven into blankets and slippers. Since murder was no longer inexpensive, moreover, the gold fillings from the teeth of the slain would serve to defray the costs.

***

How is it possible to depict a routine in a world ruled by madness? How does one even justify the attempt to describe the indescribable? The greatest painter cannot paint a sound, nor would it be possible for a musician, no matter how talented, to produce a color in a melody. I have only words. My hands shake as I attempt to find any that are adequate to the task of portraying Treblinka; my head aches at the realization that I must continue to try, even though I know that I will ultimately fail. My mind rebels at the thought that, as grotesque and inconceivable as it may seem, hell not only has rules, but a routine as well.

The camp was divided into two main sections: the upper death camp, the *Totenlager*, which contained the gas chambers, and the lower section, where I and the other so-called "work-Jews" performed our odious assignments. To assure the utmost efficiency in the main operation of the camp (namely the killing of Jews), the Nazis created a society characterized by specialization. Thus, the several hundred "work-Jews" were subdivided according to their specialty. The "court-Jews" (*Hofjuden*), were the elite victims of Treblinka, the artisans such as Arnold Blum, and those who possessed other temporarily useful skills, the tailors, cobblers, carpenters, and even the musicians (the Nazis loved their music even when it smelled of death). Also part of the upper stratum of the camp were the "gold-Jews" (*Goldjuden*), who wore an appropriate yellow cloth badge as they sorted and packed currency from various countries, along with jewelry, stock certificates, deeds, and other items of value that had been confiscated from those on the transports.

The "blues" comprised another important group in the hierarchy of the camp. Identified by blue cloth badges on their clothing, they were the first to greet the new victims as the cattle car doors were thrown open. It was their responsibility to see to it that the unloading procedure was orderly, and the trains prepared quickly for their next transport. At times this work was very difficult, particularly when the transports were severely overcrowded and had come from far distances. The blue group had to first dispose of the corpses, sometimes numbering in the hundreds, of those who had died during the journey. They carried them to the huge ditches behind the sorting square to be incinerated along with the refuse in the fire that burned there almost constantly. In addition, they were given the demanding task of cleaning the boxcars, filthy as a result of monstrous crowding and lack of toilet facilities. Finally, it was the responsibility of the blue group to bring those too ill to make the final journey down The Street of Heaven to what was euphemistically called the camp hospital (*Lazaret*), located to the east of the burning ditch. The three inmates who worked there wore red crosses on their arms to further the simulation of a hospital staff, but they did not give medical aid to the new arrivals. Their function was to position the ill person properly over the ditch while the treatment was administered: an SS bullet in the back of the neck.

The sorting commando, whose members were identifiable by the red insignia they wore, was the largest of all the commandos, and was further subdivided according to specialty. My particular group, for example, was assigned to clothing: suits, dresses, coats, etc.. It was our responsibility to separate items according to size and quality and make neat bundles of these items so that they could eventually be shipped to the Reich on the returning trains. Other sorting details specialized in shoes, briefcases, and even such items as fountain pens and bottles. While one might be inclined to find a degree of macabre humor in the idea of condemned Jews sorting out dirty, used bottles for reuse by the Aryan Master Race, I found out quickly that there was nothing funny about it. It was about my third or fourth week in the camp. While that does not seem like a long time in the ordinary course of the world, in the distorted time frame of Treblinka, where one lived from minute to minute, four weeks of survival made one a seasoned veteran.

We went through the usual morning roll call, received our work orders for the day, and were in our assigned work areas. On the previous day there had been two large transports from Warsaw, and so we were all racing about at full speed to perform our duties to the satisfaction of the watchful guards. The particular Ukrainian who was supervising in my vicinity that morning was a huge, sullen fellow, one who would strike out with his heavy whip or bare fists whenever he felt the urge to do so. Often he would continue the vicious beating until he either tired or his victim lay in a lifeless, broken heap. It was snowing lightly. I had just picked up a bundle of clothing and was on my way to the sorting barrack to ready them for shipment, when out of the corner of my eye I noticed the Ukrainian guard approaching from the side. Without looking directly at him, I increased my pace so that I would be quickly out of his range. Due to a combination of my panic, the slick ground, and the awkward burden, I tripped and fell down heavily. I got to my feet at once and began frenziedly snatching up the scattered articles of clothing. By this time the Ukrainian was only a couple of meters from me and quickly closing in. I was paralyzed. Before he reached me, however, there was a loud crashing sound just to the left. One of the workers from the bottle detail had also lost his footing on the snow and fallen; the basketload of bottles he was carrying slipped from his hands, sending a shower of glass across the surrounding area as the bottles smashed onto the hard ground. The Ukrainian shouted some curses and changed his direction at once. He reached the trembling inmate as the latter was making a feeble attempt to pick up the few unbroken bottles and place them back into the basket. As he bent forward, the guard's booted foot caught him squarely in the face, crushing his nose as if it were made of clay. I gathered up the fallen clothing quickly and ran at full speed to the sorting barrack without looking back, thankful that chance had worked in my favor again. At the time, I felt no particular pity for the poor fellow who had saved my skin by his carelessness. He and fate. It was only later that the image of his crushed face and the sound of his cries of pain became a part of my nightly torment.

I lost track of time. The transports continued to arrive, sometimes three or four a day. Unbelievably, before long there was a sameness to it all. In order to survive I had to suspend my senses, to learn how not to see the fear that flooded the eyes of the newly arrived victims, or hear the children's muffled cries of pain as they stood naked for as long as an hour or more in the freezing winter air, awaiting the terror of their final journey along the "Road to Heaven." I had to learn to shut my mind off to the present, to become an unthinking, unfeeling automaton. I could not allow myself to be human as I bundled up the soft, freshly cut hair of the women into large bales, or came across a wrinkled family photograph in the coat pocket of someone who at that very moment might be convulsing in agony as the carbon monoxide fumes choked out his life. After working feverishly from sunrise to sunset I could not allow my feelings to awaken during the dreaded evening roll call, when those who had been physically marked during the day by a guard's whip or fist were called aside and taken to the "infirmary" to be given either a bullet in the neck or a lethal injection. I was determined to do what Arnold had demanded of me: I would survive to tell the world about what was happening in Treblinka. Ironically, however, I discovered that by erecting a barrier between myself and the world in order to survive, my humanity was dying; by building a wall to shut out the horror, I locked it within myself and become an integral part of it. The sadistic assistant commandant of the camp, Franz Stangl, must have understood this numbing psychological process when writing the song that was to become a kind of anthem in Treblinka. The first stanza clearly expressed it:

> *We look directly at the world:*
> *The columns march off to their work*
> *All we have left is Treblinka:*
> *It is our destiny...*

Unlike the barbwire fences and lethal watchtowers surrounding me, the wall I had placed around my mind was far too fragile to stand for very long. Sounds and images began to find their way through the cracks that developed, and as hard as I tried to seal off the points of entry, I was unsuccessful. In spite of my exhaustion, I found it increasingly difficult to sleep. I tried to block out the present by searching out pleasant memories from the past: Lake Constance...Birgit...Karl...my family. But more and more frequently these memories were crowded out by the visions of a reality I could not ignore, even though I continued to reject it. Visions of heads exploding and faces smashed to pulp. Sobbing children, their bare feet painfully stuck to the frozen ground and their eyes filled with a fear so deep that it burned through one's soul. I was surviving, but I was not alive. *"All we have left is Treblinka..."*

***

The newly appearing signs of spring seemed almost like blasphemy. In the inverted world of Treblinka, the warming air and the lively sound of birds merely emphasized the fact that it was death, not rebirth, that reigned supreme. Death.

After a relative lull at the end of winter, the number of transports began to increase again. Each day the dark trains rolled into the phantom station. No sooner had one been processed than another arrived. As a result of the increasing demands on the workers and administrators, there was no longer any serious attempt to convince the new arrivals that they were in a transit camp. The facade was lifted. The terrified Jews, almost all from the east, were beaten unmercifully from the moment they emerged from the suffocating boxcars until the moment they were driven into the overburdened gas chambers of the upper camp. The "work-Jews" of the camp labored frenetically to keep pace, and in recognition of their labors were treated with an unusual degree of consideration by the guards and administrators. It was now a joint effort to keep the machinery of death functioning at peak efficiency, and so allowances were made. At the evening roll call, for example, the customary flogging of inmates who had been reported during the day for minor infractions was suspended; every able-bodied worker was needed for the next day's labor. For the time being, the slaves had been granted almost equal status with their masters. A macabre fraternity of annihilation had been established, and we expended all of our energies to prove ourselves worthy of it.

At the end of one morning roll call during the height of this period of accelerated destruction, a group of us from the sorting detail was called aside and ordered to the upper camp. The frightened protest of several of the veterans (assignment to the upper camp was virtually tantamount to a death sentence), was met with the assurance that we would be returned to our usual functions when the situation was normalized. What difference did it make, I thought; I had already seen the worst that this earth had to offer. Or so I thought. What I witnessed in that short interval, however, made all else I had ever seen or imagined pale in comparison. For, while death was certainly no longer a stranger to me, until then I had not been forced into constant physical contact with it; there still remained a tenuous distance between us. In the *Totenlager* this distance was bridged as death and I locked in an embrace from which neither would ever again release the other.

The stench of diesel fuel and putrefying flesh assaulted my nostrils as I marched along with the others on the tree-lined trail that ran along the western edge of the barracks, curving sharply eastward to the entrance of the upper camp. Following the SS escort, we came to a huge brick building, supported by a thick concrete foundation. This was the gas house; the structure that housed the newer gas chambers, constructed when the original three proved inadequate to the task of processing the massive numbers of Jews and other "subhumans" selected for inclusion in the Final Solution. The sporadic sound of small arms fire echoed throughout the building as we were led inside.

My blood froze as I beheld the sight that greeted us. There, in front of a set of heavy doors that had apparently been opened only moments before, was a mountain of naked, contorted corpses: women and children who appeared to have been welded together during some macabre dance of death. Several filthy, perspiring inmates worked strenuously to disengage the bodies from each other, many of which were covered with loose feces and urine. Once separated, each body was tossed onto a crude wooden stretcher held by two other so-called *Totenjuden* (Jews of the dead). Having received their burden, the latter immediately set out with it at a run. An SS officer with drawn pistol stood at the edge of the large mound of flesh and from time to time nonchalantly fired a shot into a writhing victim who had not been completely finished off by the carbon monoxide fumes.

"What is the matter, haven't you ever seen a pile of shit before?" he said, his voice badly slurred, and his lips curled in a strange, drunken smile as he studied the horrified expressions on our faces. For several moments I was rooted to the spot. I began to retch uncontrollably. I shook my head from side to side, trying to convince myself that I was having a nightmare. This seemed to amuse the SS officer even more. He took two or three steps toward me, waved his pistol in an arc and laughed loudly. Then, in a mocking tone he said, "What a pity. You don't like the decor of our pleasant little establishment, do you? And to think that we built it just for all of you." He staggered back a few steps and pumped two bullets randomly into the pile of corpses. "Now get to work or the next one will be for you!" he barked, his smile replaced by a fierce frown.

Mechanically, I and the others stepped over to the door of the chamber and began our loathsome task. The flesh of the dead was still warm to the touch. So this was the culmination. For the previous ten years I had watched God grow steadily weaker in Germany under the attack of the Nazis; in the spring of 1943, in the upper camp of Treblinka, I became a witness to His murder.

For at least a week I performed the gruesome labor of loading the fresh corpses onto the stretchers or, when stretchers were not available, carrying them on my back to the cremation ditches some fifty meters or so behind the gas chambers. There, burial details stacked them in the best burning configuration on the huge cremation grills. My clothes caked with human waste, I ran double-time, delivering the corpses to the so-called dentists, whose job it was to extract any gold fillings from their teeth before incineration. I could not allow myself to think that these burdens of dead flesh had only moments before been human beings like myself — no, not like myself, but infinitely better ones; at least they had had the decency to die.

How could I have taken part in such perfidy? And why did I continue to do the bidding of the devil? I have asked myself these questions every day since Treblinka, and have been unable to find the answers. Certainly it was not fear of death; how can one fear that which one has become? Moreover, any remaining desire to survive, at least on the conscious level, was eradicated the very moment I set foot into the gas house. And yet, when the SS man offered me the alternative of death or complicity, I chose the latter. Why? Why and why and why?

The number of transports dwindled sharply in the days following that unusual two-week spurt. Surprisingly, as the pace slowed, I and the others who had been sent to the upper camp with me were not added to the flaming stack of flesh on the cremation grid as we had expected we would be. The explanation for this was a practical one. During our absence from the lower camp, the sorting square and railroad platform had been piled up with items from the numerous transports. We were still needed to sort, pack and ready the items for shipment before the next wave of transports began to arrive.

***

Arnold came to see me one evening in my barrack. It had been some time since we had had the opportunity to speak at any length together; he was housed in the separate, medieval-style structure built specifically for the *Hofjuden* during Lalka's renovation of the camp. In his desire to create a magic kingdom, the mad assistant commandant had combined a warped sense of humor with the ingrained German need for bourgeois order. The barracks area had been constructed to resemble a miniature medieval town, complete with various streets, shops, and even a miniature Jewish ghetto.

"You don't look well at all, Heinrich," Arnold said, his forehead furrowed with concern. "You have to get hold of yourself. You know how important it is to keep yourself in good physical condition." There was an urgency in his voice.

"It doesn't matter," I replied in a dead voice. "I've reached the end of my rope. What is the point of going on like this?" I felt empty. My emotions had been blunted almost completely by the magnitude of the atrocities I had witnessed. Since my return to the lower camp I had fallen into a bottomless depression, and although I did not seriously consider suicide, I worked listlessly, subconsciously inviting the order to report to the infirmary for my bullet in the neck. I no longer made an attempt to supplement the meager camp diet with contraband food obtained from the transports, nor did I carefully shave each morning and pinch my cheeks so that I would appear young and vigorous during roll call.

"Don't give up, Heinrich." he said, holding out his hands as if in supplication. "Not now." His hands trembled. Then, moving his mouth close to my ear, he added in a low whisper, "You must hold out! I can't tell you exactly when because I don't know, but an uprising is being planned. If you can only wait, we may have a chance to escape."

I was stunned by the news. An uprising. Escape. Could that be possible? For the next few days I thought of nothing else, trying to imagine how such a thing could be carried out and what possible role I might play in it. Like a child, I fantasized the heroic feats that I would perform. I saw myself storming watchtowers and breaking through the outer gates after furious hand-to-hand combat with the SS. Escape. Away from this living hell, away from the interminable stench of death. Was it a dream?

***

My daydreams of glory and freedom were short-lived. They ended abruptly one afternoon with the arrival of a transport which included *them*. It was only a matter of minutes — ten, twenty, thirty at most — and yet I have seen *them* every day since. And every night. When the wind whistles through the trees it is *their* pleading voices I hear. When my eyes search the sky at night, perhaps hoping to catch a glimpse of the resurrected God I saw murdered in Treblinka, I see *them* instead. The stars become *their* terrified eyes, merged with the hundreds of thousands of other eyes, all weeping. All weeping. And I weep with *them*. I weep over the memories I cannot bear to keep, and from which I will never be free. I weep from the guilt that should have been *theirs* instead of mine. I weep because I am alive in *their* place; because *their* ashes are scattered in the Polish marsh lands where mine should be. I weep because the words from the "Treblinka Song" have proven to be true: "*All we have left is Treblinka. It is our destiny.*"

A passenger train transport was arriving from Germany, the first of its kind in some time. The camp grapevine had spread the word of its pending arrival earlier that afternoon, and so I and a few other German "work-Jews" managed to maneuver ourselves over near the platform during the unloading procedure, hoping perhaps to see a friend or relative and at least say a last farewell if it proved impossible to save them from the journey along the Tube. Arnold Blum stood a few meters from me, watching intently as the frightened, mystified passengers disembarked, luggage in hand, and stopped briefly to read the deceitful signs that had been placed on the unloading platform:

> *Attention Jews!*
> *You are now in a transit camp, from which you will*
> *continue your journey to a labor camp. In order to*
> *prevent epidemics, all clothing and luggage must be*
> *handed over for disinfection.*
>
> *Gold, cash, foreign currency and jewelry must be*
> *turned in at the ticket office. You will be given*
> *receipts for these valuables. Later, upon presentation*
> *of the receipts, your valuables will be returned to you.*
>
> *For reasons of personal hygiene, all new arrivals must*
> *bathe before continuing the journey.*

A few of the more levelheaded arrivals even noted down the numbers of the "porters" who took their bags, and attempted to press a coin or two into the hand of the member of the blue squad who was handling their luggage.

Presently, however, a minor commotion arose at a point halfway up the platform; several Ukrainian guards and SS converged on the spot at once. After some loud discussion and arm waving, one of the latter went off at a run. Minutes later he came striding briskly back, at his side the Assistant Commandant. The curiosity of the surrounding inmates proved even stronger than their fear of punishment; whatever was happening was exceptional, otherwise Lalka would not have been summoned. A small cluster formed at the edge of the sorting square, watching the unique spectacle unfold.

A young, strikingly attractive woman stood in front of the assistant commandant and the SS guard, while the latter examined a document she had handed them. Her delicately chiseled Germanic features were softly framed by the long blonde hair that draped down to her shoulders. At her sides, clinging to her, were two young boys of about seven and five years of age. I moved closer to them, as if drawn there like a moth to a forbidden flame. She was pointing down at the children, repeating something in a high-pitched, excited voice, but I was still too far away to make out the words. I saw her reach down and begin to fumble with the older child's trousers and then point downward. Lalka shook his head and said a few words to the SS guard. Then, after a short conversation between the two, he turned quickly on his heel and strode away. The guard, a sadistic brute by the name of Kiwe, motioned with his whip toward the building where the Jewish women from the transport were already undressing. The blonde woman's shoulders sagged; she bent down and said something to the children who were now crying loudly as they continued to cling to her. They seemed to calm down somewhat after that. Then, led by the guard, she and the children made their way across the sorting square. As they passed within a meter or two of me, she and the children suddenly turned and stared directly at me for a brief moment. Their deep blue eyes seemed to plead with me and accuse me simultaneously. Totally shaken, I rushed past them without looking back.

I saw them again briefly some minutes later, as she and the other naked women waited in line before the camp "barber shop" for their hair to be shorn. She was still holding her crying children's hands, but there was already a dead expression on her face.

Within hours everyone in the camp knew the full story. The young, blonde woman, wife of a Wehrmacht officer serving on the Eastern Front, had been on her way to visit her husband; but as the result of some incredible error, she had boarded the Jewish transport, believing it to be an ordinary passenger train. Even before she arrived at Treblinka, however, she had begun to have a foreboding of the truth. In a state of panic, she attempted to correct the mistake by producing her Aryan identity papers to the conductor on the train, but was told that nothing could be done until they reached their destination. Once in Treblinka, she had repeated her story, demanding to see the officer in charge. When Lalka arrived, she even offered as further proof that she and the children did not belong there the visual evidence that her sons were not circumcised. It was all futile. Lalka, having decided that she could not be permitted to leave knowing what she did, had ordered her and her children to be disposed of along with the others.

There were a few, those who had witnessed their own family's similar destruction, who derived a momentary sense of satisfaction from what had happened. It was as if the death of the German woman and her children had avenged the deaths of their loved ones. To most, however, the incident made it even more plain that their lives were already forfeit. If the Nazis were willing to kill their own people to preserve the terrible secret of Treblinka, no Jew had even the slightest hope for survival. As for me, the years of injustice, despair, suffering, and death merged into that single moment in which the condemned Aryan woman and her children stopped to burn *their* eyes into my tortured future. You are one of them, said that unforgettable glance; as long as you are here, alive, you are one of them. You are as much a murderer as they. At first, during my scant, nightmare-ridden sleep, I wanted to protest when their images appeared before me, to shout at the top of my lungs that *they* were to blame for this evil place, *they* were the ones who had made Treblinka possible. But in place of the words, only tears would come. Only tears.

***

In the following weeks an amazing change took place in the camp. The flow of transports became a trickle once the final survivors of the Warsaw ghetto had been fed to the gas chambers of Treblinka. Now the energies of the inmates were devoted almost exclusively to exhuming the corpses from the original burial ditches and transporting them up to the huge pyres for final disposal. The Germans were tidying things up for posterity. Soon all traces that a death camp had existed there would be obliterated. Each day (unless one of the infrequent transports arrived), we hauled the decomposed remains along as if they were pieces of rotting wood. We worked feverishly, although all of us understood that when the grisly task was completed the Germans would leave no witnesses. In the meanwhile, however, they had granted certain privileges to their slave-assistants in this final, macabre act. After working from as early as three or four o'clock in the morning until early afternoon, we in the lower camp were granted the freedom to do as we pleased within the barbwire surrounded camp ghetto. Some used the opportunity to recreate life as they remembered it on the outside. There were parties with loud, cheerful music and energetic dancing; there was lovemaking as the women from the camp laundry were permitted to mix with the male population; there were mock marriages sanctioned by the Nazi masters and even co-celebrated by them. Unable to take part, I watched the macabre spectacle with a mixture of incredulity and fascination.

Late one afternoon in mid-spring, Arnold came to see me. The instant I saw him I knew that something terrible had happened. His red-rimmed eyes stood out alarmingly against his pale, quivering face.

"What is it?" I asked, motioning him to follow me outside where we could speak above the noise of the barrack.

"My wife and children," he said simply, as we reached the street. "I have had news of my wife and children."

Arnold and I had rarely discussed our families after that initial meeting on the train to Berlin. While we both maintained a glimmer of hope for their survival, we were also realistic about the odds involved, and so avoided voicing our fears.

"News?" I said. "What kind of news?" We reached the ghetto street at the front of the barracks.

"For the last few days," he replied unsteadily, "I have been working in the upper camp, on the engine of one of the excavators." The excavators were huge, crane-like machines which were used to open up the burial trenches; there were three of them in almost constant operation during the clean-up phase. "I met a fellow there, a kapo, whom I knew from Munich. He lived in my old neighborhood." He put his hand up to his face and rubbed his eyes with the back of his fingers. "He told me that my wife and children had been on the same transport that brought him here." His voice cracked completely at that point; his knees seemed to give way for a moment, forcing him to grasp the side of the barracks building to steady himself. Then, tears streaming down both sides of his face, he groaned, "They are here, Heinrich. In this monstrous sewer. My family. At this very moment they might be melting in one of those huge bonfires up there." He lifted his eyes toward the billows of smoke that filled the sky above the upper camp and groaned again.

I could not answer. I had seen the mounds of bodies on the cremation grids, watched the faces contorting grotesquely and the bodies bursting like punctured balloons as the flames consumed them. Any comfort I might have offered would have been futile. We stood that way for a long time, each submerged in his own vision of hell. Finally, I stepped over to him and put my arm around his gently heaving shoulders.

"We can't stay here any longer," he said. "One way or the other we have to get out. The world has to learn what has happened here." After several seconds he suddenly straightened up. Then, in a voice shaking with anger and hatred he added, "And these murdering bastards have to pay their price in blood for what they have done. Every last one of them has to pay."

It was decided. We would not wait for the general uprising for which, as far as either of us knew, no definite plan of action had yet been developed. Together, Arnold and I went over the various possibilities open to us. To our knowledge there had been very few successful escapes from the camp. At least twice I had personally witnessed the results of failed attempts. In the one instance, a young Polish Jew had been discovered clinging beneath one of the boxcars of a convoy that had been emptied and cleaned. An alert SS guard discovered his hiding place just as the train was about to pull out of Treblinka for its return journey. That evening, the inmates of the camp were treated to a special entertainment — the badly beaten Pole was brought out to the roll call square, hanged upside down on a makeshift gallows, and methodically clubbed to death by two of the Ukrainian guards.

Another time, a fellow was discovered hiding in a boxcar under the stacks of clothing that were to be shipped to the Reich. His punishment was swifter. He was dragged from the car and quickly dispatched by a burst of bullets from an SS automatic weapon. Several others who had actually succeeded in breaking free from the camp had been brought back as mutilated corpses and put on public display to discourage any who might have had an idea that escape was possible. These warning examples no longer had any effect; both Arnold and I had reached the point where whether we lived or died was no longer the primary consideration.

In the following days we weighed the various options open to us. It was difficult to convince Arnold that our best chance for success would exclude any violence on our part. His understandable inclination was not merely to escape, but to leave behind at least one or two dead Ukrainian or SS guards as a message to the others that Jews could also kill. I was finally able to sway him with the logical argument that such an action would not only greatly increase their efforts to recapture us, but would also result in terrible reprisals against the remaining inmates of the camp. He finally agreed when I pointed out that violence would probably incite the Nazis to take such harsh restrictive measures that any future, general uprising might be made impossible.

The plan we finally adopted was simple in the extreme. In addition to the other relaxed restrictions, the guards now often left the doors to our barracks unlocked before morning roll call so that we could use the latrines located to the rear. We agreed to meet in the latrine in the early morning hours, and if the coast seemed clear, cut our way through the fences leading to the forest beyond the perimeters of the camp.

Twice we met in the latrine only to have our escape plan thwarted. On the first occasion, the moon was shining so brightly that it almost seemed like daytime. As we peered out through the latrine window, we could clearly see the Ukrainian guard lazily patrolling before the barracks. The second time, conditions were seemingly ideal. There was no moon, and a thick haze covered the ground. This time, however, we were stopped in our tracks when the guard unexpectedly came into the latrine to relieve himself. As one, we lowered our heads humbly and made for the door, pretending to hike up our trousers. My heart raced like an electric motor as we passed by him. Fortunately, he was too drunk to take notice of us. If he had been alert, he probably would have seen how awkwardly Arnold was walking, a result of the wire cutter he had crammed into his pants' leg. Had he stopped to search my bulging pockets, moreover, he would have discovered the large assortment of German, Polish, and even some American currency I had crammed into them, not to mention the array of gold rings and other small jewelry. All of this had come from the pockets, purses, and even the linings of the coats, suits, and dresses of the victims from various transports. It was my job to search these items in the sorting square, and to retrieve any valuables that the naive victims were planning to use to make their future resettlement more pleasant. Whereas previously I had always obediently turned in anything of value to the "gold-Jews" (to be caught with such contraband meant instant death), when Arnold told me about the planned general uprising I had begun to hold back from time to time in preparation for our future outside the camp.

The third morning was made to order. It had begun to storm late on the previous evening and continued unabated throughout the night. It was pitch-dark; there were no sentries in the area of the latrine. Already soaked to the skin, we made our way out of the latrine to the fence leading to the roll call square; still no Germans or Ukrainians in sight. With a few quick snips, Arnold made an opening large enough for us to fit through. Then, running as fast as we could across the rain swept tract, we cut our way through another fence and entered the area where the camp firewood was stored. The wind had picked up considerably. With the wind driven rain beating against us, we crossed the camp vegetable field and crouched as low as we could so that we would not be seen by the guard in the watchtower which was located some two or three hundred meters to our right. We reached the final obstacle. As quickly as we could, we cut our way through a small section of the barbwire anti-tank barriers that ringed the entire camp. The razor sharp wire tore through our clothing and skin as we tried to bend it aside. Finally, bleeding from numerous superficial gashes, we burst through and sprinted toward the forest. We were free. We had done it.

***

We ran for what seemed like hours, first in an easterly direction and then, turning south, we began to make a semicircle around the camp. The rain continued to fall, but there in the forest it was very still. We doggedly made our way forward, panting and stumbling in the semi-darkness. My lungs felt as if they would burst, and yet every kilometer we put between ourselves and Treblinka fed my growing sense of euphoria. At times I even became aware that my face had frozen into a smile.

We finally stopped to rest. Arnold reached into his shirt and produced several soggy slices of bread which we proceeded to devour as if they were a royal feast. Then we raced on, determined to get as far as possible from the camp before any search parties were sent out. Our best hope was that they would not consider us important enough for any full-scale search, and that any efforts they did make would be concentrated to the north, above the point where we had cut ourselves free. We were fairly certain that the heavy rain would wash out any traces of our footprints and make it impossible for them to track us. But we could take no chances, and so we ran on, uncertain of our ultimate destination.

By nightfall we were exhausted and hungry. It was a clear spring evening; the rain had stopped sometime earlier. For the previous two or three hours we had been making our way carefully along the edge of the woods, keeping our distance from the few small peasants' cottages that we had seen. At one point we heard voices in the distance, but we were hesitant to approach to ask for food or directions. Arnold was not even sure that his scant knowledge of Polish, gleaned from his maternal grandmother who had been a Polish-Jew, would be sufficient to make our needs clear. On top of this, we both knew that we could not count on any kindness from the traditionally anti-Semitic Polish peasantry. At about ten o'clock we decided to take a chance. We had spent the previous hour or two resting behind a large pile of rocks just beyond the tree line of the woods. In front of us was a large, freshly tilled field. Approximately three hundred meters further on we could see a dim light shining through the windows of the small cottage we had noticed earlier.

A dog began to howl loudly as we approached the low slung hut. I knocked on the door tentatively two or three times; finally, it creaked open slowly and a leather-faced peasant peered out at us. His expression was one of puzzlement and distrust as Arnold attempted to communicate with him in broken Polish. A stout woman stood behind him, peeping over his shoulder curiously. After a few seconds the peasant began to wave his arms from side to side, as one would to shoo away a swarm of annoying insects, but when Arnold held a large denomination bank note up in front of his face, his arms fell to his sides and his expression changed to one of keen interest. Minutes later, Arnold and I sat in the small shed next to the cottage, wolfing down the bread and cheese the woman had brought us.

For several days we stayed in the damp, musty shed, trying to decide what to do next. Through trial and error, Arnold managed to make it understood to our host that we needed a map of the area. Surprisingly, the latter produced an old, leather bound volume, obviously a history text, in which there was a fairly detailed map of mid-nineteenth century Poland. We calculated that we were approximately fifteen to twenty kilometers south of Treblinka, on the outskirts of a village that was not on the map, but which the leather-faced farmer referred to as Stodine or Stydine. We were totally surrounded by the Germans; our only hope was to find and link up with some partisans who hated the Germans enough to accept the help of two escaped Jews, or, not succeeding in this, to find a safe hiding place where we could remain until the Nazis were driven out of Eastern Poland.

For the remainder of the spring and throughout the summer we continued to move toward the southeast, sleeping in barns and fields, and avoiding populated areas. For the most part, the peasants were more frightened than hostile when we approached for food or shelter, and since we were able to compensate them for any provisions they gave us, we had no difficulty in that regard. In mid-July we learned from a farmer who spoke passable German that the Nazi armies had suffered a crippling defeat at Stalingrad during the previous winter, and that before long the Soviet armies would be marching through Poland. We remained in his barn for several weeks, and would have stayed even longer had we not noticed that he was beginning to become very nervous about our presence. We feared that he might eventually decide that even the high prices we were paying for his aid were not worth the danger and turn us in to the local authorities.

In late August we had a very close call. We usually stayed away from any paved roads, keeping to the woods, the dirt paths, and fields. On this particular day, however, we became careless. It was early morning. Dressed in the peasant attire we had "bought" with a gold wristwatch, we were walking along a small road about fifty to seventy-five kilometers north of Lublin. All of a sudden, as if out of nowhere, a German armored car appeared on the road in front of us. Lacking time to duck into the high weeds along the side of the road, we simply continued to walk straight ahead. My stomach jumped at the loud screech of brakes several meters behind us. I glanced over at Arnold. His teeth were clenched tightly; his eyes narrowed to slits. I turned to look at the car; a German officer jutted his head out of the window on the passenger's side and ordered us, in Polish, to approach. My mind raced wildly as we made our way over to him. I saw Arnold shove his hand into his jacket pocket where he kept the hunting knife he had bartered from a farmer. When we were just a few meters from the car the officer opened the door, stepped out, and came toward us. A large piece of paper fluttered in his outstretched hand. One could see immediately that it was a map. It was clear from his gestures and expression that he and his driver had taken a wrong turn somewhere and were asking Arnold for directions with the few words of Polish they knew.

I shall never know why I did what I did next; it was as much a surprise to me as it was to Arnold and the German captain. Looking the latter straight in the eye, I said calmly, "I am very sorry, but we are also strangers in this land."

He looked at me in amazement, and then at Arnold, whose face was still compressed tightly.

"Germans?" he blurted out, looking us carefully up and down. "What the hell are you doing here?" He frowned ominously. His free hand had moved toward the pistol strapped to his waist. "Who are you anyway, a pair of deserters?"

I shook my head from side to side slowly. "German-Jews," I replied in a clear, firm voice, without dropping my gaze. Out of the corner of my eye I saw Arnold suddenly grow rigid and feared for a moment that he would leap at the German captain with his knife. Before he could do anything, however, something remarkable happened. The frown on the officer's face instantly dissolved; he looked us over carefully once again, and then turned his eyes away as if in embarrassment. Both Arnold and I stood still, anchored there by some invisible force.

"So that is it," he said, barely audibly. "From the camp." He stood there for several seconds looking down at the ground. Now he will take out his pistol and shoot us, I thought, feeling extremely calm, freer than I had at any time since our escape. He will make us kneel and shoot us in the back of the neck. Perhaps it was what I wanted; I am not sure. I knew only that I would not go back to Treblinka. Never. Contrary to my expectation, however, his hand dropped limply to his side and he let out a deep sigh.

"I have seen what goes on there," he said softly. "It is terrible." Then, without a further word, he turned on his heel and strode back to the waiting car. As he grasped the door handle he turned to us and shook his head sadly. Arnold and I stood silently for a long time watching in amazement as the armored car slowly disappeared down the flat, deserted road.

After that we continued southward, keeping to the remote, wooded areas as much as possible. It was clear to us that we could not expect to be as lucky in a second encounter with any Germans who might chance upon us and we were in constant fear that if we remained in one place for any length of time there was the risk that the local populace might report us to the authorities. Though communication on any but the most basic level was impossible because of the language barrier, we had been able to piece together enough to determine that there was at least one other concentration camp somewhere in that part of Poland. At first the idea that there could be anything on earth comparable to Treblinka seemed impossible, but as we thought it over and discussed it, we realized that it must be so; one camp alone could never have been sufficient to accomplish the goal that the Nazis apparently had set for themselves: the eradication of the Jews. Treblinka, even operating twenty-four hours a day, could not have dealt with the large Jewish population of Poland, let alone that of occupied Europe. There had to be other such places. And it seemed to follow from this that the German captain who had spared us had not been speaking of Treblinka, but of another camp.

During the long, uneventful days in the forest, I spent much of my time recounting to myself the events that had brought me to such an unbelievable pass. As hard as I tried, however, I was unable to understand even slightly how such things could have been possible. There were brief moments when, leaning back against the bark of a tree and listening to the sound of the birds and insects, or sitting quietly at the edge of a free-flowing stream, I wondered if it had not all been just a nightmare; but no sooner did such thoughts occur to me than the grotesque visions returned. At those moments it was no longer the rays of sun that filtered through the spaces between the leaves above me; it was *their* eyes. And the sounds of nature became the dreadful screams of the dying victims in the gas chambers as they clawed their way to the top of a hideous pyramid of death for a final breath of unpoisoned air.

Arnold and I knew that we were not alone in the forest. A number of times we heard distinct human sounds in the distance, or came across the remains of a still warm campfire. But our instinct to survive, honed to a fine edge in Treblinka, kept us from seeking out the sources of these signs. We knew from first-hand accounts we had heard in the camp that there were partisan units operating throughout the country, as well as in the densely wooded areas of the adjacent Soviet Ukraine. These stories, however, were not without their dark side. One evening, a fellow "work-Jew" on the sorting commando told me a chilling tale about his experience with a particular group of Polish partisans. He gave a harrowing account of how he had escaped into the forest to avoid an Aktion — the name given to the process in which randomly selected Jews from a particular ghetto were rounded up for execution in some secluded spot or shipped to a concentration camp. After several days of aimless wandering, he came in contact with a band of partisans, and, believing himself saved, identified himself and volunteered his services to them. Instead of accepting his offer, however, they robbed him of the little money he had managed to bring out with him, beat him into unconsciousness, and left him for a German patrol to find and include in their next transport to Treblinka.

We were also aware that there were German military units in the area. The telltale signs of their presence were everywhere, from the carelessly discarded cigarette packs to the frightening imprint of their hobnailed boots on the soft forest floor. Our dilemma was magnified even further by the fear of approaching winter; at times I thought bitterly of the cruel and ironic fate that had saved us from the cremation grids only to have us freeze to death in a Polish forest. Arnold was no more hopeful than I. As the days and weeks passed he became more withdrawn. It was as if we were both waiting for an answer that did not exist. Waiting. Once again, waiting.

In November, our waiting came to an end. It was a dark, wet night. Every now and then, large, feathery snowflakes mixed in with the lightly falling rain. We crawled into the primitive shelter we had built from dead branches and leaves and covered with a few strips of tattered canvas that we had found the day before in an abandoned barn just beyond the woods. We were both very cold and hungry; that afternoon we had eaten nothing but a few half-rotten potatoes and our last small tin of herring. In the morning we would have to find a farm and barter for a new supply of food. Arnold was already asleep and was snoring lightly. I closed my eyes reluctantly, fighting back the painful visions of suffering and death that masqueraded each night as sleep.

"Good morning." An unfamiliar voice suddenly cut through my semi-sleep. It was just becoming light. I emerged from our shelter and found myself looking up into a group of bearded, smiling faces. The one who had spoken said something else that I did not understand, then laughed when he saw my puzzled expression. Arnold, who had come out right behind me, replied in halting Polish, which evoked another short burst of laughter from the others. For the first time I noticed that they were all armed. A fellow with an automatic machine pistol raised in one hand took a step forward and said, in perfect High German, "You are German?" His voice was level, but there was a palpable tension behind the question. Apparently he had drawn the same conclusion as the German captain some months before — that we were deserters from the German army.

We both rose to our feet and stood less than a meter from him. Before I could reply, Arnold looked our inquisitor straight in the eye and said, "We are Jews. We have escaped from the concentration camp Treblinka." Then, his eyes flashing, he stood there and waited for a response.

The partisan stared first at him and then at me for several seconds, as if trying to uncover some hidden truth. Then, handing his machine pistol to the fellow next to him, he stepped over to us and locked each of us in turn in a tight bear hug.

"Don't worry, brothers," he said. "You do not have to run any longer."

***

Moshe Potok, the leader of the partisans, leaned forward and spoke in a clear, deep bass voice. "The Nazis raided the ghetto in the middle of the night and began to shoot everyone on sight. They knew all about our secret tunnels and the armory we had established. Only six of us managed to escape. We linked up with a Jewish partisan unit in the woods near Zloty-Potok, and have been making as much trouble as possible for the sons of bitches ever since."

We moved deeper into the forest with Moshe and the others and set up camp for the night. After we ate I began to give our new comrades a brief summary of our escape, which Moshe translated simultaneously into Polish. This was followed by a series of questions about conditions in Treblinka. Everyone's eyes were moist as I graphically described the unbelievable things I had seen there. There was a long silence after that; apparently more than one member of the group had family members who had been taken to Treblinka or similar camps. Finally, at Arnold's request, Moshe told the story of how he and his comrades had fled into the forest from the Czestochowa ghetto early in the summer. Much of what he said was already a familiar pattern to me by now: the establishment of a Jewish ghetto; the systematic and increasingly frequent "actions" and deportations; the outright murders of Jews, either in reprisal for some anti-Nazi incident or for no apparent reason at all, culminating in the final liquidation of the ghetto. I had heard similar stories in Treblinka from former inhabitants of other Polish cities.

"Did someone in your group betray you?" I asked, wondering how the Nazis had known so much about their organization. Moshe sighed and stared into the leaping flames of the campfire.

"It was not one of us," he replied, in a sad, tired voice. "It was a German truck driver. We thought we could trust him." He shook his head and inhaled deeply. "As if one can ever trust any of them." He paused again, still staring at the fire. Then he went on. "We had paid him a large sum of money to transport weapons and partisans to various destinations, but he was working for the Gestapo. We should have known better. Many good people died because of our carelessness."

As we continued to speak, it became clear that the Jewish Fighting Organization — the name given to the combined, primarily Jewish partisan units — had been terribly weakened by the destruction of the Czestochowa and Warsaw ghettos, and now consisted only of a few cadres of between five and ten members.

"Some of our units," he said, in answer to a question Arnold put to him about the strength of the movement, "have joined up with the Polish partisans in the woods around Konyetopol. The rest of us have been forced to live here in the forest, more or less depending on the local peasants to supply us with food and other necessities. But you two shouldn't have much of a problem with that. You seem to have managed quite well up till now. You certainly don't need our help."

Arnold and I exchanged a quick, understanding glance. I reached into my jacket and withdrew the leather pouch I always kept there.

"We have had a little help along the way," I said, opening the pouch and withdrawing a fistful of paper money. Moshe whistled under his breath and then laughed as I put the money back into the pouch and handed the latter to him.

"Thank you, brothers," he said, passing our gift around to the others for their inspection. "With this we should be able to cause even more trouble for the Third Reich."

Including Arnold and myself, there was a total of eleven men in our unit. With the exception of Moshe, who seemed to be in his early to mid-thirties, they were no more than boys, although their eyes mirrored more than their chronological share of suffering. For the most part, my short-lived experience as a partisan was little different from that which Arnold and I had known since our escape from Treblinka. For the following two weeks almost all of our time was spent seeking food and shelter and keeping on the move to avoid the anti-partisan forces in the area. Our small size and lack of firepower (with the exception of Moshe's machine pistol we had only a small collection of antiquated hunting rifles and two or three questionable pistols), forced us to avoid confrontation with any German or Polish fascist troops, at least for the time being. Moshe's immediate goal was to establish contact with the leaders of a Polish partisan group that called itself *Orzel* (Eagle). This group belonged to the *Armia Krajowa*, which was the largest Polish underground movement, directed by the Polish Provisional Government in London. He hoped that they would be willing and able to supply us with arms and munitions, or invite us to join forces with them.

Through intermediaries, Moshe arranged a meeting with the representatives of *Orzel* for the following week in an area near the southeastern border with the Soviet Ukraine. Having stocked up on provisions for the journey, we set out, keeping as close as possible to the dense forests. Late in the afternoon on the third day, we were climbing the side of a small incline overlooking a picturesque mountain stream. The air was crisp and cool. I remember marveling to myself about the paradoxical contrast between nature and man. While the human race seemed to be exerting a supreme effort to destroy everything and anything on the planet, nature remained oblivious, as if supremely confident that, in the end, man would prove to be but a mild interruption in her overall scheme. As I trudged along immersed in such thoughts, I tripped, and before I could regain my balance found myself tumbling down the rocky slope.

Moshe was crouching next to me, his face etched with concern."Your leg is broken in at least two places, Heinrich." I closed my eyes and tried to fight off the wave of pain that shot from my ankle all the way up to my hip. Moshe held my shattered leg in his hands and lightly turned the lower part. "I'll have to set it as best I can and rig up some kind of splint. I'm afraid it is going to hurt." He turned my leg again, this time with more force. The pain was so intense that I cried out and lost consciousness.

It was already night when I awoke. My entire body throbbed. I attempted to sit up, but the effort sent a shooting pain through my chest that made me gasp for breath. I felt a gentle pressure on my arm and turned to see what it was. Arnold Blum's familiar face came into view, illuminated by the light of the full moon that seemed to hang just above his head like a giant lantern. In spite of the pain, I felt a strange detachment from my body, a floating, dreamlike sensation.

"Try not to move, Heinrich," whispered my friend, patting my arm lightly with his large hand. "It seems as if you may have broken a few ribs along with the leg. The morphine shot Moshe gave you should keep you comfortable for a while yet. Tomorrow you will be taken somewhere where you can recuperate." He patted my arm again and pulled the heavy woolen blanket that was covering me up to my neck. I closed my eyes again and allowed the drug to do its work.

By dawn I felt feverish, but as long as I didn't attempt to move, the pain was bearable. I rejected Moshe's offer of another injection of morphine, settling for aspirin instead. I felt very guilty for the trouble my clumsiness had caused everyone. The irony of having gone through the terrible months in Treblinka physically unscathed, only to have something like this happen during a walk in the forest, reinforced my growing belief that existence was an absurd joke.

Following a short discussion it was decided that Arnold and one of the young partisans, a smiling, red-headed fellow named Yuri, would take me to some trustworthy Polish gentiles the latter's family knew. Yuri had grown up in that region before being moved to the Jewish ghetto in Kracow. It was hoped that these people would agree to conceal me from the Germans and Polish fascists until I recovered from my injuries. Moshe and one of the other partisans made splints out of tree branches and tied them tightly to my injured leg with heavy twine. With other branches and more rope, Arnold then began to put together the litter.

"It isn't luxurious," he said, as he spread out a blanket over the bottom of his creation. "But it should be a lot more comfortable for you than walking."

I was still feeling too downcast to return his forced smile; I knew how anxious he was to get revenge for the murder of his family and felt responsible for delaying his opportunity. I gritted my teeth against the pain and remained silent. Finally, Moshe stepped over to me to say farewell. I stammered out a dejected reply and feebly shook his extended hand.

"We will see you again soon, Heinrich," he said, swinging his knapsack over one shoulder. "Before you know it, you will be dancing again, and with a little luck you will still have the opportunity to kill a few Nazi bastards. In the meantime, Yuri will see to it that you are taken care of." He turned to the young redhead and exchanged a few words in Polish with him. Then he shook hands with Arnold, turned, and quickly joined the others who had already crossed the narrow stream and were patiently waiting for him on the opposite side. I watched them slowly disappear into the dense pine forest, cursing the fate that had kept me from being able to accompany them.

We set out in the opposite direction soon after that. I groaned as

Arnold and Yuri carefully lifted me onto the litter, but once they had tied me in securely, I felt relatively comfortable, just as Arnold had promised. In addition to the blanket cushioning my lower torso, he had even thought to fashion a pillow from our old canvas strips, which he now placed under my shoulders and head.

"We'll try not to jostle you too much," he said, as he and the smiling young Pole lifted the litter and began to move carefully forward along the uneven ground.

At first our progress was very slow because of the mountainous terrain. With each step I rocked forward and clenched my fists, fighting to restrain myself from groaning as the stabbing pain shot through the right side of my chest. I could hear Arnold's heavy breathing behind me as he struggled to keep pace with the younger man in front. From time to time, Yuri gave a signal to set the litter down gently so that they could take a short rest. The rhythmic, rocking motion irritated my bladder; at least twice during those first hours they had to stop and tip the litter to the side so that I could urinate.

By the end of the first day the pain in my chest had increased and my fever had spiked. I began to hallucinate. Horrifying visions leaped out from behind trees and rocks and hung suspended in the air before my burning eyes: piles of naked corpses, with huge, ugly worms slithering in and out of their empty eye sockets, and terrified children's faces, turning black and falling to pieces, as searing flames consumed them. At one point I screamed out and struggled to free myself from the confining ropes. I had convinced myself that not Yuri, but a black-uniformed SS man was walking in front of me. On his back was emblazoned a grotesque, spiderlike swastika that was slowly transformed into a twisted, six-pointed yellow star as I watched in growing horror and fascination. I slipped in and out of consciousness, no longer aware of time or space; I was back in Treblinka. Back in Treblinka. Mercifully, a black curtain descended, releasing me at last from the torturous visions.

When I opened my eyes I was disoriented. For some time I believed that I was back in the camp barracks during the minutes before the morning roll call. This impression continued even when I saw Arnold's face peering down at me. I must hurry, I thought. I must not be late. Today we will make our escape. I tried to rise, but a pressure in my chest pulled me back onto the soft blanket beneath me.

"Thank God," sighed Arnold, who was crouching beside my cot and dabbing my forehead with a damp, cool cloth. "You gave me quite a scare." The corners of his eyes and mouth were creased with worry. I studied his face for a moment or two uncomprehendingly, and then looked down at a spot on my chest that seemed to have a weight on it; it was covered with adhesive tape. As I let my gaze travel further downward, I saw my injured leg; it was slightly elevated and encased in a white plaster cast. Suddenly, it all came back to me — the fall, the litter...

"What is this place?" I whispered, looking around curiously. We were in a dimly lit enclosure, not much more than two and one-half meters square, more a closet than a room. The smell of damp earth and mildew mixed with the fumes of the small kerosene lamp that burned weakly at my feet. As I looked up I could also see a small, square pattern of dim light just above Arnold's head.

"On a farm. I don't know the name of the nearest village, but from what little I was able to understand, we aren't very far from the border with the Soviet Union," he replied, flipping the cloth into a small bowl of water on the floor next to him. "We are in a secret cellar, beneath the floor of the farmhouse. The people who live here are friends of Yuri's family." He reached over and picked up an earthenware pitcher and a mug that were also at his feet. "Your fever finally seems to have broken. For a time there I didn't think you were going to make it." He poured some water into the mug and handed it to me. My hand trembled as I greedily drank the cool liquid and requested another.

"How long have I been here?" I asked, after having drained the second helping with a few gulps.

"Two days," he replied, filling the glass for a third time. "But it is five days since we left Moshe and the others. It's been a difficult journey for all of us."

"I'm sorry I am such a nuisance," I stammered. "It seems you always have to come to my rescue. As if you didn't have enough troubles of your own...I mean...your family..."

Before I could continue, he frowned and put his hand up. "Please, Heinrich," he said. "Don't speak like that. If it weren't for you, I would not have been able to go on. The fact of the matter is, you are the only family I have left." His voice cracked. He turned his head away from me for several seconds so that I would not see his tears.

"We had to leave the forest because we were afraid that the Nazi patrols would hear you," explained Arnold, as he recounted the events of the previous few days. "For another thing, your condition was deteriorating. I wanted to get medical attention for you as quickly as possible."

"You mean you carried me all the way here?" I asked, looking down at my plaster-encased leg.

"Not all the way," he replied. "We managed to hitch a ride with a peasant. He hid us under a pile of straw in his wagon. The way you were carrying on, though, I don't think we would have lasted five seconds if we had been stopped." He patted my cast affectionately and smiled. "Getting a doctor to take care of you was another matter, though," he said, fixing his eyes on the flickering lantern. "We had to settle for the local veterinarian. He came out in the middle of the night and worked on you for many hours."

A sudden pain in my chest made me wince. Arnold noticed this and patted my cast again.

"I'm not sure I understood correctly," he offered. "But I think the doctor said that one of your broken ribs had punctured a lung. He gave you some foul-smelling medicine to combat the infection, something they probably use on horses." He smiled again. "Getting you down here with that thing on was a major project. With all that plaster on you, you felt like you weighed almost as much as a horse. It took three of us to get you through the trap door." He pointed at the outline of light in the low ceiling. "We are directly under the family dinner table. From up there you can't even tell there is a room below. We have to be very careful. There are a lot of German patrols in the area."

When I expressed my surprise at the fact that people were willing to risk their lives to help a stranger, and a Jew at that, Arnold provided the sad answer.

"They have good reason to hate the supermen of the Reich. Their only son was in the Polish army when the war began. He was killed by a panzer shell on the second day."

In the days that followed the pain in my chest gradually receded. Our hosts, the Witowskis, shared with us what little they had from their small farm, as if we were their kin. During the day, Arnold left the cellar to help with some of the chores, leaving the trap door open so that I could have air and light. From time to time, Mrs. Witowski's face appeared at the opening; she smilingly lowered down food or drink in a basket, or returned the emptied bucket that was provided me for elimination. Some evenings her husband came down with Arnold and tried to communicate with me in his local dialect which seemed to be a mixture of Polish and Ukrainian. Even Arnold was unable to understand more than a few words, so for the most part we had to rely on facial expression and sign language to make ourselves understood. After several minutes, the stocky, round-faced farmer would shake our hands, wish us a good night, and ascend the small wooden ladder, carefully pulling the door shut behind him.

While my physical condition improved, however, my mental state worsened. Day and night the horrible visions I carried from Treblinka continued to torture me; it became more and more difficult to suppress them or concentrate on memories of happier times. I was also depressed and apprehensive over the fact that Arnold would be leaving as soon as Yuri returned to fetch him. I did not know if I would be able to endure my situation alone, or if I was worthy of survival. I had begun to regard myself more and more negatively. I felt even lower than the farm animals. At least, I thought, they either performed some useful service to justify their keep, or became, upon their deaths, a source of food. I, on the other hand, could see no purpose in my continued life or, for that matter, any great loss to the world were I to die. I clearly remember Arnold's reaction when I expressed this thought to him approximately a week after our arrival at the Witowski farm.

"How the hell can you say such a thing? You mustn't allow yourself to think that way," he replied, his voice raised almost to a shout. "I have tried to tell you this before, but I will repeat it one more time. When this is over, people like you will have to tell our story so that Treblinka can never happen again. Never again! It will be painful, Heinrich, but it is your duty, just as it is mine to go out and fight those murdering bastards with every ounce of my energy. We will beat them together, each in his own way. To say that your life or death has no purpose means that all of the other lives and deaths are useless. Our families. You don't believe that. I know you don't." His voice had become softer as he went on and was almost a whisper by the time he finished.

I shook my head, uncertain of my own feelings at that moment. "And suppose I am incapable of doing what you say?" I finally replied, speaking as much to myself as to him.

"You can do it," he said without hesitation. "There is no doubt in my mind that you can do it." He paused and then added, "Whether you know it or not, I owe you a great deal."

"I don't understand," I replied, puzzled by his unexpected statement. "I've been nothing but a burden to you. You are always coming to my rescue. In the munitions factory, in Treblinka, here."

"What you did for me was not so visible, but just as important," he countered, before I could sink further into self-pity. "Right from the first day we met on the train I was impressed by what you had to say. At first I was confused. I couldn't understand how you could have so little hatred in you, while I was almost consumed by it. And yet I was not angry with you. Since then I have watched you and listened to you very carefully — watched and learned. That doesn't mean that I intend to forgive the sons of bitches who have destroyed our families and our world. I said just a few minutes ago that I would fight, and I will, to my last breath if that is what it takes. But I will never enjoy killing, not even killing them. If I did, I would be as bad as they are. That is what you taught me. Whatever happens to me from now on, I know that in the end I owe it to myself to remain a human being. If I don't, they will have won."

I sat silently for several moments, feeling angry and ashamed; angry at Arnold for placing such a burden of responsibility on me, and ashamed because I felt unworthy. Finally, I replied, "You give me too much credit, Arnold. It isn't that I don't hate. I am certainly no holy man. My dilemma is that I don't know exactly where to direct my hatred. There are so many possibilities. Certainly I hate Hitler and the other Nazi murderers, but can it end there? Don't I also have to hate the German people for electing him to power? Aren't they proudly goose-stepping over a continent of corpses simply because he gave the command to march? And how about the French, English, and Americans for setting the stage for such a demon, and then closing their eyes until it was too late? Or the Catholic Church for its almost two-thousand-year-old policy of anti-Semitism? Or those other good Christians who waved the swastika so ardently when the Führer spewed out his venom? Shouldn't I even hate myself and other Jews like me who denied our origins and chose to wait and hope that all would be well again, instead of acting right from the beginning? Perhaps, though, the ultimate blame is God's, for allowing such a mutilation of decency, for creating such a world in the first place. No, Arnold, it isn't that I don't hate; it is simply that I do not have enough hatred to do justice to what has happened." I sat back, completely drained, fearing that I had hurt Arnold's feelings. Once again, however, he surprised me.

"Whether you know it or not, you have just proven my point," he said, smiling sadly. "You are the one who will be able to tell the world about it. You must write it all down. Every word of it. You have to, Heinrich!"

Two days later, Arnold brought me two pencils and an old ledger book that still had many blank pages, and suggested I get to work immediately. And so, in the late autumn of 1943, imprisoned in a small underground room in occupied Poland, I began the task of attempting to create form, order, and meaning out of a world that no longer seemed to possess any of these qualities.

***

Yuri's return was an occasion for mourning rather than celebration. It was late afternoon, the first week of December. I was hunched under the thick feather quilt that Mrs. Witowski had provided me, probably taken from her own bed. The smooth, heated stones that she had lowered down to me an hour or so earlier were still warm enough to keep my hands from growing cold as I randomly wrote my thoughts down onto the yellowing paper of the ledger. Suddenly, I was startled out of my concentration by loud, excited voices above. Before I had time to speculate on their source, Arnold's ashen face appeared over the half-open trap door.

"Yuri is back," he said, his voice trembling. "I'm afraid there is terrible news."

The voices continued for at least an hour. During that agonizing interval I lay on the thin cot, both frustrated over my helplessness and apprehensive about what was taking place in the room above me. Finally, Arnold made his way back down into the cellar.

"What is it? What has happened?" I asked, alarmed by the haunted look on his face.

"It is very bad news. Dead. Moshe and the others are all dead," he responded, his voice barely under control. My mouth fell open and a cold shiver ran down my spine.

"As far as I can make out from what Yuri said," he continued, "they were ambushed by the Polish group they were supposed to join. They didn't have a chance."

"Ambushed?" I repeated. "But surely the partisans..."

"They were not partisans. They were a bunch of filthy fascists!" he spit out. "Yuri learned that after wandering around several days questioning the peasants in the Konyetopol area. He knew that something had happened because there were signs in the woods that Moshe and the others had been there. Fascists! The group called *Orzel* was working hand-in-hand with the Gestapo."

"But how can he be sure that they are dead?" I asked, feeling as if the blood had been drained from my body. "How can he be sure?"

"One of the farmers showed him the graves in the forest. Their bodies were riddled with bullets. They didn't have a chance. They were gunned down like animals."

Yuri remained at the farm for a few days. I saw him only once during that time when he came down to the cellar, sat next to me silently for ten minutes or so and then left. We both understood that there was no need for words. I was struck by the great change that he had undergone in the short interval since I had last seen him. His face was drawn and pale; his eyes seemed to have lost all animation, and were fixed in the resigned stare I had seen so often in the eyes of the condemned inmates of Treblinka. Even his shock of red hair appeared to have lost its former luster.

"Did you see the lines in his face?" Arnold asked later that night." He has become as old as we." He shook his head sadly as he spoke.

"And why not?" I replied. "His blood is more than five thousand years old, just as ours is." I closed my eyes, feeling more than a little trace of bitterness over the burden that history had placed upon all of us.

Some weeks later, Yuri returned again, this time not alone. With him was another young man, a German-speaking Pole who proudly identified himself to Arnold as Pasha, a courier for a partisan group led by a former cavalry officer named Hanysh. This group, ironically, also had its base in the Konyetopol area. It had close ties, he said, with Soviet partisan organizations, and included among its members the scattered remnants of several Jewish Fighting Organization units from the Warsaw area. During the course of our conversation he confirmed what we already knew, namely that Moshe Potok and his men had almost certainly been murdered by *Orzel*, and that they had not been the first Jews to suffer such a fate. He added with youthful solemnity that this and other atrocities would soon be avenged, since the tide of battle was definitely changing in favor of the Red Army. Pasha was particularly delighted to learn of Arnold's mechanical skills, which were, he said, much needed by the partisans. Later, when Arnold and I were alone, I expressed my skepticism. I feared that if he went with the others he might be walking into a trap, just as Moshe had. As we discussed the various possibilities, however, I concluded that if the courier were not who he claimed to be, the Gestapo would certainly have already descended on us. And so, Arnold left. Another farewell. Another empty space in my life.

My sole refuge from despair during the next months was my writing. It was only while I wrote that I was able to forget the fact that I was an exile in a strange land. While I wrote I was no longer alone in a dark cellar underneath the Polish earth. The geographical and linguistic gap that isolated me was bridged by my memories. As I recaptured the precious words of my loved ones I could actually hear their voices; my grandparents were alive again, liberated by my memory; my mother and father were no longer prisoners somewhere in Bohemia, consigned to an unknown fate; Uncle Solomon's wit was transported across an ocean with the rapidity of thought, bringing a smile to my weeping soul; Karl was with me again, as were his father and Birgit. And Birgit...

***

The veterinarian who had treated my injuries came to visit me during the holiday season. Preceded by my host, he scampered down the little ladder, unmelted snowflakes still clinging to his full head of bushy, grey hair. For a man of his age (he must have been at least seventy at the time), he was extremely agile. After a cursory examination, he nodded his head happily to indicate that I was making good progress, and patted my shoulder as one might the flank of a favored horse. Then he painstakingly removed the adhesive from my chest and followed this by vigorously rubbing the entire area with a liquid that smelled like a mixture of turpentine and laundry soap. Finally, through energetic sign language, he instructed me to continue to exercise my good limbs as much as possible and departed.

Another break in the routine occurred sometime in the second week of January. It was late morning; I had just finished sponging myself with the hot water that Mrs. Witowski had lowered to me, and was about to begin my writing for the day. Suddenly I heard loud footsteps directly above me and then the excited voice of my host. I looked up just in time to see his head appear in the opening of the trap door.

"Hitler," he said, clearly agitated. Then, putting his hand to his lips to indicate that I should remain silent, he closed the door, locking me into the darkness.

A minute or so later I heard muffled voices. Although I could not hear clearly, every so often I caught a sharply uttered German word or phrase. My first thought was that the young Pole had betrayed us after all. I cursed my churning stomach, fearing that the rumbling sounds it was making would betray my hiding place. For what seemed like an eternity I sat motionless, pulling the quilt up over my face like a little child who seeks to hide from the dark by making it even darker. After several more minutes it became still. Rather than reassure me, however, the silence terrified me as much as the sound of the German voices had. My imagination was fired up. I envisioned the Witowskis' bloodied, bullet-riddled corpses sprawled out grotesquely in the room above, and convinced myself that the farmhouse had been put to the torch by the Gestapo. I felt as if I were suffocating; I began to gasp for air. In my growing panic I did not realize that I had cut off my fresh oxygen supply by covering my head with the heavy quilt. By the time my smiling host pulled the quilt from me and indicated through hand motions that the coast was clear, I felt dead.

***

My cast was removed in early February. The doctor frowned slightly as he looked at my wasted, pale limb, and proceeded to rub it thoroughly with the familiar turpentine solution. When he had finished, he smiled and pointed to the trap door, nodding his head affirmatively and gesturing to indicate that I should follow him out. Minutes later I emerged from under the heavy oak table like some huge, awkward insect. The doctor and Mr. Witowski helped me to my feet and directed me over to the sofa by the blazing fireplace. After giving my withered leg yet another rubdown, the elderly veterinarian uttered some instructions to the farm couple, shook my hand vigorously and departed. Later, as the Witowskis stood at my sides and voiced their encouragement, I took my first painful, halting steps.

The following weeks were uneventful. I spent a good part of my days before the cozy fireplace, recording many of the events that appear in the first part of this work. When my last pencil was worn almost to nothing, Mr. Witowski miraculously produced two new ones. Noticing that I had almost filled the pages of the old ledger with my copious notes, one afternoon he proudly presented me with several hundred sheets of writing paper. Where he managed to get such a treasure is still a mystery to me.

My apprehension grew with the approach of spring. I knew that as the front drew closer, there were certain to be more German troops in the area. It was not so much that I feared for my own safety (in a certain respect my life had ended in Treblinka), but I was now obsessed by the thought that I would not be able to complete my mission, that I would fail those for whom I had become a witness. I knew, too, that if I were discovered, the kind people who were protecting me would suffer. Therefore, on my own initiative, I increasingly restricted myself again to my prison-sanctuary below the earth, convinced that the Nazis had not paid their last visit to the remote farm. I wrote and I waited.

The war reached us even more quickly than I thought it would. By mid-March, the familiar, unmistakable sounds of artillery boomed constantly in the far distance, sounds that seemed to be getting closer and closer with each passing day. I continued to write, forcing myself not to speculate on what the final outcome of the military struggle would be. Every so often, moreover, my concentration became so intense that I was able to forget the terrible reality surrounding me. For those short, rare moments I was a human being again, free to come and go as I pleased, free to sit quietly in the Hofgarten, or in the Marienplatz. For those short, rare moments the clock was turned back to a time when everything that was beautiful and decent and good had not yet been submerged in the hateful cesspool that Germany, my Germany, had allowed itself to become. Heine's sad lament seemed more poignant than ever: *"Once I had a beautiful fatherland..."*

My leg had not healed properly. The weeks passed and I still could not put any weight on it without experiencing intense pain. My host eventually fashioned a sturdy cane for me from a tree branch, which I now used to hobble the short distance from the trap door to the sofa and back again on those infrequent occasions when I emerged from my prison-sanctuary. In spite of the discomfort, however, I had to smile inwardly every time I thought of my Uncle Solomon's facetious prediction that control of the world would one day be taken over by cripples. I tried to imagine what his reaction would be if he could see me. Most likely, I mused, he would have said something to the effect that he was proud to see me carrying on an old family tradition, perhaps quoted the old adage, "Like father, like son," and then given me a short speech welcoming me into the exclusive circle of limping world leaders. This indulgence in gallows humor helped to sustain me while I waited for fate to issue its final decrees.

***

This time, I did not have to wait very long. It was a warm night in the beginning of July. I had already closed the trap door, stretched myself out on my cot, and was attempting to recall the details of my first meeting with Birgit by Lake Constance which I had begun to write about earlier in the day. As always happened, however, my happy memories were intermittently interrupted by the tormenting visions that stalked me day and night. Try as I did to resist, the image of Birgit slowly metamorphosed. In her place I saw a terrified, blonde-haired woman, desperately clinging to two small children whose eyes already reflected death. Flames suddenly began to engulf all three of them, bright yellow tongues of fire that made me squint painfully as I stared into them. Shortly after this the flames began to take shape. First they formed a huge, burning swastika and then, alongside the hateful, twisted cross, a six-pointed Star of David. As I watched in terror and fascination, the two images moved toward each other, twisting and fusing in a ghastly, grotesque dance of death.

"Wake up, comrade! Wake up!" My father's familiar Russian accent echoed through the small cellar, yet the voice was not his. Confused, I opened my eyes, thinking I was still dreaming. A bright beam of light shone down into my face. I reflexively shielded my eyes with the back of my hand and forearm and sat up. It was no dream; outlined in the opening above were the face and upper torso of a stranger. He continued to play the light on my face for another second or two, then, obviously realizing the distress the light was causing me, he considerately directed the flashlight away from my eyes to a neutral spot on the floor beside me.

"Come up. Come up," he said, beckoning with his free hand. "I have come to liberate you."

I leaned back in the worn sofa and listened to the incredible news. The impossible had happened. The Soviet armies were sweeping the invincible Wehrmacht back to their Thousand Year Reich like so many dead leaves.

"I will not be content until we have destroyed every last one of those murdering bastards," bellowed the slightly drunk Russian officer who straddled the chair across from me. He leaned over and picked up the large flask that was sitting at his right foot, raised it to his mouth, and took another long drink. Then, his eyes closed in sheer delight, he pulled the flask away from his lips noisily and held it out to me. A small stream of clear liquid trickled slowly down his bearded chin. I grasped the cool vessel between my hands, took a short sip, and winced as the pure potato alcohol burned its way down my throat. My head was already spinning. He slapped his thigh and laughed as I handed it back to him.

It was already after midnight. The Witowskis had retired behind the thick leather curtain that served to set off a small corner of the room as their sleeping quarters, and were already snoring rhythmically, their deep sleep no doubt enhanced by the victory drinks they had shared with their new guest and me. I still found it difficult to believe that I was finally free; that I no longer had to keep myself hidden underground like a living corpse. The irony inherent in the situation did not escape me: the same country from which my father had been forced to flee in order to escape oppression was now responsible for restoring my freedom, thus completing an incredibly bizarre circle. This and other thoughts ran through my mind as my bearded companion told me about himself and the war.

Captain Sergei Romek was a remarkable fellow. In civilian life he had been a head librarian in Leningrad, but when the Nazis invaded his country he traded in his books for a uniform and rifle, and before long had become as fluent in killing the enemy as he was in Russian, Polish, German and French. Because of his linguistic skills, however, he had been promoted in rank and given an assignment in the rear as company interpreter.

"Sometimes I question Nazi prisoners before we put them out of their misery," he explained, his nostrils flaring. "Or I talk to the scraps of humanity they leave behind them in their death factories." He rubbed his eyes and took another long drink. "But I don't need to tell you about that." He got up from his seat suddenly and placed his hands on my shoulders. Tears fell from his eyes onto the sofa in front of me. I was a bit shaken by his emotional reaction which could only partially have been the result of the alcohol. His face told me that his reaction sprang from an inner knowledge of the abyss. But how? While I had told him of my escape from Treblinka, I had not yet had time to give him any details of the atrocities committed there. Surely these things were not common knowledge; I knew from my own experience how much effort the officials who ran the death camps expended to keep their work veiled from the outside world.

Before I could express my surprise he went on. "I have seen what it is first hand, Heinrich," he said softly, letting himself down next to me. "I have seen it."

He ran his hands over his eyes again and exhaled deeply. "Two weeks ago we liberated a concentration camp by the city of Lublin. It was a place called Maidenek. I talked to some of the survivors and saw the remains of thousands who had perished. In many instances there was very little difference between the two. It was horrible." Then, without looking at me he added, almost in a whisper, "I still cannot believe that any human being could do such a thing to another. I cannot believe that."

We continued to converse throughout the night, oblivious to time. Although strangers, our worlds had been bridged by the profound experience of suffering. Sergei, too, had experienced deep loss. I listened attentively as he told me about the relentless siege of Leningrad which had cost his country so many thousands of lives. His eyes became redder as he recounted how his father had collapsed and died on a frozen sidewalk of the besieged city the previous January. His voice cracked when he described how the latter's body, as well as those of many others who had suffered a similar fate, was left where it had fallen for more than two weeks because the survivors, themselves starving, scarcely had the strength to step around the growing number of corpses, no less remove them for proper burial. I, in turn, gave a short summary of my experiences in Berlin and Treblinka, trying to verbalize for the first time many things that were beyond the limited power of words.

It was dawn when Sergei reluctantly announced that he had to return to his company which was bivouacked close by. They would be moving on later in the day, he said, following in the wake of the Nazi retreat. In response to my question how he had happened to come to the Witowski farmhouse, he explained that he had done so on his own initiative upon learning from the partisans that a Jew who had escaped from a concentration camp was being sheltered there. My heart jumped joyfully when I heard this. It meant that Arnold might still be alive. Sergei, however, could neither confirm nor deny my assumption; he had, he said, spoken only to a Polish liaison officer, and knew nothing of the other members of the unit. Finally, we both arose and embraced warmly. In spite of the pain, I accompanied him to the door after he had said his farewells to the Witowskis. We embraced once more and he was gone. Another farewell. Another farewell.

***

I remained at the farm for several more weeks. The condition of my leg took a turn for the worse during that time; it eventually reached the point where I was unable to put the slightest weight on it without experiencing excruciating pain, and the ugly red streak that was spreading upward from my ankle indicated the onset of infection. Mrs. Witowski applied hot poultices for hours at a time, but there was no improvement, and so once more the old veterinarian was summoned. His eyes told me immediately that he considered my condition very serious. He and my host exchanged some hurried words, and then he left. Several hours later he returned, this time not in his usual horse-drawn wagon, but behind the wheel of a dilapidated, open-backed truck.

"Krankhaus," he said, in broken German, pointing down at my leg. I nodded to let him know I understood. Supported on either side by the doctor and my host, I made my way painstakingly to the truck and was virtually lifted into the rear by the two elderly men. I crawled back toward the cab and leaned against the cool metal as the doctor tied a rope loosely around my midsection and lashed it to the low wooden sides so that I could not be thrown out during the journey. Ignoring my protests, Mrs. Witowski insisted on cushioning my head and back with the feather quilt I had used during my confinement in the cellar. Then she handed me my ledger book and other papers, tied neatly together with a length of brown string. Clutching my manuscript to my chest with one hand, I used the other to wave feebly at the two people to whom I owed so much, as the ancient vehicle chugged out noisily onto the narrow dirt road.

It was only through another grotesque bit of irony that my leg, and possibly my life, were saved. After bumping along for hours on the primitive roads, we finally arrived at the small hospital in a village about forty miles southeast of Lublin. It was actually a converted warehouse, one of a number of similar temporary facilities that the Soviets had set up throughout the area to handle the numerous casualties from the front, and one which also counted among its patients and staff some former inmates of the Maidenek extermination camp. Doctor Nathan Levi was one of the latter. The son of Polish emigres, he had been a prominent surgeon in Dresden before being stripped of his profession by the Nuremberg Laws. Due to the protection of a high official in the Dresden Nazi party (he had successfully performed intricate surgery on the official's wife) he had managed to escape resettlement until the very last "actions" were carried out in his city. As was so often the case, mere chance had again prevented him from joining the other members of his transport, which included his wife, in the gas chamber of Maidenek.

"As we began to line up on the platform they asked if there were any surgeons among us," he explained, in the course of one of our long talks. "It seems that one of the *Lagerführer*, an SS lieutenant colonel, had been suffering for several days from an acute attack of inflamed hemorrhoids and was willing to suspend his racial philosophy, at least temporarily, if it meant being able to sit or shit again without agony. I operated that afternoon. On the following morning he announced to me solemnly that he had had a good, relatively painless bowel movement. I was reprieved. Such is the strange nature of divine intervention."

Dr. Levi operated on my leg three times during the next months, twice scraping the badly infected bone before he could repair the crookedly joined bones.

"You can't blame the old fellow too much," he explained, after informing me that corrective surgery had been necessary. "He is used to dealing with horses. You don't try to set their legs when they break them. You shoot them. As for your turpentine rubdowns, be happy that he just rubbed you down with it and didn't make you drink any."

On another occasion, a week or two after my last operation, he came in to see me and announced in mock solemnity, "Your Uncle Solomon will be disappointed to hear that you are not going to qualify for his club of elite cripples after all. In fact, if you continue to progress the way you have been, you will be dancing on Hitler's grave before you know it."

Our discussions were not always in such a light vein. There were also times when he would sit on the edge of my bed and we would talk of our common experiences. He told me how he, too, had been brought up in an assimilated home, and how for most of his life he had viewed his Jewishness as simply another interesting, but not exceedingly significant accident of nature, very much like the mole on the side of his face. His wife, on the other hand, had come from an orthodox family, but had defied her upbringing and married him, hoping perhaps that one day he would see the light.

"She never lost hope," he said, during one of our conversations. He was describing his arrival in Maidenek. "She assured me that if I put my trust in Him, God would save us. She really believed it. And I am almost certain that she continued to believe it right up to the moment they drove her into the gas chamber with their whips." His lips quivered as he spoke; his hands were balled to fists. Then, smiling strangely he added, "But I had no faith. Any that I might have had disappeared a long time before that. Yet I am still here and she is gone."

He became most emotional, however, when he spoke of his only child, a son whom he had not heard from for more than two years. From the way his eyes misted over whenever he mentioned the latter, I knew that his own will to survive came from the hope that they would be reunited one day.

"My boy will be nine years old in September," he said, his head bowed almost reverently. "He is living in Düsseldorf with old friends from my university days, a gentile couple who are staunchly anti-Nazi. As far as anyone else knows, he is their nephew from Bonn whose parents were killed in an American bombing raid. He is a wonderful child. Anyone would be proud to be his parent."

***

By mid-autumn everyone knew that it was just a matter of time before the Third Reich would be defeated. The daily radio reports spoke of one Allied victory after another; the armies of the western powers and Russia were steadily pushing Hitler's legions back toward the borders of Germany, closing in on both sides like the jaws of a huge vise. Even the German broadcasts, although promising ultimate victory, could not completely conceal the truth.

A matter of time. Many questions tormented me as I watched the drama unfold. Had my parents survived, and would they be spared now that the end was nearing? Where were my sisters? And the others: Judge Linsdorff, Karl, Birgit? I wondered how many human beings would still have to suffer and die before it was over, how many more death camps were still continuing their gruesome work, even though the war was lost? I already knew that there had been an armed revolt in Treblinka during the previous summer and that the entire camp had been dismantled soon after that. Dr. Levi reported this to me soon after I arrived at the hospital. Even this news had been unable to lift my spirits. I knew that although Treblinka had been physically destroyed, it would continue to exist within me and everyone else who had been there. For as long as we lived. Treblinka. The ugly towers and fences, the gas chambers and cremation grids, the rows of terrified victims being herded to their doom, the mountains of dead flesh — these terrible things were and would remain my reality, whether or not they retained material form.

By late November I was walking normally. Except for a neat, long scar along the side of my leg, extending from ankle to knee, and a slight unevenness in my step when I tired, there were no visible signs of my injury. As I recovered, I gradually made the transition from patient to staff member, and when, in the first week of December, Dr. Levi told me that he was being moved closer to the front (one of several such moves) I volunteered to accompany him. In this way we became part of the historic military advance toward the mighty Reich that had declared us unworthy and cast us out. We were going home. The strange names continued to change: Krasnik, Ostrowiec, Kielce, Praszka, Wroclaw. But regardless of the names, the scene was almost always identical. Cities and villages reduced to piles of charred rubble, horribly mutilated bodies of human beings, for the most part young men, whose screams of pain fused with those in my nightmares as if they had found a proper home there. At first I helped with record-keeping and other paperwork, but soon I was also given the assignment of circumventing the inevitable bureaucracy in order to secure the necessary medicines and equipment for Dr. Levi and the other doctors. At night, although often drained of energy, I sat wherever I could find space and attempted to transport myself back in time to continue the thread of my writing. Dr. Levi often came to me late at night and requested to see my latest work. He would sit on the side of my cot, completely absorbed in the reading. Sometimes he would ask pointed questions about a particular incident or person, as if attempting to discover some hidden meaning in my depiction of one or the other. He appeared to be searching for a key, some illuminating metaphor that might be lurking just beneath the surface of my words, one whose meaning even I, the author, had not fully understood.

The first month of the new year drew quickly to a close. It was as if time itself had become impatient and had speeded up to keep pace with the inexorable military advances that were spelling an end to the final chapter in a twelve-year tale of unparalleled barbarism. Even at that late juncture, however, we had not begun to see the full dimensions of that hell on earth. During the first week in February, I became acquainted with yet another name that, like Treblinka and Maidenek, would have to be included in the geography of the seventh circle: Auschwitz.

I made the trip from Praszka to Zabrze in a battle-worn Russian army truck. The driver, a young soldier of indeterminate rank, paid very little attention to the icy roads as he sped along, singing lustily in a deep bass voice and laughing heartily every time I threw my arms out in front of me to brace myself for a crash. As I entered the hospital where I was to pick up the load of surgical supplies for Dr. Levi, a dismal scene unfolded before me. In the narrow hallway, some on thin cots, many more simply lying on the floor covered by coarse blankets, were a number of people whose emaciated faces and vacant eyes were all too familiar to me. My assumption was confirmed minutes later by the doctor to whom I had been directed when I presented Dr. Levi's written request.

"From the concentration camp Auschwitz," he said, in surprisingly intelligible German. "They were brought here last week. Many have died already, and most of those who are left are more dead than alive. There is very little we can do for them."

I tried to get more information from him, but it was obvious that he had told me all he knew in those short sentences. Later, as I made my way back through the eerily silent hall to the waiting truck, I kept my eyes fixed straight ahead, as if fearful that I might see myself among those on the cold floor.

***

Closer and closer. The Aryan masters were being inexorably driven from the lands they had conquered so easily only a few years earlier, and were now fighting desperately to delay the total destruction of their own country. It was a time for rejoicing, and yet I felt as much pain as joy. I could not derive happiness or satisfaction from the knowledge that one by one the cities of the devil were going up in flames. It was not so simple. I knew all too well that, like the sun and the stars, bombs and bullets were impartial. Just as the former shone with equal warmth and brilliance on a death camp and a house of worship, so did the latter maim and kill both the innocent and the guilty without distinction. This thought immediately occurred to me when, one afternoon in mid-February, Dr. Levi sought me out. As soon as I saw his face I knew that something terrible had happened.

"I heard a BBC broadcast this morning, Heinrich," he said, his eyes fixed on mine in a mournful stare. "There was a massive bombing raid on Dresden three days ago. If the reports were not exaggerated, the city has been destroyed."

"How is that possible?" I said, shaken by the unexpected news. "You told me yourself that there were no major industrial or military targets there." He shook his head without answering. Only days before he had told me of his plan to return to Dresden as soon as it became possible. He had, he said, given the information about his son and the latter's benefactors to the local Russian military authorities, and had been assured that they would do all that they could to locate and protect them when the Soviet forces occupied the city. They also provided him with the necessary documents to return there once the military situation was under control.

"Totally destroyed," he repeated, shaking his head from side to side. I stood by helplessly, unable to offer any words of encouragement. It would have been futile to do so; he had also been in the kingdom of death, and knew as well as I that fate is no respecter of love or hope.

***

And then, just like that, it was over. Spring, 1945. The drum-like sound of hobnailed boots had finally been silenced; the terrifying creaking of panzers and the heart-stopping wail of Stucca bombers were gone. The war was over. The mighty Aryan armies were destroyed; the Führer was just another burned, rotting corpse. Nature, as if signalling man to follow its lead, burst forth in its annual symphony of renewed life. It was over. For many, however, it would never end.

***

In July I finally received permission to return to what had once been my home: Munich. Doctor Levi had left for Dresden several days before, his eyes mirroring both fear and hope as we embraced and said our farewells. Now it was my turn to learn what, if anything, remained of my life. As if in a dream, I stared out of the train window, the clearly visible signs of the recent conflict contrasting grotesquely with the beauty of nature in full bloom. My feeling of unreality increased as I changed trains once, twice, three times, automatically handing over my papers again and again to the Russian officials, military and civilian, who seemed to be everywhere. After more delays the journey continued; now it was the landscape of Czechoslovakia whizzing by the window, the same alternating scenes of destruction and rebirth repeating hour after hour. Yet more stops, some for minutes, others for hours. More document checks. Similar to the roll calls in the camp. Treblinka. During the pauses I tried to sleep, but each time I closed my eyes I was assaulted by unbearable memories.

Eventually, the severe Russian uniforms were transformed into the unfamiliar khaki of the American army as we crossed into the Allied zone of occupied Germany. It was all the same. Everything the same. Whether the voices demanding identification papers spoke Russian or English, they remained only voices. Voices of strangers. I was in my native land and yet I was myself an alien. As I had always been. Even once familiar names had lost any meaning for me: Cham, Schwandorf, Regensburg. I stared at the ugly, twisted piles of rubble and saw my own inner self reflected in them. A fitting homecoming, I thought bitterly, aware that this wasted land was not and never really had been my home. In spite of this, however, I felt strangely drawn here, like the Pied Piper's mice to the edge of the river. Against my will, the melody of a hateful song began to run through my mind in rhythm to the rocking train, forcing me to admit to myself that Lalka, mad as he was, had seen the terrible truth and forever inscribed it deep within my being: "*All we have left is Treblinka; It is our destiny.*"

Finally, Munich. I emerged from the train like a somnambulist, only vaguely aware of my surroundings. I might just as well have been on the face of the moon. My stomach churned wildly, whether from anxiety or hunger, I was not certain. I could not remember when I had eaten last. Ten hours before? Twenty? The morning air was heavy with the stale odor of charred wood and mildew, the latter released from the ruins of bombed-out buildings, many of whose interiors had not been exposed to the outside air for a century or more. Automatically, I made my way up Luisenstrasse, past the huge piles of rubble that had been stacked up at what seemed to be well measured intervals. Teutonic order, even in the face of annihilation, I thought angrily, uncertain whether to direct my growing rage at the ubiquitous American soldiers who seemed to radiate health and joy, or the deadeyed, zombie-like natives of the once thriving city. As I watched the silent groups of men and women carry and rake debris from the sidewalks and streets, I wondered how many of them had once stood proudly at the same curbs, arms outstretched toward one of their Nazi gods who happened to be passing, how many had raised their proud voices to passionately proclaim the reverent "Heil Hitler," how many had reluctantly thrown off their SS uniforms and tried to wash the telltale blood from their souls when they realized that the end was inevitable, how many were now attempting to convince even themselves that they were also innocent victims, forgetting in their self-pity that they had willingly and eagerly made a pact with the devil. Overwhelmed by such thoughts, I made my way past the old Botanical Gardens to Meisestrasse, my eyes purposely riveted to the ground so that I would not be mocked by nature.

By the time I turned the corner of Brienner Strasse I was trembling inwardly. I stopped to compose myself when I reached the Karolinenplatz; my destination was so very close now. I fought a growing sense of panic as I passed the blackened remains of stores and apartment buildings I had known as a child. For a moment or two I contemplated turning around and running back to the railroad station, but I immediately suppressed this impulse and began to walk again, this time more briskly than before.

Minutes later I was there; the circle was about to be completed.

Miraculously, the Linsdorff's apartment building was one of only a handful that appeared unscathed. On either side, and across the street, similar structures hovered in varying stages of ruin. Many looked as if some cosmic fist had punched huge, jagged holes into them; others had the eerie appearance of tilted concrete skeletons, ready to collapse at the slightest provocation. Hesitantly, I pulled open the heavy front door and made my way to the familiar stairway that had become my link between yesterday and today.

I raced up the creaking stairs two at a time, just as Karl and I had done so often as young boys. This time, however, it was an act of will rather than one of habit; as if by so doing I were attempting to compel fate to make my friend miraculously appear to accept the challenge of the race. As I neared the final flight I found myself actually listening for his footsteps behind me and was even tempted to turn around to chide him for falling behind, to spur him on so that he would put on his usual finishing burst of speed and pass me, thus restoring the proper order to our world. But when I reached the top there was no smiling Karl to greet me. I was alone. Slowly, my heart pounding from the unaccustomed exercise and the growing anxiety, I stepped across to the heavy wooden door and stood before it for several seconds like an errant shadow, struggling to muster the courage to knock.

"Heinrich?" Jutta's hand went up to her mouth and her eyes brimmed over instantaneously as she looked up at me. I attempted to answer, but no sound would come from my constricted throat. For a moment or two a wave of such utter weakness swept over me that I feared my legs would be unable to support my weight. And then we were in each other's arms, both of us sobbing quietly. We remained like this for a minute or longer, communicating an inexpressible mixture of joy and sorrow with our tears.

"Jutta, is something wrong? Who was that knocking?" Frau Linsdorff's familiar voice floated out toward us as if from another dimension. Still without speaking, Jutta stepped back, linked her arm in mine, and with her head resting on my shoulder guided me to the inner room.

Karl's mother sat on one corner of the sofa, an open book in her lap. My nephew sat next to her, his bright blonde hair contrasting sharply with the dark fabric of the sofa. As he lifted his head to look at us I felt as if a jolt of electricity were passing through my body. The face staring up at me was, although in miniature, that of my friend.

"My God, you are alive, Heinrich," uttered Frau Linsdorff, rising with some difficulty and stepping toward me with her arms outstretched. "You are alive," she repeated, as we embraced. Her frail body trembled in my arms. Meanwhile, Jutta had gone over to the sofa, taken her confused son by the hand, and brought him over to us. When she reached my side she stopped.

"Do you remember your Uncle Heinrich, Fränzchen?" she asked softly. I had to stifle a sob as I gazed into my nephew's steel-blue eyes. The expression on his face was a mixture of fear and curiosity.

"Pleased to meet you, sir," Franz responded formally, putting out his hand and bowing slightly at the waist like an imitation adult. I crouched down and took his small hand in mine, but before I could shake it he let go and threw himself against me, burying his face against my chest.

"Uncle Heinrich," he sobbed, as I stroked his head. My own tears flowed freely once more, as did those of Franz' mother and grandmother.

"There is still a possibility that he is alive," said Jutta, her voice cracking slightly in spite of her effort to keep it steady. "The American major I work for promised to do all he can to try to get the information from the Russians. It won't be easy. Everything is chaotic."

It was late afternoon. The two of us sat across from each other in Judge Linsdorff's study, which was virtually unchanged since the last time I had been there. We were speaking of Karl. Up to that point all of my worst fears had been realized. My parents and Judge Linsdorff were gone. They, like millions of others, had been transformed from human beings into ciphers by the Nazi machinery of destruction; they had become part of the grim statistics of death already being compiled by the victors. In a time when good fortune had to be measured by the simple fact of survival, Jutta had to be considered fortunate. The American occupation command, faced with the Herculean task of restoring order to their sector of the decimated country, had had to seek assistance from the native population. Jutta's knowledge of English, in addition to her *Mischling* status and the fact that she was the daughter-in-law of an internationally known and respected enemy of the now defunct Third Reich, had more than qualified her to join the "denazification" effort.

"The last letter we received from Karl came from the Stalingrad sector," she added, in a voice that seemed almost as far away as the place she had named. "He was assigned to a field hospital of the Sixth Army there. It is dated February, 1943, but it only arrived here in Munich three weeks ago. It was one of thousands that had been confiscated by the censors. Wait, I'll get it for you." She stood up and stepped quickly out of the room.

As I sat waiting for Jutta to return, my eyes wandered to the bookcases I remembered so well. The beautifully bound volumes that I had once looked on with reverence now seemed to mock me. The law. Had it ever really existed here? The image of an SS officer I had known at Treblinka suddenly flashed through my mind. I recalled the damp, cloudy morning he had begun a conversation with me in the sorting shed. It was during a slow period; there had only been one transport during the previous several days. His voice had surprised me considerably. It had a soft, almost gentle quality, and his command of language indicated to me that he was well educated even before he confided that he had studied law and philosophy at the University of Heidelberg. For at least two hours we spoke; more accurately, he spoke and for the most part I listened. I think that at first he really did not expect me to understand; he was simply in a sentimental mood, and was speaking to himself through me. Perhaps he was lonely; perhaps simply bored. He revealed nostalgically how, as a very young man, he had dreamed of becoming a famous trial lawyer, and how proud his parents had been when he qualified to enter the university. During the course of his monologue he quoted the philosopher Emmanuel Kant to illustrate a point he was trying to make, and was openly delighted when I ventured to offer a reply that indicated my familiarity with the latter's writings. His delight turned to rapture when I disclosed to him that I had also studied law. After that, he would go out of his way to engage me in conversation whenever there was an opportunity; on one such occasion he even went so far as to say that I was the only person he had spoken to since his arrival at the camp with whom he had anything in common.

It was preposterous, but I actually began to look forward to our talks; they seemed to indicate that there was still some hope that sanity would return to the world, that goodness could exist even in a place like Treblinka. This illusion was shattered suddenly one morning when I saw this very same man, this enlightened, aspiring philosopher of the law, fly into a fit of rage and pump several bullets into another human being's head and body, simply because the latter, like myself a member of the sorting commando, was not performing his assigned labor with sufficient speed or enthusiasm. I was standing just across the sorting square when the incident took place; close enough to see the bullets tear through the poor victim's flesh and shatter his skull into hundreds of pieces. When it was all over — in seconds actually — the SS officer looked up and saw me staring at him in horror and disbelief. For a moment or two his expression became so fierce that I was certain he was about to shoot me too. Instead, he turned abruptly on his heel and barked out an order to no one in particular to clean away the "load of Jewish shit" that was cluttering up the area. He never spoke to me again after that morning.

My thoughts then shifted to Judge Linsdorff himself, and to my parents, all three of whom had become inseparable in my mind. Although in terms of the distorted world that had existed for the past twelve years, the one was a pure Aryan and the others subhuman Jews, they were now forever intimately linked by a grisly common denominator: death in the camps. According to what information Jutta had been able to find, Judge Linsdorff died in Dachau during the previous winter. The camp records listed the cause of his death as pneumonia, as did the official letter to his widow. Was it true? How could one trust any information coming from a place such as Dachau when even those who had been there or in its obscene counterparts often had difficulty believing that it had been anything more than a nightmare?

The fate of my parents seemed more certain, although no written confirmation had yet come to light. According to the only official records that Jutta was able to obtain, my mother and father had been part of a transport of German and Czech Jews taken from Theresienstadt to Auschwitz in the summer of 1944. Given my father's age and handicap, and my mother's devotion, I have no doubt that they failed to survive the initial selection on the train platform. Sometimes I see them in my dreams, their distorted, blue faces framed by countless others. I watch grieving as they tumble out of the gas chamber door that I have just opened.

"What is wrong, Heinrich? Are you ill? " Jutta's agitated voice startled me out of my tortured thoughts. She placed her cool hand on my forehead and cheek which were dripping with perspiration.

"It's nothing. I'm fine," I gasped. I took out my handkerchief and wiped my face roughly with it.

"Here is Karl's letter," she said, still studying me with concern. "Perhaps you should rest a bit before you look at it. You don't look at all well. What you must have gone through." She was crying again; her narrow shoulders seemed to vibrate as gently as a butterfly's wings.

"Don't worry, I am fine," I repeated. "Just a bit worn out from the long train ride." I reached out and took the single sheet of paper that dangled from her extended hand.

I felt a sudden lump in my throat as I recognized my friend's familiar handwriting, the words cramped closely together so as not to waste any of the limited space on the soiled page. Some time later I copied this letter out word for word so that I could include it in this work. I offer it now:

Dearest Jutta,

The thought that I may never again see you, Franz, or the others I love is far more powerful than my fear of death. It is almost over now. Those of us who have lived through this inferno are almost relieved that the end is approaching. It has been terrible beyond description. So many young lives wasted on both sides. Destroyed by ice and steel. So many. And those poor devils that we have managed to piece back together; what will become of them? I speak not only of the thousands who have been physically shattered, but also of the remainder, the ones who have sacrificed their youth and innocence to a despicable, evil cause. What will their lives mean to them in the future, devoid of hope or faith? What will they tell their children?

No, do not mourn for me, Jutta, but for them. Be thankful, as I am, that I was fortunate enough to have come through all of this without having to take another person's life, that I did not lose my capacity to love. I only pray that our son will live in a better world, one in which kindness, and not killing predominates, one in which no one will listen to the liars who claim that glory is preferable to goodness. No matter what they say, the truth is that here in Stalingrad the soldiers of the Reich do not die with words of reverence for their Führer or Fatherland on their lips. Rather they moan, or scream out for their mothers and other loved ones, just as they did in times of crisis as little children. And there are no heroes here. Only corpses. Everywhere corpses.

It is growing late now my beloved and I must prepare for tomorrow. I have patients to tend to, even though it seems futile to do so. The Russians are about to punish us for what we have done. They have gathered for a final assault; for us their will more than likely be no day after tomorrow. Kiss Mama and Franz for me, and remember that I love you all more than this sad life.

Your Karl

"There is still hope, Heinrich, don't you think so?" Jutta whispered when she saw that I had finished reading. Her eyes were pleading.

"Yes," I replied, although inside me I was already disobeying my friend's final request: I was mourning him.

***

"Ursel and Joshua are in Palestine. They have been there for almost a year." For the first time, my sister's face relaxed into a soft smile. The sun was setting, but neither one of us made an attempt to turn on the lights in Judge Linsdorff's darkened study. As she continued to speak of her twin, Jutta's voice grew stronger. Her tone projected an unmistakable sense of pride. "She and Joshua left Europe soon after the liberation of Paris. They belong to a group that is working to establish an independent Jewish state there in Palestine. Ursel used her underground contacts to smuggle the news out to Frau Linsdorff. That was almost six months ago." She paused and smiled again, this time sadly. "If only Grandfather were alive to know that she was attempting to realize his dream. He would be happy."

I made no response, afraid that my bitterness would destroy this tiny ray of light that still existed in her soul. It was only partially true. While he probably would have taken a degree of satisfaction in the knowledge that his granddaughter sought to make the Promised Land a reality, there were too many other factors involved that made any thought of happiness impossible. I shuddered to think how he would have felt were he still alive; a survivor living out his days with the awareness that there had been millions whose dreams and hopes and prayers had gone up in smoke along with their flesh and bones, obscenely belched out into an indifferent sky through the chimneys of Auschwitz, or from the glowing cremation grids of Treblinka. No, there could be no happiness for my grandfather were he alive. I knew. He would never find peace again. Not even in the Promised Land. Not even there.

It was not until later in the evening that I finally had the courage to ask the question that had been in my mind from the moment I arrived. Jutta was in one of the inner rooms, softly singing Franz to sleep. I was still seated at the large dining room table, absent-mindedly poking my fork at the remains of the meal Frau Linsdorff had prepared from the generous supply of canned food provided by Jutta's employers in the American occupation forces.

"You must eat, Heinrich, even if you have no appetite for food."

I had not noticed Karl's mother standing next to me. For several seconds I remained silent, then, without looking up I asked quietly, "Have you heard anything from Birgit?" My stomach constricted cruelly as I waited for the reply I feared more than death itself. It was obvious to me that if there had been any positive news, Jutta would already have shared it with me; but she had said nothing. In spite of this I longed for a miracle, much like one who rereads a familiar tragedy in the futile and irrational hope that by sheer will power and desire one will be able to alter the outcome. Frau Linsdorff placed her hand on my shoulder. Still, I did not look up.

"Poor Birgit," she sighed. I closed my eyes, fearfully anticipating the curtain that was about to descend on my spirit. "She loved you so very much, Heinrich, so very, very much. When she heard that you had been taken away she could not go on." The pressure of her hand on my shoulder increased, as she attempted to steady herself for what she was about to say next.

***

I draw the soft feather quilt around my shoulders as I sit by the frosted window and stare down onto the peaceful scene below. It has been snowing for several hours already; the hypnotic effect of the gently descending flakes is deepened by the steady ticking of the large mantle clock in the adjoining room. Although it is still several hours before dawn, the thick white blanket covering Brienner Strasse magnifies the weak glow of the newly restored streetlamps, creating the illusion of daylight. Tomorrow will be the first day of 1946. I try to think back to a time when the coming of a new year was an occasion for celebration, but my mind balks, just as it does at any thought of the future. Soon, Jutta, Franz and I will be in America; the papers have been finalized. Jutta continues to cling to a thin thread of hope that Karl is still alive and that he will join us one day soon. At least that is what she says. Frau Linsdorff is in Switzerland with her other sons and promises to visit us in America at the first opportunity.

America. For me it is too late. I know that not even an ocean will be wide enough to dilute the stench of death in my nostrils. I know that not even the sights and sounds of a healthy, promising new world will be able to alleviate, let alone cure, the sickness in my soul. I know that I will never be able to dream again, that my sleep will forever be stolen by the horror and accusation in *their* eyes; eyes that are no longer distinguishable from those of my parents, Judge Linsdorff, Karl, Birgit...eyes that have become identical to my own.

1946

GLOSSARY

Abitur: The graduation certificate awarded after the successful completion of Gymnasium (see below). In order to earn the Abitur, a student must pass comprehensive examinations that include virtually the entire spectrum of Gymnasium study. A very small percentage of students achieve this certificate which enables them to attend university.

Aktion: The name given to the roundup of Jews from a particular ghetto. Those who were caught up in the Aktion were either taken to a secluded spot and shot, or shipped in sealed boxcars to a concentration camp.

Aryan Paragraph: As early as 1927, Prussian students demanded the insertion of such a paragraph into the bylaws of the university. This paragraph, which 77 percent of the students favored, would have excluded Jews from the universities.

Chamberlain, Houston Stewart: Naturalized Englishman whose anti-Jewish work, The Foundation of the 19th Century, helped to lay the groundwork for Naziism. Hitler was an ardent follower of Chamberlain's racial theories. Chamberlain was one of the first to predict that Hitler would become the leader of Germany, but he never lived to see his prophecy come true. He died in 1927.

Cremation Grills: Treblinka, unlike Auschwitz, did not have any crematoria. In order to destroy the evidence of the mass murder that had taken place there, the Nazis burned the bodies of their victims on huge cremation grills made up of long metal rails stretched across concrete pillars. They called in an "expert" to aid them in finding the most efficient way to meet their goal. Through trial and error they discovered that by placing bodies in a particular configuration, they could cremate up to three thousand at one time.

CVDSJG - Central Verein deutscher Staatsbürger jüdischen Glaubens (Central Association of German Citizens of the Jewish Faith): This organization had been founded in 1893, and was the leading exponent of the assimilationist's philosophy. The organization was very active in promoting fair treatment for Jews, and in combatting defamation and discrimination. Obviously, it did not have the power to prevent the Holocaust.

Dresden: Declared an open city, Dresden was bombed on February 13, 1945. The entire old city was leveled by the massive Allied air attack which created a fire storm that destroyed over 1500 acres. Although the exact number of deaths has never been determined, estimates range from eighty thousand to one hundred and fifty thousand. There have been many accounts of the raid on Dresden, the best known of which is in Kurt Vonnegut's novel, Slaughterhouse Five.

Final Solution: The euphemism used by Nazis to describe the destruction of European Jewry.

Franz, Kurt: Deputy Commandant of Treblinka. He was given the nickname "Lalka" (the doll), because he was so physically attractive. His outward appearance, however, belied his inner character. He was a sadist who sometimes tortured and killed inmates for little or no reason. He was sentenced to life imprisonment by a German court in 1965 having managed to remain free until 1957. During this period of freedom, he was bold enough to use his own name.

Frick, Franz: An early Nazi who became Minister of the Interior of Thuringia in late 1929. The next year, the Nazis became the second largest party in the Saxon parliament.

Fürstner, Wolfgang: The Jewish architect who designed the Olympic Village. He shot himself to death when he was later replaced as commandant of the Village by an Aryan.

Gemeinnützige Krankentransportgesellschaft: The agency set up to transport patients in asylums and nursing homes to killing centers (there were six in all). The victims first spent some time at a transit facility where they were observed before being exterminated. To further the illusion that these deeds were being done out of humane motives, each case was reviewed by "experts" whose approval meant extermination. It is remarkable how closely the Nazis later followed the procedure developed in their euthanasia program when it came time to put the "Final Solution" into operation. (See T-4)

Gestapo: When this organization was first established by Göring it was labeled the **Gestapa (Geheime Staatspolizei)**, but before long the name **Gestapo** became more popular.

Goebbels, Joseph: Nazi Minister of Propaganda.

Goethe, Johann Wolfgang von (1749-1832): Generally considered the greatest German poet.

Gold, Arthur: The famous Polish conductor who became an inmate of Treblinka. He set the camp anthem to music. It was often played by the camp orchestra.

Götterdämmerung: Twilight of the gods. In Norse mythology, this was the final battle between the gods and the forces of evil, and resulted in the destruction of all concerned, including all living creatures on earth. Heimdall was the god who announced the onset of the hostilities by blowing his horn in warning. Loki was an evil god who fought on the other side.

Grynszpan, Hershyl: Polish Jew whose parents were expelled from Germany even though they had lived there since 1914. Grynszpan had intended to assassinate the German ambassador, but the opportunity did not present itself. Thus, in another of those ironies of history, he shot **Ernst von Rath**, a secretary who was himself an anti-Nazi and was under investigation by the Gestapo.

Guertner, Franz: The Bavarian Minister of Justice. A nationalist, he used his considerable influence to insure that the defendants were given every opportunity to run roughshod over the Chief Justice and the three lackluster lay judges appointed to try the case.

Gymnasium: Roughly the German equivalent of high school plus two years of college (see Abitur).

Heine, Heinrich: Nineteenth century German-Jewish Romantic poet. Heine's real name was Harry, but when he had himself baptized (not out of religious conviction, but rather because he wanted to qualify for civil service placement), he took the name Heinrich. The poem quoted here was written in the 1840's while its author was living in self-imposed exile in Paris.

Herzl, Theodore: An Austrian journalist who founded the modern Zionist movement. He favored assimilation of Jews in Europe, but saw anti-Semitism as too strong to allow this. Thus, he advocated the formation of a Jewish state which would maintain close ties with the Palestinians. In August, 1897, he convened the first Zionist congress in Basel, Switzerland, making Zionism a worldwide political movement.

Himmler, Heinrich: Headed the SS.

Jüdenräte: Jewish Councils. In keeping with their established practice, the Nazis involved their victims as much as possible in their own destruction, and thus, in an utterly perverse way, forced them to share the guilt. The

Jewish Councils in the ghettos were an example of this. Made up of leaders of the Jewish communities they represented, they submitted lists to the Nazis of those selected for transport to the concentration camps.

Jüdische Rundschau: The official newspaper of the German Zionist movement.

Kapo: In the concentration camps, each labor detail was supervised by a Jewish foreman called a Kapo, who was often as brutal as his Nazi masters. Both the upper and lower camps at Treblinka had a Chief Kapo.

Kellogg-Briand Pact: Signed in Paris on August 27, 1928. This pact, signed by Germany and most of the major world powers, outlawed aggressive war. According to its terms, all international conflicts were thereafter to be solved by peaceful arbitration.

Kristallnacht: Night of November 9, 1938. An indication of how little opposition there was among the Aryan population can be obtained by reading Heydrich's report to Göring on November 11. Heydrich attempted to give a summary of the damage inflicted on the Jews, as well as a numerical accounting of those arrested. While he admitted that the figures were not complete, they did present a clear picture: 20,000 Jews arrested, but only seven Aryans and three foreigners taken into custody for interfering with the police action against the Jews. It would seem then that almost half as many foreigners as Germans intervened on behalf of the Jews.

Lagerälteste: Concentration camp elder, a respected inmate of the camp who was used by the Nazis to keep a degree of order among the others. The person who held this position had a relative amount of influence, but in the last analysis he was, to the Nazis, just another Jew to be ultimately eliminated.

Lagerführer: SS officer in charge. In each camp there were two or three of these who were rotated every twenty-four hours. They had virtually absolute control over the prisoners.

Law for the Restoration of the Professional Civil Service: Passed by Bundestag on April 7, 1933. This law declared anyone who had one or more parent or grandparent who was a non-Aryan as ineligible for positions in the government service. This included teachers in public educational institutions, members of judicial tribunals, workers in the postal service, employees of the Imperial Railway Administration, public bank employees, police officers, civilian employees of the army. Gradually the ban spread to other professions, including medicine and the arts.

Mischling: Approximate equivalent of "mixed breed" in English. The addition to the Nuremberg Laws that defined what a Jew was appeared on November 14, 1935. Briefly, a person with three Jewish grandparents who belonged to the Jewish community as of September 15, 1935 (the date of the original law), was to be considered a Jew. In addition, any offspring of a marriage contracted with a Jew after that same date, or any baby born out of wedlock as the result of an extramarital affair with a Jew after July 31, 1936 was to be classified as a Jew.

In the case of the child of a mixed marriage, there were other rules. If that child had two Jewish grandparents who did not otherwise fit into the Jewish community, the child was a *Mischling* of the first degree. A further division dealt with those children with only one Jewish grandparent; these children were put into a category of *Mischling* of the second degree. The Nazis never did clear up the ambiguities in this system of classification.

Night of the Long Knives: see Ernst Röhm

NSDAP - National Sozialistische Deutsche Arbeiters-Partei: National Socialist German Worker's Party.

Palästina-Amt: The agency that dealt with emigration to Palestine. For those Jews who emigrated to other European countries, the agency involved was the **Hilfsverein**. The third most important agency was the **Hauptstelle für jüdische Wandersfürsorge** which dealt with repatriation of Jews from Eastern Europe to the country of their origin.

Rath, Ernst von: The secretary to the German ambassador whose assassination set the stage for **Kristallnacht**. See Hershyl Grynszpan.

Raubal, Geli: Hitler's niece. On September 18, 1931, she killed herself in his apartment on Prinzregentenstrasse where she lived with him. Most historians agree that she, Angela (Geli) Raubal, was the only woman whom Hitler ever truly loved, and that he never got over her death. There are those, however, who claim that Hitler either killed her himself or had someone else do it. This seems highly unlikely. It is fairly certain that Hitler was in Nuremberg when it happened and obvious that had he wanted her eliminated he would not have had it happen in his apartment.

Reichsausschuss zur wissenschaftlichen Erfassung von erb-und anlagebedingten schweren Leiden: The Reich Committee for Scientific Research in Hereditary and Serious Constitutional Impairments. Hitler himself was directly involved in the establishment of the organ of state responsible for this bureau which decided the fate of the mentally and physically handicapped.

Rentebank: Established in order to stabilize the currency. This bank was endowed with the sum total of the mortgages on all the land used for agriculture and industry. The issuance of the "Rentemark" was only a stopgap measure, and was eventually superseded by the new "Reichsmark" which was backed by gold.

Röhm, Ernst: The leader of the SA. He had been with Hitler from the beginning and never hid the fact that he was a homosexual. Hitler not only tolerated Röhm's homosexuality, but even defended him when others attacked him on that basis. It is fairly clear that the "execution" of his SA leader and the others on the night of June 30/July 1, now popularly known as **The Night of the Long Knives,** was motivated by fear that the SA leader was becoming far too powerful and independent.

SA (Sturmabteilung): Storm Troopers.

Sebi, Sabbatei (Zebi): A seventeenth-century Turkish-Jew who claimed to be the Messiah. He attracted a large following in Central Europe, even after his conversion to Islam.

Sisyphus: One of the great "sinners" of Greek mythology. Sisyphus' punishment in the underworld was to roll a huge stone up a steep hill for eternity. Each time he reached the summit, the stone would roll down to the bottom again. What his sin was varies with the version one reads. In the last analysis, the provocation is unimportant, since the gods did not have to justify themselves for any punishment they inflicted.

Speer, Albert: Nazi Armaments Minister who formed a cadre of approximately six thousand honorary administrators from the composite entrepreneurial and managerial ranks of the country and a network of committees to preside over the armaments industry.

Stalingrad: The Battle of Stalingrad ended in total defeat for the German army on February 3, 1943. Those who survived from the Sixth Army, two Rumanian divisions, and a Croatian regiment, were placed in Soviet prisoner of war camps. The letters that were written by the German soldiers who took part in the battle were confiscated by the Nazi government and used as a means of measuring the mood at the front. After the war, one such bundle of these letters was published. There is also a *Deutsche Grammophon Gesellschaft* phonograph recording of the contents of a selected number of these letters.

T-4: Designation for Nazi euthanasia program. So named because the location of the office was Tiergartenstrasse 4. Conservative estimates put the number of those killed in the T-4 program at 80,000. The indirect destruction due to the work of those involved in T-4 cannot be overestimated. It was there that mass killing by gas (carbon monoxide and Zyklon B), was first introduced. Much of the personnel involved in T-4 later became the leaders in the "Final Solution," assuming positions as directors and staff of the death camps. Even some of the equipment from T-4 was later utilized in the camps: gas chambers used to eliminate the insane, infirm and deformed were shipped to Treblinka, Belzec, and Majdanek to be used on the Jews and other victims there. The facts of the euthanasia program were finally disclosed in a sermon by Cardinal Galen of Münster. The resulting pressure of public opinion led to the termination of the T-4 program in August, 1941.

Thule Society: A racist organization that advocated the struggle against "international Jewry." Three of the early founders of the Nazi Party came from the Bavarian branch of this group: Hess, Eckart, and Rosenberg.

Verordnung über die Anmeldung Jüdischen Vermögens: On April 26, 1938, Göring and Frick issued the "Decree for the Registration of Jewish Wealth." Every Jew had to register his total worth, both that which he had in Germany, as well as any holdings abroad. This included any works of art, jewelry, business holdings, pensions, and claims for support. Only holdings under 5,000 Reichsmarks were exempt from registration. Article 7 of the decree stated: "The one in charge of the Four Year Plan (Göring), can take the necessary measures to assure that the amount registered is brought into accord with the needs of the German economy." The intentions of the decree were clear to the Jews, and as a result many did not report their entire holdings as required.

Vienna Academy: Hitler failed the test for entrance into the Vienna Academy of Arts in 1907. He details the experience in Chapter 2 of *Mein Kampf*.

Zionistische Vereinigung für Deutschland: Zionist Union for Germany.